The Datch Pack.

Chronicles of Datch

By David Hallam

ISBN: 978-1-917238-14-4

Cover design by: David Hallam

Printed by Amazon

DEDICATION

For my wonderful daughter Emma.

ACKNOWLEDGMENTS

I want to say thank you to all the staff in my local public house for putting up with me sitting in the corner typing away on my laptop.

I would also like to thank Jeff for all his help with proof reading.

The Arrival

A large black ship landed covertly outside of an old warehouse in an abandoned part of the city, a ramp dropped down from its rear. A few moments later a huge jet-black monster came down the ramp followed by three men armed with pulse cannons. It turned to them and the man in the centre took a step forward,

"Ok, you know the deal, this is for my brother Traimore make sure the target dies."

The monster spoke in tones that sent shivers of fear running down your spin,

"It will be done. And the payment?"

"As we agreed, the items will be taken and unlocked before being put in safe keeping for when the job is done. Then you can sell them off world to the highest bidder."

"And what about food?"

"We'll bring you food as and when we get chance. And if you get hungry, I'm sure you can find something to eat in the city. You can contact us using the button on the generator around your neck in case things go wrong."

"I don't make mistakes."

"I'm sure you don't. Well, make yourself at home."

The other two men laughed as they went back into the ship.

The creature turned and headed into the warehouse as the ship lifted off.

School

Datch was born to a middle-income family on the solar date 485-556-749.250. He came into the universe just outside of Yuland city on the planet Bellatrix five. His parents owned a small ranch on the edge of the Great Western desert. His dad was a retired fleet officer and now at the age of 2079 was taking the easy life. Datch had ten brothers and twelve sisters all of which were scattered across the stars. A year ago, Datch had his implant installed. That gave him access to all the knowledge in the known universe.

Now he is 7 years old which was just over 15 years in Earth terms due to Bellatrix fives orbit which is 792 days. Now he has got to go to school for four days and three nights each week. The school is not like Earth schools as all the normal subjects like maths and science are given by the implant. Instead, it teaches social skills, behaviour and also implant training.

Datch woke up and opened his eyes. The sun was shining in the window above his head also the room was strange and then he remembered, this was school.

He got himself out of bed and grabbed his dressing gown before heading for the shower. The day before he had been introduced to his fellow classmates and shown around the school. Now he was sharing a room with Dapo and Hagger. Dapo was a bit shorter than Datch and had blond hair and purple eyes. He was from the city and his mum worked in the alien affairs office and both of his dad's lived off world most of the time. Hagger on the other hand was tall and skinny and only had a dad. His dad was working on the new power plant in the city. Datch and his roommates were all within a month of each other age wise but were from very different backgrounds.

This was their first full day at school. They had been told to meet in one of the lecture theatres at 11am for a basic assessment to give the tutors an idea of their skill levels. Datch had his shower and got dressed. He gave Dapo a poke to try and wake him up.

"Come on Dapo, its 10am we need to be in the lecture room at eleven" Dapo opened one eye and looked at him. Then his brow furrowed.

"Oh, err…" there was a short pause, "Datch, oh, ok."

You could see the thoughts flowing through his mind as he tried to join reality.

"You need to get up" Datch carried on. At this point Hagger started to stir.

"Erm… what's going on?" he said looking up from his pillow.

"It's ten o'clock, we need to get up or we'll miss breakfast."

The mention of food was enough to get both of them moving. Fifteen minute later they were both up, showered and dressed.

"Ok, now we're up," said Dapo "where is the food?"

Datch thought about this. He wasn't sure but he remembered turning right into the room after the nights entertainment and so it seemed to be a good guess to turn left.

"I think it's this way." Datch said as he came out of the room.

The others followed him down the corridor to the junction and on the wall were a number of arrows with names on them one of which said restaurant.

"Ah. This way," he said.

Off they went to the right and soon they arrived at the restaurant. They went in and found a table.

"Do you want to grab yours first?" Dapo said.

"Ok, thanks" replied Datch and headed off with Hagger to get food.

They had a lot to choose from but Datch went straight for the chocolate pancakes and soon they were back at the table. Dapo went and fetched his and they sat eating.

"So, what do you think this test is going to be like?" said Dapo tucking into a bread roll.

"I'm not sure, never had one before." Hagger answered.

"What about you Datch?"

"I've had a couple of tests. My dad would do them with me and they were OK. Just lots of questions that's all, so no problem really."

They carried on chatting about where they lived and what Vid shows they liked. Then it was time to go to the lecture room. They got up and headed for the door. Datch was feeling a little nervous now himself but didn't want the others to know. Dapo and Hagger were also nervous as they walked down the corridor. Halfway down was an old balding gentleman with light grey wisps of hair trying to pick up some papers that had fallen on the floor. Datch stopped to help him.

"Are you ok sir? Let me get them for you." He asked picking up some of the papers.

"Thank you, it's hard to pick things up with my back." he said.

Datch picked up the last of the papers and gave them to him.

"Are you new here?" the old man asked.

"Yes, we're just on our way to the lecture room."

"Well, you had better hurry then, you don't want to be late and thank you again."

"You're welcome, sir."

With that they headed off down the corridor and into the lecture theatre.

The lecture theatre was a large room and had small groups of tables spread out on raised platforms. Each table had a number on it attached to a post in the centre and as they went in, they were given a number and told to go to that table. The tables had six seats around each of them and a number of papers at each of the positions. The three of them headed to table number seven and sat down. Dapo was about to start looking at the papers when Datch stopped him.

"I think we should wait to be told what to do."

Dapo looked at him and put the papers back down.

"Some people are looking at them and writing things down." Dapo said.

"Just wait." said Datch.

Three girls came in together and were given their number. They came over to the table. Hagger went red in the face.

"Hi I'm Tish, I think we're with you. This is Rosey and Carina." Datch stood up and shook their hands.

"This is Dapo, Hagger and I'm Datch" They all sat down.

"Where are you from?" he added trying to make some small talk.

"I'm from Papaso, it's a village to the south of the city." said Carina.

"I live on a ranch near the desert to the north." said Datch.

"Oh, we're both from the countryside cool." she added and with that everyone introduced themselves.

A bell rang and everyone went quiet. A man stepped up on to the podium in the centre of the room.

"Welcome to all of you, my name is Mr Poe. This assessment is to find out how much you know and what sort of tutoring you will need. I should at this point inform you that the assessment started about 1 hour ago in the restaurant. Please can you remove the top sheet of the papers and put it in the box next to you without writing on it"

There was a lot of murmuring around the room as a lot of students had put their names on them. It had been part of the test.

Mr Poe continued… "Can you now put your names on the second sheet and try to answer the questions as best as you can, you can talk to each other if you wish."

With that they started to fill in the papers.

"Datch thanks for that," Dapo said, "I would have filled that in if it wasn't for you."

Datch turned to him.

"You never fill things in when you're being tested until you're told to."

Carina nodded at him, smiled and winked. Datch had no idea what she meant with the wink but her smile was nice.

The test had five pages which mostly consisted of questions about family, friends, hobbies and experiences. But some questions asked things like what is the name of the person opposite and where are your roommates from? Datch had most of the answers and any he didn't have he just asked. The test only took him 30 minutes and then he had to wait for the others. He decided to help them with theirs as the tutors had said to talk to each other. Soon they were all done and a tutor came around and collected their papers. They carried on chatting while waiting for the rest to finish.

The bell rang again.

"Ladies and Gentlemen please bear with us while we process your papers, after which we will be announcing your group captains. The group captains will be the people who already have quite good social skills. Your captains should be listened to and learnt from but at the same time if you think something is wrong then speak out. Please talk amongst yourselves while we discuss the results." At this point the old man in the corridor came in and went over to the desk.

"There is the old man who had dropped the papers in the corridor" Hagger said. They all looked over.

"Yes, he had a big pile on the floor when we came by," Carina added.

"Hmm… "Datch was thinking. "I picked them up for him and made sure he was alright."

"You look puzzled." Carine said looking at Datch.

"I think he was part of the test." he said.

There was a general chorus of "Oh..." as the thought sank in.

"That's a bit sneaky." Dapo said.

"I think it was to see if we would help." Datch concluded.

The tutors were all having a deep conversation and kept looking at the papers then around the room. Eventually they seemed to come to a conclusion.

The bell rang again and the room went quiet. Mr Poe took to the podium again.

"After a lot of deliberation, we have picked your captains. The table you are sitting at is your house and as such you will earn points for it. Your captain will help you get them. Some points are earned as a team and some as individuals. At the end of the year the winning team gets to choose their reward. Please note we will be watching you all the time so be warned good conduct gives positive points, bad conduct negative points. What is good and bad is for you to work out. Now your tutors will come around and tell you who your captains are."

With that the tutors spread out throughout the room. The old man they had seen now seemed to have got a new lease of life and came striding over to their table.

"Good afternoon." he said.

"Good afternoon, sir." said Datch standing up and the others followed suit.

"Please be seated." The old man said and with that they sat back down.

"I am Mr Doji, I will be your tutor while you are here."

"May I ask you something sir?" asked Datch.

"You may, that is why I'm here."

"The papers in the corridor, it was part of the test, wasn't it?" Mr Doji laughed.

"You are a very clever man, Datch Thome." Datch was impressed.

He had never been called a man before, little man yes but not man. Mr Doji continued.

"That is why you are going to be this team's captain. Team Datch how do you like that?" Datch was taken a back.

"Thank you, sir, but why?" he asked.

"You have by far, had a lot more experience of life than any of your fellow team mates and if I could I would pass you here on the spot but the law is clear and you have to do your two years, however I expect great things of team Datch."

Wow thought Datch then wondered just how much Mr Doji did know and wondered if bathrooms were mentioned anywhere.

"Well done, Datch." Carina said and the others followed suit.

"So, what do we do now sir?" Datch asked.

"Well, lunch would be good start then in about an hour you will have a lecture about general behaviour. Tonight, after dinner you will have some free time to spend with your new team. I would attend and make sure you're all ok, but I think looking at your record that won't be a problem. I have a feeling you want to explore anyway. Normally I would tell you all to stay on college campus for the first week, but I think you have somewhere in mind."

He looked straight into Datch's eyes. Datch felt like he was reading his mind and wasn't sure he liked it. The others were very quiet and were also looking at Datch.

"I was thinking a nice walk in the evening air would be nice." He said hoping it was the right thing to say.

"Well, be careful and can I suggest, out the front, three blocks down, then left and down to the end and then turn right."

Datch was now convinced that he was reading his mind either that or he was having a psychic premonition or something.

"Hmm…" Datch thought about the next sentence carefully.

"Well, it is nice outside, but it will depend on what the others want to do." Mr Doji smiled and gave Datch a wink.

Datch was starting to wish people would stop winking at him as it seemed to mean they knew about what was going on before he did.

"Well, I shall see you all again soon, enjoy your walk." With that he got up and left them to chat.

"What did he mean by all that?" Dapo said.

"I have some friends in the city and was planning to go and see them when I got chance. He just pretty much gave me their address and I have no idea how he knew."

"Wow, now that's really strange." said Carina.

"Do you think we should?" said Hagger.

"You just heard what he said, he pretty much told us to go," Tish added.

"Yes, I suppose he did." Datch concluded.

Team Datch went off to have some lunch and to get to know each other a bit better. Carina seemed to be the top girl, so Datch decided to make her his number two much to Hagger's annoyance due to the fact they were girls. Datch pointed out that they maybe girls but they were just as smart as he was so that was that. Carina was now sitting next to Datch. He thought he should be doing something but had no idea what. They finished lunch and headed off to the next lecture.

Datch was bored. The lecture was basically what to do and what not to do in public and how to behave towards other students. His mum and dad had taught him all about this when he was younger. The lecture went on about males and females and how to behave when around them which at one-point made Hagger go very red. Datch realised that he hadn't had any experience with members of the opposite sex or how to deal with them. He thought about this a bit while the lecturer went on to how to order food and drinks in a restaurant but Datch was still thinking about Hagger and realised that it was likely due to Hagger being an only child. His mum had been killed in an accident when he was young and his dad had raised him on his own. This was something Datch decided to work on fixing and as he was sort of in charge of him anyway, it was his job.

Finally, it got to dinner time and the Datch pack went to the restaurant. They all seemed to be watching Datch more now which made him feel a little uncomfortable but he figured that it would soon wear off.

"So Datch, where are we going tonight?" asked Dapo. Datch stopped eating his Hacks in a bun and looked up.

"It's a secret and are you sure you want to come?"

"Want to come!" said Carina, "After all the cryptic talk between you and Mr Doji, we wouldn't miss it."

The others all nodded in agreement.

"Ok, but you need to dress casual."

There was a number of blank looks from Dapo, Hagger and Tish.

"What's casual mean?" asked Hagger.

"Carina will show you Tish, I'll sort these two out."

Carina nodded.

"Ok let's finish up dinner and meet outside the main doors in say thirty minutes?"

Carina had a slight frown on her face.

"Ok, make it forty-five." The frown went away.

"Cool, that will give us chance for a shower." she said.

They finished eating and headed back to their rooms.

Datch looked at the other two.

"So, what cloths do you have?" he asked

Dapo opened his draw and showed him. This was going to be harder than he thought. After a few minutes he selected a pair of jeans and a T-shirt with a car on the back. That was Dapo sorted, now it was time for Hagger. He was even harder and ended up with a tropical shirt that looked like a Hawaiian reject and some green shorts. Datch went for shorts and T-shirt with a bike on the front, also his jacket. Finally, after a lot of muttering they were ready, just in time too. They headed down to the main entrance and found Carina, Tish and Rosey waiting for them.

"Sorry if you have been waiting long but I think I need to take these two out shopping as soon as possible." Datch said walking over to girls.

"We've only just got here ourselves." Carina said.

The girls looked great. Carina was wearing a nice top and a short skirt, as was Rosey. Tish had a T-shirt and shorts on.

"Ok, let's go." said Datch.

They started to head down the road. Datch sort of knew where they were going because he had been studying a map but the directions from Mr Doji helped. They headed three blocks down and turned left.

"Well, aren't you going to tell us where we're going?" asked Rosey butting in to the small talk that was taking place between Datch and Carina.

"We are nearly there now just wait and see."

Datch was being very coy about their destination and the others were a little nervous. None of them had been out in the city alone before. They got to the end of the road and turned the corner. Three doors down stood a bar. Outside were two bikes that Datch recognised and above the door was a sign saying 'The Barbers Inn'. Datch headed for the door.

"Are you sure we should be going in there?" Carina asked. "It looks a bit rough."

"If you want you can stop outside but I'm going in."

The others thought about this and figured that if the tutor had told Datch how to get here it couldn't be as bad as it looked.

"Ok, we're in."

"Right, when we go in just follow me and stay close. Oh, and don't talk to people you don't know, that will mean everyone."

With that they walked through the door.

The Barbers Inn was a small bar as far as the city was concerned. The lighting was dimmed down and the music was a mix of rock and blues. The bar had a number of small alcoves with tables in and a long bar ran along one side of the room with stools along the front. A vid was on the wall showing a sport channel and there was a number of drinkers sat along the bar. At the far end was a large biker in a leather jacket who was standing talking to a tall skinny man. The jacket had writing on the back. Datch went walking straight across to him.

"What are you doing?" Carina said now worried that they could get into trouble.

Datch took no notice and walk right up to the big biker and poked him in the back. The biker turned around wondering who had prodded him. He looked at Datch and grabbed him with both hands lifting him up in the air. The others were about to run for the door when he spoke.

"Datch, how's it going? It's good to see you dude."

The others had just frozen to the spot.

"I'm good Tank, how's it with you?"

"I'm good dude, still getting over the party though." he said laughing. He put Datch down and the other biker turned around.

"Hey Datch. We wondered how long it would take you to find us." he said.

"Hi Fred, how's it going?"

Fred looked around at the others.

"I'm good thanks, I see you have brought some friends with you."

"Yes, please let me introduce them."

He waved at the others to come over which they did somewhat nervously.

"This is Carina, Rosey, Tish, Dapo and Hagger, this is Tank and Fred, they are both good friends of mine and very cool dudes."

"Very pleased to meet you sir." Carina said cautiously.

Tank laughed.

"You don't need to mind your P's and Q' in here love."

"So, what are you drinking Datch?" said Fred.

"Have they got Gruck's by any chance?"

"They sure do, on the rocks?"

"Yes please, but no little boats please."

Fred laughed, "What about your friends, would they like the same?"

Datch turned to them and nodded they nodded back.

"Yes thanks."

A few minutes later they all had a large glass of Gruck's with ice in and the girl's drinks had small umbrellas in as well. After a number of questions about the party. Some of which made Datch go a little red. The chat turned around to school.

"So how are you finding it?" Tank asked after complimenting Carina on her hair.

"It's ok I suppose." said Datch "I've been made team captain but I don't know why really."

Fred looked at the others.

"What do you think to Datch so far folks?" he said to the rest of them.

There was a consensus that he was doing well especially as they were now sitting in a bar drinking and it was only their second night at school.

"Who wants nuts?" Tank asked.

At which point a number of bowls appeared on the bar. As they started eating the newly arrived nibbles the door opened and another biker came in. He spotted Datch and came striding over.

"Datch dude how's it going?" said Peebop patting Datch on the back so hard a number of nuts ended up behind the bar.

"I'm good, I think." he said as he almost choked.

There was another round of introductions and someone put a bit more upbeat track on the sound system.

"Is Clax coming in as well?"

"Yes, he'll be along in about thirty minutes, He'll be shutting his shop about now." said Tank.

"How's school?" Peebop asked, Datch went through it all again.

"So how did you find this place?" Fred asked with a grin.

"It was really weird; the tutor knew that I was planning to come here tonight and I don't know how." Datch had a puzzled look on his face.

Tank paused while chatting to Dapo and Rosey.

"Well maybe I can solve that." he turned to look over to the corner.

"Hey Jep, stop hiding and come over here." He shouted.

A figure rose from the darkness of the booth and an old looking man emerged into the light and came over. It was Mr Doji. Datch looked at him.

"So that's how you knew all about me." Datch said.

Jep laughed.

"Yes, I have known these guys for a few years and when they told me about your escapades in Traxsent and then this week when they told me about the Asmove and the starship Carpaycus, Well I made up my mind and pulled a few strings so I would be your tutor."

Datch's jaw dropped and he went very red. The bikers were all laughing and Jep was as well. Datch's team weren't sure what was now going on other than there seemed to be a lot more to Datch than they thought.

"Sorry Datch, I hope we haven't embarrassed you too much." said Tank handing him another glass of Gruck's.

Datch was now turning back to a normal colour and was now smiling again.

Jep looked at the rest of the students.

"Well team Datch, your leader is quite a role model, I'm sure you would like to know who your captain really is?"

They all turned to look at Datch.

"Err…" he said.

He now understood how Commander Isbar felt when he did the toilet thing to him.

"Come on Gang, let's go over there to the big booth and Datch can tell us one of his adventures, another round of drinks Jim and one for yourself." said Tank patting Datch on the shoulder again.

They were just sitting down when Clax walked in. He grabbed a drink and came over to sit with them. After the good to see you Datch and another round of introductions all eyes turned to Datch.

"Well, come on, tell your friends about Asmove then." prompted Fred with a grin.

"Ok" said Datch feeling that he had no choice.

"I hadn't long had my implant when my dad's old captain invited us for a trip on his starship and…"

Datch continue to tell the story and Tank filled in the bits that he tried to miss out. It took about an hour to tell the Asmove tale. Team Datch was somewhat stunned but very impressed. Carina had moved closer to Datch and was now almost sitting in his lap. He decided to go to the toilet at the same time Fred did.

"I think Carina likes you Datch." said Fred.

"Err… you do, I sort of like her?"

"Good, word of advice man to man."

Datch liked the man-to-man bit.

"Just let things happen, don't rush it."

Datch wasn't quite sure what he meant but said yes anyway. This was all new to him as he had never had a girlfriend and it looked like he was about to get one. His mum had told him all about the whole sex thing and some basic information and his dad had also put his bit in. He thought about it and decided that he would go with Fred's guidance. He was here after all and therefore could help out if he got stuck. They went back out to the bar and sat back down. They carried on chatting and it was soon eleven at night.

"Oh crap, we're going to get into trouble, we were meant to be back half an hour ago." Carina said.

"Don't worry, I'll walk back with you and explain you were all being educated." Said Jep.

It wasn't far from the truth either. They had certainly leant a lot about Datch and as far as Carina was concerned, he was a super hero.

They finished their drinks, said goodbye and promised to come back at the same time the next night. This time Jep was going to walk down with them. That way it would be classed as and educational excursion and they could go back when they wanted as long as it was before midnight.

They got up and headed back to the school. On the way Carina put her hand in Datch's and Datch decided to go along with it like Fred had told him to. It was a nice feeling after all. It also seemed to make Hagger go red for some reason which amused him.

They finally got back to the school. Sure enough, Jed had a quick word with the security officer and they were allowed through without any problems. They said good night to each other and Carina gave Datch a peck on the cheek. He wasn't sure what to do then remembered what Isbar had done when Jarna had kissed him. He gave her a kiss back. They went to their rooms after arranging to meet up for breakfast. The first lecture wasn't until eleven so they didn't have to get up early.

Datch got into bed and thought about Carina. He liked her and had some strange feelings when she touched him. She sent shivers up his spine but he didn't know why. He made a mental note to have another talk with Fred about her.

Next morning, he got up early. There was a message light flashing on his vid com so he went over and viewed the message. It was from his mum. She had left a vid message saying that they had tried to call but he was out and to call back when he had chance. He called her.

"Hi, mum"

"Hi Datch, I tried to call you last night but you didn't answer."

"Sorry mum, I was busy with my team."

"Your team?"

"Yes, I've been made team captain and its now team Datch."

"Well done, but how did you do that…"

The next five minutes were spent with Datch talking about the school and the test. He left the bar out as he thought he might get in trouble for that. His dad came on looking like he had been up late and congratulated him for getting team captain. Datch said he would ring in the morning again as he had a late lesson.

"Ok Datch, well take care and we're here if you need us, remember that."

"Ok mum, talk to you tomorrow, love you." with that the call ended.

Datch turned to the task of getting the male part of team Datch out of bed. Soon they were all up and heading down to breakfast.

As they walked into the restaurant the girls waved at them and they headed over to the table to sit down. Datch ended up sitting next to Carina.

"I wish I was at home; I really fancy some ice-cream." he said looking at the menu.

"Ice-cream?" Carina asked.

"Yes, Ice-cream, chocolate ice-cream, I really fancy some."

"Ok what is Chocolate Ice-cream?" she said.

"Well, it's sort of..." he tried to explain it but decided to ask his mum if he could have team Datch around for a sleepover and then they could have some ice-cream with dinner.

"Maybe you can come to my house for a sleepover and we can have ice-cream for the sweet."

There was a consensus of opinion that a party at Datch's house would be cool especially as he had a pool and his own bar.

After breakfast they headed to the lecture room. The mornings lecture was titled 'What to do and what not to do in a restaurant', Datch thought it was going to be boring but they covered etiquette in various places on and off planet. On the planet of Okab six for instance you were expected to burp loudly to show your appreciation for the food. The louder the burp the more you liked it and therefore it was a good idea to drink fizzy pop with your meal. He made a mental note to tell his mum about this fact the next time she told him off at the table. They finished for lunch and headed to the restaurant. On the way in Datch asked the waiter about burping and was told that it was not polite in this establishment.

They had their lunch and headed off to the next lecture. Then it was dinner time and Mr Doji came and joined them.

"Well, how is team Datch today?" He asked.

There was a number of comments that the lecture was a bit boring and another question about burping. They finished their food and arranged to meet outside the front at seven thirty. With that they all headed back to their rooms to freshen up and get changed ready for the night's festivities.

Datch and the boys headed outside and found Dr Doji was waiting for them. The girls soon came along and the group headed off to the Barbers Inn. Carina was holding Datch's hand again and now seemed to be sitting next to him every chance she got. Datch really had to talk to Fred and find out what to do. As they walked along Datch was talking to Dr Doji.

"Are we meant to be going in bars?" he asked.

"Well, normally we would not suggest it until the second year but with your experience I think it would be good to set an example to the others."

"Do a lot of the lectures happen in the bars?"

"Some do, it's an important part of the social experience, most of the bars around the campus have a lecturer in them. they even mark students on how they interact with the population."

"Hmm…" Datch thought about this, "Are you marking us now?" he asked.

"No, not at the moment. That won't happen until you have covered social interactions."

They arrived at the bar. It was a little busier tonight, Tank, Fred and Clax had taken over the large table they were sitting at the night before. They got their drinks and sat down. Again, Carina was at Datch's side. Fred looked at him and could tell he was a little out of depth.

"Datch, your dad called me today and wanted me to ask you something, can I have a quick word with you?" Datch nodded and they went and sat at another table.

"I can see you're a bit unsure how to react to Carina?" he said quietly.

"I don't know what to do?" said Datch sounding a little worried.

"Do you like her?"

"Yes, quite a lot."

"Well then this is what you do…" five minutes later they went back to the table and Datch was smiling. He sat down next to Carina and put his hand on hers. She looked at him and smiled.

"So Datch," said Dr Doji who was now called Jep because they were in the bar. "What's this about the Dancing Jaxx, I should like to point out that it's Karaoke night tomorrow so we could all do with a heads up on your style." Datch looked at Tank.

"What can I say dude, you have a rep." Datch wasn't sure what rep meant.

"Rep?" he said.

"Yes, reputation dude, you're a bit of a party animal and have no fear of anything."

The other bikers all nodded in agreement and Datch was about to say something about the bathroom incident on the Carpaycus but changed his mind.

"Ok then, I'll tell the story of the Dancing Jaxx and The Mountain."

The bikers looked at each other and wished Jep hadn't said anything. Datch was just about to start when Peebop came walking in looking a bit down. He got a drink and came over to sit down.

"What's up man?" He looked into his glass.

"We've lost another two bots this week, I don't know what's happening to them. One minute they were working on the new power system and the next, they had gone."

"Oh, sorry to hear that dude,"

"That makes eight now and no trace. They just walked straight off site and vanished."

"Well, don't worry dude, Datch is about to tell us about the story about the Dancing Jaxx." said Fred trying to change the subject.

"Is he including the skiing bit?" he asked looking slightly worried and could see his street cred taking a nose dive at any moment.

"I think so mate, sorry."

He got back up, went to the bar and came back with a stronger looking drink. Jep was now very interested as he hadn't heard about the mountain yet and judging by Peebop's reaction it was going to be priceless.

"Ok, Datch off you go?" said Tank taking a large gulp of beer.

Datch started to tell the tale and on one or two occasions various members of the group turned funny colours. Also, at one point everyone turned and looked at Fred who just went very red and said 'look it was cold' this was followed by a chorus of laughter. Team Datch were starting to join in now and Datch noticed Jep was watching them but didn't seem to be paying him the same attention though. It was more how they were joining in that was catching his eye. The evening went on and it was soon time to head back to the school. Again, Datch was holding hands with Carina all the way back. They arrived back at school and went in.

Datch and Carina slowed down along the corridor as the others went ahead and around the corner towards their rooms. Datch stopped and turned to Carina. She looked into his eyes and smiled. Datch did as Fred had told him and moved closer to her. He put his arms around her and kissed her on the lips. It sent more shivers down his spine. They kissed for a few seconds before stopping and Datch looked at her trying to gauge if she liked it. She looked at him back,

"Was that, OK?" He said slightly puzzled.

"I think so, but let me have another one to make sure."

They kissed again.

"Yes, it was." She said with a big smile of her face as they came up for air.

They walked back up the corridor and to her room. He gave her another kiss good night before heading back to his room with a spring in his step.

He walked into the room and sat down looking at the starport through the window. Dapo walked over to him.

"Are you ok Datch?" he asked.

"Yes." he said still looking out the window.

"You kissed her, didn't you?" Datch looked around.

"How do you know?" he said wondering if they had been peeping around the corner.

"It stands out a mile. You're looking all starry eyed and have a smile on your face from one ear to the other. The holding hands and the slow walking, it was going to happen."

Datch looked at him for a second taking in what he had said,

"Was it really that obvious?" he said.

"Yes. So, I take it you and Carina are boyfriend and girlfriend then?"

"I suppose we are."

He didn't want to talk anymore. He just wanted to saver the moment and turned back to the window. Dapo said something else but he took no notice. His thoughts were with the kiss, the softness of her skin against his and her smell, he let out a sigh and went and got in bed.

The next morning, he got up and went to call his mum. The thought entered his head of whether to say anything or not. He decided not to and wait until the right moment. He told his mum about the lessons and a bit more about team Datch, then she asked the question.

"So, what have you been doing at night?" Datch thought about this and decided to tell the truth.

"Hanging out with, Team Datch, our tutor Dr Doji (Jep), Fred, Peebop, Clax and Tank." There was a pause. His dad just walked in as he said it.

"So that's why you went off with a spring in your step, don't tell me you have been partying every night?"

"No dad, as Mr Doji said, we are learning social interaction, anyway its karaoke tonight and Jep, sorry Mr Doji told us to get there early." his mum looked at his dad.

"Well, if the tutor thinks its ok it must be." His dad said shrugging his shoulders.

"Oh," he said trying to make it sound like an afterthought "I want you to meet team Datch, so can you come a few minutes early and can you bring my bike to pick me up tomorrow, I want to look cool."

They carried on talking but Datch switched the conversation to the view out of his window and the lessons he had for today. The call ended and he set about getting the others up for breakfast. Back at the ranch, his mum and dad looked at each other.

"He's not telling us something, I can tell." said Tansya.

Dechow turned to her.

"I think you're right, but what?"

Tansya shrugged.

"I'm sure we'll find out." she said and headed off into the kitchen to get herself some breakfast.

The restaurant was very busy but they found a table and sat down. A few minutes later the girls turned up. Datch waved them over and Carina came and sat down next to him. He asked her what she wanted for breakfast and went and got it for her along with his own. The others were looking at each other and then at Datch and Carina.

"What's the matter?" Datch asked,

"So, are you two an item?" Tish asked.

Datch looked at Carina who gave him a little nod and smiled.

"Yes." he answered.

He went back to eating his breakfast. Hagger asked Dapo what an item was to which he whispered in his ear and Hagger went red again with embarrassment. Datch decided to get Fred to talk to Hagger about the whole girl thing and hopefully stop him going red so much. More to the point he was now trying to work out how to introduce Carina to his dad.

They got up and headed out of the restaurant. Carina gave Datch a kiss for getting her breakfast and Hagger went red yet again. They headed off to the day's lectures with Datch considering changing Hagger's name to Beacon on account of his redness or hazard after the red lights that flash on and off.

Datch was a big help to the team. He schooled them on what to do and what not to do. Some of which might have been a bit wrong but it was a lot closer than most of the other students. The rest were now taking in every word he said. It was a bit worrying for him as he didn't know everything and felt that he now needed to. He pondered the problem for a while and decided to ask Jep at the break. They finished the first lecture and went to lunch. Afterwards he went and had a chat with Jep which made him a lot happier. Jep had told him that there was not always a right or wrong way to do things. So just trust in yourself, gauge things and hope for the best. He also told him he was not to mother them too much and don't let the captain thing go to his head.

The next lecture was what to look out for in bars and clubs. This consisted of a number of lecturers acting out scenes and various scenarios. Each team had to go up and handle the situation. Then the rest of the teams got to vote on the outcome and say what they would have done. It was in fact quite good fun.

Soon it was time for dinner. They didn't hang about. Dinner was finished in thirty minutes and then back to the rooms to get ready for the evening. Datch had been busy talking about what they should wear and asking them what songs they liked, he was really in his element now. They met outside, but ended up waiting for Jep before heading down to the Barbers Inn. This time Datch had his arm around Carina and he found it a bit awkward to start with but they soon worked it out.

They walked into the Barbers Inn and went over to the big table. Datch got the drinks in as his mum and dad had given him some credits to spend if he needed something. They sat down ready for the nights thrilling instalment. Datch was sitting next to Carina and this time she was leaning against his shoulder. The conversation started about what songs people liked and Datch went through his list before finding a couple that Carina liked. He made a note of them for later. It turned out that Rosey had also done Karaoke once and had a couple of songs she liked whereas Hagger and Dapo didn't want to do it at all. Neither did Tish, but after a bit of persuasion gave in and agreed to do one song. The bikers came in and picked up their drinks on the way to the table.

Datch had given the barman credits for them as they had got the drinks the last two nights. Fred looked across at Datch and Carina. She had her hand on top of his and he smiled to himself. The karaoke started up about nine o'clock and it wasn't long before the place was full. The music played and the place started to buzz.

"Wow, this is really cool, let's dance." Carina said taking Datch's hand and dragging him off to the small dance floor. They started to dance to one of the songs that they both knew and soon were swaying together on the dance floor.

"Err Fred, you have talked to Datch about the whole girl thing, haven't you?" said Tank wondering just what Fred had told him.

"Yes, don't worry, he knows the ins and outs, also the dos and don'ts."

"Good, because I don't think the planet could handle two of him."

There was a general sigh of relief from around table, well from the adults anyway. Team Datch were slightly puzzled by the comment.

"He seems to be getting the hang of the dancing with her anyway?" said Jep.

"Datch doesn't have a problem with dancing, just wait till later." said Clax looking across the dance floor.

Datch had Carina in his arms and was now cheek to cheek with her. The song finished and they kissed.

"Yep, no problems there." Said Fred.

"Eight out of ten, I would say." Added Tank, team Datch were just looking stunned and Hagger had gone red again.

Datch and Carina came back from the dance floor and sat down. Carina had a hot flush and Datch was sweating. They both took a really big drink.

"Was that, ok?" asked Datch getting his breath back.

"Which bit?" said Hagger trying to exert himself a bit.

"Err, the dancing." Datch said going a bit red himself.

"Eight out of ten." said Fred jumping in before anyone else could embarrass the young couple.

"Yes, now who wants another drink?" said Tank changing the subject.

The evening went on and Datch went up on stage. He did one of his rock songs and by the end of it team Datch were once again stunned. Datch put his arm out and beckoned to Carina, she was a bit reluctant but Fred gave her a push. She went over to the little stage. Datch put out his hand, she took it and stepped up next to him.

"I'm bit scared" she whispered.

"It will be fine, just watch the vid and follow my lead, most of all just enjoy it." He handed her a mic.

The vid started to show the words to the song and the music started to play. Datch started to sing and Carina joined in, it was a little bit disjointed to start with but she soon got the hang of it and then Datch started to dance with her while singing. Soon they were both dancing and Carina forgot about the rest of the crowd. It was just her and Datch singing together. The others watched in awe as the young couple danced and sang on the stage making it their own as if under some magic spell. Then at the end of the song they kissed again. The bar erupted with applause and Tank threw in a few whistles for good measure.

Jep was sitting looking somewhat impressed.

"Who taught him to do that?" he asked.

"I have no idea; I don't even know how he does it?" said Clax.

"His mum and dad said he learnt to do it in the shower." added Fred helpfully.

"The shower?" asked Jep.

"You should see him with the band, it's really something else." Peebop said.

"He has a band?" said Dapo catching up with the conversation.

"No, I think the band in the Dancing Jaxx sort of has him, but it's a bit of a grey area."

"Oh, that one." said Rosey joining in and trying to sound like she knew something.

It was now Datch and Carina's second song. Datch was again leading and the crowd was now joining in as well. Rosey grabbed Dapo and dragged him onto the dance floor. Then Tish not to be out done grabbed Hagger and dragged him up as well. He tried to tell her he couldn't dance but it didn't work. The four of them started dancing in front of the stage. Well three of them anyway. Hagger was just trying to keep up and not fall over. The music carried on and the song came to the end with a big crescendo, Datch and Carina leaped into the air and landed in front of the rest of the team to another round of applause. They headed back to the table somewhat out of breath.

"Well, I can see you're on form." said Fred looking at the pair of them.

"What a rush." said Carina who was rather red in the face.

The night carried on and Rosey did her song and got a big round of applause. Then they called Datch's name again and this time he had a grin on his face.

"Oh no! I know that look." said Fred.

"Err what look?" asked Jep puzzled.

The rest of the bikers looked worried and started to debate running for the nearest toilet but it was too late. Datch came on the mic and asked the whole table to come up.

The bikers only comment was "Oh no, not again," as the whole bar turned to look at them.

Soon the whole gang was on stage. Hagger looked like his worst nightmare had just come true. The bikers had dragged Jep up as well. If they had got to sing, so had he. Team Datch assembled behind Datch and Carina, Datch turned around.

"You're just doing the chorus, me and Carina are doing the song, just enjoy it."

He turned to face the front and nodded. The music started and the bar shook to the rhythm, even the bar staff were dancing. It took two choruses before Hagger finally got the idea but then opened up. The song ended to rapturous applause and cheers as they came off the stage and headed back to the table. A round of drinks came from the bar and a large bowl of nibbles. They sat there getting their breath back. Hagger was looking a little pink which made a change from red. Jep looked like he had been hit by lighting and the rest of team Datch were all drinking and looking like they had just eaten too much chocolate. The bikers just sat looking at each other.

"Well, we knew that was going to happen, didn't we?" said Tank. The others all nodded in unison.

"Does this normally happen?" asked Jep finally getting his breath back.

"Well, Datch is a sort of magnet to it and to answer your question, yes, quite a lot." Replied Tank.

The drinks were going down very well and it wasn't long before team Datch were back on the dance floor.

"I'm thinking of calling in sick next week." said Clax.

"You own your own shop; how can you call in sick? You would be talking to yourself." asked Tank.

"No, not to work, to the bar."

"Oh, I see what you mean." said Tank.

The bikers thought about this and finally Fred spoke.

"You can't and neither can we, we can't let Datch loose on the city, it would be defenceless, we'd have to move planets or something!"

There was a general consensus of agreement. Jep was starting to think that maybe taking on Datch might be harder than he thought for totally the opposite reasons than normal.

After a couple more songs team Datch came wandering back to the table and Jep pointed out that they had better be heading back soon. They had another drink before saying their goodbye's and arranged to meet up the following week. With that they left the bar and headed off back to the school. Datch and Carina walked along hand in hand while the rest of them were chatting away. They were still buzzing from the bar when they got back to the school. Datch and Carina were left on their own to say good night and after a few minutes went to bed.

Next morning Datch packed his bag and headed off to have breakfast. Carina was waiting for him.

"Here is my vid com, call me if you like?" she said giving him a kiss.

Datch smiled at her.

"I will, it's going to be a long time till next week."

She gave him another kiss.

"I want you to see my bike before you go home." he said with a smile.

"Oh, and my dad." he added as an afterthought.

They went in and started to have breakfast, soon the rest of the team turned up, then Jep came over and sat down.

"Well team, it's been an interesting few days and I have been very surprised by all of you. I mean that in a good way. If you carry on like this, school will not only be fun but judging by last night, exciting as well."

Datch thanked him for letting them out as did the others. They finished their food and decided to all wait outside for their parents to turn up.

The Home Coming

The morning was bright and sunny. The space port was busy as usual and there were a lot of people coming and going in the streets around the school. Datch made sure everyone had his vid com and said he would ask his dad about having a 'err what was it, ah yes' a team building party at his house with a pool party included. He sat next to Carina with his arm around her enjoying the sun light. Then in the distance the familiar roar of bikes. This time there was two of them. They dropped down to the edge of the parking area and came to a stop. There was only one rider as the second bike was on auto pilot. The rider got off and came walking over. He was a tall man of medium build and was wearing a jacket similar to the bikers at the bar. He pressed the button at the side of his helmet and it folded away into his collar.

"Hi dad" said Datch standing up, Carina stood up with him.

Dechow looked his son up and down, then looked at Carina. it didn't take any working out what was going on there.

"Hi Datch, looks like you have been having a good time at school, who are your friends?"

"This Dad is team Datch, this is Carina," she stepped forward and held out her hand, Dechow shook it.

"Please to meet you sir." she said.

"You too." he said.

"And this is Dapo and Hagger."

They stepped forward and shook his hand, Hagger had gone red as usual.

"And finally, this is Tish and Rosey." They stepped forward and shook hands.

They had just finished introducing each other when Dapo's and Tish's parents showed up. There was another round of hellos and before that was finished Carina's mum turned up to fetch her. Hagger had a message to go home as his dad had to work and couldn't fetch him. They all said their goodbye's and Datch got a peck of the cheek from Carina. He got on his bike and put his helmet on before starting it up. He followed his dad as the bikes rose into the air and headed off out of the city. As they cleared the edge of the city his dad came on the headset.

"I take it Carina is your girlfriend?" he said.

There was a long pause while Datch debated his options.

"Yes." he finally said.

He felt he needed to say something more so plumbed for

"She comes from a farm near Papaso in the south"

The conversation carried on at a somewhat cautious pace. Datch was trying to make sure he didn't say anything his dad wouldn't like as he wanted him to like Carina and the team. He was also being careful about what he said especially when it came to the Barbers Inn and only said that the team had been there with his tutor on an educational outing where they had met the bikers.

The bikes left the suburbs behind and were soon flying over the fields below. The desert could be seen in the distance as they flew over the small village and then the ranch was in sight. The bikes started to drop lower and Datch could see his mum waiting for them on the veranda near the pool. Datch and his dad brought their bikes around and they landed next to the veranda steps. They got off and Datch ran over and gave his mum a hug.

"Hi mum." he said.

Dechow came walking up behind. After a few minutes of Datch telling her about the school, the team and Jep. Dechow spoke,

"Err Datch, don't you have something else to tell your mum?"

Datch looked a little awkward. He didn't quite know how to put it and he looked at his dad. Dechow stared back at him with a look of 'if you don't I will' on his face.

"Erm." He paused "I might have a girlfriend."

He paused waiting for some sort of inquisition but none came.

"It's Carina," he added.

His mum just gave him another hug and smiled at him. Datch wasn't sure whether this meant it was ok or there would be trouble later, but decided to leave it like that and take his stuff indoors.

"Told you he was hiding something." Dechow whispered to Tansya as they walked in the house.

The next day Datch got up and headed down to get breakfast. He watched the latest episode of Star Warrior and then decided to see if he could talk to Carina. He didn't know why but he was missing her a lot. He entered the code in the vid com and after a few seconds a lady answered.

"Hello, Can I help you?"

"Yes mam, please can I talk to Carina?" the woman looked at him.

"Who can I say is calling?"

Datch was starting to sweat a bit.

"It's Datch mam." he said in his best voice.

"Ok, please wait I'll get her for you."

She turned away from vid com and shouted up the stairs, then tuned back to Datch.

"I take it I'm addressing her team leader?" she asked.

"Yes mam." he was about to carry on when there was the sound of someone half running and half jumping down the stairs at the other end of the vid com. Then Carina came into view looking a bit out of breath and she had her T-shirt on backwards.

"Hi Datch." she said half nudging her mum out the way.

Her mum relinquished control of the vid com and walked off out of the room saying he sounds like a nice young man to someone Datch hadn't seen.

"Hi Carina, how are you doing?"

"I'm good, how about you?"

"Yes, am I ok to talk?" She looked over her shoulder.

"Yes, my mum's doing something in the kitchen and dad's just gone outside somewhere."

"I'm missing you; it's only been one day and I can't wait see you again." he said.

"Me too," she said and blew a kiss at the screen.

"I've been learning another one of the songs you like." she said.

"Cool. Maybe we can do that next week."

The next fifteen minutes were spent mostly with small talk. Datch also decided to spend some time in the shower later. It was the best place to learn songs after all.

Tansya came down the stairs and could hear Datch on the vid.

"Morning Datch." She said walking into the bar to find out what he was up to.

"Oh, hi mum." he said looking a little red. He thought for a moment.

"Mum come here a minute."

She went over to him. On the other end of the vid com was a young woman with red shoulder length hair, she had deep green eyes that sparkled in the light from the vid com and a light brown complexion.

"This is Carina mum."

Datch stepped to the side a little so Carina could see his mum.

"Please to meet you mam." she said.

"Yes, Datch has told us about the team, it's very nice to meet you, you live on a farm as well, don't you?"

The conversation carried on for a couple of minutes before his mum made her excuses and then headed off into the kitchen to get some breakfast. Datch turned back to the vid com.

"I'll have to go soon. My dad will be up and he wants me to give him a hand with one of the fences."

"Oh." she sounded a bit down hearted.

"Yes, but I'll call you in the morning again, about the same time if that's ok?" She started smiling again.

"That would be great I'll make sure I'm up tomorrow, have you said anything about us?" she said.

"Err, I didn't have to, my dad worked it out when he came to pick me up. I think he spotted my arm around you and the kiss. They both seem to be cool with it I think."

"I think my mum suspects something but hasn't said anything yet."

"I'm going to try to get my parents to let me have a team building weekend. At least that's what I'm going to call it, I would invite the bikers but they are still getting over the last party we had."

"Are your parties that bad, no good, err you know what I mean."

Datch laughed.

"Yes, some of them can be quite an adventure or so I'm told." he was smiling.

He could hear his dad moving about upstairs so he said his goodbyes and blew her a big kiss but it still took about five minutes more until he finally disconnected the call.

Dechow came down stairs. He had decided to take Datch down to the bottom field to have a chat about girls. It was something he had planned to do for a while. He was still trying to work out how to put things after he had finished his breakfast and decided just to go for it. He called Datch and they walked down to the field. Datch seemed to be in a very good mood for this time in the morning. Dechow got the spare fence posts and gave Datch the hammer and nails to carry, He was trying to work out how to start the conversation as it was a long time since he had told Datch's brother Dydinyon about the opposite sex. They started putting the fence posts in.

"So, Datch, how are you getting on with Carina?"

"Ok dad."

"I know it's all new to you but if you want any advice, I'm here. We can talk man to man if you want?" He thought it sounded ok.

"It's ok dad, you don't need to tell me, Fred's explained everything." Dechow looked at his son.

"Really? What everything?"

Datch could see the look of surprise and relief on his dad's face.

"Yes. Well, all the important bits anyway." He carried on knocking the nail into to post.

"Oh. That's ok then" he paused,

"What about the kissing thing?"

"Yep."

"Dancing?"

"Yep."

"Baby making and not making?" There was a small pause and Datch went a bit pink,

"Yes." he said.

"Err, and this was all on the educational trip?"

"No, the following night when Tank got me to tell them about the Dancing Jaxx and the mountain." Datch suddenly realised what he had said.

"Oh, so you went to the Barbers Inn twice then?"

"Yes, but our tutor said it was a really good learning experience and was with us all the time we were there."

"Hmm."

Datch turned back and hammered a nail in extra hard to avoid the conversation.

Dechow gave up but decided he was going to have a word with Fred next time he bumped into him. Still, it had just got rid of all the awkward questions that he hadn't wanted to talk about. They carried on putting the fence up and finished just before lunch. They went back to the house to get some food. Tansya sat looking at them eating their sandwiches.

"So, did you two have a good chat while you were down at the field?"

"Yes, mum it was cool. Can I go in the pool?"

"Yes, but take it easy until your lunch has gone down." she said.

With that Datch went off to get changed.

"Well?" she said.

"I didn't have to say anything. Apparently, Fred is his new Guru and has told him everything he needs to know."

"Really? Are you sure?"

"Yes, I even tried to catch him out and couldn't."

"Wow, He's a bit of a surprise,"

"Yes, Datch is turning out to be different that's for sure."

"Not Datch, Fred!"

"Oh, yes. I have to say, he's given Datch all the important bits."

With that they finished their lunch and went outside to join Datch who was now in the pool.

The rest of the weekend was spent talking about school and the Barbers Inn although Datch was careful about how much he said. Also, a bit more about team Datch then he brought up the team building party at the house saying the school had talked about them and thought getting together out of school was a good idea. His mum asked what it would entail and Datch came up with the idea of learning the others to ride bikes. Dechow thought it might work and also through in the idea of some sort of team event but they would need to think about it a bit more. It would be a two-day event taking place over the weekend.

Datch would get up early each day to call Carina and then spend the next half an hour talking to her. The time he spent in the shower also seemed to be longer than normal but after Traxsent, no one dared to ask why.

Home is good but school is better

It was soon time to head back to school. His parents had come around to the team building event as long as the other parents agreed to it. Datch had already got his mum to talk to Carina's mum and so a date had been set for two weeks' time. Datch got up early and headed down the stairs. He had his breakfast before putting his bag on his bike. Tansya came down shortly after followed by his dad. After having to leaver, him out of bed on the first day it was a nice change to see him eager to get there, even if it was only because he wanted to see Carina. After breakfast his dad took him to school. Forty-five minutes later the bikes came into land outside of the school. Datch was the first of the team to arrive and said goodbye to his dad before taking his bag to his room. He then headed back outside to wait for Carina.

The next two days went by with lectures during the day and nights in the Barbers Inn with the bikers. On the second night they were sitting in the bar when Peebop came in looking down in the dumps, he got his drink and sat at the table looking into his beer.

"What's the matter mate?" asked Tank sitting down next to him.

"We lost another bot today; I'm getting a lot of pressure now to find out where they are going and we don't have a clue." Datch was listening.

"Don't you have a vid of them?" he asked.

"Yes, but it just shows the bot stopping and then making off into a tent and vanishing."

"Someone must have transported it out." said Hagger who was also listening.

"No, the bots all have transport locks on them so they can't be transported off site without the system being shut off. We looked in the tent and even scanned for any residue, but nothing was there."

Datch was getting very intrigued.

"Could I see the vid please, I might have an idea."

"Do you know anything about bots?" Peebop asked.

"A little, my dad taught me to use one when we built the bar. If these are the same someone must have got close to them."

"Well, ok, at this point I'll take any help I can get."

He pulled out a small vid com from his pocket and replayed the vid of the bot disappearing.

It showed the bot fetching some cabling and then going back to the edge of the site to get some more. As the bot got next to the fence it stopped and sat down then got up and walked out of the site and into a tent on the road outside. The vid bot flew around to the tent but it was empty except for a few small stools where the workers would sit for a break.

"Hmm," said Datch "I see what you mean, could you play it again but with a closer view of the bot please." Peebop did as requested.

As the bot got to the corner there was a branch or something that flicked across the screen. The bot sat down and then after a short pause got up walked off the site into the tent and was gone.

"I can't see anything." said Hagger who was trying to be helpful.

Datch sat backdown next to Carina.

"I don't know either." he said.

The evening carried on and everyone tried to make Peebop feel better. Tish even got him a cookie because as she put it "Everyone feels better after a Cookie."

Datch seemed a little bit distracted, Carina was worried as he wasn't paying her as much attention as normal.

"Are you OK Datch?" She said looking into his eyes, he snapped back to reality.

"Oh, err, yes, sorry, I was just replaying the vid of the bot's disappearance in my head, I'm sure I'm missing something." he had a look of frustration on his face.

"Oh, I thought I had done something wrong."

"No, no, I was just thinking, sorry." With that he gave her a kiss and joined back in the conversation.

The evening finished and plans were made for the following night, Karaoke night.

The following day team Datch had implant training in the morning. Datch found it a bit boring as it was about knowledge recall and recording memories, both of which he knew how to do already. Following lunch, it was street behaviour and as such the class was taken off into a number of busy streets and put through their paces. It was interesting as Datch spent most of his time checking out the local shops and found a number of outfits for Hagger and Dapo, one for himself and a nice top for Carina. He also found a shop doing custom T-shirts and ordered six of them with 'The Great Adventure' on the front and 'The Datch Pack on tour - Born to Party' on the back. He was going to get some hats as well but then thought it may be over kill. The evening arrived and it was time to head down to the Barbers Inn.

They arrived at the bar and sat at the big table. The drinks were brought over by one of the barmen. They were getting to know them and the bar staff were now more than happy to bring the drinks over for them. It was great because they just had to put their hand up and another round would appear. Datch had been practicing one of the songs that Carina liked and was planning to surprise her with it. It wasn't long before the bikers turned up.

Fred, Tank and Peebop were trying to work out how to get out of going on stage but Datch was having none of it. Clax had tried to say he was ill but totally failed to pull it off and therefore was going to have to do a forfeit of some sort. The Datch pack weren't sure what a forfeit was but it sounded like fun. The music started and Datch was first up. He shouted into the mic. "Let's get this party started." and the music blasted out.

Tank turned to Fred.

"You know we might have created a party monster."

Fred looked at Datch then back at Tank.

"No, he was like it when we met him, But now he's no longer on the leash. "

"Do you think the planet will survive?"

"Well, if not I have an uncle on Alcyone three who I can live with."

Datch hit a high note on the stage and a woman at the back of the bar screamed.

"Does he have a spare room?" Asked Tank.

They turned back to the stage, Datch finished his song to a huge round of applause and came back to the table.

"So what song are we doing?" asked Carina,

"It's a surprise and you know it so don't worry." he smiled at her and gave her a kiss.

The kissing was now a lot more relaxed as Datch and Carina's confidence was growing along with their relationship.

The night moved on and soon it was time for Datch and Carina to go up. They took to the stage and the words 'Star Lovers' appeared on the vid. Carina turned and gave Datch a big smile. It was a rock ballad and Datch was in his element and soon the bar was vibrating to the sound of the music. This time though he wasn't singing to the bar, he was singing to Carina. He looked straight into her eyes singing his heart out. At this point two more bikers came into the bar. They got some drinks and headed over to the table.

Tank turned to look at them.

"Err, Fred?" he said and poked him in the ribs.

He turned to look at Tank and spotted the other two.

"Oh, this could be awkward."

The two bikers came and sat down.

"Hello Fred, Tank, Clax, Peebop." The tall biker said

"Hi Dechow, Tansya." said Fred, others all said hi in a slightly sheepish way.

The song carried on and at the end Datch took Carina in his arms and kissed. The bar went wild, cheering and screaming. Datch and Carina took a bow and headed over to the table. They got to a few steps away when Tansya turned around, Datch froze to the spot for a second.

"Err, Hi mum."

"Hi Datch, looks like you're having fun."

He tried to weigh up whether he was in trouble or not, then his mum smiled and so he figured not. Jep in the meantime was trying to melt into the background which considering he was between Tank and Clax was not an easy task and he totally failed.

"Yes, mum, can I present Carina, this is my mum and you've met my dad."

"Hello, it's nice to meet you." Carina said.

"Yes, you as well." Tansya said, his dad stood up and shook her hand.

"So, are you going to introduce us to the rest of your team?" he said.

Datch then went around the table and introduced everyone including Jep who had given up trying to hide as there seemed to be a very large Tank in the way.

"So, what brings you here?" Fred asked when he thought it was safe to do so.

"Well, Datch wants a team building weekend at the ranch, so we thought we had better get to meet the rest of the team first. We guessed you would be here tonight so I booked a room upstairs overnight."

He was just about to ask what sort of food people liked when Datch and Carina were called back to the stage. Carina smiled at Datch and mouthed 'Pay back'. They were handed the mics and the song title came on the screen, Datch smiled. the music played and they started to sing.

It was like watching magic happen on stage. Tansya had a tear in her eye as she realised her little boy was not her little boy any longer but was Carina's. There was something electrical about their performance. She could see Datch was firing off Carina and she was bouncing off him. It was like they were one person split into two and even Dechow couldn't take his eyes off them. As the song went on Datch didn't take his eyes off Carina, as they danced around each other on the stage. Then they turned to the audience and raised their hands and the bar erupted. Finally, the music finished and another round of applause, cheering and clapping. They took another bow and then came back to sit down. There was no denying it Datch and Carina were a couple and when they were together it was magical.

"Mum, is it still ok for the team building?" Datch looked at his mum.

"You mean party! and yes, get everyone's vid com and I'll call their parents." She had seen through Datch's team building, but was ok about it, as long as they behaved.

"Cool." Datch said.

He put his hand on Carina's and sat watching the karaoke. Rosey was up next and did another rock song. The evening carried on with song after song. Tansya and Dechow chatted to team Datch and got to know them. Soon it was time for the last song of the night and Datch's name appeared on the Vid. The bar started to chant, 'Datch, Datch, Datch'. He got up and headed to the stage with Carina in toe. Clax hid under the table and the rest of the bikers looked into the bottom of their glasses. Datch and Carina were on the stage and waved at the table.

"Please can I have a big round of applause for our backing singers." he said pointing at the table, they all started to get up.

"Someone help Clax up, he's fallen under the table." said Fred.

Tank pulled him out and marched him up to the stage.

"I would like to welcome my mum and dad; they will be helping out as well."

There was another cheer from the crowd.

"Ok, are we ready to rock?" a huge cheer came back.

"I can't hear you, ARE WE READY TO ROCK?" with that the bar erupted.

The song started and the music blasted out, the bar was moving to the rhythm of the music. Even the bar staff were again dancing behind the bar and singing along. Finally, after the second encore they headed back to the table.

They sat having their dinks and now the music had quieted down they sat chilling out.

"Don't you have to be back at school?" said Tansya.

"We're ok till one in the morning mum, we have a special pass, Jep sorted it out for us, he said as I had already a lot of experience, we could have it this year instead of next." Jep just nodded.

He was feeling a bit worn out and was starting to have second thoughts about the Datch pack. He had thought it would be a nice easy team to manage, just sit back, watch them chat and act mature. Easy. However, he had forgotten that the more mature students know how to party and team Datch seemed to be taking things to the limit. At the rate things were going, he wasn't sure he would make the end of the trimester let alone two years.

"Are you ok Jep?" Tansya asked.

"Oh, fine thanks, I'm just getting my breath back that's all," he smiled.

"I know the feeling." she said.

They had another round of drinks before heading back to the school. It was strange for Datch leaving his mum and dad behind and heading back through the city, still he had Carina on his arm and it felt great.

The next morning Datch got up and went to have some breakfast. Carina was there with Rosey. He went over and gave Carina a peck on the cheek before sitting down. They chatted a while and soon Hagger, Dapo and Tish arrived at which point they all had breakfast. They had a couple of coffee's and carried on talking a bit before finally heading outside.

The rest of the parents were waiting apart from Hagger's dad. Hagger had got another text message telling him that his dad was working again and couldn't get away. Tansya suggested that they take Hagger home. He was a bit reluctant until Datch said he could give him a ride on the back of his bike and with that Hagger agreed. After a round of goodbyes and a covert kiss to Carina, Datch got on his bike and Hagger got on behind him.

Datch fed Hagger's address into the Nav Con and soon they were airborne. Hagger's home was only about five minutes away from the school but would take him about fifteen to twenty minutes by public transport to get there. They landed outside the apartments and Datch was going to carry his bag in for him but Hagger said the place needed tidying up and he was fine. Datch was a little puzzled about it but got back on his bike and said goodbye. The bikes took off and headed down the street and out of site. Hagger watched them go before heading inside.

The apartment was small and had only one room which consisted of a main seating area, a small galley kitchen and a small shower cubical in the corner. Hagger looked around. There were empty fast-food cartons littered about and a pile of cloths laying in the floor near the shower booth in the corner next to the toilet. The place smelled of stale food and body odder. Hagger sighed, put his bag on his bed and started to pick up the mess.

Datch got home and went and sat in the bar. It was about ten minutes later when his dad came in and sat next to him.

"What no pool?" he asked.

"I'll be there in a minute, it's just something Peebop showed me, I'm trying to work it out."

His dad looked puzzled.

"Show me." he said, Datch looked at him.

"I can't I recorded it with my implant." Dechow smiled.

"You can still share it if you want to, you just have to tell your implant to copy to and then look at me, I'll then accept the transfer and be able to see what you're looking at."

Datch did as his dad said and then they were both looking at it.

"I don't know Datch, its very strange, I can't see anything, maybe you could try the alien database, but I've never seen anything like it." he shrugged.

"Ok dad, Thanks for having a look anyway." He looked at it again and decided to try to draw the branch.

He was trying to work out if it could have brushed it. He paused the playback a few times, each time drawing the shape. Afterwards he put them together and came up with a black crooked stick with a point on the end. What a weird branch he thought, he gave up and headed to the pool.

The rest of the weekend was spent with calls to Carina in the morning and then planning the team building event for the following weekend in the afternoon. The event was now turning more and more into a Datch party but there still had to be team work involved. However, even if you stretched the words team and building over an entire light year the word party would still have appeared somewhere in very big letters.

His mum and Dad called all the parent's and arranged to pick them up. After a bit of a discussion Datch was going to be allowed to pick Carina up on his own as long as she called her mum as soon as she arrived at the ranch. Datch was made to promise to behave himself on the bike and come straight back. His dad was going to pick up the rest of them in the truck.

Datch kept going back to the drawing of the branch. There was something about it that was bugging him. He coloured it in brown but it still wasn't right, there were no places for leaves to go. He decided to go and have a look at the site while he was at school. It was only five blocks away and he could get the team to come with him.

During the next week, Datch and the team went to the lectures during the day and partied at night in the Barbers Inn. On the second day Datch told the team to meet him half an hour earlier than normal as he wanted to go somewhere on the way.

Datch and the boys went and picked up the girls before heading outside.

"So, what's with the detour?" Asked Rosey.

"You know Peebop's site where the bots keep disappearing, it's only about four blocks from here. I want to have a quick look on my way to the Barbers to see if I can spot anything."

Datch looked at them.

"You don't have to come if you don't want to, but I want to help Peebop if I can." He added.

"Well, I'm in, Peebop is a nice guy and if I can help I will," said Carina.

There was a consensus of agreement and soon they were all walking down the road discussing the case of the missing bots.

"So, what do we know?" asked Dapo looking at Datch.

Datch raised an eyebrow and sighed.

"Well, there is the vid of the crime, the tent and the fact it's happened nine times now without a single clue."

"So, what are we going to look for?" asked Tish.

"I want to see the tree, there is something about the branch that doesn't look right, I recorded the vid using my implant then replayed it a few times last weekend, I showed my dad too, but he didn't know."

"You can record things!" said Hagger trying to catch up.

"You can share them?" asked Carina.

"Yes, you can share them if you want to," said Datch squeezing her hand gently.

"Oh right." she said.

Datch smiled at her and winked.

"So, we're looking for clues then, that's cool." said Tish.

"Yes, look does everyone know how to record things with their implants like we were shown last week?"

"Err, I'm not sure. I think I must have missed that bit." said Hagger.

"Ok, I'll go through what I know about my implant." Datch said with a sigh.

This was hard work. The following three blocks were spent with Datch explaining how to do this and how to do that. The rest were now hanging on his every word and he felt like a leader. It was strange, the team that he had only known for three weeks was now following him.

Finally, they came to the site. It was over half the block and it took a while to find the tent were the bot disappeared. They stood looking at the corner of the site.

"Are you sure this is the right place?" said Carina looking puzzled.

"Yes, I think so" said Datch replaying the vid in his head and trying to work it out.

"Err, well the tree is missing."

They looked at the site. It bordered a large building which had a solid concrete wall stretching up three stories and other than a piece of white frayed rope hanging down from the top had nothing on the side of the site. At the base of the building was a pile of rubble and some stacks of construction supplies. Datch looked at them. No sign of a tree, he must have got the wrong spot. He turned to Carina.

"Look at me and when your implant asks if you except say yes."

Datch sent her a copy of the vid and then turned to each them in turn and did the same.

"Now replay it and tell me what you think?"

There was a bit of a pause and then Carina turned around in a circle,

"I see what you mean but the tree should be there." She said pointing to the rubble at the foot of the building.

"Yes, that's what I thought."

He went over and looked in the hut. He was now recording everything. The stools were all covered in dust apart from the one in the middle which was a bit odd, maybe only one workman came in for a break. After all the site had its own rest area with food, drinks and even showers so why come to the hut?

"Datch," said Dapo "Why do they need the hut?"

"Hmm, that's a good question, I don't know."

He looked down under the stool in the middle of the hut. There was a heavy metal access cover underneath it which looked like it hadn't been used for years. Other than that, there was nothing in the hut apart from the dusty stools.

"Does anyone see anything odd or out of place?"

Everyone had another look around for good measure.

"Well, let's head to the Barbers." said Datch.

He put his arm around Carina and headed off down the street with the rest in tow.

The Barbers inn was its normal self and they now seemed to be getting a reserved sign on the big table. They sat down and then discussed what they had seen going over the clues one by one. It wasn't long before the bikers arrived and after they had got their drinks Datch turned to Peebop.

"Peebop, we went to look at the site where the bot disappeared today. Why did you remove the tree?"

"You went there. Why?" he asked.

"I wanted to have a look to see if I could see anything," said Datch.

"We want to help if we can," added Carina.

The rest of The Pack all nodded in agreement. Peebop looked at them for a moment,

"Well, as for the tree, we haven't moved it, it should still be there."

"It's not there, and there is no sign of it being there," Dapo said joining in.

"That's odd, so what is on the video then?"

"I'm not sure but it looks like this."

Datch pulled out a small vid com that his mum and dad had got him for school things. He showed them an image of the stick that he had drawn. Carina thought it was a very good drawing but it was not a branch. Tish looked at it and thought it was a bit of pointy metal.

"Could someone have poked it and caused it to go nuts?" she asked.

"No, the bots only respond to living things, they would have to touch it with their hand and we would have seen that." Peebop said.

They sat staring at the picture and looking perplexed. That was until Rosey who had only been half paying attention got a good look at it.

"It sort of looks like one of the legs off the flying spiders that we kill when they come in the house."

Datch turned and looked at her.

"Look, I'm sorry, I just don't like spider's."

"No, hmm... you just gave me an idea." he said.

Datch stopped and looked into space. He asked his implant and it responded with 'There are three sentient arachnoid species in the known universe, two of which live in the third galaxy and one in your current galaxy, all three are of low intelligence and most never leave their home planets, they are aggressive and have also been known to feed on humanoids.'

He blinked and looked back to the table.

"Hmm, what if it was an arachnoid?" he asked. Clax shook his head.

"No, arachnoids are not allowed on this planet, they have a nasty habit of eating people, so they are banned from the star system."

Datch sighed again and put his vid comm back in his pocket. The conversation turned back to normal things like 'Star Warrior' which the bikers seem to have all got hooked on and had to watch it before coming to the bar. Clax had even started selling 'Star Warrior' merchandising in his shop and Tank had started doing 'Star Warrior' hair styles which seemed to be going down quite well.

Across town a homeless tramp broke into a disused warehouse looking for somewhere to sleep. It was dark and dusty with a few empty boxes scattered about and a strange smell in the air. The tramp walked over to one of the boxes and was about to make a bed for night when something moved in the shadows. He tried to make it out from the darkness and for a moment he thought he spotted something. It must have been about four metres tall and then it vanished into the shadows again. He felt he was being watched and decided to find somewhere else for night and made his way across the floor towards where he had come in. He was nearly there when there was a noise above his head. He looked up. Two pigeons on the roof heard a stifled scream and the dull thud. They decided to move to a new building on the grounds of not becoming a dessert.

The next day the Datch pack were getting quite excited about the weekend. Carina was trying to get Datch to tell her what he had planned but he wasn't giving anything away. Even when they arrived at the Barbers in the evening all he would tell them was to bring their swim suit and some nice clothes. Hagger was a bit quiet and didn't seem as excited as the others so Datch took him to one side to find out why.

"What's up?"

"Err," he was looking embarrassed, "I don't have a swim suit and I don't have much in the way of nice clothes other than the bits you got me the other day," he said quietly.

Datch smiled at him.

"Your part of my team and I've got your back. We'll get up early tomorrow and order some bits to be delivered to my home, I'll put them in your room for you when you arrive, Ok?" Hagger started to look happier.

"Are you sure it will be, ok?" he said.

"Yes, you can help me get a nice dress for Carina while we're at it?"

"Err, I don't know anything about girls' dresses."

"Well, neither do I, so we can work it out together." Hagger was now smiling again.

They went back to the rest and carried on chatting until the karaoke started, then it was time to party.

The next morning Datch was up early with Hagger. They sat in front of the vid com chatting and saying things like 'err really', 'Are you sure' and 'they don't do they?'. By the end of it, Hagger had been given a lightening course on the opposite sex and clothing styles. He also had a swim suit on the way along with two other outfits and Carina had a lovely top with matching skirt as well as a dress all of which Datch had arranged to be delivered to the ranch. They turned the vid off and got Dapo up before heading off to breakfast. Hagger had a very big grin on his face now. In fact, it was the happiest Datch had seen him and he had a bounce in his step. They had just sat down when the girls came in.

Datch got up and gave Carina a peck on the cheek and helped her get her breakfast.

"What have you done to Hagger?" she asked.

"Why?"

"He's grinning like a clown that's just sat on a Whoopee cushion."

"Oh that, I just had a bit of a chat with him this morning and gave him a bit of a boost." Carina looked at Datch.

"Datch you are a really amazing person; I know now why I love you." Datch stopped. It was the first time she had said that. He looked into her eyes and gave her a kiss on the lips.

"I love you too," he said.

They stood still looking at each other.

"Are you two going to be standing there all day?" Shouted Rosey.

With that they went and sat down.

They finished their breakfasts and headed back to their rooms to get their bags before heading outside to wait for their parents.

"Does everyone know what time they are being picked up?" Datch said.

There was a general chorus of 'yes' and then it was time to go home. Datch took Hagger home as his dad couldn't come again and then headed home with his mum and dad.

He told his mum about the cloths for Hagger and she was ok with it and added some credits to his weekly allowance to cover them and the other items. Also, she said that as he was team leader, she would talk to his dad about increasing the allowance to cover certain extra costs!

Team Building

Next morning Datch was up early. He had to get the bar ready and had to sort out the plan for the desert. By mid-morning everything was in place. The parcel he had ordered had arrived and the bits for Hagger were placed in his room. Datch had wrapped up the dress and bits for Carina and put a little card inside saying 'with lots of love Datch x x'. He headed to the bar and made sure the box with the T-shirts was there along with a set of matching Grucks glasses. He also turned on the psychedelic palm tree but decided to keep its brightness down so it didn't cause anyone retinal damage. It was then time to go and fetch the guests.

His dad was going to pick up Rosey, Tish and Dapo and Hagger and he was going to collect Carina. He went out and got on his bike and started it up, his dad had followed him out.

"Datch, Remember, no showing off. You promised. Just do as I told you."

"I know dad, I'll come straight back."

He started up the bike and fed Carina's address into the nav com. He put his hand up to his dad and took off. He rose above the ranch and headed off in the direction of the city. He had made a route to skirt around the western edge of the city to get to her farm so he could miss most of the busy streets. He engaged the nav com and accelerated. The ranch soon vanished in the distance and the city got larger.

The bike's automatic system took over as he got close to the city and the bike slowed down and slotted itself into traffic. It took about fifteen minutes to get around the city before the fields appeared again and the bikes automatic systems let Datch have control back. He gave the bike a kick of speed and followed the nav com.

The fields were rolling along bellow and here and there a small forest would break up the checked pattern of green. Then in the distance a small farm appeared. It was about the same size as Jed's farm who live over the hill from the ranch. He backed off the thrusters and as he arrived, he came in for a soft and slow landing on the drive way. He stopped the bike before making sure he got off in the safest way he could and then started to walk to the door.

The door opened and Carina came out.

"Hi Carina, your taxi awaits." He said walking up to her.

"Let me take you in to meet my mum and dad first." She said and took him indoors.

Inside Carina's mum was standing in the kitchen making some bread.

"Mum, this is Datch."

"Please to meet you, mam." he said.

She looked him up and down then smiled and came over to him.

"Yes, it is nice to meet you, Carina has told us a lot about you,"

He was then taken out of the backdoor and over to the barn, Carina's dad was there.

"Dad, this is Datch."

"Ah, so you are Datch,"

"Yes sir."

"I hope you are going to take good care of Carina this weekend?"

"Yes sir, I will. I promise."

"Good." he said.

There was then a bit of small talk before Datch was taken back to the house. Carina had a rucksack with all of her bits in for the weekend and after her parents had told Datch to be careful about six times they got onto the bike. Datch pressed the home button on the nav com and started the thrusters. Carina put her arms around him and held on as the bike rose slowly into the air and headed back towards the city. Both of Carina's parents watched as the bike headed off making sure Datch was not going too fast.

They flew on for a couple of miles and then Datch said "Hold tight!"

She gripped him tighter and he opened up the bike. Carina gave a little squeal as the bike accelerated. Ten minutes later the fields gave way to the city scape and the bike slowed down again.

"Why have you slowed down?" she asked.

"It's the city, the bike is on auto until we reach the other side." he said.

They carried on talking as the bikes auto pilot took them around the edge of the city. Once on the other side the bike beeped in Datch's ear to let him know he was now able to take control.

"Ok, hold on tight."

He accelerated again. Carina hadn't been to this side of the city before. She watched as the city scape changed to fields and then in the distance was the desert.

"What a view." she said.

The bike flew on and soon they were over the little village. Then ahead Datch could see the ranch and started to slow down. The bike dropped down lower and Carina could see the pool, the bar, the barns and the paddock. Datch brought the bike around and landed outside the kitchen.

"Welcome to my house." he said getting off the bike.

"Wow, this is amazing." She stood looking around. "You made it sound like a normal house."

Datch looked at her.

"Well, it is, it's my house." he said a bit puzzled.

She gave him a hug and a kiss. Datch took her bag.

"Mam, would you care to follow me to your room."

she laughed.

"Why sure, lead the way sir."

They headed up to the back door. It opened and his mum came out.

"Hi Carina, you made it here in one piece then?"

"Yes mam, I had a very nice ride thanks to Datch."

Tansya smiled.

"It's just Tansya, we don't stand on ceremony here."

"Ok Tansya." she smiled.

"I take it Datch is showing you to your room?"

"Yes."

"Good. If you need anything don't hesitate to ask, ok?"

"Thanks, Tansya. I will."

With that Datch took Carina to her room. When they arrived at the door Datch opened it and waved Carina in. She walked in and there on the bed was a box with a bow on it.

"Datch, what's this?" he went a little pink and smiled at her.

"It's sort of a present, I hope it's, ok? I sort of guessed the size."

She sat down and opened the box.

Inside was a red and pink dress with a floral pattern in gold, it was made of a light fabric that was designed to be cool in the sun.

"It's beautiful." She said and gave him another kiss.

She looked at the shorts and T-shirt next.

"Oh Datch, you shouldn't have they're all beautiful, I love all of them." she gave him another kiss.

"But why?" she asked.

"Err, because I wanted to." he said looking a little unsure of himself.

"Thank you so much, I don't get new clothes that often." and yet another kiss.

This time the kiss had a very large hug included. Datch was starting to think if he bought her enough clothes, he may suffocate but it would be worth it.

They headed back down stairs. Carina went and called her mum to let her know they had arrived ok. Afterwards Datch got them both a drink and they went outside to sit on the big sofa on the veranda. Datch put his arm around Carina and they sat looking out towards the city.

After twenty minutes there came the noise of the engines in the distance and over the fields his dad's truck could been seen approaching with the rest of the team. They got up and went to meet the others. His dad landed the truck on the driveway and the occupants spilled out like a tidal wave.

"Wow, Datch this is so cool." they said pretty much in unison.

He took them into the house to say hi to his mum and then showed them to their rooms telling them to get into swim suits. Last to his room was Hagger. Datch went in with him and showed him the bits. He couldn't thank Datch enough, in fact Hagger seemed far too happy about a few new clothes. Datch wasn't sure why but he wanted to find out. So, he planned to get to the bottom of it by the end of the weekend.

Fifteen minutes later. Datch, Dapo and Hagger were sitting by the pool when the girls walked out. Hagger went very red and tried to cross his legs. Dapo's jaw dropped that far that it was nearly on the floor and Datch was just starring at Carina. He didn't know why but he felt like he needed to take a shower.

"Wow, you look stunning." he said to Carina.

She had a cream and pink bikini on and had a sun hat with a daisy tucked in the top.

"You don't look bad yourself." she said smiling at him.

"Please come and sit down."

Datch looked at Hagger,

"Oh, and hurry before we have to throw Hagger in the pool to stop him bursting into flames."

There was a bit of a snigger as the girls came and sat down.

"So, what do you have planned for the weekend?" Rosey asked.

"Well, I'm glad you asked. This afternoon is chilling by the pool followed by a bit of karaoke in the bar."

"What about the team building?" asked Rosey.

"That start's tomorrow after breakfast. You will all be learning to ride bikes. My dad has sorted it out, so I don't know what he has planned. Then if all goes well, we'll be going rafting on the river the day after."

"What river?" said Dapo looking around.

"The one in the desert."

"Do you get rivers in the desert? don't they dry up or something?" asked Hagger.

"Not this one, oh, and we have to make the rafts first."

"Right. Now we need to make sure everyone can swim. I know Hagger doesn't know how so we need to work together and help him."

Hagger stared at the water and forgot about being red.

"Hagger, you're with me in the shallow end, come on and get in to the water." Datch said.

Hagger was looking very apprehensive. Datch got up and jumped in the pool followed by everyone else. Hagger came reluctantly over and got in next to Datch and Carina. Carina went just a little bit down the pool and the others spread out in circle. Hagger was shown how to swim and after a few attempts and several lungs full of water he started to go around the pool from person to person. Each of them grabbed him to make sure he didn't sink. Tansya watched out the window.

"He's turning out like you." she said to Dechow who was sitting relaxing on the sofa watching a vid.

"He's looking after them, just like you with your command."

Dechow got up to have a look.

"Yes, he is making sure they are all ok." he said and smiled before going back to the vid.

The afternoon carried on and once Hagger had got his confidence the pool turned into a water war and by the time Dechow went out to start the barbeque everywhere was wet and most of the troops were lounging on the sun beds recovering from the conflict. Carina had settled down under the umbrella next to Datch. Rosey and Tish were sitting at a table talking to Hagger and Dapo was floating around the pool in one of the inflatable chairs. Tansya came out with a bowl of salad and some flat breads. Dechow put some Jaxx steaks on the grill and it wasn't long before they were all tucking into the food.

"I hope the food is ok." Tansya said.

"Yes Tansya, it's great thanks." said Carina eating another bit of steak.

There was a general chorus of nodding and various people waving food in the air. After finishing off the Jaxx steaks and then progressing through the sweets. They headed off to their rooms to get freshened up ready for the night's karaoke.

Datch had a shower and hurried back down stairs. He headed straight into the bar and put his plan in motion. He went over to the karaoke set up and fetched the boxes out from behind it. Each box was covered in silver paper and had a name on it. He moved them to the table in front of the bar which he had placed there in the morning. It had nine chairs. He put his box next to Carina's and then placed the rest how they normally would sit at the Barbers Inn. He took a step back to admire his work. There was a knock at the door. He turned around. It was Jed from the next farm. They had only got their new house a week and a half ago after the storm destroyed it at the solstice. Jed had been living at Datch's until they had got the replacement finished and he was also Datch's friend. There was about a year's difference between them and Jed was due his implant in about another month and a half. Datch thought it would be good for him to see that it would be alright and you could have a lot of fun. He opened the door and let him in.

"Hi Jed, how are you?"

"I'm good Datch, where is everyone?"

"Oh, the others will be down shortly."

Tansya came around the corner.

"Oh hi, Mrs Thome, err, sorry Tansya."

She laughed.

"Hi Jed, Make yourself at home."

He went over and sat at the bar.

Datch got him a Gruck's.

"So how is school going?"

"It's great, some of the lectures are boring but we have a lot of fun in the evenings and my friends are cool."

"Are you talking about me?" came a voice from behind him.

He swung around. It was Carina and she had put on the dress Datch had given her. She looked amazing. Datch went to her and escorted her over to the bar.

"Jed, this is my girlfriend Carina."

"Hello." he said.

"This is my friend Jed from the farm over the hill, I've known him since I was about two."

"It's nice to meet you." she said.

Just then Rosey walked in followed by Dapo. Datch went around the back of the bar.

"Everyone want a Gruck's then?" he said.

The reply was yes with two on the rocks. Just then Hagger and Tish came through the door with Datch's mum. Datch poured out everyone's drinks apart from his mum who got her own. It was a cocktail and was quite hard to make. His dad had tried to show him but without much success.

He introduced everyone to Jed and they went over to the table.

"Wow what's this?" said Dapo spotting the boxes,

"Open them." Datch said grinning.

They opened the boxes and inside was a T-shirt. It had a picture of the six of them bursting out of a green cloud on the front with 'The Great Adventure' underneath and their name was on the right breast. Then on the back it had the words 'The Datch Pack on Tour' then underneath 'The Barbers Inn – Born to Party', Datch had also selected the colours so that everyone would like them. His mum had helped him a bit with the design.

"Hey, we have our own T-shirts, that's so cool." said Tish "I love the colour."

There were general voices of agreement and people holding the shirts up and showing each other. The music started and they were chatting away when there was a noise like thunder from outside. Datch got up to see what it was. The shadow of a bike flicked across the pool and then the roar stopped.

"Oh, it must be dad." he said sitting back down.

Then the doors at the end opened and a silhouette of a big biker stood in the doorway.

"So, where's the party Dudes!" he boomed across the bar.

"Tank!" shouted Datch.

With that, three more bikers appeared and came walking in.

"You can't have a party without us dude, it's the rules." Said Tank laughing.

The rest of the pack got up and welcomed them. It turned out Datch's dad had asked them to come and help out the following day with the bikes and maybe come to the river if they felt like it. The party started to swing and soon people were singing and dancing.

The evening turned into night and the music was turned down and soft songs were put on. Rosey was talking to Tank about doing her hair when they went back to school. Tish, Jed, Dapo and Hagger were playing cards with Fred and Clax. Fred was currently losing and Tish was pulling his leg about it much to the entertainment of the others. Dechow was chatting with Peebop. Datch and Carina had snuck away to the veranda overlooking the desert. They were sitting arm in arm on the sofa listening to the six-legged things that make a chirping noise at night. Tansya looked out of the window to check they were ok and then went back to the others that were sitting on the new veranda looking out towards the city.

"Are they ok?" Dechow asked.

"Yes, they are just sitting together on the sofa looking out across the desert like we do sometimes, I think they want a bit of time to themselves."

She smiled but there was something sad about her.

"Are you ok?"

"Yes, I think it's just hit me. Datch isn't a little boy anymore. Now he's starting to make his own way in life." She sighed.

"He is growing up fast. It will only be another two years before he is an adult. Think of all the nice evenings and quiet nights we can have to ourselves." He smiled at her.

It started to get late and the gang was getting tired. Rosey got up and said good night. Then she stuck her head around the corner and said good night to Datch and Carina. They said good night to her before going to join the others. It wasn't long before more people headed off to bed. Datch walked Carina to her room and gave her a kiss good night. He walked back down to the remaining party goers and sat next to Hagger.

"Are you enjoying yourself?" he asked him.

"Yes, it's great, I wish I could do this every night, It's so much better than home."

"Don't you have a very good view at home from your bedroom?" Datch was digging.

"I don't have a room, just a bed and a box underneath for my things." Datch stopped.

He was taken by surprise and didn't know what to say.

"Err, I bet it's a nice bed though?" trying to recover the situation,

Hagger let out a sigh.

"It's just a bed, my dad only has a one room apartment, well one room and a shower, I have a little bed in the corner and my dad sleeps on the couch."

"Well, you can come here whenever you want." said Tansya stepping in to rescue Datch.

"Wow, you mean it?"

"Yes."

With that Datch changed the subject to what they had been up to at school so Jed would know all about it. Soon after that the party ended and everyone went to bed. Dechow took Jed home.

The next morning Datch was up early. He was so early in fact that he had time to watch a whole episode of 'Star Warrior' before anyone else surfaced and that was his mum. He went over to her and started talking about Hagger.

"Maybe his dad doesn't earn much in the way of credits." she said.

"Yes, but only one room, that's why he didn't want me to go in."

They carried on talking until the door opened and Tish walked in.

"What's for breakfast then?" she said smelling the air.

Before Tansya could answer she continued.

"Oh, I know that smell, you have Jaxx rolls and orange sauce too."

"I take it by that you would like one?" said Tansya

"Oh yes please I love them, is it ok if I have two? I'll help do the washing up." She had a big smile on her face.

"You don't have to do that; I have a kitchen assistant for that." She handed her two rolls.

It wasn't long before the rest turned up and they all went in to watch the episode of 'Star Warrior'.

Dechow came in and grabbed a coffee and a couple of rolls. Fred wandered in and grabbed a cob, Tank and Clax weren't far behind and then Peebop was following up the rear. They grabbed their food and all headed outside with Dechow.

Dechow went out to the barn with Fred and fetched out two boxes, he pressed the buttons on them and they folded themselves away revelling two more bikes.

"So, what's the plan big man?" said Fred.

"I know this spot in the desert where I taught Datch to ride, we'll take them there on auto and then Datch can help us teach them. It's his team at the end of the day."

They moved the bikes around to the end of the bar and Dechow went and shouted for them to come out.

After a few moments Datch came out followed by Carina and then the rest of The Pack.

"Oh cool." said Tish looking at the bikes.

"Ok Listen up. Carina you're with Datch. Tish and Rosey, you're on the yellow one. Dapo and Hagger, you're on the green one. Now all pay attention, the bikes are on auto pilot at the moment and will follow behind me. Datch please don't go charging across the desert, you can have fun later. Tank and Fred will be helping Tish and Rosey, Peebop and Clax will be helping Hagger and Dapo, I will be over seeing things and Datch will be helping Carina. Ok everyone got that?"

"Yes sir." said Tish getting on to the bike, the others all nodded.

"Ok then, mount up!"

Everyone headed to the bikes apart from Tish who was already sitting on it. Datch took Carina over to his bike and got on with Carina climbing on behind him. The others followed suit and soon everyone was ready. Dechow started his engine and the other two bikes started up. Datch and the rest of the bikers started their bikes.

They took to the air and headed towards the desert. Datch opened up the throttle a little and his dad followed suit. They didn't go as fast as Datch would have liked but he was doing as he was told. It wasn't long before the sands of the desert were going by underneath them.

"Wow, this is amazing Datch, I've never been to the desert before, there's so much sand." said Carina in Datch's ear.

"I'll have to see if we can come here more often, but it will depend on my mum and dad."

The sand went by below and a bird that was sitting on a sand dune spotted Datch heading towards him and decided to hurry up and fly away in the direction of a tree it had been calling home for the last three months.

Datch dropped the bike down to a wide-open area on the desert, there was a tent in the middle of it. He pulled the bike up next to it and stopped the engine. The rest of the bikes came in and landed behind.

"OK, first up is Carina, Hagger and Tish. Datch will show you what we want you to do." Datch got on his bike and slowly did a wide circle then pulled up slowly next to his dad.

"Now, please can the first three get on the bikes." Datch got off and put the bike in safety mode. Carina got on and soon the three bikes were lined up.

"Ok, listen up, the controls work like this…" he explained how each of the controls worked.

Datch was showing Carina. Each of the bikers took one of the others and pointed to the bits as he went through them. Dapo and Rosey were shown Tanks and Fred's bikes. It was soon time for the pack to have a go and the bikes were started.

First up was Carina. She moved away slowly and then gave the bike a little more speed. As she started to turn Hagger headed off slowly down the course. Then it was Tish's turn, she accelerated and took the first corner. She was a bit wide but ok, by this time Carina was coming back towards them. She slowed down and stopped. She looked over just in time to see Tish over take Hagger. Tish turned into the straight and came towards them. She got to fifty metres away and hit the brake hard. the bike went into a corkscrew and after the third rotation came to a stop upside down in front of everyone. Tish looked green.

"Ok, folks, Tish has just demonstrated how not to brake."

Dechow pressed a button on a hand set and the bike righted itself. Tish got off and headed for a seat wobbling a bit. If it was possible to be both red and green at the same time Tish would have done it. Hagger came in and stopped next to the other bike.

"While Tish gets her breath back, Rosey you're up."

The next few hours were spent with them taking it in turns to learn to ride the bikes, After Tish's error she soon got the hang of it and then it was time for the time trials, the bikers headed off to set positions on the top various dunes in a three-kilometre circle and the race began.

An hour later they were all sitting in the tent having a cold drink, Dechow stood at the front.

"Well done all of you," he said "You have all exceled yourselves, now there can only be one winner and it was very close between all of you, the winner is," he pauses and took a breath. "Dapo with Tish a very close second."

There was a general clapping and everyone agreed that a good time had been had by all. After finishing off the drinks they headed to the bikes and mounted up ready for the trip back and a very welcome dip in the pool. This time the limiters were switched off and the bikes were under rider control. Datch and Carina took off first followed by the rest of The Pack.

Datch accelerated and there was a roar of engines as the bikes thundered across the desert. Datch grinned to himself. This was his pack now and the sky was theirs. The bikers and his dad were at the back watching to make sure everyone was ok. The desert turned to scrub followed by fields and then the ranch was up a head. They came into landed near the barn. They touched down safely and after shutting the bikes off, team Datch ran inside and went to get changed for the pool. The bikers and Dechow hit the bar.

"That bad?" said Tansya sticking her head into the bar.

"No, it went very well in fact. It was just so hot out there we really needed a drink." Dechow said with a smile.

The others were all nodding and watching while Dechow poured the beers. There was a loud splash outside and a lot of laughing. Tansya got six glasses of Gruck's and took them outside. That night there was a bit more singing and Datch got out his guitar and managed to play a song for everyone and considering he had only been doing it for a few weeks, he didn't do a bad job. It was a much quieter night as they were all tired from the day's activities.

Datch went over to talk to Hagger again and after a bit of general chat he turned the conversation around to his dad.

"Why is your dad always at work?" he asked.

"He's not, he spends a lot of time in the casino near the space port."

"So, what do you do with yourself when he's not there?"

"I watch the vid and do the cleaning; he gets mad at me if it's not clean when he gets in."

"Oh," Datch looked down at his drink. He was feeling really sorry for Hagger now as his main problem in life was how to get ice-cream for breakfast.

"It's ok, he was alright until my mum died then some men came and took our big apartment and we had to live in that one."

"I thought your dad had a good job?"

"He does, he just spends all his money in the casino." He paused, "Look can we changed the subject?"

"Yeh, sure, no problem."

They started talking about the next day's adventure. Dechow had got a spot sorted out for the raft building on the river and it was about ten minutes ride from Soto. They were going to have a race against the bikers and Dechow. First ones across the river and back wins and Tansya was going to be referee to make sure there was no cheating. It started to get late and everyone headed off to bed so they could get an early start.

Next morning everyone was up by ten o'clock and having food in the bar area. By half ten they were all on the bikes flying across the fields towards the desert. The Datch pack were out in front with Datch in the lead. He had the nav com working so he knew which way to go. The fields turned in to sand and the desert rolled by below. Datch gave his bike a kick of speed and the others followed suit. The bikes thundered across the desert and then in the distance a thin green line could be seen snaking across the sands. As it got closer the green line turned into trees and bushes and then through all the greenery was the river. The bikes approached and landed on the grass near two large piles of wood, rope and plastic barrels.

They all had a drink and Tansya gave both teams five minutes to talk before the build started.

"Are you ready, 5 4 3 2 1 Go!" she said and blew a horn.

The two teams started getting the barrels and setting them out. Datch split his team up into tasks and it wasn't long before the rafts started to take shape. Dechows team was going for a streamlined shape so they could get across the water faster. Datch on the other hand was making sure everything was secure as he didn't want Hagger falling in the water halfway across. Planks and bits of plastic were tied together and Datch's team made some oars out of planks and poles. After two hours of work time was up.

The two rafts were taken to the water's edge and carefully put in making sure they both floated. This point on the river had been chosen because it was wide and you could see up and down the river easily. It had the sandy beach on one side and trees on the other.

On two of the trees opposite were two pieces of brightly coloured cloth and the idea was to use the rafts to get across the river to their piece of cloth and bring it back. The first team back with their piece of cloth would be the winner.

"Ok teams you both know the rules so get ready." said Tansya.

The two teams got on to the rafts. On Datch's raft Hagger was put in the middle in case things went a bit wrong. Rosey was put in charge of the rudder with Hagger helping to navigate. Dapo was at the front ready to get the cloth. Tish, Datch and Carina were on the oars. Dechows raft didn't have anyone on the rudder as it appeared not to have one. Fred being the smallest was at the front while the rest had planks of wood to paddle with.

"5 4 3 2 1 GO!" Tansya watched as both teams paddled furiously.

The rafts headed off towards the centre of the river and then the current started to get hold of them. Rosey compensated and kept the raft on course. Dechows raft was out in front but now seemed to be starting to veer off course and was starting to turn up stream. Dechow shouted at them to try and get it back on track but all that happened was the raft started to spin around in circles. Datch's raft started to pull ahead and was soon quite a bit in front. They reached the far bank and after a bit of manoeuvring Dapo grabbed the cloth. Dechow had closed the gap and was close behind, soon they had the cloth too.

Datch whispered something to Rosey. She nodded and started to head partly up stream. Dechow thought he had it in the bag and they started to slow down to make sure they didn't go into a spin again. Datch's raft reached the centre of the river with Dechows raft now just ahead of them. Datch looked at Rosey and said now. She turned to head down stream. Carina and Datch both started to paddle together with Tish now helping Rosey with the rudder. The rivers current took hold of the raft and it started to pick up speed quite quickly. The raft was soon moving quite fast. Rosey and Tish turned towards shore and they shot past Dechows raft as if someone had given them an engine. The raft reached the beach with nearly two lengths to spare and went on to the sand and stopped, Dapo fell off the front, he got up brushing the sand off and gave Tansya the cloth.

"We have the winners!" she shouted.

The other raft landed on the beach and Dechow held out his hand for Datch to shake it.

"Well done son, very well played."

Datch took his hand and then was unceremoniously lifted up and thrown in the water. His team responded be trying to throw Dechow and the bikers in the water.

The next five minute were spent with all the contestant's getting thrown in the water one way or another and finally after a lot of laughing the teams got out of the river just as a boat came by. They all ended up sitting on the beach drying off in the sun and a round of drinks was passed out.

"Ok who is up for a late lunch or early dinner?"

They pulled the rafts up the beach and placed them in a pile under a tree. Dechow would come back with the truck later to get them and tidy up. They got on the bikes and headed down stream to Soto.

Soto was a small village on the banks of the river and mostly catered to tourists and the river folk. It consisted of a number of hotels and modest housing. The roads all led to the river and along its banks were shops, restaurants and bars which surrounded parks. They landed in a parking area next to one of the riverside parks and walked over to a seating area that had some shade. Even though it was only about four weeks after the winter solstice the temperature was starting to hit 26C and the sun was already very strong. Another two months and the temperature would be in the mid-thirties.

They sat down and ordered some lunch. When food came, they sat eating and watching boats on the river. It was a while before anyone could be bothered to move. The rafting followed by the food had made everyone really relaxed. Datch asked if it was all right to take Carina for a walk along the path next to the river and Tish wanted to come as well. The others just wanted to sit until their food had gone down a bit more.

The three of them headed off down the path. Tish went a little bit in front so Datch and Carina could have a bit of time together. Datch waited until they were over the other side of the park and then put his arm around Carina. Tish was quite happy looking at the river. Datch pointed out the wind ships and the cruise ships, then went on to tell them about when he came with his mum and dad.

They had never seen the desert or the river before. They had heard about it in stories and seen it on the vid when the great race took place once a year. Datch was enjoying having them with him. It was great to have his own friends and especially Carina. They found a seat and sat watching as a wind ship came slowly gliding by, its sails catching the light breeze. Eventually Tish wanted to go back so they set out for the park. It took nearly thirty minutes to walk back.

"Come on you three, it's time to head back to the ranch." Dapo shouted across the park.

It didn't take long before they were heading across the desert at speed.

Half an hour later they arrived back at the ranch and it didn't take long before they were all in the pool. Dechow headed inside with Tansya and the bikers chilled out in the chairs under the sun umbrellas.

"I could just murder a beer?" said Tank.

"I'll go and get them," said Peebop, "Fred, Clax what about you?"

They nodded in unison. Peebop got up and headed inside, five minutes later he came out carrying the beers and followed by Tansya who was carrying a large tray of dishes.

"Ok Team Datch, Chocolate ice-cream all round!"

Datch leapt out of the pool as if it had suddenly become red hot. Carina quickly followed him as did the others.

"What's Ice-cream?" Said Tish looking at the brown balls in the dish.

"It's cool, just eat it." Datch said.

"This is what you told me about isn't it?" Carina asked.

"Yes." said Datch with his mouth full.

Carina put some in her mouth and after few seconds her eyes lit up.

"Wow, this is good." She said putting another spoon full in her mouth.

The others followed suit and it wasn't long before it was all gone.

"That was nice," said Tish "Where did you get it from?"

"My dad found it on another planet with a really dull name and worked out how to make it."

"We so have to come here more often." said Rosey licking her lips.

"Is there any more?" asked Hagger

"You can have some more if you like." said Tansya.

There were six bowels placed on the tray and a lot of smiles,

"Ok Datch, please can you come and help me."

He went with his mum inside and Carina followed as well. They got some more ice-cream and Datch got some drinks from the bar. As they walked back through Carina stopped to help Datch carry the drinks. A small movement caught her eye behind Datch. She looked closer. In a glass bowl which was fixed inside the wall was a white mouse. It was looking at her and twitching its nose.

"Err Datch, did you know you have a mouse in your wall?" she said without taking her eyes off it.

"Oh, that's Bob. He's my pet and if you look around the room, there are more of the globes. he runs between them in little tunnels we made for him, I'll see if he wants to come out if you like."

Datch turned around to look at Bob. Bob then decided that it was time to disappear and exited up the tunnel in the direction of the chicken.

"Hmm. It looks like he doesn't want to come out." he added

"You never mentioned him before." She said "how old is he?"

"He's nearly eight now, but I've only had him about six months."

"I thought mice only lived for two or three years?"

"They do, but Bob's special, you remember me telling you about Asmove in the Barbers Inn?"

"Yes, but you didn't mention Bob." she said.

Datch went on to explain,

"You remember Big D. Well, Bob was his but he couldn't take him where he was going. So, I was allowed to look after him. He's genetically engineered and Big D said he should live for about fifty years."

"Oh wow, does he do any tricks?"

"My dad taught him to start the music on the sound system at the solstice but other than that I don't know."

Bob appeared at the globe near the chicken. Checked the coast was clear and then began dragging a fresh pile tissue into place over the hole he had made, He liked his home but also found that the outside world was fun. He was after all a very clever rodent and needed a bit of entertainment now and again.

Datch and Carina headed outside with the drinks as Bob seemed to want time to his self. The next day everyone had to go home so they made the most of the rest of the afternoon and evening. Tansya did some buffet food for the evening and there was another karaoke session in the bar. Bob was nowhere to be seen.

When things don't fit

In a quiet street on the north side of the city there was a warehouse. It was not a very big building but had a loading bay to one side of it. Above the main doors was a sign stating "Jucks and Jeans whole sale meat venders" in big red and gold writing. The sun glinted off it in the early morning light. Down the side of the building something moved in the shadows and then ran up the wall onto the roof. There was a crash as a sky light was broken and soon after the alarm start to sound. Ten minutes later the civil authorities arrived just in time to meet to owner and together they went in.

Inside they were greeted with the sight of devastation. The main meat locker was wide open and meat was thrown across the floor. It looked like something had torn the place apart. The strange thing was that the entry and exit had been through the sky light and the alarm had only been triggered when the locker door was ripped open.

The officers scratched their heads. No DNA was found apart from that of the meat and owners. There was no sign of a ladder or any other means of exit through the roof and the door's hinges had also been broken in two without any sign of tools being used. They scanned the area and found nothing. The only thing was a smell of rotten meat which they put down to waste skip outside. Far below them a dark shape moved in the tunnels under the city.

The next day Datch sat watching the vid. Team Datch had gone home a couple of hours ago and he was bored. He was used to playing by himself but after going to school and having the team around him. He missed the company and it was boring not having people to play with. He switched to another channel just as the news came on. There was a piece about a big visit by the president who was coming at the end of spring to open the new power plant that Peebop was working on. Another story was about a strange break in involving meat where the only thing taken was Half a Jaxx, and finally, a piece about some drug lord who after having his memories replaced by the courts went on to work for a hospital as a doctor and had saved twenty-five people when the city was hit by a storm just before the solstice.

He turned it off and went outside to his bike. He got on and flew off over the hill to Jed's farm.

Bob watched him go and went for a nap in the globe behind the bar. He had spent the night down at the barn annoying an owl. The Owl now had concussion after the mouse it had been chasing ran through an invisible hole in a piece of glass that hadn't been there ten minutes earlier.

Datch got to Jed's and they went off playing in the barn. They couldn't go outside in the meadow as his dad had been spraying pesticides nearby to get rid of some critters on the crops that he had just planted. They spent a while climbing about and then started building some signs for a race track around one of the fields outside.

"Datch, you know your implant, did it hurt at all when you got it?" Jed's was soon to have his and was thinking about it.

"No, it didn't hurt. It was a bit like having bubbles going up your nose but in your head instead. Then you see the memories your mum and dad want you to have, it was really amazing."

"Oh, what about school?"

"That can be a bit boring but Carina and the rest of them make it fun and you do get to do cool stuff with your implant."

"And it really doesn't hurt?"

"No, it's fine. When you get it, I'll show you some cool stuff if you like." This made Jed feel a bit more relaxed about it.

They finished painting a right turn sign and moved onto
the pit entrance. They carried on messing about in the barn
until Jed's mum came out and told Datch that his mum
wanted him back for dinner. He said his good byes and went
home.

The next day Datch was back at school and the gang was
back together. The lectures this week were all about off world
etiquette and how some aliens had odd rituals. They were
shown how to access the cultural database with their
implants. It was for a change very interesting and Datch was
almost hanging on every word. Carina was also very keen as
she wanted to go off world someday. The second lecture was
covering rare races such as the millipedes of Saiph two. They
took over two million years to become intelligent and now
have a reputation for making very good footwear. When it got
to the end and they asked are there any questions Datch
stood up.

"Sir, what about the arachnoids, what are they like?"

The professor looked at Datch and took a deep breath.

"Well, Datch, if you did meet one you wouldn't need to
worry about etiquette. They are very aggressive and would
eat you for lunch without thinking." Everyone laughed a bit
and then the professor continued "If you see one and don't
have a very big gun in your hands, you had better run like hell
and hope it's already had lunch." People started to laugh
again and then they realised the professor was very serious,
Datch sat back down.

"You still think it's an arachnoid?" said Hagger quietly to
Datch.

"I'm not sure, from what I have read, they would have no
reason to come here and there would be a lot of dead people
around."

The lecture finished and they went off to have dinner.

That night the Barbers Inn was its normal self. They got there first and sat down at the big table. The bar staff were now putting a big reserved sign in the centre of it. They had been there about twenty minutes when the bikers came in.

"I see the president is coming to open the new power plant." Datch said to Peebop.

"Yes, there is going to be a lot of fuss and we are behind schedule thanks to the missing bots, we still don't have any leads on what happened to them."

"What nothing?" said Rosey taking a sudden interest.

"No, nothing. We did get a short transmission from one of the locators but it only lasted a few milli seconds, not enough time to get a fix on the position, the signal didn't even have any GPS data just the ID code. We don't even know if it was still in the city as the transmission was very weak."

"I wish I knew how to get hold of the captain." Datch said.

"Have you tried sending him an email?" Said Fred.

"Err. No."

"I don't think he would come half way across the galaxy just to help me find some missing bots." Added Peebop.

"I suppose you're right." He looked a little down hearted.

"Well let's look at what we have." Carina said and then continued,

"One, the bot's all vanished in the same way. Two, there was a branch of a tree on the vid that flicked in front of the picture just before the bot vanished. Three, the tree didn't exist. Four, the branch looks like a weird stick. Five, at least one of the bots is still somewhere near the city." They all looked at the table thinking.

Hagger lifted his head up a bit.

"So not only do we have missing bots but we have lost a tree as well." he said.

"We're missing something, I'm sure." said Datch in deep thought.

"Yes, the tree." repeated Hagger with a grin and let out a little laugh.

"Well enough of this tonight, lets change the subject and talk about something fun." said Tish.

The subject turned to sport which was on the vid above the bar. It was the intercontinental wind surfing race, the racers had to traverse the continent on surfboards with sails attached. It was a national past time with the winners being hailed almost as heroes.

The next couple of weeks went by and it was time for the first team scores at school. They had to sit a couple of tests and also the tutors gave them scores on conduct, behaviour and attitude. The team's score was an overview of how all the team members were progressing.

Datch's team came out top but had dropped a couple of points because of the restaurant. Hagger had not said please on a couple of occasions. They were pleased about it and Datch was thanked by everyone even though he didn't want it.

They went off to the Barbers Inn to celebrate afterwards and arrived a little later than usual due to the scores being handed out. The bikers were already sitting at the table and they went over and sat down. Peebop was sitting quietly looking into his beer.

"What's up Peebop?" asked Carina.

"We lost another bot today, they were told not to send them over to the corner, but someone did. Ten seconds later, no more bot, we questioned the guy who was operating it but he said that he had received a call from head office telling him to do it, we checked and there was a call but it was untraceable, and head office didn't know anything about it."

"Don't you have security codes or something?" asked Hagger.

"Yes, but apparently the caller knew them."

"Maybe someone stole them from someone. I know my dad keeps them written down on bits of paper so he doesn't forget them. I've been told to destroy them if I find them laying around." Hagger added.

"It's a possibility, but I doubt it, the codes are changed every week."

They all sat looking at the drinks.

"Well, let's try and liven the place up, Solar Ball anyone?" said Tish.

"Yes, "Said Datch "Are we doing teams or playing singles?"

"Teams" said Carina grabbing Datch's arm, Tish grabbed Hagger and Dapo, Datch picked Rosey, Fred and Tank, Peebop and Clax went with Tish.

The game was in the centre of a circular area about three metres in diameter. It was a holographic game and expanded out to the walls of the building when in play. The game was a cross between polo and pool with mallets. The player must hit a white ball into one of the coloured balls and put the coloured ball in one of the nets. The holographic balls were the size of normal footballs and the virtual playfield could be huge with all sorts of terrains.

Datch pressed the virtual start button and started to enter the players' names. The bar staff looked over and reached for their virtual crash helmets. They had seen the way team Datch played. If the balls had been real the bar would have to be rebuilt every time they played. Luckily, everything was holograms. However, even they can be scary when you're trying to serve a beer and a ball comes crashing through the air in front of you. The virtual helmets deflect the balls and hopefully puts people off hitting the balls towards the person wearing it. That is apart from team Datch. Datch had worked out that the helmets would act like a post so if he had a difficult shot and could use one of the bar staff as a post to deflect the balls, he would.

Datch was up first. A play field opened up across the bar. It was an alien jungle and they were standing in a clearing with the coloured balls scattered around and also up the trees. The trees also had the nets in various places behind them and also in the branches. A number of the locals sitting at the bar decided it was a wise move to head for the chairs at the back.

Datch took his shot. The ball shot through the air hitting a bright orange ball sitting in a low branch which in turn shot almost straight up and headed into the net above.

"Hmm, going for the easy one first." said Tish as she stepped up for her turn.

"I'm just making sure to warm up." he said with a smile.

Tish stepped up to take her shot. She took aim and hit the ball hard. It shot straight at the barman who had turned around to serve a customer. Unfortunately for him he turned back just a second before the ball hit him and tried to duck but it was too late. The ball hit his virtual helmet in a flash of light before shooting across the bar and knocking the green ball into the net behind the tree that was currently growing out of their table.

"Beat that!" she said.

Carina took her turn hitting the white ball across the bar. The bar staff ducked and the ball hit the optics and ricocheted towards the tree near the door which had a purple ball on one of its lower branches. It made contact just as Jep walked through the door. The purple ball flew straight through him and hit the opposite wall before landing in the net above the bar for double points.

"How about that then." said Carina with a smile on her face.

Jep came walking over to the table still blinking after having a bright purple ball travel through him.

"I can see we're in a sporting frame of mind tonight." he said putting his hand up to the bar staff.

"I would say, why don't you do that at school but to be honest, I'm not sure the rest of the school could handle it."

Hagger was up next. He was good at this because as he put it. When his dad was out, there wasn't much do other than play games on the vid. He went for the yellow ball above the stage and put it in the net near the table. The game carried on with most of the customers watching the game very carefully. This wasn't so much because they were riveted by the game play but more because they wanted to know when to duck.

After two games and an overall draw. The game was abandoned for a while and they all headed back to the table for a drink and a sit down. The bar breathed a sigh of relief and people went back to chatting and watching the vid. Some of which were now rubbing their necks which had gone a bit stiff from being turned the opposite way for nearly half an hour.

The night finally came to an end and it was time to head back to school. They walked back up the street from the bar. Carina was a bit more clingy than normal and was holding

Datch quite close. Rosey also seemed to be a bit closer than usual as well.

"Err, are you ok?" Datch asked.

"I'm not sure, I just feel that someone is watching me."

"Me to." said Rosey.

Datch looked around. It was dark but the street was well lit. He checked up and down the street but it was empty apart from them.

"I can't see anyone." he said.

But now they had mentioned it he felt someone was watching them. The hairs on the back of his neck were tingling as if someone was stroking them the wrong way. The rest of the team could tell as well and were looking about as they walked along.

"Well let's get back to school." They quickened up the pace.

Up above the lights in the darkness of the shadows a head turned and watched them go up the street. There was a stifled squawk as a pigeon that was sleeping on a gutter suddenly became a light snack.

The next day Datch went off into town with Carina at lunch. They had a longer break than normal as the afternoon lecture was going to be a simulated state dinner and they were going to have to show they had been paying attention to the mornings lecture. Datch took her to a few shops and bought her a gold chain with a fire jewel on it. He was going to get her an Iridium chain but it was too expensive and his allowance wouldn't cover it. They walked along a bit further and found themselves next to the construction site. They stopped to look again at the spot the bots had disappeared.

The area was clear a part from a few bits of tattered plastic and you could see some small depressions in the ground but no sign of the tree. Nothing Datch thought. He looked up and there were two pieces of worn rope hanging high up on the building next door. A bit fell off and Datch caught it. It was soft with a shiny look and fell apart in his hand. He put what was left in the empty bag from the chain and placed it in his pocket. They had a last look around and then headed up to the park next to the space port.

The space port was as busy as usual with ships of all shapes and sizes landing and taking off. They sat and watched them for a while.

"I want to go into space one day." Carina said, "I want to see what's out there."

Datch pulled her in a little closer,

"I'll take you there." he said with a smile.

She turned to him and looked into his eyes and at that moment she knew he meant it and would somehow make it happen.

They sat arm in arm watching the ships and enjoying the afternoon sun. They talked about the stars, space ships and the flowers planted in the bed in front of them.

The weekend soon came around and Datch sat pondering the missing bots. He decided to send what he had to the captain. He composed a message on the vid and added the images that he had recorded in his implant. He had learnt how to do that at school. He also added that no one had a clue what had happened and if he had any ideas. 'Oh, and sorry for disturbing him.' It would take a few days for the message to get to him but he didn't know who else to ask and poor Peebop was looking so down lately.

The next couple of weeks went by and Datch's team was getting a bit of a rep. A number of other teams were trying to catch up, one of which was team Zorm. They were a nice enough group and did try very hard. Datch had even helped them out on a couple of occasions and they had become quite good friends with them. Jep pulled Datch into one of the offices at lunch and asked if his team would take them out one night. He said he would come to the bar as normal and bring their tutor along as well.

"What night do you want us to take them? Karaoke night would be good fun."

Jep looked at him.

"Err, no, not karaoke night. We want to see how they behave in a normal setting, not scare the willies out of them and cause premature deafness at the same time."

Datch thought about this and wasn't sure that his singing could cause deafness.

"Well, what about tomorrow night?" Jep put his head on one side trying to work out if there was anything planned for the following night.

"Err, isn't it Tanks birthday?"

Datch scratched his head.

"No, that's next week and don't tell him we know, we've got him a surprise cake."

"Oh, it is the cake that's the surprise isn't it, not what's in it?"

"Yes, it's a chocolate cake ok, oh and we have some balloons with his age on."

Datch was grinning and that was never a good sign, the bikers had warned Jep about the grin.

"So, just the cake and the balloons?"

Datch nodded but he was still grinning. Jep looked at him unsure whether to believe him.

"Ok." He paused just in case Datch wanted to add anything else but nothing came. He continued,

"Back to the matter in hand, so tomorrow night then?"

"Yes, I'll talk to The Pack and we'll look after them."

Datch's grin turned into a smile that was nearly as bad.

"The Pack?"

"Yes, we decided to be a pack instead of a team when in social settings. It sounds cooler and looks better on the T-shirts,"

Jep hadn't noticed the T-shirts. Well, he had seen them but not noticed the writing on the back.

"OK..." he said then after a moments contemplation he continued,

"Right, we will be sitting at the back of the room where I was sitting on the first night you were there. I will place some credits at your disposal as after all the bar will be a classroom for the evening and I want you to have a good night, I will however, be watching how you look after them and taking notes."

Datch knew what he meant. They were going to be scored on how they treated others. Still entertaining was Datch's thing and he loved doing it.

"Ok, this is how we are going to set it up, their tutor will sort out the later passes and will tell them that they are going to be allowed out as long as they stay with you... "

he continued to explain the plan and made sure Datch understood what to do.

Datch came out of the office. The rest of The Pack was loitering with intent on the other side of the corridor. When they saw him come out Carina came over followed by the others.

"Everything ok?" she asked slightly concerned.

"Yes," said Datch grinning, "We have to talk."

They went outside and sat on the grass and Datch explained it all.

The next day, team Zorm was given a special assignment and told to meet outside at seven fifty dressed casually. They told Datch that they we're going to be allowed out as well. Datch didn't say anything and just smiled.

At seven fifty Zorm's team came out through the main doors. Their tutor was standing next to the fountain and they went over to him. He started to talk to them and explained the ground rules. They were going to be accompanied by some fellow students that would act as their guides and that they should listen to them. At this point the main doors opened and the Datch pack came out and they were wearing their T-shirts.

"Well, here they come now."

Team Zorm turned to look at the escort. There was a bit of a silence before Zorm spoke.

"We're coming with you?" he said slightly stunned.

"Yep." said Datch with a grin.

Their tutor turned to Datch.

"Try to bring them back in one piece please." He said with a slightly worried look on his face.

"Don't worry sir, we'll take good care of them."

The whole of The Pack was grinning which was more unnerving than if they had all been carrying swords dripping with blood.

"That's what I'm concerned about, well off you go, see you in the morning."

"Well come on folks let's go."

"Where are we going?" asked Jen, one of team Zorm.

"Don't worry we know a place." Said Carina as the crowed headed off out into the city.

Jep walked up behind their tutor and tapped him on the shoulder, he turned around.

"Hi Jep," he said "I hope this isn't a mistake."

"It will be fine, Datch is going to take them the long way around so we can get there first. The bar staff have also been informed and the bikers as well. So, let's get moving so we can get our drinks in before they arrive." With that they set off in the direction of the Barbers Inn.

There had been a lot of rumours around the school about team Datch's evening trips. They were the only team in the first year to be allowed out without a tutor. They were said to be going to secret meetings or were very rich and had been given special permissions. Everything from spy training to working the bars had been floating about. No one knew because the rest had not been let out yet and the second years were in school on the days when they were not there. Now team Zorm was about to find out what they did.

The group came to a junction and turned right down a street. At the next junction they crossed straight over and there in front of them stood the Barbers Inn, they walked up to the doors.

"We're not going in there are we?" said Zorm who was very apprehensive. "Won't we get in trouble?"

Datch looked at him, he looked very insecure.

"Yes, we are going in there and no you won't get in trouble as long as you behave." Said Tish trying to sound about a hundred years older than she was.

"Are you sure?" said Japor who was standing next to Hagger.

"Yes, you could say we come here a lot and even Dr Doji comes in here sometimes." said Datch.

Zorm looked at him.

"He does?"

"Yes, shall we go in, I take it you all like Gruck's?"

There was a round of nodding.

With that the party walked through the doors. The bar was having a quiet night until they walked in. The bar staff had been busy preparing things and the large table had been extended to accommodate the extra members. The sports channel was showing orbital racing. Datch told Zorm's team to follow Carina to the table and went over to the bar to order the drinks. Bins was serving and told him that he'd sort it for him and put it on the tab for the night. Datch could feel Jep's eyes on his back but didn't look round.

Jep read the writing on the back of Datch's shirt, 'Born to Party'. Well, there was no arguing with that he thought to himself.

As the group headed across to the table team Zorm were hanging at the back.

"There's someone sitting at that table." said Sadey.

She could see four bikers sitting hunched over their beers.

"They're cool." said Dapo walking up and tapping Tank on the back. He turned around.

"Hi dudes and dudets." He looked at team Zorm, "So are these your fellow warriors?"

There was an awkward pause and then Carina stepped in.

"Tank, what did we say last night."

He looked down at his beer and tried to remember.

"Err, was that before the drinking game or after?" he asked.

"It was sort of after."

Fred was sniggering to himself. Carina thought about it.

"Ok, I'll let you off." she said, "Everyone, can I introduce our good friends the Barbers Angels. This is Tank, Fred, Peebop and Clax."

There was a general round of introductions and they all sat down. Then the drinks arrived along with Datch. The conversation was a little awkward to start with but soon the new comers got the idea. It got to nine thirty and Datch stood up and cleared his throat.

"Ok time for some fun. Zorm your team versus my team."

"What are we playing?"

"Solar Ball!"

Datch started to head for the game followed by the rest of the pack. The bar area suddenly cleared and there were a few raised voices of 'we need to take cover' and one of 'oh no not that!' which seemed to come from the dimly lit area in the corner and the voice sounded familiar.

The bar staff put on their helmets ready for the onslaught and the game started. This time the setting was a volcanic moon which was alarming to some of the customers as their tables suddenly became molten pools of bubbling lava, at least in a visual sense anyway. Zorm was given the first go. Datch knew they played it at school because they had told him about it one lunch time.

The bar was soon full of balls flying about which caused a number of muted screams as the balls hit the lava in front of people causing virtual lava to splash up in front of them. Also, a couple who happened to walk in from the street went white and needed the toilet because they stepped through the door into a pool of lava just as it erupted. The game was now starting to become a spectator sport and a number of the locals were taking bets on who would win. If anything, excluding people needing the bathroom in a hurry, the game was in fact increasing custom.

Team Datch won the first game and the next game was pulled up. This time it was underwater which also seemed to have the effect of making people want to use the toilet. It had sea creatures which were more than happy to swim around the bar making the place look like a giant aquarium. Datch took his shot. The speed was slower now and the ball floated across the bar hitting a jellyfish before being redirected to the purple ball that in this case looked like a bubble and on impact in a net it appeared to go pop. The game only had one small incident which was when someone came out of the toilets and walked into a giant octopus that was swimming by at the time. The result of the collision was that they needed the toilet again.

The second game went to Zorm's team. Carina did have to tell them to quiet down a little as they were getting a bit excited but they listened and dropped the volume a bit. Datch had told them on the way down he had been asked to report back about their behaviour. He figured that way they would listen. The third game was a solar system and the planets were the balls with the star being the net. There were asteroids and meteors flying around which were bumping into each other causing the bar to look like a shooting gallery.

The game progressed and it came down to the last two players. Tish and Dando. Dando walked over to take his shot. He hit the orange planet over to the brown one that in turn headed straight into the sun for a double. Tish was now under pressure and had to make a double at least to cause a tie. She took her shot, knocking the green one into the purple. The purple just missed the sun and started to curve out again. Zorm's team started to celebrate but the ball was still in play. Datch was watching it intently as was Tish. The ball flew past the bar just as a comet came across the room. It hit the planet sending it spinning towards the centre of the room and the star. It entered the pull of the star and was sucked straight into its heart for triple points. The game bleeped and Datch's team was declared the winners. Datch got another round of drinks and they headed back to the table.

The group carried on talking and soon it was time to head back. This time they went the short way. Datch and Carina still had the feeling someone was watching them. They quickened up the pace and soon were back at school. Security put their hand up to Datch and the gang. Team Zorm started to get their passes out and the security officer pointed out that if they were with Datch it was fine. They said their good nights and everyone except Datch and Carina headed back to their rooms. They went around to the big windows looking out towards the space port and sat talking for a little while before kissing good night and heading back to their rooms.

The shadows moved and a dark shape dropped down to street level. A bit further down the road a tramp was trying to get comfy in a doorway. There was a thud and a crunch before the shadow was gone back into the darkness. The doorway was now empty except for a few bits of paper that blew away in the breeze.

The next morning Datch was called to Jep's office, he knocked on the door and waited.

"Enter," came Jep's voice from behind the door and he walked in.

"Ah Datch, come and sit down, we were just discussing your outing last night." Jep was sitting with Zorm's tutor in the comfy chairs near the window.

"Is everything alright sir?" Datch said trying to resist the temptation to call him Jep.

"Yes Datch, the only issue Mr Waddo had all night was when his drink momentarily disappeared under a fountain of erupting lava just as he was going to pick it up."

"Err, sorry sir." said Datch who was now sitting down.

"Don't be sorry Datch, it was quite funny really." Mr Waddo added.

"Yes," said Jep, "we were both very impressed by how your team behaved last night, you corrected Zorm's team when they were going to over step the mark and at the same time you did it in a nice way. You can tell your team that they have got a platinum star for all their efforts."

Datch looked at Jep and then at Mr Waddo.

"Yes Datch, I was very impressed, in fact to the point where we will no doubt be asking you to do the same again soon. Oh, if Zorm's team want to go with you again would it be, ok?" asked Mr Waddo.

"Err... Yes Sir. "

Datch was still trying to stop grinning after finding out about the platinum star. Jep looked at Datch thoughtfully.

"Maybe not karaoke night though, at least not yet." he added.

"Karaoke night?" asked Mr Waddo.

"Yes, karaoke night, I don't think they are quite ready for that, let's just say that Datch has his own style and well it's a sight to be seen."

They turned to look at Datch, he felt a little uncomfortable.

"Well, it is a bit loud sir."

Datch was recalling last week's karaoke.

The Pack had ended up dancing on the bar while singing a very lively rock and roll number while Jep and the bikers did backing vocals standing on top of the big table. Jep really didn't want that to get out. The news of The Pack had started to spread around the city and people were coming into the bar just to see The Pack perform.

"Datch, well done again and I'll see you later." said Jep.

Datch got up.

"If you see Zorm outside, please send him in."

"Thank you, sir. See you later." Datch opened the door and walked out. Zorm was standing outside.

"You can go straight in; they're waiting for you." Datch smiled at him, Zorm looked like he was bricking himself, so Datch added, "It's fine really."

Datch headed off down the corridor and he knocked on the girl's door, Tish opened it.

"Hi Datch, what's up?"

"Meet outside near the fountain in ten minutes, I have big news."

"Ok, I'll get the others," she shut the door and Datch heard her shout 'Datch needs us outside in ten minutes, Move it people!'

He went back to his room and started to get Hagger and Dapo up and moving.

"Why can't you just tell us now." said Dapo.

"Because I can't, just get ready we have five minutes." Hagger came walking out the bathroom and fell over Dapo's towel. Datch helped him back up and soon they were ready. They headed off down the corridor and met the girls on the way out.

"So, what's going on?" Rosey asked Hagger.

"I don't know, he wouldn't say."

They got to the fountain and sat down on the grass, Datch stood in front of them.

"So, come on then, tell us what's up."

"Ok, I was called to Jep's office this morning. I went in and Zorm's tutor was there as well, they told me that they had been very impressed with how we looked after Zorm's team, they are going to give us a platinum star."

"What!" said Carina.

"A platinum star!" she got up and gave him a massive hug and kiss. The others all got up and there was a general round of everyone congratulating each other.

"Oh, my mums going to be so pleased." said Tish.

"Yes, my folks will be really happy." Added Carina.

Hagger was a bit quiet.

"Hagger, are you ok?"

"Yes, it's just I wish I could tell my mum; my dad won't care." Rosey put her arms around him and gave him a hug and a kiss. Hagger went red but at least he was now grinning.

"So, when are we getting it?" Rosey asked.

"I don't know, I was just told we're getting it, I suspect it will be at the end of trimester assembly, that's only three weeks away."

"Well, I think we had better party tonight to celebrate" said Dapo.

"Sounds like a plan." said Tish in agreement.

"Folks, it's Karaoke night tonight," Carina pointed out.

"Oh, in which case we'll have to party more than normal then." Added Dapo.

"I'm not sure the bar can survive anymore partying than we did last week without having to be remodelled afterwards." said Datch with images of the previous week flowing through his head.

They had a couple of hours before they had a lecture so they went to one of the outdoor bars down the street for a Gruck's to get into the spirit of things.

That night the Barbers Inn vibrated to the sound of The Pack. The place was rammed and they did six songs to start with then had a break for a drink and then another seven songs. People were watching them instead of taking part.

It was something else. They moved together and sang in almost perfect harmony. The bikers singing had improved as they had got the hang of it. The bar was buzzing, people were coming up and asking them for pictures with them. It was really crazy. The bar had even put a bouncer on the door and in the window was a poster saying tonight 'The Pack'. Finally, the bar started to calm down and the gang were all sitting around the big table.

"Have you told the bikers?" asked Jep.

"No not yet, we didn't get the chance the crowd was already here." Datch replied.

"Told us what?" asked Tank.

"We have been given a platinum star for last night."

"Congratulations all of you." he said and was followed by the others.

"Another round over here please!" said Fred putting his hand up and waving at the bar.

The barman came over with the drinks and the manager as well and asked if he could talk to them, Datch asked him to sit down.

"Hi all, if you hadn't noticed the bar has been getting a lot busier since you have been doing the karaoke and people are now coming just to see you folks, I have a proposition for you all." He stopped and waited for a response.

"We're all ears," said Fred figuring he might get a free beer or two.

"Well, OK, hear me out, I would like to pay you to perform, that is instead of the karaoke, I would put up a stage and you could perform say five songs then have a break and then another five, you did eleven tonight so that shouldn't be too much, what do you think?"

There was a bit of a discussion and then Fred spoke.

"How much are you thinking of paying?"

"Ok, What about forty credits each?"

"Hmm, "said Fred who had appointed himself as manager due to the fact he worked in insurance. No one is sure why this qualified him but it seemed like a plan.

"What about fifty credits and free drinks while we perform?"

The manager looked around the bar at all the people and then back at them. He had been in the business too long to miss out on a good thing.

"Ok, fifty credits each and a free bar on the night, I'll cover the advertising and any overheads, how's that sound?" There was another discussion and then they turned back to the manager.

"OK Jim, you have a deal." Said Fred.

"That's great, could I ask one more thing?"

"Yes, what is it?"

"Could you go and pose over there for the posters and can you sign this for my wife, she's a fan."

Datch suddenly realised that this was not just fun anymore. They were making other people have fun and enjoy themselves. People were following them and it blew his mind.

He gave Datch a card to write on and Datch put 'We love you Angi signed The Pack'.

They got up and headed into the middle of the bar to have their photos taken. After a few issues with people not smiling or pulling faces etc. Jim finally got the photos he wanted.

It's a universal constant that if a large group of people are having their photo taken, someone will A) have to pull a face, B) make rabbit ears over someone's head or C) pick their nose at the wrong time.

They had another round of drinks on the house to celebrate the deal. Datch did ask that no one tell his Mum and Dad but just invite them to the night before the end of trimester assembly. The rest of The Pack agreed this was a good plan and they would do the same. Datch made the bikers promise not to say anything and to make sure his mum and dad came. It would give them a couple of weeks to get the hang of it. They finished their drinks and headed back to school.

In the morning Team Datch were all given sealed letters to be given to their parents, Datch's dad came to pick him up as normal and Datch gave him the letter but told him not to open it until he got home, they took Hagger home again as his dad was not around as usual. Then they headed back to the ranch and home. His mum came out and gave him a hug.

"Well, how's my little man doing?"

"I have a surprise for you and dad." he said grinning.

"What is it?"

"Dad open the letter."

Dechow took the letter out of his pocket and broke the seal and unfolded the paper. He started to read it to himself and then he looked at Datch and smiled.

"Dad, read it out."

"Ok, ok." his dad cleared his throat.

'Dear Mr and Mrs Thome, it is my great pleasure to tell you that Datch and his team have been awarded the platinum star for outstanding behaviour skills, His team has not only displayed exceptional social skills but has been instrumental in helping other students improve their skills as well. We are very pleased to give Datch and his team this award and would like to invite you to the end of trimester assembly when the award will be given to them. Please accept our congratulation and we look forwards to seeing you there. Signed Dr Doji Datch's Tutor.'

Tansya gave Datch a big hug.

"Well done," she said "I'm so proud of you."

When Tansya put Datch down his dad grabbed his hand to shake it and pulled him in for another hug.

"Well done, you have made me proud of you again."

Datch wasn't sure how to react. He did feel very important and asked if he could have some ice-cream. His mum went and fetched him a bowl full.

"Oh, I was talking to Tank last night and we wondered if you would come down the night before and stop over at the Barbers Inn?"

"I don't see why not; do you want us to bring some ice-cream for the others as a bit of a gift?"

"That would be cool mum."

That weekend Datch had a lot of ice-creams, in fact that much he felt a bit ill.

The next week was The Packs first paid gig. The Barbers Inn was full and the vid screen outside was displaying pictures of The Pack along with phases like 'On stage tonight' and 'An unmissable act'.

The Pack went in and was escorted to the rear by a couple of bouncers. The big table had been moved to the back of the bar and a screen put across in front of it. Tank and Fred were already there sitting down having a drink. There were already a number of large Gruck's waiting on the table for them. Soon Clax, Jep and Peebop turned up. Datch stood up and handed out some bits of paper.

"Ok, this is what we thought we would do."

They sat looking at the sheets. Datch, Carina and the rest of The Pack had worked it out that lunch time.

"It looks ok to me." said Tank.

The others all nodded in agreement, it was then that Datch noticed.

"Err, you guys all have the same hair style."

Clax cleared his throat ready to speak,

"Yes, it was Tank's idea and the colour will wash out later." They all had green hair apart from Jep who didn't have any so they gave him a green wig and matching jacket.

"Well, ok then." said Datch slowly "Anything else we should know about?"

"No, apart from Fred having a tattoo with 'The Pack rules' over a skull and cross bones." Datch raised an eyebrow.

They had about an hour before the first set so they carried on chatting and drinking, they even got some free food. It arrived at nine o'clock and was time to perform. Jim went on stage,

"Ladies and gentlemen please put your hands together for the pack."

Datch and Carina headed out from behind the screens first followed by the rest. As they stepped out the crowd cheered. There must have been about two hundred people in the bar. Carina grabbed Datch's hand and moved in closer. They got to the middle of the stage and Datch raised his and Carina's hand. The crowd cheered at them again. Datch had been watching some vids about concerts and had studied what to do. He grabbed the mic and yelled into it.

"Are we ready to PARTY?"

The crowd screamed back "Yea!"

"I can't hear you, are we ready to PARTY?"

They screamed back even louder.

"Ok, then let's do this!" a beat started up.

"Hi, I'm Datch and this is The Pack, Carina my GF, Rosey, Hagger, Tish, Dapo, and on backing Tank, Fred, Clax, Peebop and Jep."

Each time the named member would put their hands in the air and the crowd would cheer. Then it was time for the first song. It was one of Carina's favourites 'Shoot for the Stars.'

They started singing and the crowd was joining in. The buzz was incredible. By the time they had finished the first set they were feeling like they could fly. The bouncers had to close the doors because the bar was full. People were dancing in the street outside. They went behind the screen and sat down to have a drink.

"Wow, that was exciting and what a rush." Dapo said getting his breath back at last.

"Yes, just a bit" added Rosey.

Datch, Carina, Tish and Tank were standing in front of a large fan which they had just set to full power.

"Well, Datch what do you think, did you like that?" asked Fred.

"It was cool, I wish we could get some more cool air. I think I'm steaming."

"Me too." Added Carina.

Just then Jim the manager came in.

"Well folks, it looks like you're a hit, we're having to turn people away because the bar is rammed, is there anything I can get you?" Datch thought about ice-cream but changed his mind.

"Err, some fresh air?" Carina asked.

"I'm not sure how fresh it is but you can have the back door open if you like."

He waved at one of the bouncers who opened the door and checked the yard. He nodded to give the all clear and the party headed outside.

The yard was a bit of a mess with empty barrels of beer, bottles and plastic containers lying about and it smelt a bit as well. But the air was cooler than inside. Datch and Carina sat together on one of the beer barrels drinking their Gruck. The others picked various barrels and containers to sit on. The bouncer parked himself on a barrel near the back gate just in case.

"That's better." said Tank who was starting to cool down at last.

"Well, I think we can class the first set as a success." said Fred with a grin.

"Yep, I can't disagree with that." said Jep who had been reluctantly talked into doing it.

"I thought it was great." said Hagger finally getting his voice back.

"Well, we've got to do it again in fifteen minutes." Datch added. Carina was resting her head on his shoulder.

"I just need to cool down a little more and I'll be ready." Said Rosey.

"Is this going to be marked on?" asked Tish.

"Err, no, I think this should just be our thing. I'm not sure the school would approve of me helping students become rock stars." Jep had his serious face on just to make sure everyone understood.

They sat having their drinks. Datch and Carina had a kiss and were told that it was hot enough already without them steaming things up further. It was soon time to head back in for the second set.

They had a final drink before heading out on stage. Datch and Carina did a duet to start with and then they ramped it up. The bar vibrated and pulsed with the rhythm. The final song of the night was 'We Can't Get High Enough' and the crowd were singing the words along with them. It finished to cheers and shouting. Some woman threw her underwear at Tank who automatically caught it before realising what it was and Fred was being eyed up by a woman who was not wearing very much at all. They headed back behind the screen and out the backdoor to cool off.

"Wow, that was so cool." Said Tish.

"Yes, it was cool." said Datch in agreement as the rest of The Pack nodded.

"I would have said more on the hot side than cool." added Clax who was trying to wring out his shirt that looked like he had just put it in a bucket of water.

"Ugh, that's a bit wet." said Carina.

"Well at least some woman didn't throw their knickers at you." said Tank pulling a face.

"Yes, but you did catch them, why did she do that anyway?" asked Hagger, Fred whispered something in his ear and he went red again.

"Really?" he said. The others just nodded slowly.

"Well, next week I'm going to wear something cool, these shorts were ok but made me sweat a bit, it's a skirt for me I think." said Rosey.

"I think we need to have a talk about costumes." Carina said and Datch agreed.

"Yes," he said, "I think we need to have something cool to wear that allows us to move freely. Everyone, have a think about it and we came sort it out after the weekend."

"Sounds like a plan." Added Fred.

"There's a shopping outing coming up next week, I could make it part of the course work. It would give me chance to pick some bits out, what about animal skins?" said Jep.

They all turned to look at him and Carina was trying to get the image of Jep wearing a furry thong out of her head.

"Ok, it looks like it's calming down in there, let's head back inside." Datch said.

He wanted another drink.

Tank stuck his head around to check the coast was clear in case a woman was looking for him.

"Yep, looks safe, err, I mean alright." he said.

They headed back inside to the big table. The bouncers put the screens away and they were able to see the bar again.

The room was thinning out now and they could see the bar for the first time in two hours. It looked like the woman who was lacking her garments had gone home much to Tank's relief. A few people came over to thank them for a great night and tell them how much they had enjoyed it. It gave Datch a good feeling inside. Carina was almost sitting on his lap again and she was making sure everyone knew he was with her. Jim came over and gave them all seventy credits each.

"I thought it was fifty credits?" said Datch.

"Yes, but I have just had a week's takings in one night, you deserve a bonus." Jim said while handing out the credit chits.

They chatted some more while they chilled out and it was about another hour before The Pack headed back to the school. When they arrived Datch and Carina went to the big window for a bit of them time.

"Sorry, I'm a bit sweaty." Datch said.

"That's ok, I'm a bit that way myself."

They sat arm in arm.

"Did you enjoy tonight?" he said.

"Yes, it was too hot but fun never the less."

"That's what I thought too, and when those people came up and said thank you to us for a great night, I felt so good about it."

"I know what you mean, it was a good night."

"I think I'll message the Snowmen about it."

"The Snowmen?"

"Yes, the band in the dancing Jaxx."

"Oh them, I remember now."

They carried on talking until security came around and told them it would be a good idea to go to bed.

At the weekend Datch's mum said for some reason they were having trouble getting a room for the night before the assembly. Datch said he would get Fred to have a word with Jim. He nearly let the secret out but just managed to save it.

Every morning he would call Carina and spend an hour on the vid com talking to her. He would put the vid on, normally the news channel so his mum didn't hear anything. The news was boring with stories about the homeless decreasing in the city or a redevelopment of an old area of the city and things like that. One story was about a new genetic crop that would boost the farm yields allowing more to be exported off world. oh, and the arrival of a new starship with a new type of drive system that was meant to be more efficient. Datch made a note to look out for it.

Life is full of Surprises

It was the last week of the trimester. The assembly was three days away. The previous weeks gig had gone well with the new style of clothes going down well. The Pack had green shorts for the boys and skirts for the girls. They had very light T-shirts with 'The Pack' on them for everyone. Tank had a big hat with a fan in who by now had lost about 4 kg in weight by sweating and was starting to cause a slip hazard. He had also taken to wearing dark glasses because the same woman had thrown some more items of clothing at him and he was worried in case she came in and found him at some point. The rest of them had tried to point out that the glasses probably wouldn't help, but they did make him feel better so that was ok. The manager Jim had sorted out a room for Datch's mum and dad. They were very surprised not only to get a room but had somehow ended up with an upgrade to a suite for the same price.

The gang were still refining the song list. They had added a biker's song to the list so Tank, Fred, Clax and Peebop could take the front of the stage half way through the second set and give The Pack a chance to cool down at the back. They were getting a fantastic buzz on stage but it was very hot even with the air con running flat out. The bar was so full of people that Jim had to put on four extra bar staff just to cope.

They sat at the big table enjoying a cold drink and watching the sports channel. It was the semi-finals of the orbital racing. In the last heat some one's dart hit a boulder and exploded killing the racer. The med team said he should make a full recovery and be ready to race next season.

Hagger was surprised, "So you mean when they die, they don't die?"

"Yes," said Fred, "at the moment of impact their brain is transported out and put in stasis until a new body is grown for them, then the brain is put into the new body. The racers have new bodies on standby so it only takes three months before they are racing again."

"Oh, so if I die, I'll get a new body?"

"Well sort of, normal people have to be careful, you only get four bodies not counting the one you have and you have to go to a medical centre to be transferred, so if you die by accident you may end up staying dead. Hasn't anyone told you this before?"

"Err, no," said Hagger.

"Me neither." Added Tish who had been listening intently. The next fifteen minutes were spent explaining the whole life span thing, life and death and why you shouldn't tell people they are too young because they might actually be older than you.

Finally, they got back to the matter in hand, the racing. The current champion was leading but they wanted the racer in third place to win as he happened to be from Yuland city and was a local boy. The first two racers went through to the nail bighting final the following week. Datch never really used to watch the sport much at home but he was really loving it. Carina was cheering along with him and he thought that was very important and also was liking it a lot. The racers entered the last section of the course. Carina was squeezing Datch's hand as the racers dodged the small orbiting boulders. Their thrusters were running flat out and it was neck and neck right up to the finish line. Finally, they were over it, the slow-motion feed showed that the champion and the local boy had crossed the line in joint first with, the second racer missing out by only a thousandth of a second. They all cheered and shouted at the vid, it took a few minutes to calm down.

"Peebop, I got a message from Don today concerning your missing bots." said Datch.

"How does he know about them?" asked Peebop a little confused.

"Well, I sort of asked him about them and sent the vid that you had to him."

"Oh, what did he say?"

"Well, he thinks it's a very interesting puzzle and wants Isbar to scan the site where they disappeared."

"Err, I'm not sure my boss will like the IPSF getting involved, he's a bit cross with me already."

"Don't worry, Isbar's going to do it as a tourist so no one will know, oh and he's coming for a beer tomorrow with Don." Datch stopped and waited for the reaction, there was a pause and then.

"You do know last time we were drinking with them it took me three days to get over the hangover?" said Clax looking straight at Datch.

"I did tell them not to get you drunk because we have a gig the following night, and before you say it, they have been told to keep hush hush about the gig."

There were a few sighs of relief.

"Who is Isbar and Don?" asked Carina.

"Err, Isbar is the 1st commander on the starship Carpaycus and Don is the captain." Said Fred.

"You mean we're going to have a starship captain here tomorrow!" said Carina who started getting excited.

"Shh. Don't stay anything. They are coming incognito." Datch added trying to calm her down then continued, "But yes, the captain and Isbar the 1st Commander. Oh, they asked if you could bring your vid com, they want to have a look at the vid of the site."

"Ok, but I don't know what use it will be, the local government officers couldn't find anything." Peebop said looking a bit down.

"If anyone can solve it, I'm sure they can." Tish added trying to make him feel better.

"I suppose so" he said.

"Anyway, they're coming around eight ish, The Carpaycus gets in at lunch time but they have to sort out the crews shore leave as they are here for six days. Anyway, on with the fun." Datch added.

"How about a game of Solar Ball?" Tish asked.

"I'm in," said Hagger.

They got up and headed for the game. The bar staff grabbed their helmets.

The next day Carina was a bit excitable. Datch was wishing he hadn't said anything about Don. Tish and Dapo were ok but Hagger was very nervous and Rosey couldn't work out what to wear.

"Look trust me, they're just normal guys who happen to work in space, really, stop worrying about what you look like and what you'll say."

Datch knew what the captain's idea of casual dress meant and incognito was not a word he would use.

They had their dinner and headed off to get changed. It didn't take long, well apart from Rosey who changed cloths three times and did her hair twice. Datch had talked Carina into not over doing it and getting dressed in a nice skirt and top. Datch and Dapo had their normal shorts and T-shirt on and then spent five minutes sorting Hagger out. They managed to get him to the point where he wasn't panicking and had told him about twenty times that they were normal people. Finally, they headed outside to meet the girls. Rosey looked like she was about to go to a formal dinner or something but Tish had followed Carina. They waited for Jep, he came walking out wearing a short-sleeved shirt with a bowtie and knee length trousers, Datch sighed. They were in for a shock.

They headed off to the Barbers Inn and for some reason it didn't take as long as normal to get to the bar. When they went in the bikers were already there and like Datch were wearing their normal clothing. They sat down and the bar staff brought their drinks over. As the time got near to eight 'O'clock and the door opened they would all look around. Well apart from the bikers and Datch. Datch would just give the door a quick glance and then go back to his drink and talking to Carina.

At five past eight the door opened and two people walked in one was wearing a very loud orange and yellow shirt and shorts which looked like they should have been in a flower show. The other was wearing desert-coloured shorts, shirt and what can only be described as an adventure's hat as it had stickers all over it. Both had sunglasses on and carried a touristy bag. They both stood out like sore thumbs. The girls looked and then turned back to the table. Datch put up his hand and the two of them came over. The Pack looked at them.

"Err Datch, is that them?" asked Tish in disbelief.

Datch stood up. Don and Alex came and shook his hand.

"Hi Don, Hi Alex." Datch said, shaking their hands.

"Hello Datch, so is this team Datch?" said Don smiling.

"Everyone, I would like you to meet Don and Alex. Let me introduce everyone."

Datch turned and started to go around the table.

"This is Dapo and Hagger, they are my room mates," they saluted and Don reciprocated, "This is Tish and Rosey." Tish shook his hand and Rosey started to bow then changed her mind and went for a handshake which led to a little amusement. "And this here is my girlfriend Carina."

"It's a great pleasure to meet you, young lady." Carina blushed and went to shake his hand.

He lifted her hand up and kissed the back of it.

"This here is Jep, he's our tutor." Don shook his hand.

"Have you managed to teach Datch anything yet?" he asked in a joking way.

"Err, I'm not sure." he said suddenly realising that in fact he had learnt more from Datch than the other way around.

"And of course, you know the bikers."

"Good evening gentlemen," there was a general round of "Hi Guys" and Tank waved at the bar staff, "couple of large cold beers please."

"Well, let's get the business out of the way before the fun starts, shall we?" said Don.

"Sounds like a plan." said Datch the next half an hour was spent going over everything they had found so far, once they had gone through it all Don sat back in his seat.

"So, what do you think?" said Peebop.

"We need to do a few more checks. The commander, sorry, Alex took some readings at the site earlier and needs to feed them into the ships computers, it's slightly puzzling and I can see why Datch wanted my help, tell me have there been any other strange crimes or things disappearing in the city?"

"Hmm," said Peebop thinking, Datch turned to Don

"Well, there was the break in at the meat venders the other week and also a thing about the homeless disappearing, do they count?"

Don had a very serious look on his face.

"They might, look I have an idea but can't tell you with any certainty at the moment. in the meantime, until I've been able to check it out, don't go out in the city at night on your own, the bigger the group the better."

"Can't you tell us anything?" said Jep now somewhat concerned.

"Ok, if my hunch is right your city has a spider problem."

"So, when Rosey said it looked like a spider she was right?"

"Look, keep it to yourself because I don't know if it is an arachnoid yet and as to why it would want bots, I have no idea, all I'm saying is to stay safe. If it is here, it won't go after groups of people because it won't want to be seen, also I will need the sensors on the Carpaycus to find it and that's if it's not shielded in some way. so, at this point just stay safe, ok?" everyone agreed.

Jep said he would tell the school he had heard rumours about a madman attacking people alone in the street. That way the school would tell the students to go out in groups only and wouldn't ask too many questions.

"Oh, and Datch, I was wondering, myself, Comm... Alex and Fizz want to come to the gig, any chance of a ticket or two?" said Don changing the subject, Datch stopped to think about this.

"Err, I'm not sure they do tickets yet. Hold on." He put his hand up and waved at Jim who was checking his stock behind the bar, Jim put down the vid com he was holding and came over.

Datch whispered in his ear.

"Really?"

Datch whispered something else.

"Well, I can put them on the table with your mum and dad, would that be, ok?"

"Perfect." said Don.

"That's it sorted then. Please can you get here early though, it gets quite busy, say seven ish, oh Datch can you all come in the back tomorrow, you know where the back-gate is don't you?"

"Yes" replied Datch.

With that Jim went back to checking his stock behind the bar.

"So, what else do you do here for fun?" asked Alex.

"Glad you asked?" said Datch getting up, "Solar Ball anyone?" the party headed to the game. Jim headed into the office and the bar staff put their helmets on.

Across the city the arachnoid stirred and its large bulk uncurled slowly from its resting place high up in the attic of a disused building. It was jet black and the size of two large Jaxx with long spindly legs which moved silently across the rafters. Two large pincers extended from either side of its head and in the centre was its bone crushing jaws. On the top of its head was an array of small round eyes that allowed it to see perfectly in the dark.

It moved to a vantage point on the top of the building to look for prey. Its masters had forgotten to bring it food again. It was annoyed and hungry. Time for the hunt it thought to itself. It moved out across the city in search of fresh meat using the darkness as cover. It soon spotted a tramp sleeping in a box under a tree in one of the many parks. It moved closer, silently climbing from tree to tree until it was in the tree above the tramp. It waited until the right moment and then it struck causing some nearby birds to take flight. A moment later the box was empty and the park was quiet again. The arachnoid climbed up a nearby building, its prey cocooned, hanging limp and lifeless under its large body, it pulled itself up onto the rooftops and headed back cross the city to its nest in the attic.

The next morning Datch was up early. It was going to be a busy day. The morning lecture was a long one about holiday dos and don'ts on interstellar cruises and it turned out to be a very boring lecture. Especially the bit about stops on Welly four. Why anyone would want to go there he had no idea. The afternoon lecture was a bit more interesting; it was all about haggling for goods and they had to do some practical assessments which got everyone laughing. Datch managed to sell a table to another team in exchange for a grandmother and a bag of sweets. It was then time for dinner and then they had to get ready for the nights gig.

At the Barbers Inn, Dechow and Tansya were tucking into a nice steak dinner. Jim had put them on the table near the stage in a spot where they couldn't see the posters. They had asked him what the band was but he just said it was a local group of singers and they would be on stage about eight. He also said it would get busy and if they needed a drink to wave at the bar and someone would come over. The big table had disappeared and been replaced with some smaller ones.

Their table had three extra seats and a reserved for Datch in the middle of it. It was also next to the screen that ran across the bar next to the stage, the stage was about 3 metres by 2 metres and had a number of mics and stands on it. Jim had put up a lighting bar above the stage and barriers in front of it to stop the crowds pushing forward.

"It must be a popular band, looks like they have bouncers on the doors." said Dechow.

"Yes, it certainly looks like it's going to get busy, I hope Datch gets here soon or he might have trouble getting in." replied Tansya.

It got to seven thirty and the bar was filling up quite quickly. Jim went around the back of the stage and opened the backdoor, a hand came over the gate and opened it, Datch and The Pack came walking in,

"How's it looking?" said Tank walking in.

"It's filling up nicely, should be a full house tonight for sure." Jim replied.

"Is my mum and dad here?" asked Datch.

"Yes, they are on a table just in front of the stage." Datch thought for a moment.

"Err, tell them I'm running a bit late and will be there as soon as I can, I have a feeling they might call me otherwise." Jim looked at him.

"Ok, I will, I've put your drinks on the table and I'll come and announce you at eight, please can you be ready."

"Yes, we'll be ready, don't worry."

They sat down and had a drink. Datch went and had a look through the little hole on the screen.

"See what he means, its nearly full already."

Carina put her arm around him. He turned and gave her a kiss.

Out in front of the stage the bar was getting very busy. The bouncers were manning the door when three people came in. It was Don, Alex and Fizz. They got some drinks from the bar and were shown over to the table with Dechow and Tansya.

"Well look who we have here?" said Don loudly. Dechow turned around quickly.

"What are you doing here?" he said.

"We're on shore leave and heard that they had a good band on, what about you?"

"Oh, Datch comes in here and we're meeting him, his team has got an award for outstanding behaviour."

"I'll have to congratulate him later." He added.

Fizz was looking at the stage and trying not to make eye contact. She had been told not say anything and was trying not to give the game away.

"Why don't you sit with us, I'm sure we can get another couple of chairs for Datch and Carina."

"Thank you we will." They carried on talking and the bar got packed.

At eight Jim got up onto the stage. The lights dimmed and the spot lights came up. He picked up a mic.

"Ladies, Gentlemen and fellow humanoids, Welcome to the Barbers Inn, it is my great pleasure to introduce tonight's Band, please put your hands together for THE PACK!" the music started and The Pack came running on stage.

Dechow and Tansya looked open mouthed then turned to Don, Alex and Fizz who were all cheering. Don looked at Dechow and tapped his nose with his finger and smiled.

The music filled the bar and soon people were dancing. Fizz got up with Alex and were going for it at the front of the stage. This just made Datch and the gang encourage the dancers more. Soon half the pub was on its feet. By the time the first set came to an end the bar was buzzing and the place was full to breaking point.

The Pack disappeared behind the screens. One of the bouncers came over and took Tansya and Dechow around to the back of the screen. There sat Datch and the gang getting their breath back and having a cold drink.

"Hi mum, Hi Dad." said Datch casually "So what did you think?"

"Err, it was very good but when did you start this?" asked his mum somewhat shocked by it all.

"Well, it just sort of happened about four weeks ago. I didn't want to say anything until we were happy with the way things were working. I planned to invite you down but then with the platinum star, it just sort of worked." She looked at him.

She realised that in the last four months he had grown up a lot. He was now coming into his own and had a group of friends around him that would look after him and be there for him.

"So," said Dechow, "What does your tutor think to all this or haven't you told him?"

"Ask him yourself, he's doing backing vocals." Jep stood up and tried to dry the sweat off his hand.

"Err, hello again. To answer your question as his tutor, it is a good grounding in social interaction, and on a personal note it's also a lot of fun." Dechow thought about this and was about to say something then changed his mind.

"Oh, well that's ok then." he said instead.

There was a few 'hello' or 'Hi, how are you doing?' from the rest of The Pack and then Dechow turned to Datch again.

"Err, so you invited the captain and Alex, but didn't tell us?"

"Well no. He came about Peebop's missing bots and then asked for tickets."

At this point Dechow gave up. He knew when he had no chance so graciously threw in the towel.

Datch went on to explain how they ended up with the gig and how the bot investigation was going. Dechow was a bit alarmed when he found out it could be an arachnoid involved but went with what Don had said. The bouncer told them it was time for the second set and escorted Tansya and Dechow back to the table.

"So, has Datch brought you up to speed?" asked Don.

"Yes, do you really think it could be an arachnoid?" Dechow said.

"Everything is pointing that way, the only thing I can't work out is why it would want bots."

"That is very odd, bots are not much use to an arachnoid, so why take them also how did it do it?" the conversation stopped there as the music started and The Pack went onto the stage.

It wasn't long before the dance floor was packed again. Alex and Fizz were up dancing and even got Tansya up as well. Dechow sat with Don watching the proceedings. It got to half way through the second set and as planned Tank, Fred,

Clax and Peebop came to the front of the stage and did a rock song that bikers liked. Apparently, the bar liked it as well judging by the whistles and cheers. Unfortunately, so did the woman at the front and Tank ended up with another pair of underwear. Luckily this time he ducked, however Jep didn't. The song finished and The Pack was back up front. They were looking very refreshed. Jim had come up with the idea of putting towels in the freezer which seemed to work well and cooled you down quite quickly.

The set carried on and got to the last song. It was one they knew the crowd loved and would go nuts over. Sure enough, as the first few notes played the place erupted. The cheering and whistling was so loud Jim had to turn the PA up even louder. The crowd were singing the song with them and the dance floor was packed. The song finally came to an end and the crowd shouted and whistled. The Pack headed behind the screen and back to the big table. The bouncers moved to the front of the screen.

"Is it ok if we go behind?" asked Tansya,

"Yes, but can you just wait a few minutes until the crowd dies down, they are a little volatile at the moment mam."

She could see what they meant.

It didn't take long before people started heading home and the bar started to empty. After about twenty minutes the bouncers removed the screen and moved the big table against the smaller table in the bar. The Pack wandered in through the backdoor and sat back down at the table. Before they could start talking Jim came over.

"Another good night for both of us. I have a hundred and twenty credit's each."

"Cool, thanks" said Datch watching as the credits were transferred into his account.

They we're now making quite a lot of credits. In the four weeks they had been singing they had made four hundred and eighty credits and the free drinks went down well too.

"So Tansya, what did you think?" Asked Carina eager to get in there first.

"It was very good, I really enjoyed it. I just wish Datch had given me some warning so I was wearing the right shoes."

"I'm starting to see quite a different side to Datch." Said Dechow looking across the table.

"Actually," said Don wading in "He reminds me of you a few hundred years ago, you liked to party and you always looked out for your friends and colleagues as well."

"He's a smaller version of you for sure." Added Alex.

Dechow had to agree, Datch was like him in so many ways.

"Yes, I suppose he is." He said looking at Datch who was currently introducing Fizz to the bikers.

"So, I take it Datch has told you about his award tomorrow?"

"Err, yes we were in here last night talking to Peebop about the missing bots" Alex said.

"We arrived in orbit yesterday morning and the mystery had got me puzzled and myself and Commander Isbar – sorry Alex, wanted to have a look around."

"When do you head out?"

"Not for another four days yet. We're getting some supplies and the crew are on shore leave, so we're making the most of it."

"Did you want to come tomorrow?" asked Tansya

"I would love too, thanks." Don said.

"What about you Alex?"

"Err sorry no, I'm heading up to Traxsent for a couple of days."

"Jarna by any chance?" she didn't need an answer, the smile on Alex's face said it all. He just nodded.

The evening carried on until well after midnight. Don, Alex and Fizz said they would walk back with Datch and The Pack as their shuttle was at the spaceport and so Dechow and Tansya headed off to the bed.

Next morning, they were all up early and had arranged to meet in the restaurant for breakfast. There was an air of excitement about the place and the students were all looking forward to the break. It was only three weeks but it wasn't school. The assembly was at ten fifty and they had to be there at ten twenty-five to settle down before the parents arrived. Datch had a large bowl of muesli with fruit in it. He had taken a liking to it on the Carpaycus and now both him and Carina had it every morning. Sometimes Rosey would even have some. Dapo, Hagger and Tish were pancake people with lots of syrup on. It was soon time to head off to the main hall. Datch was very excited about the awards bit as were the rest of his team. It was a big thing to get a platinum star especially in the first trimester, they didn't hand them out very often so to get one was very impressive.

The main hall was a large circular room with a stage at one end and had a high ceiling with lights scattered about it in clusters. The walls were a cream colour and had pictures of previous principals hanging on them like a legion of warriors overseeing the proceedings. Around the room were tables and chairs, each of which was allotted to a team. It was set out like an awards evening would be and even now it was another lesson of sorts. The students filed in and went to their allocated seats. The room was buzzing and Team Datch had a table at the front. The table had twenty seats around it and named places for the students and parents, for some reason Datch's table seemed to have been given a posh chair with 'Captain Don Ronediamar' on the place setting.

Team Datch sat down.

"Well, it looks like Jep told them Don was coming." said Carina looking at the chair.

"He won't like it you know; he likes to relax when on leave, just ask him about the party at my house." said Datch with a sigh.

"Err, does Jep know about the party at your house?" asked Dapo.

Datch thought about this for a moment.

"Hmm, maybe not unless the bikers told him. Still Don won't want any fuss."

They sat looking at the stage. It was bigger than it looked from the back. There was a set of eight steps going up to it and two rows of twenty chairs on each side of the podium in the centre. They sat making plans for the next week. Even though school was out they still had the gig at the Barbers Inn. Carina, Rosey and Dapo had squared it with their parents. Hagger said his dad went out every night at six and was never back until three in the morning if he came back at all so he wouldn't miss him anyway. Tish however was a bit reluctant to talk to her parents. She didn't know quite what to say and was hoping a good word from the other parents would do the job.

Soon the hall filled up with students and after a few moments the parents started to file in looking around for their son or daughter. The first of team Datch's parents were Dapo's mum and dad. They came over and Dapo introduced them to the rest of the team and helped them to their seats. Then it was Rosey's turn followed shortly afterwards by

Carina's mum and dad. Then it was Tish's turn. Hagger's dad had sent a message saying he wasn't coming. Finally, Datch's mum and dad came in accompanied by Don. He was certainly not incognito now. He had put on his dress uniform and two members of his crew took positions on either side of the main door. There was a general mummering in the crowd and craning of necks to see where he went to sit. Datch's mum and dad came over and sat down followed by Don. A number of the parents got up and attempted to bow or salute then realised he had sat down.

"Err, Don, I thought you were incognito?" Datch said quietly in his direction.

"Well, that was yesterday. Today it's something special so I got dressed up, oh and I have a surprise for you all later." He smiled.

The other parents at the table were introduced to him. Soon the Tutors walked out on to the stage and sat down. The principal came out and walked up to the podium.

"Ladies, Gentlemen, students and honoured guest's, it gives me great pleasure to start this assembly. We have a lot to cover so..."

The assembly went on with reports from the tutors and the various results. The overall rating for the year so far and what was planned for the next trimester. Finally, it got to the rewards bit. A number of teams won an award for conduct or extra effort in this or that subject. Then it came to the last group of awards. Team Zorm had got an award for best improved team and then it was time for the best team overall.

"This award is for the most mature and sensible team. This team has shown excellent behaviour and has stood out from the rest, please put your hands together for Team Datch." The was a round of applause and Datch and The Pack got up and went on to the stage. Jep stepped forward and had a box with him. He stepped up to the podium.

"It has been my pleasure to tutor these fine students. They are very mature individuals and have shown outstanding behaviour, I was asked a few days ago if I was teaching them or they were teaching me. I had to stop and think about it. Datch and his team have showed me how to enjoy life and be mature at the same time. It is my great pleasure to give you the Best Team award please step forward." They did and each of them were given a golden medal to a round of applause when they received them. The principal stepped back up to the podium.

"Please wait team Datch." he said, "Ladies and Gentlemen it is also my honour to give out a special award. This award is not given out very often and is only given to a special team. This team in front of you not only have exceled in their attitude and behaviour but have been passing on their skills to fellow students and a couple of weeks ago they were given the task of looking after Team Zorm. They took them to one of the local bars and demonstrated how to behave and helped to teach their fellow student what to and what not to do. We had two of our tutors watching them the whole time and they were so impressed they came and told me what had happened. We felt that their behaviour needed to be rewarded and therefore I take great pleasure in giving the Platinum Star to team Datch." He turned to face the Team.

Jep came over to him with another box and opened it. Inside there was six small shinny stars. He walked down the row and shook hands each one of them and pinned a star on their tops. After the last one he turned to the rest of the hall.

"Ladies and gentlemen put your hands together for Team Datch."

There was a huge round of applause and some muted cheers. Finally, they headed back to the table and sat down. The principal thanked everyone for coming and announced that there would be refreshments in the restaurant for anyone who would like to stay for a bit. With that people started to filter out. Don stood up and raised his hands to indicate the table to wait for a minute.

"I have a little surprise for you all. When I was here the day before yesterday Carina told me, she dreamed of going into space and so I've arranged for a small reception onboard the Carpaycus for Team Datch and all of your parents."

He gave one of the officers on the door a signal and the officer nodded back.

"What, we're going into space?" said Carina and Dapo almost at the same time.

"Yes, if it's ok with your parents that is?" at this point the parents didn't seem to have much choice considering their now somewhat excited offspring were grinning and they nodded their approval.

"Well, that's sorted then. If you will please follow me to the shuttle."

They headed outside through the main doors towards the carpark. There in the middle of the parking area was a large shuttle with four officers standing outside and a hand full of the school's security officers keeping people way from it as it was attracting quite a crowd. Datch and Carina were walking next to Don, Carina was squeezing Datch's hand with excitement.

"Err Don," said Datch "Have you got ice-cream?"

Don laughed.

"Why did I know you were going to ask that. To answer your question, yes, and the ships chef has been busy trying things out since last time you were onboard. The crew seems to like it and he has a few flavours he wants you to try."

They arrived at the shuttle and the officers saluted. Don saluted back and walked up the ramp. The officers also saluted Datch and Dechow. They saluted back. Datch realised that they were the crew that had been to Asmove with him. They went onboard. It was one of the larger shuttles and had thirty-two seats set into four rows of eight, two on each side. Datch and Carina went and sat next to Don at the front. Dapo and Tish sat behind them with Rosey and Hagger on the opposite side. Dechow and Tansya filed in behind along with the rest of the parents. Soon the four officers came in from outside and sat at the back. The rear doors closed and the engines started up.

"Datch, I would like you to meet the pilot, this here is Hycrax the one who died on Asmove."

The pilot turned to look at Datch.

"Please to meet you." he said.

"Please to meet you too." Datch said and looked at him for a minute.

"Can I ask you something?"

"What?"

"Did it hurt?"

"What the dying thing?"

"Yes."

"No, didn't feel a thing." he said with a smile, then turned back to looking out the front of the shuttle.

The engines built up power and then the shuttle started to move, Datch felt Carina squeezing his hand as the shuttle left the ground.

"Wow, this is so cool." said Rosey as the shuttle pointed its nose skyward.

The shuttle's engines whined loudly as it headed up through the atmosphere. Team Datch were transfixed by the view out of the windows. The sky started to get darker and then the stars appeared. The planet was below them and passing by at a considerable speed. They had left the atmosphere and were now in space.

One of the four orbiting space stations came into view below and then the shuttle turned towards the stars. In the distance a bright light could be seen. As they got closer the light got bigger slowly turning into a huge starship. It was white, long and sleek with letters on the side six decks high which spelled out the name 'CARPAYCUS'. Everyone had gone quiet in awe of the view outside the windows. The shuttle flew alongside before turning into the landing bay. Datch looked out the window. A group of transport shuttles were on the flight deck, three of them. One of which looked very new. The shuttle landed near the entrance to the main corridor. Datch recognised it from last time he was onboard. There was a clunk as the docking clamps engaged and the crew got up and opened the door. Don got up and turned to everyone.

"Ladies and gentlemen, Welcome to the Carpaycus if you would like to follow me to the reception." He went to the door.

"This is so cool, we're on a starship!" said Carina in Datch's ear.

"I told you, we would see the stars." he said with a grin.

"Is this your dad's old ship?" She asked.

"Yes, he was 1st commander here for over a hundred years."

They followed Don up the corridor and into a pod. The pod headed off through the ships maze of tunnels and soon arrived at the reception suite which was on the front of the ship. They followed Don in and were greeted by some of the crew Datch had met last time he was onboard. Fizz was there looking a bit more crew like now. The reception suite was a large room with an enormous window and there in front of them was the planet below shining bright against the stars. It was breath taking. Team Datch ran over to look and watched as the planet scooted by. There was a cough from behind. They turned around and everyone was looking at them.

"Err, sorry we've never seen the planet like this before." Tish said

"It's ok." said Don smiling. "This is meant to be a treat for you, please come over here and we'll get the formalities out the way then you can look outside all you want."

They walked over to him.

"Ok, Ladies and Gentlemen, I would like to start by welcoming you all to the Carpaycus. I have done this as a little treat for team Datch, as the principle has already said, they are a very mature and intelligent group. If they stick together, I have a feeling they may even shake the universe. I have known young Datch for most of his life and he seems to have a spark inside him that spreads to the people around him. Team Datch have that fire and have shown what they can do. I know they will all become amazing people and it is our job to nurture them and help them grow. I have seen team Datch in action and found myself thinking wow how did this happen. Needless to say, from school work to singing on stage they excel, to all six of you, keep up the good work and well done."

There was a round of applause, Tish's mum looked at Tish and mouthed 'singing' Tish just nodded. Hagger had gone his normal colour and was glowing like a warning beacon.

"Ok let's have some food and you can enjoy the view." Don said, he waved his hands and the doors opened and half a dozen crew members came in carrying trays of food, then a strange trolley was pushed in.

Datch went over to look at it. It had a glass top on with a hinge so it could be lifted up, inside were eight compartments with different flavours of ice-cream.

"Oh wow." said Datch now starting to drool.

"You like it?" came a voice from behind him and he turned around, it was Qwots the chief engineer.

"Yes, it's really cool."

"The chef wanted a way to keep the ice-cream frozen while he was serving it in the restaurant so I came up with this. It keeps it ice cold and can be wheeled about."

"Hmm I wonder if my dad can make one to go outside next to the pool."

"If you like I can send him the plans?"

"That would be so cool, thanks!" he said. At that point the chef came in.

"Ahh Datch." He said putting his arms out. "So good to see you again. How are you?"

"I'm good thanks. You?" Datch said while being hugged by the chef.

He didn't like being hugged by a strange man but had been told that on some planets it was a normal greeting.

"Yes, I'm good and have been very busy with Ice-cream. The crew love it. So, I have been trying things out and have some ice-cream for you to try and tell me what you think."

He said grabbing a spoon and a dish.

Datch looked at the ice-cream and noticed there were little labels on the compartments.

Chocolate | Renar Berry | Tarli fruit | Purpur | Talitop Berry | Laypar | Ginjin | Sipa Berry

A scoop of each was put in the dish just as Carina came up behind Datch and put her hands around him,

"You're wonderful." she said then looked down.

"Oh, ice-cream!" she said grabbing a dish and handing it to the chef.

"Who is this?" said the chef.

"This is my girlfriend Carina."

"It's very nice to meet you mam, let me fill your bowl."

Once they had the ice-cream, he sat them down.

"So, tell me what you think?"

They tried the chocolate. Yep, big thumbs up.

Then the Renar Berry. Yes, that was good as well.

Tarli fruit was next, that was good.

Next was Purpur, he had not had that before. It was a sort of strange spearmint flavour but was missing something.

The chef looked at their faces

"It needs something doesn't it?"

"Yes, Hmm I think I know." said Datch and took a bit of chocolate and mixed it up.

He took a taste "That's it." he said and gave the chef a taste.

He savoured it for a moment "Yes, that is good, thank you."

Carina did the same and nodded in agreement.

Then came Talitop Berry, this was a sort of black current flavour and got the thumbs up.

The Laypar was a sort of lemon taste and had a bit of a strong flavour. Both Datch and Carina wrinkled their noses.

"Err… that's a bit strong." said Datch and Carina nodded in agreement then added.

"I think it would be ok at about half the strength." she said, Datch nodded.

"Ok, that is good. Next is the Ginjin"

The Ginjin made them both pull a face. It was very gingery and made you feel like your nose was about to implode. It got a big thumbs down.

The chef put his head on one side then nodded.

Last but not least was the Sipa Berry. This was quite nice but also quite plain with a hint of vanilla, it got a thumbs up.

"Thank you both, I'll take the Ginjin off the list and adjust the Laypar" he said.

"Well, it might work with a curry?" said Carina smiling.

He smiled back and then took the Ginjin back to the kitchen.

They grabbed some food and headed over to the window where everyone else was talking and looking out. The planet filled about half the window and was scrolling past below. Currently you could see the Great desert and a few cities scattered around its rim. Team Datch stood eating ice-cream and watching the scene out of the window.

"I never thought the planet as being so small." said Rosey.

"Yes, I know what you mean." said Dapo.

"So, which is the bit where we live?" asked Hagger.

Fizz who was standing close by pointed at a spot to the bottom of the desert.

"It's just there, if you look carefully, you can see the glint from the spaceport as the ships take off." she said.

Carina and Datch were looking up into the inky blackness above.

"So where is Asmove?" she said turning to him.

"Err…" he was about to say that one there but changed his mind. "I'm not sure to be honest. When we left orbit, we headed to the sun and then sort of up, so it must be up there somewhere I guess."

"This is amazing." she said giving him a subtle peck on the cheek.

"I want to explore out there one day. All of my family live in the stars and my dream is to have a ship of my own one day." he said looking out.

"Well, I think it's time we went and tried to talk Tish's mum and dad into letting her sing next week."

"Yes, let's do that, then I'm going to ask Don if I can take you to the Stellar auditorium." Carina Looked at him,

"Stellar auditorium, what's that?" she asked

"If you think looking out here is cool, wait till you see that." He was grinning, they had only been dating for three months but she already knew that grin. It meant just you wait and see as I blow your mind.

They walked over to Tish's mum and dad who were talking to Dechow and Don.

"Err, could we talk to you please about Tish?" Her mum smiled.

"Yes, I thought you might. Your dad and the captain here have been very enlightening and before I say anything else can I say well done on the awards and thank you for everything you have done for Tish."

Datch was getting the feeling that she now knew a lot more than he thought. She continued.

"I take it you have come to ask if she can sing next week?" Datch was a little surprised but Datch being Datch wasn't fazed by it.

"Err, yes mam. If it would be alright that is?" he said trying to sound as grown up as possible.

"Well, she can come on one condition."

Condition he thought.

"Ok?" he said slightly worried.

"We want some tickets to see her perform." Datch let out a sigh as did Carina.

"I'm sure we can sort that. I'll talk to Jim when I get back to the planet. Dad can we call in on the way home." Dechow thought about this and figured that it was a good excuse for a beer and so said yes.

"Thank you, mam, I'm sure you will have a great time." Datch added.

"Maybe we should invite all the others as well?" Carina said.

"That sounds like a good plan, let's go and ask."

With that they headed off to see the other parents.

Half an hour later they were sitting with the rest of team Datch staring out the window. The ship was now in the night side of the planet and they had got a new game called spot the city and name it. Fizz was being the quiz master and was having a great time. It was far better than working in stellar cartography. Datch had asked Don about taking Carina to the Stellar auditorium but he said they didn't have time as they would soon have to head back to the planet. They played the game a bit longer and then dawn happened on the planet below. The star's light bursting through the atmosphere sending rainbows racing across the sky. The sight was stunning as the light hit cloud tops and mountains. Then the sun's light drained down into the hills and valleys bringing the morning to the people below. Datch and The Pack watched in awe as day dawned.

Don tapped a glass.

"Ladies and Gentlemen, I would like this to last longer but I'm afraid it's time to head back to the planet so if you would like to finish off your drinks the shuttle will be ready for departure in about 30 minutes so no need to rush as you have plenty of time, I hope you have enjoyed this little visit, I'm pretty sure team Datch has."

Team Datch were sitting with big grins on their faces.

"Thank you all for coming and no doubt our paths will cross again."

With that Datch and Carina went back to watching some more of the planet go by while drinking a glass of Gruck.

The reception came to an end and they headed back to the shuttle. This time Don stayed with the Carpaycus and watched them aboard the shuttle. The doors shut and it took off out of the bay. Just then an officer came walking up, he stopped and saluted.

"Err sir, I think I have found the anomaly you were looking for, but it's very faint and I can't get an exact fix on it, it is definitely some sort of scattering field."

"Thank you, lieutenant, where is it?"

"Somewhere in the south side of the city in an industrial area, best I can get is an area around one kilometre, sorry that's all sir."

"That's ok, well done, just keep scanning that area and see if you find anything else."

"Yes, sir." With that the lieutenant saluted and headed back up the corridor the way he had come.

Don watched out of the observation window as the shuttle headed back down to the planet, 'I wonder what you're hiding down there.' He thought to himself and then headed back to the command deck.

The shuttle started to hit the upper atmosphere and the plasma trails could been seen streaking across the shields.

"I love this bit." said Datch to Carina, "It gets very intense in a minute."

The plasma started to spread right across the shields making it look like they were passing through a wall of multi coloured fire. Then the shuttle started to shake a little and the pilot reduced thrust. Almost instantly the plasma started to fade and soon they were passing through high cloud. Below they could see the city spread out like a huge disc around the spaceport. The shuttle banked way from the centre and dropped down onto the campus where it had left from a few hours earlier and landed softly. The crew opened the door and helped everyone off. After a number of goodbyes and see you next week the various parents took their respective offspring home. Hagger was left standing on his own looking a bit down.

"Do you want a lift home so you can see your dad?" Dechow asked.

"Yes, but my dad won't be back till this evening and then he will be in, eat and then out again off to the Casino."

"Tell you what, why don't you come with us to the Barbers for a drink and then we can take you home after, that way you won't be on your own for so long."

"Oh, that would be cool, Thanks Mr Thom… sorry Dechow." he was smiling again.

He came over and got on the back of Datch's bike, his dad got on his bike along with his mum. They headed off to the Barbers Inn.

It was mid-afternoon, the bar was still busy with tourists and had a very chilled out atmosphere.

They walked in and Jim was at the bar putting up a new display under the optics, he turned when he heard the door go.

"Hi, Datch what are you doing in here at this time?"

"Well, we wanted a drink and also I need a favour." He said walking over to the bar with the others in tow.

Datch explained about the following week and Jim agreed to sort out a table for the parents. After which they headed over to a table and sat down with their drinks. Soon after Jep walked in and came over to sit with them.

"I Thought you would still be on the ship?"

"No," Dechow said, "We had to come back as Don only had a few hours spare."

"Did you have a good time?"

"Yes, it was great thanks." said Hagger, Datch nodded in agreement.

"So, are we all set for next week?"

"Yes, and we have guests." said Datch

"We do?"

"Err yes, all the parents are coming to watch."

"They are?"

"Yes, it was mine and Carina's idea after Tish's parents wanted to come to see her."

"Can I ask one thing then, please don't put me near Tank, I had to shower twice after that woman's undergarments hit me."

"OK, go at the end next to Peebop, Then Fred will get them, he keeps saying it is only a sign of affection."

Datch, Hagger and Jep all laughed.

"Err, was that a private joke?" asked Tansya.

"Well, sort of. Fred keeps telling Tank that the woman who throws her underwear at him, likes him, but he won't say anything to her and Fred pulls his leg about it." said Datch.

"So, what are you going to do with your holiday?" asked Jep changing the subject in a hurry.

"Well, I'm going over to Carina's for a couple of days and she is coming over to mine for a weekend, mum and dad are letting me take my bike out on my own now as long as I behave and let them know where I am. Also, we have the gigs of course."

"Hagger, what about you?" Hagger looked a bit down.

"Err, other than the gigs, not a lot. My dad will be out all the time. He used to do things with me but then last year he started spending all his time at work or the casino."

Hagger sounded very lonely.

"I'll come to see you and we can do stuff if you like?" said Datch.

"That would be cool." He smiled.

They carried on chatting for a bit and then Jim came out from the room at the back of the bar and walked over to them.

"Sorry too interrupt but, I have had some more posters printed what do you think?" He opened up a poster.

Datch looked at it. It had a picture of The Pack on stage and they were surrounded by smoke and light with 'The Barbers Inn Presents' across the top and then across the bottom 'The Pack' in big green letters. Datch thought it looked really cool as did Hagger and even Jep was very impressed.

"Hey you got my good side and nice effects." Jep said.

"Err what effects? That was a photo from last night."

"Oh wow, I'll have to try to get and watch myself then."

The term 'watch myself' happened when a band fell through a temporal distortion at the end of one of their gigs and ended up falling out at the beginning of their second set and were able to watch it from the balcony.

"Can I have one?" asked Datch.

"Yes, sure I have forty of them." He gave him one.

"I want to send it to Talia."

"That would be nice Datch, she'll like it." said Tansya.

"Who is Talia?" asked Jim.

"She's a friend in Traxsent and she's part of a band called The Snowmen."

Datch, Tansya and Dechow went on to explain about the trip to Traxsent and the Dancing Jaxx. Jim had heard the Bikers talk about it but hadn't really been listening. Now he was all ears. After another round of drinks, it was finally time to go home. Jep went over and sat at the bar to wait for the bikers. Dechow and Tansya headed back to the ranch and Datch gave Hagger a lift home before heading off home himself.

The Sleep over

The following week, Datch had been invited over to Carina's farm to stay. He was getting a bag ready for the trip when his mum walked in.

"Datch, make sure you have at least three spare changes of clothes and all the stuff you need for your gig. Have you packed your toiletries?"

"Yes mum, I've been packing my stuff to go to school and this is easier, I know what I need, oh, can I have some ice-cream before I go?"

"Ok, but make sure you have everything. It's for Carina remember, you need to look good, behave and mind your manners with her parents."

"I will mum, I promise."

With that he went back to packing his bag. His mum and dad were both in the kitchen when he came down. He had the feeling he was going to be told to behave yet again. He was right. They went through a list of dos and don'ts but he was only half listening as he had now heard it about ten times and could tell his mum and dad it all word for word. After the lecture he had his ice-cream and sat with his dad on the veranda. His dad decided to talk to him about girls. Not that he needed a chat about girls as Fred was a walking encyclopaedia when it came to the opposite sex. But it was nice his dad was showing an interest. Meanwhile his mum went upstairs to make sure he had remembered everything.

She walked into his room and checked in the on-suite. Toothbrush, body wash, deodorant and fluffy towel were all missing. Then she turned back to the bedroom. She looked around and there on the bed sitting on the pillow was Snugs. Snugs was the little fluffy toy which had gone everywhere with him and now it was left on his bed.

"Datch," she shouted down the stairs," What about Snugs?"

He didn't really think about it but he didn't need it anymore. It was sad but he had Carina now and she was always in his mind.

"No, it's OK mum Snugs can stay here this time." He shouted back up

She stopped and gave the little toy a pat on the head and a little tear came to her eye. She wiped it away before heading down the stairs and out to the veranda.

"Well, it's nearly time for you to go, you don't want to be late."

"Yes, I know."

He stood up and gave his mum a big hug and then gave his dad one as well for good measure. With that he went in and picked up his bag before heading outside to put it on his bike.

"I'll see you at the gig, I've got a duet I want to try with Carina and I'm going to play my guitar."

His mum suddenly realised that he had already put it on his bike.

"Oh, are you sure your good enough now?" she said hoping that he wouldn't make a fool of himself.

"Yes, and I've asked Carina's mum and dad for an honest opinion, so as not to embarrass Carina."

"That sounds like a very good idea. Do we know the song?"

"It's the one I did with Talia; 'Star Lovers' except this time, I'm really playing the guitar."

"Well, that will work, just try not to get to carried away will you." Tansya had seen the vid of the song and it was a little bit raunchy to say the least.

"Ok, I'll see you in three days." He said getting on the bike like he had been riding it for years.

"Call us when you get there so we know you're ok."

"I will mum."

With that he started the bikes systems and then with a wave he fired up the thrusters and then headed off skywards.

The trip was uneventful. He skirted around the city to avoid the traffic. It was early afternoon and with the sun beating down it was too hot to rush. So, for once he followed his mum's advice and took his time. It was about an hour later when he spotted Carina's farm in the distance. As he approached, he could see Carina waiting outside for him. He banked around and came in for a very soft landing on the drive at the front of the house where she was standing. He stopped the bike and got off.

Carina came running over to him and put her arms around him. There was a big kiss and a hug. Finally, after they were forced up for air Datch was taken over to the house where her mum was waiting for him.

"Hello, it's nice to see you again Datch, did you have a good trip?"

"Yes mam, it was very relaxing thank you."

"Just call me Pabi and my husband's name is Jata."

"Ok mam, I mean Pabi."

"Carina, show Datch to his room please, then you can show him around."

With that Carina took Datch upstairs. The house was quite
old and the stairs creaked as Datch went up them. The house
was a bit more compact than his and it had a small hallway
with a narrow stair case leading up to the bedrooms. Carina
led the way to a room at the end of the landing. It had an on-
suite bathroom and a nice size bed. Datch put his bag down
and then they headed back along the landing. Carina opened
another door.

"This is my room." she said.

Datch looked inside. The room was covered in pastel
shades and she had her own vid on the wall so she could
watch it in bed. The window looked out across the fields
towards some woods in the distance. It was a lot tidier than
his room that was for sure. His bedroom looked like an
explosion in a clothes factory most of the time.

"I like your room it's really cool" he said, he hadn't thought
about the colour of his room but now he liked the idea of
pastels himself and made a mental note to talk to his dad.

They headed back down the stairs and Carina then took
him around the ground floor. He had seen the kitchen when
he came to pick Carina up for the team building, so they
skipped that and went straight to the lounge. The room was
quite large but at the same time cosy. It also had a lot of floral
patterns and pastel colours including the chairs and sofas. At
the far end was a real open fire but it didn't look like it had
ever been lit. They headed through to the dining room and
this was also very floral. Thinking about it Datch realised that
the whole house was similar colours throughout. The dining
room had a large sliding door which opened into the garden.
Outside was a large slabbed area with a barbeque in one
corner and some sun chairs to sit on.

After looking around the house they went outside to the
barn. Carina's dad was in there sorting out an agricultural bot
that had not been working correctly.

"Hi dad, Datch is here." Carina shouted across the barn. he stopped grinding a bit of metal and looked up.

"Hello Datch, welcome to the farm."

"Thank you, sir,"

"You don't need to call me sir, its Jata. You don't happen to know anything about bot's, do you?"

"Err, I know how to operate them but that's about all Jata, sorry."

"Don't be sorry, this dam thing keeps bending its front rota and I don't know why."

"My dad has shown me how to run diagnostics if that helps." said Datch trying to be helpful, Jata thought about this,

"Maybe you could just try it on this thing."

"Dad, he's our guest." Carina said trying to pull Datch away before he got to dragged into bot repairs.

"It's ok, it will only take a minute." Datch said trying to make a good impression.

He walked over to the bot and pressed a couple of buttons, the panel lit up and he put his hand up and thought 'Diagnostic tests'. The bot started to cycle through its system,

Power systems ok.
Motor systems ok.
Drive systems ok.
Sensor systems ok.
Control systems ok.

Datch looked at the bot. The righthand rota was not currently fitted as Jata had it in his hand. He lifted his hand again thought 'Sensor Diagnostic Tests' the bot started to run a sensor diagnostic. It slowly went through each sensor pack in turn. It got to the righthand rota and carried on saying everything was alright. Datch lifted his hand again and thought 'Righthand rota sensor Diagnostic tests'. The bot responded with sensors ok.

"I think I know what the problem is." Jata looked at him.

"What?"

"The sensor pack on the righthand rota is not working correctly, it should have come up with an error when I tested it. You're holding the rota in your hand so it should have said it was missing but it thinks it's still fitted."

"Let me have a look." Jata said moving over and pressing the buttons himself, after a minute he turned back to Datch.

"I see what you mean, no wonder it's been chewing up the rota arms. You can come again."

He went off to see if he could find a spare one and Datch and Carina went out to look across the fields.

They walked up a small track to the brow of a hill and stopped, sitting on a wooden fence.

"You see across to the woods and then from there to there." She said pointing to a hill and then across to another hill on the opposite side. "That's all our farm, you see down the bottom there where the stream runs along, I have a special place to show you. It will have to be tomorrow but I have my chores to do first."

"I'll help you." said Datch trying to sound as helpful as possible.

It was agreed and they had a slow walk back to the farm arm in arm.

The next morning Datch lay in bed and waited until he heard movement downstairs. He got up, had a shower and got dressed. He went down to the kitchen to see if there was anything to eat. Carina's mum was there making some breakfast.

"Hi Datch, what do you like for breakfast?" she asked.

He was about to say Ice-cream but then changed his mind.

"Err, what have you got?" he asked.

"Well, I'm doing a fry up for Jata. So, we have some Jeader slices, some Jeader sausages, fresh Hiphip eggs from our own Hiphips, some fried Dorts, mushrooms and Fried bread." Datch thought about it and decided to go for the lot.

"That sounds really nice."

"Do you want two of everything?"

"Err, no, one of each will be nice thanks, I think two might be a bit much for me."

"So, do you know what Carina has planned for you today?"

"I'm going to help her with her chores then we are going to her special place she said."

"Ah yes, down by the stream, I sometimes go there myself. It is really nice and relaxing. Make sure you take something to sit on."

She put a plate in front of him. He looked at the pile of food in front of him and was glad he only asked for one of everything. He tucked in and was just eating his sausage when Jata came in with a grin on his face.

"It works!" he said walking up and patting Datch on the back which almost caused a bit of breakfast to fly across the table.

"Err what does?" said Pabi.

"The bot, Datch you were right it was the sensor unit. Its working great this morning. You'll have to show me how to do the diagnostic thing."

"I'll write it down for you." said Datch after swallowing his mouth full of food.

"That would be great thanks."

He sat down and a huge plate of food appeared in front of him. Datch carried on eating his and was just washing it all down with a glass of juice when Carina came walking in.

"Morning Datch, hi mum, hi dad." she sat down.

Pabi put a plate of food in front of her which was the same size as Datch's but without the mushrooms.

"Did you sleep ok?" she asked Datch.

"Yes thanks, really well." He smiled at her.

She was a bit slow responding.

"Is everything ok?" he said. Pabi stepped in.

"Yes Datch, Carina just takes a little time to get going in the morning that's all."

"Mum!" she said.

"What, you do take a while."

There was an awkward pause before Carina carried on eating. Datch watched as the sleepy Carina turned into normal Carina during the course of breakfast. When she had finished, she got up and turned to Datch.

"Let's go." she said.

It wasn't so much a request but more of an order. Datch automatically got up and followed her outside. They got to the barn and Carina grabbed him. Datch wasn't sure what was happening and then he was pulled in close and given a very big kiss.

"Err, Sorry about in there, I just need a bit of time first thing. I should have warned you."

"That's ok." he said still trying to get his breath back.

"Let's get these jobs done so we can go out."

"OK, what do we have to do?"

"Well, we have to get the Hiphip eggs, Feed the Jeaders and then check the silo's temperatures and humidity levels, it should only take an hour if we get a move on."

With that they headed off to the Hiphip's. Datch had never had to do farm things before. Yes, technically the Ranch was a farm but his dad looked after things. Anyway, it was run more like a hobby than anything else. He had been to Jed's farm over the hill to play sometimes but Jed did tend to come to the ranch most of the time. He never did find out what farmers did, that was until now.

Datch followed Carina into the Hiphip run. It was a small field with a net around the sides and over the top to stop them flying away. Along the sides were a number of nesting boxes that stood on legs at about chest height, they were just right to reach in and take the eggs. Carina had a basket with her and as they collected the eggs, she carefully stacked them inside it. Datch counted as they went around. They had sixty-five eggs by the time they had finished.

"That's a lot of eggs, what happens to them now?" He asked.

"Well, most of them go to the up-market restaurants in the city. They pay a good price to be able to say they use farm fresh eggs. They say they taste better than the artificial or factory farm one's."

Datch had to say that the one at breakfast did taste better.

They took them over to a shed at the entrance where they had come in. Carina put sixty of them into little boxes four at a time and the remaining five she left in the basket for them to pick up on the way back.

They moved on to the Jeaders. They were quite large animals with large tusks and they grunted a lot. They had their own field with a number of troughs dotted about. Each trough had a pipe which ran back to a large hopper next to a raised platform. Datch and Carina climbed up the steps at the back of it.

"Why is this bit up in the air?" he asked.

"Let's just say the Jeaders can be a bit nasty especially when it comes to food."

Datch looked at them. They did have rather nasty looking tusks.

"So how do we feed them?"

"Their food is in that hopper and when I press the feed button on the panel the food goes along the tubes to the troughs, watch."

She went over and pressed a button on the panel and the machinery made a chugging noise. Then there was the sound of something going through the pipes before the food poured out into the troughs. The bores went running over to them pushing each other out of the way as they went. The food was a mix of feed pellets, food scraps, various vegetables and also some supplementary vitamins.

Carina explained that the food waste came from the local village and the farm. The vegetables were the ones that would not be good enough to sell. The bots would dig them out and bring them to the silos where the contents were held in stasis until it is used.

Datch never realised things were so complicated. He was use to asking the kitchen for food and it appearing. Yes, he knew fruit grew on trees and the meat came from animals. But he just thought they just did their own thing until they were ready for eating.

"Ok, we just need to check the silo temperatures." she said.

They headed off down past another barn and to a row of six silos. Each had its own control panel which showed the status of the silo.

"This one's ok." she said looking at the panel.

They went along the row and checked each one in turn. A couple of them needed a slight adjustment but it didn't take long before they got to the end of the row. Carina turned to Datch.

"That's it, we just have to take the eggs back to mum and then we can do our own thing."

"Cool." said Datch.

They headed back to the house via the Hiphip's to pick up the basket. When they got back Carina told her mum how many eggs they had and gave her the five that she had kept. She then explained that she had to alter silo three and five again. Her mum said she would get her dad to have a look at them. With that all done Carina ran upstairs to grab a bag she had packed earlier. While she had gone Pabi picked up another basket.

"Here you are," she said handing it to Datch, "Just a few snacks and drinks to keep you going till dinner time."

"Oh, thanks." he said and looked inside. It looked like a full picnic.

Carina came down stairs with a large rucksack over her shoulder.

"Are we ready?" she said looking at Datch.

"Yes." he said and with that they went outside.

Carina put her hand in his and they left the farm buildings and headed down a track that ran down the side of the field.

The sun was hot as they walked along the track. It went over a rise and then downhill towards some woods at the bottom. It was nice being just the two of them and they walked along chatting about just about anything. At school there was always someone else around and even at Datch's team building they had only grabbed a few moments to themselves. They were now alone. They followed the path to the bottom of the hill where it ran over a bridge. Underneath was a small brook bubbling along. They crossed and followed the path into the wood. Carina led the way and after a couple of minutes branched off through a little narrow path between the trees.

The path soon opened out into a clearing where the brook flowed through. The ground was higher on one side and the brook had formed a large pool with a waterfall which was about two metres deep and around five metres across. The sun shone through an opening on to a green grassy area. Carina led Datch over to it and put the bag down along with the basket. She opened the bag and laid out a big blanket on the grass. They sat down and Carina got a couple of drinks out of the basket and gave one to Datch. They lay on the blanket enjoying each other's company. Datch was feeling a little nervous and trying to remember what Fred had said. That was it 'Just let things happen'. So, he put his arm around her and gave her a kiss. They carried on kissing for a bit and Carina ran her hand up and down his back. Datch's hairs stood up on the back of his neck and it made his head fizz. This was strange but really nice. He went to kiss her again but she pushed him away playfully and stood up.

"I'm hot, if you want me, you'll have to chase me." she said laughing.

She took her dress off and only had her pants on underneath. Datch got a full view of her body before she ran over and jumped in the pool.

"Come on then!" she laughed,

"Err, I don't have a swim suit?" he said trying to work out what was going on.

"And why would you need that?" she said grinning. Finally, Datch got the hint and stripped off and ran into the pool after her.

After a lot of splashing about they ended up cuddling each other. Datch's head was a torrent of feelings which where fizzing and popping inside his brain. This is amazing he thought. He felt so good. They got out and Carina led Datch back to the blanket. They were both acting on instinct now and started to get to know each other intimately.

Two hours later they lay there on the blanket talking about what had just happened and after a little while they got up and went back in the pool to cool down and freshen up. Afterwards they sat there eating the contents of the basket in their underwear. It was strange. Something had just changed. Before they were just boyfriend and girlfriend now their relationship had move up to a new level and it felt so good. They spent most of the afternoon there before heading back to the farm with a big spring in their steps.

They walked into the kitchen, Pabi was just starting to cook dinner, Carina's dad was still out on the farm somewhere.

"Do we have time to practice the song we were on about?" asked Carina.

"Yes, I would think so, dinner will be about half an hour."

Datch went up the stairs and got his guitar and then the pair of them went out into the garden to practice. They had gone through the song six or seven times when Carina's mum came out to get them for dinner. It was what Datch's mum would call a good wholesome meal. Meat, vegetables and Kella, all followed by a piece of homemade cake. Datch liked it so much that he had a second helping. Then after it had gone down it was time for the song. Datch pointed out that they would have backing singers at the gig and put the music on. They started to sing.

After they had finished both Carina's mum and dad said it sounded very good and it was ok to perform it on the stage. With that they sat watching the vid for a while before heading to bed. The next day was going to be a long one as they had the gig in the evening and then Datch was taking Carina home with him for a couple of days.

The next morning, they had breakfast and afterwards Datch helped Carina with her chores before they headed off on the bike to the local village to get some bits for her mum. They stopped at a café to have a drink.

"What do you think the other parents will think?" Carina asked taking a drink.

"I hope they like it, your mum and dad did so that's a start. It's Tish's mum and dad I'm worried about."

"I think they will be ok when they see her having fun, they are just looking out for her that's all." Said Carina trying to reassure him.

"Hmm, I hope so or we're going to be one down next week."

"It will be fine, I'm sure."

They finished their drinks and got back on the bike ready to head back to the farm. They were just about to set off when a shuttle flew in low over the village. It was jet black and had none of the normal markings showing. It also had some very large engines on the back.

"That's strange, we don't normally get shuttles flying over here." said Carina.

"That's not all, why is it flying around the hill instead of over it when there is nothing else about?"

They watched as it flew along the valley past the wood and out of sight heading in the direction of the city.

Datch started up the bike and they took off flying straight over the hill and back to the farm. There was no reason that Datch could see that would affect the shuttles path.

They arrived back at the farm and Carina's mum had made them some Jeader rolls before going off somewhere. They took them outside and sat in the garden eating them.

"Does your mum just make the food and clean?" Datch asked.

"No, she doesn't clean, we have bots for that. She does the accounts for the farm and any ordering of animal feed and also handles all the sales orders. My dad handles the bots, planting, harvesting and the animals."

"Oh wow, it sounds a lot harder than I thought."

"It might look easy but its hard work. There is a lot of work behind the scenes that people don't see."

They finished their rolls and Carina took Datch up to her room. They lay on her bed watching the vid and having an occasional cuddle or two. The afternoon soon went by and it didn't seem long before Carina's mum was calling them for dinner. They had asked for a light meal because of the gig. They had learnt the hard way that it was not a good idea to go on stage with a full stomach. It tended to make you feel ill after a while. She had done them a salad with Jeader slices and some more rolls.

"You sure that is going to be enough?" she asked.

"Yes, we don't want to much or we'll feel sick." replied Carina.

They finished the food before Carina and Datch headed off to get their bits together. Pabi turned to Jata.

"Is it just me or does Carina a lot happier than normal?"

"I can't say I've noticed." He said and went back to watching the vid.

The news was on and he liked to keep up to date. There was an article about how there was no longer anyone homeless in Yuland city. The chief overseer was saying it was due to his polices but when questioned he didn't know where they had all gone.

Datch and Carina came back down stairs with their bags. Datch picked up his guitar and went outside to put everything on the bike. They were heading off earlier than Carina's mum and dad so they could drop their bags off at the ranch and still be at the Barbers Inn an hour before the gig. That way they wouldn't get mobbed by the crowds.

Datch said thank you to Carina's parents for having him and they got on the bike and headed off towards the city.

In the city Fred got on his bike and headed around to one of his friends. His friend had a small blue shuttle he hired out for joining's, parties or special functions. Fred had arranged to borrow it to pick up the rest of The Pack and their parents. He had even put on a smart shirt to look the part. He got into the cockpit and programmed in the addresses and pressed the start button. The shuttle headed off in the direction of Hagger's. He was first and was on his own as his dad was busy again. They all felt sorry for him and Datch was trying to be the best friend possible to him as were all of them. The shuttle arrived at Hagger's and he was waiting outside. Fred opened the door and he jumped in. He was looking a little worried.

"What's up dude?"

"My dad is drunk and can't find something, he sometimes lashes out when he's like that, can we go."

Fred shut the door and instructed the shuttle to head to Rosey's house next,

"Will he still be mad when you get back?"

"No, he'll go to the casino and it will be the early hours before he gets in, he'll just crawl into his bed and sleep."

"You sure you're ok dude?"

"Yes, I'll be ok." He sat in one of the seats and sighed.

Fred checked the shuttle was on course and changed the subject.

They picked up Rosey and her parents and then went and picked the rest of them up. By the time they got to the Barbers Inn, Datch's bike was already outside the back door along with his dad's and the rest of the bikers. Fred parked the shuttle outside the front of the bar and opened the door. Rosey led the way into the bar. Another large table had been placed next to the stage with a barrier around it and a sign saying 'Reserved for VIP's'. Tansya and Dechow were sitting at it having a drink. Fred asked what everyone wanted to drink and went over to the bar. The parents all went over and sat down while The Pack went around the screens. Jim brought the drinks over and told the parents to press the button in the centre of the table if they wanted anything.

Back stage, Datch sat with Carina and the bikers chilling. They already had their T-shirts on. The others went behind a little screen and changed themselves. When everyone was back Datch stood up.

"Hi folks, Tonight is going to be the best night ever. So, let's have some fun. Now there is a small change to the normal set. The song 'Star Lovers', we have been practicing it and I'm going to be doing it with a guitar."

"Are you crazy?" asked Tish.

"No," Said Carina, "Me and Datch performed it last night in front of my mum and dad, they thought it was great." said Carina with a grin.

The Pack looked at each other.

"Look, it will be fine trust me. Have I ever let you down?" said Datch.

They all shrugged.

"Ok, if everyone is happy, we'll do it at the end of the first set?"

There was a general consensus of ok we'll give it a go.

Rosey kept looking over at Carina who seemed to be a bit more attached to Datch than normal, she finally gave up and went over.

"Err, are you two, ok?" she asked.

"Yes, we're both great thanks." Datch nodded in agreement.

Rosey gave them a sideways look with a slightly puzzled frown. The conversation got back to what people had been doing and there was a round of catch up before Jim put his head around the screens.

"Hi folks, it's a full house again, are you about ready?"

"Yes, we're good and you need to plug this in to the PA." he looked at the small box, it had a flashing light on it.

"Oh, you have a guitar. Cool." He went back around to the stage plugging the box in as he went past.

The house lights dimmed and a spot light focused on Jim.

"Ladies, gentlemen and VIP's, are you ready to party?" there was a loud cheer.

"I can't hear you, are you ready to PARTY?" there was a really loud cheer.

"Bring on 'The Pack'." he shouted. The crowd roared.

The lights flashed and a beat started thumping out. The Pack came running on stage and took up their positions and went straight into the first song.

The place vibrated to song after song. The dance floor was packed and then it came to the last song in the set. Datch went off one side of the stage and Carina the other. The music started with a beat and then Carina was lit up by a spot light and started to sing. Datch came on stage with the guitar and started to play. The crowd went nuts. The song bounced between Datch and Carina and then The Pack joined in. Datch and Carina got closer and closer on stage battling out until the song reached a peak. The guitar squealed and they kissed. The crowd were now having to be kept in check by the bouncers. The song finished with Datch and Carine singing together in perfect harmony. The crowd roared.

"We'll be back shortly folks." Datch shouted as The Pack left the stage.

They sat around the table at the back with cold drinks and cold towels.

"Well, that worked." said Tank who had steam coming off of him. Everyone else nodded. Rosey came over and sat next to Carina.

"Ok, now I know something has happened, you two were electric out there, so?" Carina looked at her.

"Me and Datch have just had a couple of days together and have got a bit closer and that's all I'm saying." she looked at Datch and smiled.

"Me too." he added and quickly went back to his drink before anyone could say anything.

You could see the frustration on Rosey's face. She wasn't going to give up and turned to look at Tish who had been listening to the conversation. she just shrugged her shoulders.

"Well, something has happened, you both were very shall I say explicit. In fact, you couldn't have been anymore so if you had tried."

"It was fine." said Fred wading in to save the day," and if they don't want to talk about it, they don't have to." He winked at Datch.

Datch smiled back.

Rosey finally went quiet and gave up. The subject was changed to other things. The break was soon over and they were back on stage. The rest of the gig went on as usual and this time Clax got hit by the underwear. Tank was now starting to wonder if she had any left or just went out each week to buy more. The second set finished and the crowd started screaming 'encore, encore' Datch had a quick word with the rest and then the music started again. This time it was another duet but it was boy's verses girls with the bikers doing the backing for both. At the end of the song the boys took the girls arm in arm and kissed. Well, Rosey, Tish, Dapo and Hagger did a sort of peck in the cheek. Datch and Carina did a full-on kiss. The crowd went nuts, screaming, cheering and applauding. The Pack left the stage. It took about ten minutes for the crowd to calm down, Jim stuck his head around the corner.

"Err, I have some of your, err groupies at the side of the stage asking for autographs, err any chance of signing a few?"

"Yes, I don't see why not." said Fred looking around at the others. They all nodded.

"Ok follow me I've got all the bouncers down this end so you won't get rushed."

Hagger turned to Tish, "Err… Autographs?"

"Yes, we just sign our names on bits of paper, just do what we do and you'll be fine."

He looked a little nervous so Rosey put her arm around him. He looked happier but had now gone pink again. Dapo thought that was a good idea and put his arm around Tish. She started to resist and then changed her mind going along with it. Tank looked at the other bikers hopefully thinking that if the woman saw him with another man, she would stop throwing things at him. The others shook their heads. They headed out to the side of the stage. The bouncers formed a line to hold people back as Jim got a number of tables and made somewhere for them to sit.

They sat down and Jim gave them a pen each. He then gave the fans some of the posters that he had got printed for advertising and then had them file past the Pack so they could sign them.

After the first couple went by, they got the hang of it. Most of the people said how wonderful they were, a number tried to give their favourite member a kiss and some even managed it. One young woman gave Hagger a big kiss and yes, he went red but then seemed to have a very big grin stuck on his face. The woman who threw her underwear at Tank came along and Tank was sort of trapped and tried to hide under the table. When she got to him. She stooped and whispered in his ear. Tank went red much to the entertainment of the others. She winked at him and blew him a kiss then moved on down the row. It took about twenty minutes before Jim ran out of posters and had to close the signing. It was a good job too, Datch thought his hand was about to fall off.

"Wow, that was a lot." said Rosey now forgetting all about Datch and Carina.

"Yes, I can't believe all those people think we're great" said Hagger still grinning from ear to ear.

"That was extreme." said Carina, "and the number of people who said we make a great couple and asked if it was real? We kept having to tell them yes and kiss to shut them up." Datch was just nodding.

"Yes, we noticed." said Clax just as the bouncers opened the screens and joined the tables together.

The bar was starting to empty a bit now and they were able to sit with their parents.

Datch stood up and raised a glass.

"I would like to say thanks to everyone tonight. It's been a fantastic night."

He raised his glass and everyone followed suit.

"So, what did everyone think to the show?" he said sitting down again.

There was a lot of 'it was great' or 'It was not what I was expecting but fantastic anyway' even Tish's parents had really enjoyed it.

"How long have you been doing it?" Rosey's mum asked.

"Well, it started about ten weeks ago with a really crazy Karaoke night that sort of snowballed, Jim asked us to sing the next week." Rosey said.

"Yes, and then we loved it and were getting paid to have fun." Added Carina.

"Then more and more people came and the last four weeks have been like tonight." continued Rosey.

"It is just one night a week?" asked Tish's dad.

"Yes, only one night and it's always the last night before they come home from school." said Fred quickly before anyone could suggest anymore.

Then the conversation switched back to the nights gig and some of the highlights.

Datch got up and went off to the toilet. Fred took the opportunity and followed him.

"I need to ask, you and Carina, you are being careful, aren't you?"

Datch thought about it.

"Does it stand out that much?" he asked starting to feel they had a big sign above their heads.

"Err, yes, just a bit and after that song with Carina well you might as well put a sign around your necks."

"Oh, well, yes we are fine, she has her inhibiter turned on." He said smiling.

"You're not going to tell me anything else, are you?"

"No." Datch did his shorts back up and wandered back out into the bar grinning.

Carina turned to him as he sat down. He whispered what had just happened and Carina smiled and laughed.

Jim came over and gave them their credits.

"Wow, this is two hundred."

"Yes, I think I need a bigger bar." he said looking around.

"You have a builder friend who does remodelling don't you Peebop?"

"Yes, do you want his id?"

"Yes please, I've had an idea and wondered if he could help."

Peebop gave him the vid com id and Jim went off heading in the direction of the office.

Jep got up and said 'good night.' He had to be up early as he was off to visit his sister in the morning.

They had another round of drinks and then Fred said he would take everyone home. With that everyone said good night and got in the shuttle outside. Datch and Carina watched as the shuttle headed off and then climbed on Datch's bike and his mum and dad got on his dads. They took off and headed across the city. Datch looked at the display and there was a black bit on it for a few seconds, then it was gone. Thirty minutes later they arrived back at the ranch and headed straight off to bed; it was one thirty in the morning after all.

The next morning Datch got up and headed down to find some food. He got himself some waffles and syrup and then had a thought.

"Kitchen please can I have some pancakes with Tarli sauce and a glass of Renar Berry juice please."

The kitchen delivered the food and drink. He got a tray out of the cupboard and put everything on it. He then headed up the stairs at the side of the bar to where Carina's room was.

Datch knocked on the door and waited. There was a sleepy 'Come in' from the other side of the door. He opened it and walked in. Carina was lying in bed with just a thin sheet laying on top of her.

"Breakfast in bed for my beautiful girlfriend." he said walking over and sitting on the side of the bed.

"Wow, for me, thank you."

She sat up and the sheet dropped off. She gave Datch a big hug. It turned out she wasn't wearing anything at least on the top half. Datch swallowed and suddenly felt a bit warm. He gave her a kiss and handed her the pancakes.

"This is really nice and you remembered what I like."

"I thought you would like it." he said smiling and trying not to look down.

Carina suddenly realised that he was feeling a little uncomfortable and pulled the sheet up to cover her chest, Datch relaxed.

They sat eating breakfast and chatting about the night before and about the fact everyone wanted to know what had happened. They couldn't believe it stood out that much. After a while Carina got out of bed and gave Datch another hug. He went all hot around the collar again. She pulled his shirt off and his shorts down before running into the shower laughing.

He took the rest of his clothes off and followed her in.

Afterwards they laid on the bed for a few minutes before getting dressed and heading down to the kitchen with the tray.

Tansya was already in the kitchen when they came in.

"Oh, I was just about to ask you what you wanted to eat?" she said noticing the tray.

"Datch brought me breakfast in bed." she said with a bit of a smile on her face.

"You are honoured, I don't think I've ever had that." Tansya said looking at Datch who went a slight pink colour.

"So, what are you two going to do today?" She asked.

"If its ok with you, I want to take Carina out for a ride on the bike and maybe a picnic?"

"Hmm, ok but make sure you're back for dinner, what do you want to take with you?"

They gave the kitchen a list of things they wanted and Tansya found a picnic basket to put it all in. Datch grabbed a blanket to sit on and took it all out to the bike. They climbed on and started it up. Datch entered the coordinates into the nav com before turning to wave goodbye to his mum and then they headed off skywards.

Just as they disappeared Dechow came walking in the kitchen.

"Morning" he said yawning.

"Morning" she said putting a coffee in front of him, he looked around.

"Err, no Datch?" he said a little puzzled.

"They have gone out on the bike for a picnic, oh and he gave her breakfast in bed." Dechow raised an eyebrow.

"He did?"

"Yes, and I'm not sure but I think they had a shower together."

"Err. They did?" Dechow was currently having trouble keeping up with the conversation.

"Yes." he finally caught up.

"Err, that's what Fred meant last night when he said they were getting on really well, the duet with the guitar… Oh." a light came on in this brain.

"Err, you don't think they had been busy do you?"

"I don't think so yet but I think it won't be long."

"I need to have a talk with Fred and find out just how much he knows. I'll head to the Barbers Inn after breakfast, he said he would meet up with Clax for lunch in there."

"Well don't go upsetting things, they seem to be a good match for each other, we just need to know that we won't be having any little Datches or mini-Carinas running around any time soon." Tansya instructed.

"Ok, I won't." with that he started to tuck into his breakfast.

Datch and Carina were high in the air heading out towards the desert and then the sand was flying by underneath them. Thirty minutes later a green ribbon could be seen ahead of them.

"Are we going to the river?" Carina asked.

"I thought it would be nice, just the two of us."

"Yes, it sounds good."

They flew down and landed in a parking spot near one of the parks. They got off and headed down to the river bank. Datch carried the blanket and Carina had the basket. They found a nice spot just up from the water and partly in the shade. They laid out the blanket and sat down. Datch got a couple of bottles of Gruck's out and opened them. They sat chatting in the sun shine and enjoying the view. It was great, they felt really relaxed and happy.

"What do you want to do when school is finished?" Carina asked.

"Hmm, I want to explore the universe, so I suppose join the fleet and save up enough credits to buy a small ship."

"That sounds cool, I wonder if they would put us together if I joined?"

"I don't know, I think they try to put couples together on the same ship even if they're not working together. What would you do?" he asked.

"I think I'd like to be one of the people who explore planets."

"I'd like that to." Datch added.

After a while they went for a bit of a paddle in the shallow area next to the bank. It was nice to cool their feet down. They didn't have a towel so they sat drying off in the sun while eating the picnic.

"I've been thinking about the whole bot thing with Peebop, Don said the spider could be hiding under something to stop sensors." said Datch.

"Yes, and?"

"Well last night on the way back my bikes sensors had a black spot on them for a moment, When I asked the bikes computer why there was a black spot, it said the sensors were unable to penetrate that area."

"That sounds odd, you had better let Don know, I'm sure it will help him out."

"When I take you back to your house, I want to fly over the same area and see if the spot's still there."

"Ok, but I don't think we should get too close."

"Yes, neither do I. Arachnoids can jump."

The rest of the afternoon was spent chilling next to the river. They sat watching the boats and wind ships going by. Oh, and a fair bit of cuddling was involved as well.

It was getting quite late before they headed back across the desert on the bike. Datch flew high and gave the bike a big kick of speed, He wasn't sure if Carina was holding on to him tightly because of the speed or if she just wanted to.

They got back just as Dechow starting the barbeque.

"Hi mum." said Datch walking through the door.

"Oh, hi you two, that was perfect timing, another five minutes and I was going to call you. Your dad's just about to start cooking so you have a few minutes to freshen up if you want."

"That would be great Tansya." said Carina. The pair of them headed up stairs and put on their swim suits. Two minutes later they were in the pool cooling down. They sat in the inflatable chairs watching Dechow cook the food.

"Food's ready." He shouted.

They got out and dried themselves off.

Dechow had put a rectangular table up on the patio area near the hot tub. It had a big umbrella over the top of it to keep the sun off and Tansya had set out four place setting each with a wine glass. There was a salad bowl and a bottle of non-alcoholic wine in a bucket with ice. Datch and Carina went to sit next to each other on one side of the table and had just got in their seats when Tansya came out carrying some fresh bread and placed it in the middle of the table. Then Dechow came over with the meat in a big glass dish.

"Dig in, I'll pour the wine."

Dechow picked up the bottle and filled up the glasses.

"So, what did you two get up to this afternoon?" said Tansya starting the conversation.

"We went over to the river." said Datch.

"Yes, it was really nice." added Carina.

"Oh, was it where we were last time?"

"No, it was in the park on the opposite side, we got a spot under one of the trees near the water just down from the Jaja grill." said Datch.

"I know where you mean, was it busy?"

"Yes, but still relaxing." Said Carina.

The conversation carried on a bit and then got on to the night before.

"Err, we couldn't help noticing you two seem a lot closer now?" said Dechow.

"Why does everyone keep asking that?" said Datch.

"Well after the guitar duet it sort of stood out. If you two had got any closer they would have had to turn the lights out."

"Oh, Yes, well we're getting on great thanks." Said Carina.

"I've got to ask this, but you are being careful, aren't you?" said Tansya.

"Yes, mum we are." said Datch gong a bit pink.

"Well, that's good."

"So, what's your plans for next week?" said Dechow quickly changing the subject.

"If its ok, can we do the same as this week?"

"I don't see why not, it's nice having you here Carina." said Tansya.

"Thank you, I like being here." Carina added.

"That's sorted then." said Dechow.

They finished eating and then moved to the veranda to watch the sun set over the desert. Dechow went into the bar and brought out two non-alcoholic cocktails for Datch and Carina and a Traxsent star burst for Tansya. He had a beer for himself. They carried on chatting well after the sun had gone down. It started to get late and Datch's mum and dad headed inside to give Datch and Carina a bit of space. They sat cuddling until well after midnight and finally Datch walked Carina back to her room and kissed her good night.

The next two days went by and then it was time for Carina to go home. She thanked Datch's mum and dad for having her and then they got on the bike for the ride home. Datch took the long way back flying over as much of the city as he could. Then over the east side the sensors showed a black area. It was about two kilometres from the school. Datch pointed it out to Carina. There was not much there. Just a few old warehouses, an old abandoned factory of some sort and an old water pumping station. They flew over it making sure they stayed quite high up. It all looked deserted with some of the roof missing from one of the warehouses. Nothing to see but the bikes sensors didn't like it one bit and the computer was flashing up warnings. Datch recorded it using his implant and they headed off for Carina's.

The next three weeks were pretty much the same. Datch would go to Carina's for a couple of days and then they'd go to the gig and then to Datch's. Datch would fly over the warehouses each time and each time the sensors would act up. He sent the images to Don. Carina was also spending more and more time at Datch's. Instead of two days it ended up being five days by the end of the holiday.

The Missing person

The next trimester started and The Pack was back at school. It was an easy start with a couple of recap lectures and a test. The first night back they headed down to the Barbers Inn as normal. The streets were as busy and it was starting to get hot in the city now that summer was starting to approach. This trimester lasted until the start of summer and then there was an eight-week break before the next one to allow for the heat. Temperatures could reach forty-five degrees at the peak of summer in the city. So, people tended to keep out of it or go on holiday to slightly cooler parts of the planet. Pretty much all normal city life in the peak of summer became nocturnal.

The Barbers Inn was its sleepy midweek self. Tank and Fred were propping up the bar talking to Jim when Datch wandered over with The Pack.

"Hi guys, how's it going?"

"It's going good dudes, how's school?"

"Good thanks." said Carina sticking her head on Datch's shoulder. He didn't even react to it.

"I think we'll need the big table tonight Jim." said Fred.

"Sure thing, I'll bring the drinks over?"

"Can I have some non-alcoholic wine please?" asked Carina.

The Packs heads all turned to look at her like she had just grown any extra arm or something.

"Wine? Really?" Tish asked.

"Yes, I've been drinking it with Datch's mum, it's quite nice." Jim butted in at this point.

"Err, we have red, white or Rosé? it's all normal wine but the processor removes the alcohol so pick which you like but not the expensive ones please, I want to sell them with alcohol."

"I'll have a sparkling Rosé please."

Datch had a thought.

"Err, can you do that with beer?" he asked.

"Yes, if you want."

"Err, Can I have one of what Fred's got without the alcohol please?"

"Ok, anyone else?"

Dapo went for Datch's idea, Rosey and Tish followed Carina while Hagger stuck with the Gruck's.

They sat at the table looking at their drinks. The beers had a proper head on them and the wine was in tall slim glasses with bubbles going up the sides of the glass. Datch picked up his beer.

"Here's to The Pack being back in town." he said lifting his glass.

Fred lifted his and tapped it against Datch's and Tank did the same followed by everyone else. They were all saying how nice the drinks were when Jep walked in and came over to the table.

"Oh, four weeks off and you're all on the beer!" He said looking at the drinks.

"There's no alcohol in them, so it's ok." said Dapo feeling a bit defensive.

"Well, ok then." He said turning to order a large brandy.

"So, what we going to do for an encore this trimester?" he said sitting down with his drink.

"Encore?" said Rosey.

"Well, Yes, let's see, you formed a band and got the platinum star then went into space and had dinner on a starship, so you've got to top it this trimester." he said laughing.

It suddenly dawned on them that he was joking. Datch looked at him 'hmm' he thought. One thing you should never do to Datch or Dechow is wave a red flag at them as things would happen.

"Err, Save the Planet?" Datch suggested with a straight face.

Jep looked at him and for no reason he could think of started to worry about the planet's welfare. Just then Peebop and Clax came wandering in.

"That's it then, the gang is all here." Said Tank.

"So, how's it going?" said Clax strolling up.

There was another round of hellos before the gang settled back into their normal conversations.

"Oh, guess who I was talking to earlier?" Clax said to Datch.

"Err, who?"

"Only Talia," Carina suddenly was all ears. "Your mum sent her a vid of the gig a few weeks ago."

"Who is Talia?" Carina asked.

"She's the lead singer of the Snowmen; she was the one that got me on the stage."

Carina looked at Datch and he found himself feeling he had to explain more but then a light came on in Carina's mind.

"Oh, the Dancing Jaxx." said Carina and started smiling again.

"What did she think?" said Datch.

"Well, why don't we ask her, I have my vid com with me." Clax happily said pulling it out.

Clax pressed some buttons and the screen lit up saying 'connecting please wait'. After a few seconds the screen switched to an image of Talia,

"Hi Clax." she said "What's happening?"

He moved the vid to the centre of the table so she could see everyone.

"Hi Talia." Datch said.

"Oh wow, is that you Datch?" she turned to look over her shoulder.

"Hey everyone it's Datch." She said to whoever was behind her.

A moment later the rest of The Snowmen appeared on the screen.

"Hey dude how's it going, Talia showed us your vid from the gig, is that The Pack behind you?" said Jarna taking over.

"Yes, let me introduce them," Datch went around the table one by one until he got to Carina, "and this is Carina, my girlfriend."

"Oh, it's great to meet you all and especially you Carina, you hold on to Datch he's one of a kind."

"Thank you, I will." she said.

"We've only got a few minutes to chat, we're on stage in twenty minutes." Talia said.

"What, you're in the Dancing Jaxx?" Datch asked.

"Yes, look" she lifted the vid up and moved it around,

"Hey Datch, I see you have been practicing the guitar. You'll have to come back here soon, maybe you can bring The Pack for a guest act with us."

"That would be cool. But I'm not sure we could get there." said Datch.

"Can't you talk to Don, Jarna is still dating Alex and if he's coming up, maybe you could all get a lift off him."

"I don't know, I'd have to talk to mum and dad and the rest of The Pack would have to talk to their parents."

The next ten minutes were spent talking to everyone and finding out how The Pack had become such a hit. No one was quite sure how they ended up with so many people coming to see them. Then it was time for The Snowmen to go on stage so they had to go.

"Well, what did you think?" Datch said to Carina.

"Yeh, they seem really nice."

Datch turned to the whole table,

"What do you lot think about a gig in Traxsent?"

"Traxsent, is that where the Dancing Jaxx is, it's up north somewhere isn't it?" asked Rosey.

"Yes, about an hour's flight in one to the Carpaycus shuttles or five hours by the continental shuttle."

They all agreed that it was a nice idea but it needed a bit of planning. Datch said he'd have a word with Don next time he came to visit.

After a while the bar staff went running for cover as it was time for some Solar Ball.

That week after school had finished Carina headed to Datch's and stopped for a couple of days.

In the morning they were sitting on the sofa in the bar half watching the vid and half cuddling each other when the news came on and for a change there was a big headline. 'Third missing person reported'.

"Hey look!" said Datch.

Carina turned to look at the vid.

The report went on to say that a third person had disappeared without a trace. The missing person had been a farther of three and was happily joined to his wife. His wife said that he had only gone out for some groceries from the all-night shop and he hadn't come home. The local security services couldn't find evidence of him anywhere in the area and even the scans for his implant turned up nothing. The security services were appalling for anyone that had seen anything no matter how small to come forward.

Datch turned to Carina.

"You know what happened." he said.

"Yes, the spider." A shiver went down their spines and Carina pulled Datch a bit closer.

"Do you think we should call them?" she asked.

"No, they wouldn't believe us, I'll message Don, this is starting to get really bad." He said looking worried.

He went over to the vid com.

"Please send a message to Captain Don Ronediamar onboard the starship Carpaycus."

"Please wait." it said, then after a few moments,

"The starship Carpaycus is out of range, please note transmission time will be approximately four weeks. Do you wish to proceed?"

"Yes, please attach a copy of the news report about the missing persons on channel Yul17, message starts, Don I think this is the work of our spider, we're getting a bit worried now, please respond soon. Message ends."

He went back to Carina on the sofa.

"He must be a long way away; it's going to take four weeks for the message to get to him." he said sitting down.

"Oh, so what do we do?"

"Wait for Don and do what he said, stay in groups."

"Can't we warn people?"

"I don't see how, we'll talk to Jep and the bikers next week, they might know what to do to get the word out."

They sat staring at the screen lost in their own thoughts before going back to having a cuddle.

The following week The Pack were all sitting down after a rather fun game of Solar Ball which had resulted in the bar ending up full of holographic bubbles. This was much to the annoyance of the bar staff who were trying to serve at the time of the bubble explosion and then couldn't see what they were doing for two minutes until the bubbles went pop. After they had stopped laughing and got their breath back Datch brought up the spider.

"So, you have all seen the news about the missing persons, I think it's the spider." he said and Carina nodded in agreement with him.

"Yes, it could well be, but why start now?" said Fred.

"I don't think it has, remember over the last few months that the tramps and homeless have been disappearing, I think it was feeding on them and now they have all gone it's finding other food supplies."

"Oh, I never thought of that. So, you mean anyone who goes out on their own late at night could end up as dinner." said Jep.

He now had a look of horror on his face.

"If that's true, it's not good, but how do we warn people, the security forces won't believe you or me. They think it was a murderer or something like that. The last thing they want to hear is that murderer is about three metres tall, is armour plated with eight legs and likes having folks for dinner." Added Clax.

They sat looking at each other quietly and then Hagger put his hand up. They all looked at him.

"I know this may sound silly, but on a vid I was watching a few weeks ago. The hero called the news channel anonymously and told them about the murderer."

"Err, right so how did he do that?"

"I don't know, he just put this thing on his vid com to scramble the signal." They sat for a minute contemplating what Hagger had just said.

"It's a nice idea, but how to do it without the scrambler thing?" Tank asked.

The others looked at each other and then at Datch. He was thinking.

"That's a really good idea! Even if people don't believe it most of them won't go out on their own anymore just in case."

They sat looking at each other thinking for a couple of minutes trying to work out how to do it and then Datch had an idea.

"What if I get my brother Dydinyon to do it. He lives three-star systems away and could use a public unit wearing a disguise. They would have a lot of trouble tracing him even if they wanted to." The others sat looking at him and thinking.

"Well, it might work. But would he, do it?" said Clax.

"I think so."

"Err, so let me do a recap, we're planning to get Datch's brother to put on a disguise to call the news station from another planet and tell them that a spider is going around eating people." Said Jep summing it up.

"Yep." said Datch.

There was a lot of nods from around the table and then for some unknown reason they all started grinning. Jep was about to say something else but decided not to and just go along with it.

"I'll talk to him this weekend. It's this week that he comes to visit."

With that they got up for another game of Solar Ball. This time it was the volcanic moon again. The rest of the customers went and got their drinks from the bar before it was covered in molten rock. They had seen this one before.

The rest of the week was uneventful. At the weekly assembly the principal told everyone that they should not go out alone at night and the larger the group the better. Jep gave Datch a knowing nod.

After dinner it was time for the gig. The Barbers Inn was packed again and the gig went very well with another autograph session after it. They seemed to be getting around two hundred credits a night now. Datch's own credit account was looking very healthy for someone who was at school. Hagger had even brought some of his own clothes now and there seemed to be something going on between him and Rosey that didn't make sense. They would try and wind each other up and get angry with each other but always seemed to smooth it over in the end. Dapo and Tish seemed to be just really good friends and behaved like they were brother and sister. They were always helping each other out.

The weekend came and Datch asked Carina's mum if Carina could come over and meet his brother. She agreed and Datch picked Carina up a couple of hours before Dydinyon was due to turn up. The flight back to the ranch was spent talking about how to approach him about the call. They called in at the Barbers Inn on route. Fred had sorted out a bottle of Dydinyon's favourite poison and left it behind the bar for them to pick up. They collected it and headed to the ranch.

It was a hot afternoon. Tansya was in the pool floating around on an inflatable chair when they arrived. They went inside and headed straight up stairs to Datch's room to get changed. They still had their own rooms but they didn't want to waste time and five minutes later they were back down and in the pool.

"Carina, has Datch warned you that Dydinyon does tend to drink a lot?"

"Yes, he said he sometimes gets very drunk and Datch finds him sleeping on the veranda most of the time."

"Yes, he does tend to sleep outside. In fact, I think he hasn't slept in his room for over four years."

"I can't remember him ever sleeping in the house." Datch added trying to be part of the conversation.

"Well, Dechow will be back with him soon. His shuttle got in about fifteen minutes ago so another thirty minutes and they will be here. I've told Dechow to tell him to behave so he will."

"Is Dydinyon your son as well?" Carina asked

"Yes, both him and Datch are mine." she said smiling.

"Where does Dydinyon live then?"

"He has a job on Hamal four. He is a transportation coordinator for one of the central city hubs. The job is quite stressful but pays well, also he gets discounted flights so every couple of months he takes a week off and comes home. He tends to let himself go a bit when he's here. I think it's sort of a destressing thing."

"Oh, but doesn't it take a while to get here?"

"Yes, it's about a day and a half normally so he gets a good five days with us."

Datch got out of the pool and dried himself off.

"Who wants a drink?"

"Yes please, Datch. Can you get me a glass of the non-alcoholic wine? Do you want some Carina?"

"Yes please." she said.

Datch went inside to get the drinks and was soon back with two wine glasses and a large glass of Gruck for himself.

They sat under one of the umbrellas letting the light breeze keep them cool. The sensor outside of the house was reading 31C and that was in the shade. Then came the sound of engines in the distance and the pickup could be seen in the sky above the fields. It came in low over the barn and landed next to the back door. Dechow and Dydinyon got out and went inside. A few minutes later they came back out from the bar carrying a drink each and headed over to the pool.

"Hello Carina." said Dechow as he walked over to where they were all sitting.

"Hi, Dechow" she said.

"This is Dydinyon, Datch's brother."

"Hello," she said.

"Hello" he replied.

He was not what Carina thought he would look like. He was about the same height as Tansya, brown hair with green eyes and he looked around middle age. For that body anyway. He was slim build but had a bit of a belly on him.

"Hi little bro." he said looking over at Datch.

"Hi." Said Datch while trying to drink his Gruck in a cool manner.

The next hour was spent with Carina and Datch taking a sudden interest in what Dydinyon did. Tansya and Dechow just thought it was down to them now being a couple and also growing up very fast. Unlike the six to eight years, it takes on earth, most Bellatrixian children go from the start of puberty to full on adulthood in about a year and a half. The implant increases their mental abilities and accelerates their learning capacity.

They had a barbeque for tea and spent the evening drinking and chatting. Datch had never really spoken to Dydinyon before. Yes, they talked sometimes but Dydinyon was nearly two hundred years older than Datch so the conversations were a bit limited. This time however, Datch had grown up a lot. What with Carina, The Pack, their gigs at the Barbers Inn and also school not to mention the platinum star. There was a lot of things to talk about that Dydinyon found interesting or amusing. Datch and Carina sat chatting away with him most of the night.

The sun set and the cooler night air was a nice relief from the blazing daytime temperatures. Tansya and Dechow were surprised at how well Datch was suddenly getting on with his brother. Datch even suggested they all go out for a picnic on the bikes. That met with everyone's approval so they agreed to head out to the river then next day and spend some time there.

The next morning there was a knock at Datch's door. It was Carina. She came in closing the door behind her before coming over and sitting on the bed. Datch put his arms around her and gave her a little tug. She laid down next to him.

"What about your mum?"

"She won't be up for an hour yet and my dad won't get up until she is."

Carina relaxed and cuddled in more. After about half an hour of enjoying each other's company, they ended up talking about how to get Dydinyon to carry out the plan. They decided to wait till he had a few beers and then bring up the spider while Dechow was there. That way when they asked him about the call a bit later, he would know it wasn't a prank. Finally, they got dressed and headed down for breakfast.

It was time for the picnic. Dechow was going to take Dydinyon on the back of his bike, Carina was with Datch and Tansya was on hers along with the picnic basket. They mounted up and headed off into the desert. As it had been Datch's idea he had the choice of where to land. He chose the place he had taken Carina to a couple of weeks before.

The desert was getting very hot during the day now that summer was coming. They flew across the sand and the heat haze caused the desert up ahead to shimmer like water. Datch's bike was showing a ground temperature of forty-three degrees centigrade. In the distance Datch could see the familiar green line of the river snaking across the desert. The bikes came in low and circled before landing next to the park. The spot under the trees where Datch had sat with Carina was still free so they laid out a big blanket in the shade. Datch, Dydinyon and Dechow went off to get the drinks while Tansya and Carina setup the picnic.

It was nice under the trees. They kept the sun off and there was a nice cool breeze from the river. The men came back with the drinks and also had a couple of bottles of non-alcoholic wine on ice to go with the food. They sat chatting and relaxing. It was a couple of hours before Datch dropped the spider into the conversation.

"Yes, the Barber Inn is great, it's just the walk back to the school we have to be careful about." said Datch trying to casually drop it into the conversation.

"Err, the walk back? it's not that far?" Dydinyon said about to pull Datch's leg.

"It's because of the spider." Said Carina.

"What spider?" he asked now puzzled.

"Well," said Dechow reluctantly, "The city appears to have a spider problem. Don is looking into it."

"The shuttle said there was a madman on the loose killing people."

"Yes, the security forces think that but we have enough evidence to indicate an arachnoid is on the loose."

"But shouldn't you call someone?"

"No, I don't think they would listen to us at the moment, we need more evidence."

"Oh, so what are you doing Datch?"

"Well, we're doing what Don said and making sure we're in large groups when out at night, that way it won't attack. The school has told everyone to do the same saying the murderer is going after people on their own. I just wish people knew what we do." he said.

"Yes, me to, I hate to think of what that man's family are going through." said Carina.

Everyone agreed it was not nice but as Dechow said there was nothing they could do so they decided to change the subject and talk about the river instead.

That evening Datch and Carina cornered Dydinyon in the bar while Dechow and Tansya were outside.

"Err, we've been thinking about the spider thing." Datch said. Dydinyon raised an eyebrow.

"Yes, and what have you been thinking?" he'd had a few beers by this point but was far from drunk.

"If someone was to say, call the news station." he said and then Carina joined in "Yes, from a public vid on another planet, so it would be anonymous."

"Yes, that's all well and good but they would see their face." He said now somewhat intrigued by what they were saying.

"Not if they were wearing a disguise." Datch said.

"And using a voice modulator." Carina added.

"And just where would the person get that all from?" Datch and Carina both had a grin.

"Err, in the box in my bedroom." Dydinyon looked at them both.

"You want me to do it, don't you? I could get in trouble if I'm found out."

"Yes, but think of the people it could save if you do it." Said Carina who by this point was smiling and making puppy dog eyes.

"Err, well I don't know?"

"Please do it for us?" said Carina.

She was putting on her best look and the one she knew would make her dad agree to anything. It dawned on Datch at this point that it was very likely that he would never be able to say 'No' to Carina. This was certainly the case for his bother at this point. Dydinyon's brain gave up working and decided to go for a walk in lala-land.

"Ok, but you'll have to get some vid credits for me and tell me what to say." He said giving in to the female onslaught.

"I have them all in the box upstairs. An old man's disguise, a one hundred and fifty vid credit, the modulator, the statement to the news channel and the ID to call, all in a nice small box to put in your bag. And to steady your nerves a bottle of your favourite brandy." Datch instructed him.

"We'll give you it tomorrow, then you can put it in your bag so you don't forget."

"Does mum and dad know about this?"

"Err, no." replied Datch.

"But it's to save all those people." Added Carina who was now pretty much unstoppable.

"Ok, Ok, can you get me another beer, I think I need one." Datch obliged and fetched him one from the bar.

With that they went outside to join mum and dad.

"Where have you three been?" Tansya asked as they sat down.

"We were looking at Bob. Oh, and can I put the brightness up on the palm?" Said Datch attempting to change the subject as fast as possible.

"NO!" said both Dechow and Tansya at the same time.

"Oh, well can I put some music on?" he said knowing that it had worked but just wanting to back it up.

"Yes, but please put relaxing music on." Said Tansya.

"Ok, Carina do you want to help me choose?"

"Sure." she said getting up again.

They went inside.

"Do you think he will do it?" asked Carina when they were out of ear shot.

"I hope so, we need people to stop going out alone at night so it gets forced out into the open and seen by a vid." He added.

They sorted out some music and went back to the others who were by now talking about some place on Hamal four that had hot volcanic vents in the restaurant that they cooked the food over.

Two days later Datch sat watching the vid with Carina. She had managed to get her mum to let her stay until they went to school as long as Datch came over and helped her dad on the farm for a few days the following weekend. The news came on and there was yet another disappearance. This time it was a woman who had gone out of a bar after an argument with her boyfriend and just vanished. The security forces had managed to get the last few minutes of her life from the external memory storage attached to her implant. It showed her walking down the street and then the image started to get fuzzy before just stopping completely. Dydinyon had been in the kitchen trying to put his brain back in shape after the night before and heard the news. He put his head around the corner of the bar to watch. The security forces still could not explain how she died or where her body had gone. They had ruled out the boyfriend as he was still in the bar when it happened and a scan of his implant had proved he had nothing to do with it. The security forces were asking for anyone in the area who might have seen or heard anything to come forward.

Datch turned and spotted his brother looking through the door.

"Hi bro, you see what we mean? We have to do something."

"Yes." said Dydinyon with a sigh. "I'll do it, I promise bro."

They sat watching the vid. Carina had moved closer to Datch and was holding him tight. Datch could sense she was scared by it all. He was as well when he thought about it.

The next day Dechow took Dydinyon to the space port in the morning and the rest day was spent chilling in the sun around the pool. Carina was now starting to feel at home and it was almost as if she was part of the family. Datch had also changed in the way he talked about things. When Carina was about, he felt more confident and his dad didn't always correct him. It was suddenly like being an adult and having a voice.

Breaking News

In a darkened room at the back of a seedy bar. A group of four men sat around a table. The one wearing a suite and smoking a large cigar spoke.

"We need you to arrange for us to acquire two more items later this week."

A small man wearing a short sleeve shirt looked nervous,

"I can't, they are not letting them out of the centre area now."

"Well, find a way."

"They have left orders that if anyone calls or orders them to go out. The security guards are to be informed straight away." The small man was now getting scared.

"So, how do we get them then?" the large man was not going to take no for an answer.

"The only way would be to take them from the central core. But the guards go around in pairs and they have surveillance vids all over the place, the only place you wouldn't get recorded is inside the centre of the main compound."

"So, we get them from there."

"We can't get there without going past four or five surveillance vids and the perimeter fence, even if we did get to them, it would be impossible to carry them out."

The large gentleman stood up and looked thoughtful for a minute.

"Ok then, you will have to help our friend get in then?"

"Well, I don't know how unless he can fly. The security guards are also hanging around the central core a lot these days because of the murderer that's on the loose."

The large gentleman looked straight at him and gave him an evil grin.

"Let's just say, if they meet our friend, they won't need to worry about a murderer."

Then he laughed and the other two men joined in. It sent shivers running down the little man's spine.

"Err, Can't I just show someone?" he was now very scared.

"Here are two thousand credits. You will meet our friend just down the street from the power station. There is a dark alley, two buildings down. Meet him there in four days at midnight."

"How will I know him?"

"Oh, you'll know him, there is no doubt about that."

The small man plucked up a bit of courage.

"Please can we make this the last time; I'm going to get found out."

The large gentleman looked him up and down.

"Ok this will be your last run, Now leave us, we have things to discuss."

He waved his hand at the door, the little man got up and left in a hurry. The three remaining men pulled close around the table to discuss the plan.

The Pack went back to school and as normal they headed down to the Barber Inn in the evening. They arrived outside only to find a large skip sitting in the street and some scaffolding attached to the front of the bar. A big sign was attached to the front,

Open as usual
We are currently having
Improvement work carried out.
Sorry for any inconvenience.
The Barbers Inn.

They walked in. The inside now had half of a second floor. Well, a sort of balcony thing going around the outside of the room anyway. They walked over to the bar where Jim was leaning looking at the works.

Jep who had walked down with them had to ask.

"Err Jim, what's going on?"

"Well, I have been trying to work out how to get more people in the bar and then it hit me, put a balcony around over the top of the seating area."

They all looked up.

"Yes, that sounds good but where are the stairs?" asked Rosey.

"Oh, err they should be over there." he said pointing at the blank piece of wall.

They scratched their heads.

"Err, how did they put that bit up without the stairs?" asked Hagger pointing at a large bit of balcony.

It was sitting virtually in mid-air and fully carpeted with a table and chairs on it. The only thing that appeared to be holding it up was a thin post and a bracket attached to a small piece of wall.

"Oh, it's not a good place to sit at the moment is it." Jim said suddenly realising that it may fall down. "They were meant to have left it safe."

He went running off into the office. They got their drinks and went over to the big table giving the new construction a wide birth. After a few moments Jim came running out of the office with another sign and put it carefully on the post. it said:

Please do not touch or lean
on this post. It is currently under
Construction and may fall down.

He went back to standing at the bar.

The Pack were on their second round of drinks when Clax and Peebop came running in.

"Mind the Post!" shouted Jim as they narrowly avoided it.

"Wow, you're in a hurry."

"Yes, we had a bet on with Tank and Fred, Last in buys the beers." said Clax.

Tank and Fred came trotting through the door somewhat out of breath.

"Mind the Post!" shouted Jim again.

"We had to park the bikes down the street because someone had put a skip in our parking space." Tank panted back at him.

At this point Clax looked up.

"Err, what's that?"

"Apparently, it's a balcony." said Datch in a questioning tone.

"Oh." said Peebop.

They sat staring at it for a moment. It was at this point Tank and Fred got to the bar to order the drinks. Tank turned around and looked up.

"What the Jaxx is that?"

There was another discussion at the bar with Jim about the validity of the balcony while the drinks were poured. Once loaded up with beers they headed over to the table.

"Err according to Jim, it's so more people can fit in the bar." said Tank still looking at the renovations.

"He did say we might get more money." added Fred.

"Datch, did you and Carina sort things out with your brother?" said Clax changing the subject.

"Yes, he's going to do it." said Datch.

"Ahh, good." said Fred.

They sat talking about the remodelling of the bar and then it was time for a game of Solar Ball. This made for interesting play as the new alterations had not been mapped into the games play field. This caused some odd effects such as balls flying through the walls and going through the parts of the balcony only to bounce off the ceiling. The post only got hit the once by a person who ducked trying to avoid a ball. After Tank and Clax held it till it stopped shaking. A number of chairs were put around it to stop it happening again.

The next two days went by and the balcony was finished in time for the gig. The Pack had just arrived and sat down behind the screens when Clax came running in nearly knocking them over.

"What's up with you?" said Jep grabbing his drink to save it.

"Datch, Datch, look." He pulled out his vid com and turned it on.

The vid com was set to channel Yul17 and was showing a news report;

"Fellow citizens of Yuland City, Yul17 News today received an anonymous report that the city has an arachnoid on the loose. The person stated that the monster has been here for a number of months and has been feeding on the homeless in the city. The beast also has a scattering field stopping it being detected. We asked the security services to comment and their response was, 'We have no evidence to prove this and our current warning stands, we are unable to contact the caller as he or she was off world and appeared to have called from a public vid com.' We here at Yul17 received the call earlier today and the caller was very specific about certain details and appeared to know a lot about the creature. We are advising people not to go out alone at night and stay in large groups. It is likely that it will only attack people on their own for fear of being found. Please stay safe. This is Tara Jexx for Yul17 news." The report finished.

They sat looking at the screen.

"He bloody did it!" said Jep.

"Yes, and the other news channels have picked it up as well." said Clax.

Tank, Fred and Peebop came in the door and walked over.

"Flipping Jaxx Clax. I never knew you could move that fast." said Tank arriving at the table.

"Have you seen the vid?" asked Datch.

"Yes, Clax nearly shoved it up our nose when we went to meet him, your brother came through, let's hope it helps."

"I'm sure it will, even if it only stops one person dying it's got to be good." everyone nodded.

Tank looked around.

"Well at least the bar looks finished now."

"Yes, Jim said they finished it just before lunch. He wanted to make sure he had it ready for tonight. Did you see the stage?" said Datch.

Tank stuck his head around the screen to have a look.

"Oh, it's bigger and the light system seems to have gained a few extra lamps, not to mention the PA speakers seem to be mounted on the walls now."

"Yep, he told us just before you got here that he can get an extra hundred and fifty people in here now, oh and look up." He did.

"Wow, we have our own aircon." said Tank with a big grin

"Ok, let's sort out the set list, oh and does anyone else play anything because I have a plan to do more songs?"

"Well, I sort of play the drums." said Tish looking a little sheepish.

"Why does that not come as a surprise." said Fred smiling.

"I did play the synth in my last body. Can't say I've tried it in this one yet." Added Clax.

"Err, I'm trying to learn the guitar like you?" said Dapo.

Datch thought about this and then after a pause.

"The crowd, really likes the guitar bit. So, let's all go to my house this weekend and see if we can sort out a few songs, I'll sort it with my mum and dad. Carina is going to be on a hand drum. Rosey, do you think you can do that to?"

"Sure, what about Hagger?"

"Hmm, I did the recorder?" he said looking apologetic.

"Ok, time for an upgrade, a synth whistle, I'll get one for you. Tank, Jep, Peebop, Fred, what about you?"

"I'm happy on backing vocals." Tank said.

The others nodded in agreement

"Ok. That's cool, now tonight this is what I think…"

They sat sorting out the set list. Soon the bar was full and it was time for them to go on stage.

They ran on stage and straight into the first song and as it finished the roar from the crowd was louder than normal. They carried on and the bouncers were having trouble keeping people back. The first set finished to thunderous applause.

"Err, "said Carina sitting down, "that was loud."

"Yes, just a bit." added Rosey who was trying to stop her ears from ringing.

Just at that point Jim came around the corner carrying the drinks.

"Hey folks, I was wrong about the extra one hundred and fifty. There's just over five hundred people out there."

"Bloody Jaxx!" said Fred nearly spitting his beer across the table.

"Yes, and we're still turning people away outside." Jim added.

"Wow, that's a lot of people." Rosey said somewhat taken a back.

"Just wait until the end of the night." Jim said with a grin.

Fifteen minutes later they went back on stage for the second set.

By the end of the night the PA system was running flat out and a number of officers from the security services were outside just in case there was any trouble or a mini riot. They also thought it was a good idea to come in the bar for a drink and check that everyone was behaving.

There was the normal autograph signing session afterwards including one signed to officer Tyker with love.

The Pack finally got behind the screen and sat down; it was about fifteen minutes before Jim finally appeared to sort out their credits.

"Sorry, I was selling tickets for next week, here's your credits."

He gave them five hundred credits a piece.

"Five hundred!" said Hagger almost losing his voice.

The others sat in looking at the credit transfer slips.

"If we keep going like this, I'll be able to give up my day job." said Clax.

"Me too." added Peebop staring at the slip.

"So, I take it, that's Ok then?" asked Jim.

They all just sat nodding slowly.

"Good, I'll just go and get you some more drinks, I think you might need them."

"Err, what for?" said Fred still looking at his slip. But Jim had gone.

Ten minutes later he was back with another round of drinks and another round of slips. These were all for fifty credits each

"What's this?" asked Fred.

"For the photo signing and people are now asking about your T-Shirts, Can I get some more made? I think we can sell them for twenty-five credits a piece, of course, you will get a credit each per shirt sold."

"That sounds fine." said Datch looking at both slips.

Finally, they started talking again, pulling themselves away from the slips. They sat in the bar until one in the morning chatting and discussing the weekend before heading back to the school.

The following night a small skinny man walked down a street looking for an ally. He found the one he was looking for. It was very dark and two long shadows stretched into dark voids in the ally. He looked up and down the street checking that no one was about and then he nervously stepped into the darkness.

"Are you here? Big Tel sent me."

There was a noise like tiny little pads being placed softly but firmly on the walls and then onto the floor somewhere in front of him. Then came the voice.

"YESSS... I'M HERE."

It sounded deathly cold and was like a thousand icicles being stabbed into your spine with every syllable. The small man shuddered with fear.

"Err," he said shaking in his boots, "I'm to show you how to get to the central core."

"YES, I KNOW, SHALL WE GO?"

"Err, yes?" he said now wanting this to be over as soon as possible.

A long spindly arm was extended out into the light and wrapped itself around the little man like a steel cable. He wanted to scream but couldn't. It lifted him up into the air and then took him into the shadows.

"STOP SHAKING, I'LL LOSE MY GRIP." Said the voice as it climbed up the building in the darkness.

It reached the top very quickly and then the little man was able to see the true horror of the voice.

It was a spider well over four metres long and jet black. It had got the little man wrapped up in one of its legs and had curled it close to its body. The man wanted to run but knew he wouldn't make two steps before he was dead. He made up his mind that when he got home, he'd call big Tel and tell him that was it. Then leave town in a hurry. In fact, no, leave the planet then call big Tel from a very long way away. That would be better.

"SO, WHERE ARE WE GOING?"

"Err, over there, but we can't go down because of the vids below."

"ARE THERE ANY ON THAT TOWER?"

"No, why would we put any up there?" He wished he hadn't asked.

The spider turned its rear towards the tower and fired a length of web straight at the tower, it wrapped around one of the metal girders and the creature attached the other end to the building they were on, the web was only about ten millimetres in diameter but as strong as steel.

The creature then turned upside down and started to move across the webbing. The little man was now laying on the creature's body. It was hard like a concrete floor. The creature soon was over the three hundred metre gap and on the tower.

"WHERE TO NOW?"

The little man was trying not to crap himself especially now that the spider was facing down head first and that meant he was as well.

"Err, "he said in a shaky voice, "Do you see the roof to the left, that is the central core, the bots will be kept in there. We can get in via that hole over there." He was now, way past scared.

They moved down the tower and onto the roof. The spider put the little man down and commanded in a voice that sounded like it came from a crypt.

"YOU WILL WAIT HERE!"

The little man was so scared that he couldn't have moved if he had wanted to. The spider disappeared inside.

The little man watched as two security guards walked into the building. He got ready to run thinking they would find the spider. There was a yell from inside followed by a very short stifled scream and then silence. Five minutes later the spider was back carrying two big bots under its body.

"Err, what happened to the guards?" he said and then noticed blood around the creature's mouth.

"THEY WERE QUITE TASTY."

The little man lost control of his bladder and wet himself.

"How are you going to carry me and the bots?"

"BEFORE THAT SOMEONE WANTS TO TALK TO YOU."

The creature moved a disc on its collar so the little man could see it and then touched the side of it. The panel lit up and said connecting. A man appeared on the panel, it was Big Tel.

"Ah, well done on showing our friend the way in, I would like to say it's a pleasure working with you but you have become a liability. Please accept my apologies for not being there myself but I've other business to attend to."

"What! No! wait!" The vid com went blank.

"AH, DESSERT!"

The spider climbed back up the tower and across the web carrying the two bots. Its stomach full. It took the bots to the designated spot and placed them on the manhole cover and watched them disappear before returning back to its nest to sleep off the meal. He quite enjoyed humans. They had a nice refreshing taste but could give you indigestion if you swallowed them too quickly.

The weekend came and Datch sorted out a rehearsal session at the ranch. He had cleared the barn for them to use as a rehearsal room and had sorted it so they could stay over. That way they could chill out in the evening and then try again the following day.

Soon the Pack was together and having a drink next to the pool before going to practice. Peebop was very quiet.

"What's up Peebop?" asked Datch.

"Two more bots were stolen last night and two guards are missing."

"What?" Datch said.

Everyone suddenly went silent.

"Didn't you see the News Channel, the thieves broke into the central core and took two of the big bot's, not only that but two guards have simply vanished."

"When you mean vanished you mean dead?" said Rosey somewhat bluntly.

They all could imagine what had happened.

"Err, yes I suspect so." He said looking down.

They all sat in silence for a few minutes.

Datch stood up and cleared his throat.

"Ok we all pretty much know what happened and we can't change anything today so let's focus on why we're here and take our minds off it." he's paused while the others turned to look at him, "Ok, I have been doing some thinking and with a bit of work we can do these five songs, 'Space Dust', 'Wilde Wind', 'Rocking the City', 'Hot City nights' and finally 'Someone to Love'. I know we have been singing them but do you think they are ok?"

"I think they're ok, what about our song 'Wind in Your Hair'? It's a similar riff to 'Space Dust'." said Clax.

There was a general feeling that this would work if they could do the others. Datch wasn't sure what a riff was but agreed anyway and planned to ask his implant later. He put the songs on the sound system and set them for repeat. This was so they could try things out before going and making a lot of noise. After an hour of messing about they went down to the barn.

The barn had been set out like the stage at the Barbers Inn. Datch had even set up a screen so it was realistic. He had borrowed a small PA system and set it up with the help of his dad and had got some stands for the instruments. Tish put her drums up at the back, Dapo put his guitar next to Datch's, Carina and Rosey put their drums up on two small stands, Clax set his synth up on the right, Haggar was given his synth pipes and finally a row of mics on stands were put up along with various other mics dotted around.

"OK. Everyone apart from Jep get on stage." Said Datch taking control.

"Err, why?" said Rosey.

"He's going to tell us if we look cool." Replied Datch.

"I am?" Jep said, a little doubtful about what cool was.

"Yes, and then someone else will and we'll take it in turns until we're all sort of happy." There was a bit of a pause while this sunk in and then people started taking their places.

Jep stood looking at the stage and scratched his head.

"It doesn't look right." He said cocking his head to one side

"Which bit?" asked Datch.

"Err." he thought about it, "Well if Rosey moves a bit that way," she did, "Hmm and Carina you as well."

The whole process carried on and took about twenty minutes before everyone was happy. The final line up was as follows:

Clax and Hagger on the left then Carina next to Datch followed at the Back with Tish, then came Dapo on the other side of Datch with Rosey next to him and then Peebop, Tank, Jep and Fred.

They were ready to try the first song; it didn't go well.

"Hmm." said Datch. He had another think, "Let's try this how I learnt to do it with Talia, first Tish start playing the drums."

She did and after a few bars,

"Clax, get your synth to add the base line."

He did,

"Right Carina and Rosey you join in now."

This was working better Datch thought,

"Now me and Dapo."

And finally, he gave a nod to Hagger and the backing group. It didn't sound half bad.

"Right let's try that again. This time from the beginning. Everyone listen to Tish, she's the key I think, if we all stay in time with her, we should be ok."

They tried again, this time it was a little better. They did the song over and over for the next two hours until it was sounding ok. They decided to take a break and went over to the bar to chill for a bit.

They sat having a drink in the sun when Tansya came out.

"I take it you're having a break. I could hear the music up here and it's starting to sound a lot better. Would you like any snacks?" she asked.

"Yes please, mum." said Datch who had already downed half a glass of Gruck.

"Do you want them here or in the barn?"

"Err, here I think." The others all nodded.

She left and they sat talking about the song and how they could make it work better. Dapo still needed to work on his guitar a bit but it was passable. Hagger had worked out it was easier to play the synth whistle than a recorder and had managed to do alright. He was mostly for effect than anything else. Tish was great on the drums with Carina and Rosey were doing very well too. Clax, well he was very good and backing vocals were as good as ever.

Ten minutes later Tansya was back with a tray of food. It didn't last long.

They finished their drinks and headed back into the barn. This process carried on for the rest of the afternoon and part of the evening. The next morning it started all over again. By lunch time they had most of the songs sorted and thought another two or three weeks practicing and they should be ready to try at least one or two of them on stage but made a point of still having the backing music going to be sure.

By mid-afternoon it was time for everyone head off home and also for Datch to head over to Carina's farm to help her dad for a couple of days. This time he was going to stay there until it was time for school.

A Friend in Need

Datch arrived at school with Carina on the bike. They parked in his allocated spot and grabbed their bags before heading inside. Datch took Carina to her room before heading down to his. He walked in and Dapo and Hagger were already there.

"We need to talk." said Dapo.

Hagger was sitting very quiet on the bed.

"What's up?"

"It's Hagger's dad."

Datch went over and sat down next to him.

"What has he done?" Datch asked.

Hagger turned to look at him.

"He's not come home since last week."

"Does he do this a lot?"

"No, he sometimes may not come back for a couple of days but he's never been away for this long."

Hagger had tears running down his face.

"Oh, have you told anyone yet?"

"No. I didn't know what to do." Datch turned to Dapo.

"Go fetch the girls." He got up and ran out the door.

"Look he might just have met someone or something?"

"No, He went out late at night and said he would be back in the morning, I tried his vid. I know something has happened to him."

"I'm sure, he'll be back."

Hagger broke down and started crying. Datch put his arm around him and tried to comfort him. Just then the girls came running in followed by Dapo.

"Dapo, sorry but can you go and see if you can find Jep and bring him back." said Datch.

Datch explained what was going on to the girls.

"I think we should call the security services." said Carina and Rosey nodded.

"They might send me off to my mum or dads' families, they both live off world and I've never met them, you're the only friends I have." said Hagger sobbing.

"Hmm, we have to do something, let's see what Jep says."

They sat on the bed looking after Hagger. The girls were brilliant. Five minutes later the door opened and Dapo walked in with Jep, Datch brought Jep up to speed.

"Oh, I see." he said, "Well we're going to have to contact the authorities that is certain, but maybe we can sort something out as to where Hagger goes, I know Tank, Fred and you Datch have extra rooms at your houses, it might be possible for Hagger to stay with one of you. I'll contact the security services and call your parents Datch, maybe we can sort something out tonight in the Barbers."

"Ok, but what do we do now?" Datch asked.

"Well, I'll go and make the call, oh and I'll get all of you exempt from this afternoon's lecture. You just stay here until I come back with security. Oh and no one mention the spider."

With that he left the room and hurried off up the corridor. Fifteen minutes later he was back with two security guards and an officer form the security services.

"This is officer Plade from the security services, he needs to talk to Hagger. I've also spoken to Tank who has said it's ok for Hagger to stay with him for now until either Hagger's dad is found or something more permanent is sorted out."

The Detective turned to Hagger.

"Hello Hagger, I'm Detective Plade for Yuland city security services. I need to ask you a few questions about your dad. Would you like someone to be with you while we take the details?"

"Can Datch come?"

"Yes, if you want him to. Please can you both follow me to Professor Jodi's office where I can note everything down."

Jep turned to the rest of them.

"You folks stay here until we get back. Right, if you would like to follow me."

Jep lead the way up the corridor towards his office. Datch had his arm around Hagger making sure he was ok. They reached the office and went in. There was another officer sitting down and she got up when they came in.

"This is officer Tartar and she will be assisting me. Please sit down and I'll try and make this as quick as possible." said Detective Plade.

They sat down and detective started to ask some questions.

"What is your fathers full name?"

"Err, Yuter Hagger Bartow"

"Do you know his ID?"

"No." the other officer was entering the information into a vid com.

"Ok so when did you last see him?"

"About five days ago."

"Five! Why have you waited so long to call us?"

"Well, my dad goes up to the casino a lot and sometimes he doesn't come back for a couple of days."

"Oh, I see, ok well, what does he do for work?"

"He's working on the new power plant; he's a task controller." The officer glanced at the detective with a knowing look.

"Do you know where he was going?"

"He said he was going to meet someone."

"Oh, do you know where?"

"No, I thought it would be at the casino as he spends a lot of time there."

"Ok, do you know what he was wearing when he went out?"

"Err, his black shirt and trousers I think."

"Ok, is there anything else you can tell us?"

"I don't think so, he's dead, isn't he?" he said starting to cry again.

The officers looked at each other. Datch put his arm back around him and tried to comfort him.

"Err, we don't know that, look the officer will do a quick scan for his implant."

The detective gave the other officer a nod and she pressed a few buttons on a vid com she had. After a few seconds the computer beeped.

"The computer is showing the last connection to be five days ago." She said and gave a knowing glance at the detective.

"I'm sure we will find him. Ok, I think that's all the questions for now, do you have somewhere to stay?"

Jep jumped in, "Yes, he will be with the school for the next four days and then he's going to be staying with a friend. I'll give you the details afterwards if that's ok."

"Yes, that will be fine. Ok you can go; I think we have everything we need for now. However, could we have a look around your apartment later if we can't locate him, it may give us a clue."

"Yes." said Hagger still sobbing a bit. "Can I go and get some more of my things?"

"Yes, but please do not touch any of your dad's, they could give us a clue into what has happened." Hagger nodded.

"I'll go with him and help get his stuff" said Datch.

"I think that might be a good idea." added Jep.

Datch and Hagger left the office and went back to their room.

When they came in Dapo and Tish were laying on his bed. Rosey was sitting in a chair looking out the window and Carina had made herself comfortable on Datch's bed.

"How did it go?"

"Well, they can't detect him anywhere." Datch said.

Hagger went and sat back down on his bed.

"Carina, I need you to come and give me a hand with the bike a minute,"

She got up and followed him out of the room. He stopped a few steps down the corridor and turned around.

"They think it's the spider, they didn't say it, but his implant went offline at the same time the power plant was broken into with nothing since. I think he must have walked into the spider somewhere."

"Bloody Jaxx, poor Hagger. What are we going to do?"

"I'm going to take Hagger to get some of his things from his apartment so if you can tell the others while I'm gone and tell them not to mention the spider when we get back."

"But then what?"

"We'll go for a walk down to the park near the space port. It always helps me when my head mixed up."

"Ok, and be careful." She gave him a kiss and a hug before they went back to the room.

Datch walked in and emptied his bag on his bed.

"Err, Carina any chance you could sort this out for me?"

"Yes, no problem, you go and look after Hagger." she said.

"Come on Hagger, I've got a bag."

They left the room and headed up the corridor in the direction of the bike.

Carina waited until they were gone and then told the others about what Datch had found out. They sat looking at each other with no one quite sure what to say. The mystery had seemed like a game until now but after this, it hit home hard. They were all feeling a bit frightened and also now wanted the thing dead.

Datch and Hagger arrived at Hagger's apartment. They got off the bike and went inside. The place was tidy but very small.

"You sure he's not been back?"

"No, he always makes a mess and then gets me to tidy it up."

"Oh, well let's get your stuff."

They went over to Hagger's bed and he opened the bottom. There was a selection of clothes and a small box. Hagger lifted it up very carefully.

"This is my mum's stuff." He said opening it.

Datch looked inside. There were some pictures and jewellery also a little locket with some of his mum's hair in it.

"Oh wow, this is so nice."

They looked at it for a few minutes with Hagger showing Datch the pictures of his mum before closing it and placing it carefully in the bottom of Datch's bag. They put Hagger's clothes carefully around it to protect it and then put various other bits on top making sure not to damaged anything. Hagger grabbed another bag and filled that up. Then picked up a picture of him with his mum and dad and put that in. Datch felt so sad for him. He was watching him go around picking up bits of his life. A life that would now change forever. Datch made up his mind to find the spider no matter what.

They had just about finished packing when there was a knock at the door. Hagger turned on the vid to see who it was. It was the detective from the school. Hagger opened the door.

"Yes," said Hagger.

"Oh, hello, sorry to disturb you but we want to have a look around."

"That's ok detective, we're just about finished getting his stuff." said Datch.

They went and got a couple more bits and then the bags were full.

"Do you need us to stay?"

"No, we can lock up. We just want a quick look through your dad's things in case it gives us any clues, do you know where your dad kept his documents?"

"Err, yes. I think he kept all his stuff in the cupboard over there, it will be locked though."

"That's fine, we can sort that out. Do you need a hand with anything?"

"No. We're ok but is it alright to come back later for more bits?"

"Yes, that's fine, we'll only be an hour."

"Ok, thank you sir." said Datch.

He helped Hagger out the door with the bags and down to the bike. After loading it up they headed back to the school.

Carina was just about finished sorting Datch's clothes out.

"Err, doesn't it bother you touching his underwear?" said Rosey.

"No, why? I've touched a lot more of him than that." Rosey looked at Tish and mouthed 'I told you.'

They watched while she finished off putting the things away.

"Can I ask something?" said Dapo.

"Yes." said Carina.

"How do we talk to Hagger?"

She thought about it a bit and then said,

"I think we need to try and keep his mind off it, but if he does start talking about it, make sure you listen."

"Oh, ok."

"Rosey, I know Hagger likes you so he might open up to you."

"Does it stand out that much, and yes I know, I'll be there for him." she said.

"He needs us more than ever now, so let's try and be the best friends we can."

They sat watching a vid when the door opened. Datch and Hagger came in followed by one of the security guards carrying the bags. He put them down next to Hagger's bed. Datch picked up the bag with Hagger's mum's box in and very carefully put it on the chest of drawers next to Hagger's bed. They said thank you to the security guard and he left them saying if they needed anything just call the desk. As he left, Jep came in.

"Hi folks. I know this maybe isn't the best time but it may be a good idea to call your folks so they know what's going on. I'll come and sit with each of you, so they know you're alright."

They all nodded.

"If you feel you need someone to talk to the school councillors are also on hand. Ok, come to my office one at a time and we'll get the calls out of the way. You can then do as you wish. You're all excused from all lectures today."

They took it in turns to go to the office and soon they were all back.

Datch turned to everyone.

"I don't know about the rest of you, but I think I need some fresh air."

"Yes, but where to?" asked Dapo.

"Well, I thought we could head up to the park and then go down past the market and end up in the Barbers Inn."

"That's ok with me," said Rosey getting up "What about you?" she said turning to Hagger.

"I guess so." he said.

"Come on then, let's go." she went and took his hand.

The others all got up and followed Rosey and Hagger as they went out the door and headed towards the main doors. As they passed the security desk Datch stopped and told them where they were going in case anyone needed to find them and to ask Jep if he could call Jim and give him prior warning they were coming.

They headed out into the sunshine and took a slow walk to the park, stopping at a drink's vendor on the way to get a bottle of Gruck each. They sat in the park watching the shuttles, interplanetary cargo ships also the odd passenger liner going to and from the space port. Hagger was very quiet even for him. Rosey gave him a hug which seemed to cheer him up a bit. They chatted but it was hard to think of things that wouldn't make Hagger think about his dad. After sitting for half an hour, they headed in the direction of the Barbers Inn via a couple of shops as Carina and Rosey thought a bit of retail therapy would be good.

The first shop was a clothes shop and rather cool one at that. They spent some time sorting out a new look for the gig and they made sure Hagger was very involved in the discussions hoping that it would help take his mind off things for a while.

As they now seemed to be doing quite a lot of rock songs it was decided to go with a biker type look. Leather jackets and jeans. Datch had the shop print 'The Pack' in big letters on the back with a picture of them on stage underneath. On the front they had their names in a rocky type font. This caused quite a bit of debate as to what was a rocky type font and they came up with a sort of gothic looking one. It was going to take a little while so they arranged to have them delivered to the Barbers Inn later.

The second shop was a cake shop. This was Tish's idea as cakes always made her feel happy. So, five minutes later they were walking up the street eating cookies and generally messing around. Even Hagger laughed and they took that as a good sign they were helping.

They finally got to the Barbers Inn. Jim had seen them coming up the street and got their normal drinks ready for them. They came in and Jim showed them to their table.

"Datch," he said, "could I have a quick word with you at the bar."

Datch followed Jim over to the bar. When they got there, Jim turned to Datch and in a quiet voice asked.

"Jep's called and told me what happened, how's he doing?"

"He's very upset, we're trying to take his mind off it as much as we can."

"Yes, that sounds like a good idea. If there is anything I can do, just let me know. Are you folks hungry? I can sort you out some food if you like."

"I'll ask them, I think we'll try a game or two of Solar Ball I'm hoping that helps."

"Yes, it might. I'll give the staff a heads up."

"We don't really know what to say to him?"

"No, it's always hard to know what to say, I'm over eight hundred and still don't know."

They both sighed.

"I'll go and find out what they want to eat."

"Here, take a menu. If you want something else just ask and I'll see if the chef can do it, Ok?"

"Ok, thanks Jim." he said and headed back to the table.

They sorted out the food and then got up to have a game of Solar Ball.

By the time the first game was over the food was ready. They had just about finished eating when Tank came in through the door. He came striding over and stood next to Hagger.

"Hey dude, so sorry to hear about your dad." he patted Hagger across the shoulders.

"Thank you." he said almost choking on a piece of fried hacks.

"I know you don't want to think about it at the moment but, if you like, you're welcome to come and stay with me for as long as you want. I've got a couple of spare rooms."

"Thank you again, I'll have a think about it." Tank sat down next to Datch which was unusual as Datch tended to have Carina on one side and Rosey on the other. However today Rosey was making a point of sitting next to Hagger.

They finished eating and decided another game of Solar Ball was in order. At least now the techies had been in and recalibrated the system so the balcony was included. This now meant new skills were needed to get to the nets at the top. The game was also able to put caves and cliffs in now that it had two floors to work with.

This playfield was new. It was full of floating rocks and also had strange creatures that kept hopping about the bar and in and out of the caves which the game had put in the alcoves. The nets to catch the balls were scattered around the bar and some were even up on the balcony. They all started to enjoy themselves. Hagger found it funny that he could whack the balls at the creatures and they would hit them with their heads sending them ricocheting across the bar. This was not as much fun for the bar staff who were now unable to gauge when balls were going to hit them.

They had a couple more games and then Jim called Datch over to the bar. His vid com was on and Jep was on the screen.

"Hi Jep."

"Hi Datch, how is Hagger?"

"He's ok, we've been playing a bit of Solar Ball, that's taking his mind off things I think, we're trying to stop him thinking about it."

"Ok, as long as you're looking after him."

"He's one of us, there's nothing I won't do to make sure he's ok."

Jep looked at Datch's image. He meant what he said. They were a family of sorts and if one was to get hurt or in trouble the others would be there for them.

"I know you would Datch, you're doing very well. Will you be back for dinner?"

"I think we'll stay here; it seems to be keeping him happy if that's ok?"

"Yes, I'm sure that will be fine given the circumstances, I'll talk to the principle myself, he was asking about him, oh and I'll see you in a couple of hours."

"Ok Jep, see you in bit." With that Jep disconnected.

Jim turned to Datch.

"You meant that didn't you, the bit about he's one of us."

"Yes, he's part of The Pack."

"You are a very good friend to them Datch, don't let anyone tell you any different. oh, and if you want some more food just let me know."

Datch nodded and walked back across the bar to join the others at the table. Jim watched him go and he realised that he was looking at not just a group of friends but a single entity made up of the people around that table. 'Wow, I wish I was part of that.' he thought to himself as he went back to sorting out the meat delivery.

They sat getting their breath back from the game and the subject changed to the rehearsal at the weekend. They were just discussing the third song when Datch's mum and dad walked through the door.

They got their drinks and headed over to the table.

"Hi everyone." said Tansya sitting down. There was a chorus of various hi or hellos and then carried on with the debate about the third song. It wasn't long after that Fred, Clax and Peebop came in shortly followed after by Jep and he had the principle with him. They got their drink and came over to the table.

"Hi all, this is Principle Hasgo."

"Hello all. Sorry to intrude, but I wanted to make sure Hagger was alright."

He sat down.

"I can see now he is in very good hands." He turned to face Hagger.

"Hagger, if there is anything that I can help you with my door is always open, it doesn't matter what time it is, if you want anything I'm here."

"Thank you." he said starting to look a bit unhappy again.

"Now please carry on with whatever you were talking about."

"It might be a good idea before we get going again if we sort things out, then we can try and have a good night." said Fred.

"Yes, that's a good idea." added Tank.

They all looked at Hagger waiting for him to say yes or no, he wasn't sure what to do so he shrugged his shoulders and said "I guess so."

The options were laid out on the table so to speak; Option 1 – Tank's apartment. He had a large Three-bedroom apartment on the ground floor with a private garden and communal pool. It was also quite close by just on the edge of the suburbs. Option 2 – Datch's house. Pool, fields and a bar or finally Option 3 – Fred's villa. It had two bedrooms and was located in the suburbs over to the west side of the city. They all showed him pictures apart from Datch's. He had already seen the ranch inside out.

"I like everyone's, but I think if its ok with everyone I'll go for Tanks. His place is not far from here and I like it in the city. It's all I've ever known. Thank you to all of you for being so kind now my dad's gone."

He was about to burst into tears again but Rosey put her arm around him and gave him a hug.

"Well, your dad could still be found." Said the Principle.

"We all know what's happened to him, it was the spider." said Hagger starting to cry again.

Rosey gave Hagger another hug and tried to calm him down. The principle looked at the others. They were all starring into their drinks.

"Err, is there something I should know?" he said.

"Jep, I think you need to go and have a talk with your friend over there." said Fred.

"Yes, I think he should know. Please if you could follow me, I'll bring you up to speed." He got up and the principle followed him over to one of the little booths at the side of the bar.

They sat down and Jep started to explain what has been going on. Back at the table. They managed to calm Hagger down again and get back to Tank's apartment.

"So, would you like the back bedroom looking out into the garden, I like to call it the green room or the front one that looks onto the street which is the blue room?"

"Which is the biggest?"

"Err, I think they are about the same but if I was you, I would take the green room, there's not so much noise at the back." said Tank after having to think for a moment.

"Do I need to get a bed?" asked Hagger, Tank laughed.

"No, both rooms have double beds already and have full independent climate control."

"A double bed? I've never been in a double bed. Wow." he thought about this "Is it ok if the others can see my room?"

"Yes, in fact why don't you folks help him move in?"

There was a general consensus of opinion that it was a good idea and they would be more than happy to help. Hagger was starting to cheer up again and even smiled when he found out about the bed.

"Can I have friends around?" Tank looked at him.

"Yes, but no wild parties ok." He said smiling at him. "Oh, and try to put your dirty washing in the basket in the corner of your room, I have a maid who comes in three times a week. She will take all your clothes and wash them for you and she'll clean your room too. She will be in the day after school so I will introduce you."

"Cool, I have a double bed and a maid. So, I don't have to clean?" Hagger was now grinning.

"No. but please pick your things up or the maid will get cross."

"Ok." Hagger was getting excited about this now.

Tank carried on explaining all about his new home.

Dechow took the opportunity to go over to see how Jep was getting on. Jep had just about finished explaining about the spider and how they knew about it.

"Why can't the security services just scan for it, surly they must have by now?" the principle was saying as Dechow arrived.

"Maybe you can answer this better Dechow?"

"Yes, the reason they can't find it is that it has a localised scattering field generator, this is very high tech and causes any sensors to show up a negative image, they could look for it but won't find a thing."

"So how do they find it?"

"They don't, the starship Carpaycus can see the scattering field from orbit and might be able to locate the generator itself."

"Oh, I see, so we can't do a thing at the moment?"

Jep looked at Dechow and then said.

"Well, Datch manged to get the story to the news team on Yul17."

"Oh, that was Datch, I thought it was from off world?" asked the principle.

"Datch got his brother to do it for him, he's a very resourceful youngster."

"Yes, I'm coming to realise that." He sighed, "So you have all known about it for a while then?"

"Yes, about ten weeks but we couldn't go to the security forces because they just wouldn't believe us. Don gets back with the Carpaycus soon and will be able to prove it to them I hope."

"Don? Oh, the captain, I see. When is he back?"

"The last I heard was that it will be at least another two or three weeks."

"So, what do we do?".

"Just tell everyone you know to stay in groups at night and not to go out alone. It's just eaten the two security guards and Hagger's dad so it's not going to be hungry for at least a week and a half maybe two if it lays low." Dechow sighed.

"Oh," the principle looked into his drink in the same way the others had.

"Well, you know the truth now." said Jep.

"Yes, but I wish I didn't. I'll head back to the school and call an assembly to make sure the students all know to stay in groups. Jep, can you keep me informed of any developments."

"I will sir."

He finished his drink, said his goodbyes to everyone at the other table and also reminded Hagger that if he needed anything just to ask. Then headed out of the door. He stopped to look up as he went out before hurrying off down the street.

As they sat down The Pack got up for a game of Solar Ball leaving the bikers, Jep and Datch's parents at the table.

"So," said Fred "He knows everything?"

"Yes." said Jep.

"Good, at least he'll try and ram things home with the students."

"Yes, but there's not much else we can do, we don't even know where it's lair is to warn people to stay away."

"It wouldn't make any difference. All of the city is it's hunting ground." said Dechow sighing again.

The game of Solar Ball carried on as they sat and talked. The occasional ball flew across the table. An explosion erupted from the top of Clax's head at one point making Tank duck. The noise in the bar was punctuated by the occasional scream from people who weren't watching what the game was doing.

"Well, it's good to see them getting Hagger's mind off things." said Tansya taking a sip from her drink just as a creature appeared right in front of her nose. Peebop was unfortunately sitting opposite and got sprayed as she spat out the drink.

"Yes, it is." He said wiping her drink of his face.

The creature on the other hand went running across the bar headbutting a ball onto the balcony before disappearing into the wall opposite.

Finally, the game finished and The Pack came back to the table. Dechow stood up.

"Datch, Come and help me with the drinks please."

Datch was about to say the staff will bring them over when he saw the look on his dad's face. He got up and followed him. They reached the bar and his dad sat down on one of the stools.

"What's up dad?"

"Me and your mum are worried about you, are you ok?"

Datch looked at his dad. It was normally his mum who asked things like this.

"Yes and No. Yes, I'm ok. I just need to make sure Hagger is, and No, I want that monster dead for what it's done."

Dechow put his head on one side as if weighing up what he had said then came to a conclusion.

"Well, it's only right that you should feel that. The beast has hurt one of your team, but promise me you won't do anything stupid?"

"I promise, I know it would kill me without a second look. I just want it gone."

"We all do Datch, we all do. But there are somethings we must leave to the professionals."

"Ok dad." Datch was looking a bit down.

"Look, you just keep looking for clues the way you have been. They will all help Don kill it when he gets here."

Datch nodded.

"I know it's hard. Just remember me and your mum are always here for you, if you want to talk just come and find us."

"Ok dad, it's just I'm meant to be looking after them and I feel I'm letting them down."

"I know Datch, I've lost people from teams I've been in, it happens. You couldn't have stopped it, so don't beat yourself up about it. Just look after your team, just remember what I said."

"Ok, I will"

"Anyway, it looks like you're being missed."

Datch was just about to turn to look when he felt a pair of hands slide around his waist and smelt Carina's perfume as she put her chin on his shoulder.

"And what are you two talking about?"

"Nothing much." he said turning to face her.

"Well, I had better go back, I'll be in trouble if I don't." Dechow left knowing that Datch was in good hands with Carina.

"So, lover, what's going on?" Datch gave her a kiss.

"My dad just wanted to make sure I was ok, that's all, they are worried about me."

Carina stopped and thought for a second.

"You are ok, aren't you?" she asked.

"Yes, how are you doing?"

"I'm ok, I have you." she said smiling.

He gave her another kiss and a little hug.

"Come on, let's head back over and make sure the others are." he said.

When they got back to the table Tish and Dapo had their arms around each other. It wasn't much of a surprise really. They had been getting quite friendly lately. He smiled across at Tish. She saw him look and smiled back at the same time giving Dapo a gentle squeeze.

They ordered some more food and were making quite a good job of keeping Hagger's mind off things. Jim came out with some complementary starters. The plates seemed to have lots of garlic bread and Hacks wings in barbeque sauce. (Some of Hagger's favourites). Needless to say, they didn't last long and even Hagger seemed to have got his appetite back. Once they had gone the main course came out. They had ordered seven very large pizza's and three buckets of fries. It took them twenty minutes to eat their way through it and after which they all sat there looking stuffed. What followed was a number of comments about being 'stuffed' and various parties rubbing their stomachs to emphasis the point. Dechow decided it was time for him and Tansya to head off home.

"Well, we would like to stay here but we should be getting back. We'll pay Jim for all the food on the way out, just try and have a good time."

"Yes, and if you need us, you know where we are." added Tansya.

Datch went and gave his mum a hug. She looked in his eyes, he had an unsure look which she hadn't seen since he was little.

"Go get 'um Datch." she whispered in his ear.

She gave him another hug and he gave her a big smile, then grinned.

Dechow and Tansya left and The Pack was alone.

"Ok," said Fred "I saw the look, what are you planning?" Datch frowned.

"I'm not sure yet, but we need to find out where the spider is hiding for when Don gets here, then he can kill the monster."

"So how do we do that?"

"Well, when I was on my bike the nav com was playing up as I flew over part of the city, I think it was the scattering field interfering with it."

"And where was that?"

"Well, it was sort of over that way and covered three city blocks"

"Oh, that's a large area, so how do we find out it's address without getting eaten."

"I don't know but I might have an idea, I need to think about it."

"Ok then, but don't do anything without telling us first, we're all in this together OK?"

"Ok." He said and then cuddled Carina which always made him feel better.

The conversation changed to discussing songs to learn and then the next heat of the summers Jet surfing race came on the vid above the bar. This time it was in the jungles on the other side of the planet. This looked like it was going to be a lot of fun as there was an unlimited supply of trees to hit to start with. Not to mention the hidden cliffs, ravines and sudden flocks of birds. The previous year's race in the jungle had seen half the racers die before it finished. This had meant the following race was a bit low on numbers as some of the racers had to wait for new bodies. This stage was along the Trimax Canyons which was a very fast and dangerous course.

The racers were going through their prefight checks before the start which gave everyone around the table a chance to have a toilet break and resupply their drinks. Also, two obligatory bowls turned up on the table containing nuts and fried snacks.

"So, shall we make this more fun?" asked Fred.

"Err, in what way?" Asked Datch.

"Well, normally we all root for the same rider. Why don't we write down the names and put them all in a bag, then we can all pull out a rider and that's the one you cheer on. What do you think?"

"That sounds fun." said Carina. The others all agreed

Jim was asked for a bag and some pieces of paper to write the names on. The names were then put in bag and then passed around the table for each person to pull a name out.

This was quite good fun. There was a number of groans as some of them found out who they were supporting, but as Fred pointed out anyone of them could win because of the nature of the course.

The race started and the leaders soon started to break away from the main group. They flew along the first ravine hugging the far side. They came to the first tight turn, two of the leading group over did it and smashed into a cliff face with big explosions. The rest of the racers were hot on their tails. A flock of birds took off as the leaders flew past causing the racers behind to take evasive action. A number of them got hit but carried on going causing the racers behind them to go through a flurry of feathers. They pushed on through the jungle landscape with the table was cheering them on. Finally, they reached the first check point and stopped to refuel, the commercial breaks came on and everyone sat back in their seats.

"This is more fun." said Hagger who was quite pleased he had one of the leaders.

Tank was allowed to pick another racer as his was now part of the rock face after the first turn. They were just waiting for the race to come on again when the door opened and team Zorm walked in. They went and stood at the back near the bar. Datch spotted them, Zorm was looking at them so Datch got up and went over to them.

"Hi Datch." said Zorm.

"Hi, Zorm, what brings you to the bar?"

"We wanted to come and see if Hagger is ok. The principle just called and emergency assembly and told us about his dad."

"What did he say?"

"He said that Hagger's dad had been murdered by the killer and to be understanding during this difficult time for him. We've also been told only to go out in large groups and to stay together. It's horrible what's happened." Said Zorm.

"How is Hagger doing?" asked Japor.

"He's doing OK, we're trying to keep his mind off it."

"That's good, I think. How are the rest of you doing?" she said.

"It's upset us all, how did you know we were here?"

"Datch, your team is always here, it's where you live!"
Added Zorm with a smile.

Datch looked at him and thought to himself 'I suppose we
do.'

"Did you want to come over, we're watching the race?"
Datch asked.

"Are you sure? We only came in to make sure you were all
ok."

"Yes, I think it will be fine, I think Hagger would like to
know everyone is thinking about him." he turned to the
nearest barman.

"Please can you get these all a drink and put it on our tab."

The barman nodded and took everyone's order.

"Ok, come on." said Datch. Team Zorm followed him over
to the table.

"Hagger, I have some friends to see you."

There was a round of greetings and a lot of sorry to hear
about your dad and then the bag came out. After a couple of
minutes everyone had a racer and the rules were explained.
Basically, root for your racer not anyone else's. They had just
settled down again when the second stage was ready to start.

The next hour was spent watching and cheering the racers
on. Some of which exploded and some found themselves
sitting in a tree while their boards carried on without them or
even ended up having a bath in river after hitting a water fall.
When the race had finished Zorm turned to Datch.

"Well, we had better be heading back, it's getting dark and
the principle said he wanted us back before dark."

"You can stop with us if you like, then we can all walk back
together."

"I'm not sure security with be happy with that."

"Hmm. One second."

He opened his vid comm and pressed a few buttons. The main security desk at the school came on the viewer.

"Oh, hi Datch, how are you guys doing?" asked the security guard.

"We're ok thanks Tinsun. Is it ok if team Zorm stays out with us, we will all come back together so it will be a big group?"

The security guard turned to the supervisor and checked.

"Yes, that's not a problem, just make sure you all stay together on the way back."

"We will, thanks." With that the link closed.

"There you go, all sorted."

"You're on first name terms with the security?"

"Yes, of course." said Datch smiling.

They sat talking and then Solar Ball was on the cards again this time though only Hagger, Rosey, Japor and Dando got up to play. Datch sat with Carina. Zorm and Jen seemed to be getting on very well now as well.

"So, was it really the murderer that got his dad?" Asked Jen.

"Yes, it was, I just wish we could find it for the security forces so they could kill it." said Datch.

"Don't you mean he or she and isn't killing someone a bit harsh?" she said.

"No, it needs to die." said Carina.

"Why do you keep saying it?" said Zorm.

"Datch!" Fred stepped in "Be careful what you say."

"Ok, so what are you not telling me?" said Zorm.

"I've said too much as it is, sorry, but what I will say is that the news story about the arachnoid, watch it again." Zorm looked at him and Carina, their faces said it all.

Zorm realised that they knew a lot more than they were saying and a cold shiver ran down his spine. He was about to press the point when Jen stopped him.

"Let's change the subject, we never found out what your mums and dads do, I guess yours is something to do with the federation after that starship captain showed up at the end of last trimester?"

Datch went on to explain about his parents and then one by one everyone else around the table did the same. The conversation carried on and there were a few more games of Solar Ball.

They were sitting down after a rather hectic round of Solar Ball getting their breath back when Datch suddenly had a thought.

"Zorm, did you say your dad made force field generators?"

"Yes."

"Do you think he would know anything about scattering fields?"

"I don't know, why?"

"I've been doing some experiments at home and am trying to work out how to see through the field I've made and wondered if he had any ideas?"

"Well, I can ask him if you like,"

"Thanks, I'm really stuck."

Then after a few more games it was time to head back to bed. They left the bar and headed towards the school. The streets seemed to be a lot less busy now. People seemed to be heeding the warnings on the news channels and most of them were in groups. They took a steady walk back to the school. Datch wasn't worried tonight as the spider had eaten well and wouldn't be hunting for food for at least for a week. They arrived back at the school and everyone headed to their rooms except for Datch and Carina who did their normal vanishing act for half an hour. When Datch got back to his room Hagger was sitting on his bed.

"Are you ok?"

"No, I miss my dad." Datch went over and put his arm around him.

"I know, but you have us, we all feel for you and want to make sure you're ok." Hagger nodded. "We are The Pack and we stick together."

"I know, but it doesn't stop it hurting. I don't know what is going to happen to me. What if my mum's or dad's folks want me to live with them, I'm scared!"

"Hey, look you're old enough to make your own decisions and by the time they cut though all the red tape you will be able to just say No."

"What if Tank doesn't want me after a while?"

"Tanks not like that, He will have a place for you as long as you need it. So, don't worry about that."

"Are you sure?"

"Yes, now let's try and get some sleep? We missed the lectures today but I don't think they will let us do it again tomorrow."

"Ok, I'll try."

With that Datch got himself undressed before getting in bed. Hagger laid down and after a few sniffles fell asleep. As soon as Datch knew Hagger was asleep he went off to sleep himself.

The next morning, he was woken up at seven thirty by Hagger who was sitting looking out the window. He was just picking up a book he had dropped on the floor. Datch got up and went over to him.

"Are you alright?" he asked.

"Sort of, I couldn't sleep, I just kept thinking about my dad."

"Do you like pancakes?"

"Err, yes, why?"

"Well, why don't we get ready and go out for a walk, I know a great pancake café just down the road?"

"Ok," he said with a sigh.

They got dressed and left Dapo snoring in his bed. Datch wrote a note saying 'gone for pancakes. The security guards were surprised to see them as students didn't normally get up before nine. They watched as Hagger and Datch walked off up the street. They were chatting about anything and everything. It was quite peaceful at that time in the morning. Some of the cafés were open but most people hadn't made it out yet so the streets weren't that busy. Also, most people worked from home and only the city workers tended to go to offices or supply companies. They also started at four in the morning when it was cooler and finished at lunchtime.

They turned the corner and just down the road was a shop with chairs outside, 'Flambo's Pastries palace' it said above the door. They went in. The shop had a very big selection of freshly made pastries with various fillings and different styles, also a selection of cakes with fresh cream and fruit on the top but more to the point pancakes! They selected some chocolate pancakes and got a cup of coffee each to go with them before going outside to sit in the sun.

"This is nice. How did you find this place?"

"Oh, I didn't, Carina did, we have been here a few times for breakfast and I like sitting here watching the people go by."

"It is kind of cool." said Hagger looking about.

"Yes, we sometimes have sat for an hour or more just watching people go by and chatting."

"I must have been past here a hundred times but never stopped." Hagger said stuffing a pancake into his mouth.

"Why not?"

"I suppose I never had any spare credits or my dad told me to come straight home."

"I know you're, missing your dad but trust me things will come right."

"I know, part of me is sort of relived that he's gone."

"Why?"

"Well, he never did anything with me. My mum used to take me out to the parks and swimming, dad didn't. He just made me clean the apartment and make sure he wouldn't have to do anything. Credits were also short as he used to spend them all at the casino."

"I sort of guessed that he didn't treat you very well, all the times I took you home, you sort of trudged into your apartment."

"Yes, but I still miss him."

"I know, we'll get the monster for you, I promise."

"You have a plan, don't you?"

"Err, well sort of."

"Sort of?"

"Look I'll tell you, but you must promise not to tell anyone, I don't want anyone else involved in case it goes wrong."

"If it's dangerous we all should know."

"No, I'll tell you, but you must keep it to yourself. Now promise."

"Ok, I promise." Datch pulled his chair closer.

They talked and talked then at the end Hagger said,

"That's a lot of ifs and buts."

"I know, that's why this is between you and me ok?"

"Ok."

They sat back in their chairs and watched as the people went by. Hagger talked some more about his dad and how he was treated. Datch felt very sorry for him. He spotted Carina in the distance, Rosey and Tish walking down the road.

"I thought you might be here." said Carina walking up "why didn't you call for us?"

"Err, it was seven thirty in the morning, I didn't think you would be up. Anyway, we left a note."

"Oh," she paused, "Ok I'll let you off then." with that she went in the shop with Tish. Rosey pulled a chair up next to Hagger.

"Did you leave Dapo at school?" asked Hagger.

"No, he's coming, Carina thought you would be here after the note, he was still putting his trousers on when we left." Hagger sniggered.

"What's up with you?"

"You saw Dapo in his underpants." He said smiling.

"Well yes, the ducks were quite funny." she smiled "anyway, how are you?"

"I'm doing ok now, Datch has made me feel a lot better."

"That's good, we're all worried about you, you know?"

"I know." at this point Carina came out the shop carrying a tray with more pancakes, pastries and four coffees.

"What are you two smiling about?" Carina asked seeing the look on both Hagger's and Rosey's face.

"The ducks." she grinned.

They pulled another table next to the one that Datch and Hagger were sitting at and all sat around it, at this point Dapo came trotting up the road.

"I've made it." he said getting to the table, "what did I miss?"

"Err, I'm not sure." said Tish patting the chair next to her.

He sat down still slightly out of breath.

"You know next time; can you get us all up or at least tell us where you're going. The note just said gone for pancakes." Tish said.

"We just needed a walk and decided pancakes were in order, that was all."

"Ok, Pancakes are good!"

The Move

After the lectures Tank called the school and asked if Hagger wanted to come and see his new room. He could bring some of his stuff as well if he wanted to. Then afterwards they could head to the Barbers for dinner. Hagger said that would be great. Datch and Carina took some of his bits on his bike and Tank turned up with his truck. They all helped put the rest of the bits in the back of the truck before getting in themselves. Tank set off with Datch and Carina following behind on the bike.

They flew over the Barbers Inn and out towards the suburbs. It only took a few minutes before Tank brought the truck in to land. The apartment was part of a two-story block. There were a number of them set in a circular pattern with a Pool in the middle. Each had their own parking area and private gardens. The upper story apartments had the private gardens on their roofs. The pool had a barbeque area and an automated drinks vender. They got out and waited for Datch and Carina to land.

"Ok follow me." Tank said heading towards one of the apartments.

He walked up to a light red door with a yellow flower painted on it. Tank opened the door and walked in.

"Welcome to your new home Hagger." he said.

There was a central corridor that ran from the front of the building to the back door with rooms spread out on either side.

"These two rooms are the front bedrooms; I use this one here as an extra salon for special customers but I can swap it around if you don't like the one at the back and this is my bedroom. It's best not to go in there until the maid has been in tomorrow."

Hagger looked inside the spare one; it was bigger than his entire apartment.

"And this is the Bathroom"

It had a large bath, walk-in shower, toilet and a walk-in body dryer. It was finished off in nice pastel-coloured tiles. They carried on to the next room.

"This is the kitchen." Announced Tank looking pleased with himself. The kitchen had an island in the middle and just about every piece of cooking equipment you could think of, it also had some sliding doors that led to the room next to it.

"Err, do you have to cook yourself?" asked Datch.

"No, the kitchen is fully automated, but sometimes I like to do it myself especially if I have guests, so I made sure I had everything." They moved down the corridor.

"And this is your room Hagger."

It was the same size as the one at the front, it had sliding doors that lead out into the large garden, on the inner wall was a large fitted wardrobe with a mirror and set of drawers. The bed was a king-sized double bed, it had a built-in light and on the opposite wall from the bed was a large vid.

Hagger's jaw dropped open,

"Really, this is all mine?" He stopped and stood in the doorway looking around.

"Yes, it's all yours if you want it?"

"Oh, yes please, Tank."

"Ok then, I just need you to come and register with the computer."

Hagger followed him over to a console in the corridor and stood in front of it while the computer scanned him.

"Ok, that's done, you're now officially living here, ok follow me and I'll show you the lounge, the outside living area and the garden."

"Oh wow," Hagger was grinning from ear to ear.

They walked into the lounge, it had a vid wall, three large sofa's, mini bar and two coffee tables, it also had a very plush carpet.

"We have to be careful of the carpet or Jarsa the maid will moan at us. I put muddy foot prints on it once and she didn't speak to me for a month."

"Ok, no muddy foot prints." repeated Hagger.

"And don't drop crisps, there is a hand-held vacuum in the little cupboard over there just in case."

"Right, got it."

They walked across the room and out through a set of sliding doors before emerging onto a large covered patio area with chairs, sofa's and a jacuzzi in the corner. Also, a barbeque with built in flat bread oven and off to the right was the back door which led into the corridor.

The garden had a long lawn which widened out as it went down to the fence at the bottom. It had an automated gardener to keep the grass in perfect condition and a wicker work fence running down both sides then across the bottom. It had five sun loungers just in front of the patio with a table and an umbrella. A reflective shield had been fitted to keep the garden private.

"This is so cool." Hagger said looking very excited.

"Well shall we get your stuff in?"

"Yes please." Hagger said.

The party moved back out to the truck and unloaded it into Hagger's new bedroom. It didn't take long and then they were on their way to the Barbers Inn for dinner.

They sat eating their food and Hagger was talking about his new room and how he was going to have a bath for the first time ever when Fred, Clax and Peebop came in.

"Hi dudes, I'm at Tank's now." Hagger was very bouncy; it was as if someone had just set the genie free from a bottle and now it was having a party in Hagger's head.

"I take it from that we'll need another sun lounger?" said Fred.

"Yes, I've just ordered one, it arrives tomorrow." replied Tank.

Hagger then proceeded to tell them all about his new room and Tank's apartment even though they had been there a hundred times or more. It was making him happy so they didn't mind.

It was decided after the third time Hagger announced the fact that he was having a bath that they would all help him move in when school finished for the week. Another call to their parents was in order to clear it so they could all help with Hagger's main move.

Then before Hagger could start going over it all for the fourth time Rosey suggested Solar Ball. They all breathed a sigh of relief and headed for the game.

The next day they woke up at around 9am. Hagger asked if they could go to the pancake shop again. Hagger got Dapo up while Datch went and got the girls organised. Thirty minutes later the six of them were sitting outside the pancake shop eating various pancakes and drinking coffee. Hagger seemed a bit happier and had certainly slept better.

"So, what's the plan today?" asked Rosey.

"I'm not sure yet, but we have a lesson on the northern tribes of the tri alpha star system and that is followed after lunch with one about high dinning in Gater three part of the Hatt-Gamma star system." said Dapo.

"I didn't mean at school."

"Oh."

"The racing is on again tonight, stage eight. It should be interesting, it's over the lava fields." Added Datch.

"Err, maybe we could rehearse some of the songs?" said Hagger.

"It would be good but where? We can't just do it at school or at the bar." Said Carina.

"Hmm, what about asking Jim if he knows anywhere?" added Rosey.

"Ok, I'll ask him tonight." said Datch.

"Datch look!" said Carina raising her voice and pointing up. Datch looked up.

There, flying just above the building was the black shuttle they had seen in the fields. It was staying very low and Datch suspected it was just below normal scanning height for the cities scanners as it was almost taking the tops off some of the buildings. It turned at the end of the street and started heading out in the direction of Carina's farm again.

"That was weird." said Tish.

"You're telling me, they shouldn't fly that low surely?" asked Dapo.

"Yes, I think it was trying to avoid being detected." added Datch.

"But why?" asked Tish.

"I don't know, but me and Carina saw it flying low near her farm a few weeks ago."

"They must be criminals or something." said Rosey.

"Yes, but very rich ones." said Hagger.

"Why rich?" asked Carina.

"Well, that's a custom ship, you can't buy them without a lot of credits."

They all turned to look at him.

"Err, I like watching vids about space ships, that's what they call a 'Black Shadow'. It can travel an interspace factor of sixteen and has a range of four hundred light years."

They were all just staring at him. After a pause Datch spoke.

"Err, anything else you might know?" he asked.

"Well, they are very manoeuvrable and normally used by people who don't want to be seen, mainly the rich and famous. That's why it's called the black shadow. They cost about forty million credits to buy new and are made to order only."

"Hagger, I'm very impressed." Datch said smiling at him, Hagger grinned.

Datch sat thinking, things still didn't add up.

"What's the matter Datch?" asked Carina seeing the look on his face.

"I thought for a moment it might have something to do with the bots, but it can't."

"Why?"

"Well, I thought the spider was stealing the bots to take off world for some reason. But that ship has confused me. If that ship is involved, why would someone like that want to steal bots with that sort of money when they could just buy them?"

"Oh, I see what you mean." They sat looking at their drinks.

They finished their breakfast and headed back to the school still thinking about the ship.

Across the city the arachnoid stirred in its nest. It didn't like being woken up and just wanted to sleep until it was time for the next meal. There was just too much noise in the city and also lots of annoying humans around. It looked outside of its nest and checked the warehouse for any light snacks that may have wondered in before curling back up to sleep. It was going to be another week before it needed food again.

The next morning the Pack had breakfast at the school before going to attend the normal lectures. After that it was gig time and they headed down to the Barbers Inn using the back door to get in. They sat at the back of the screens having a drink before the first set.

"So, I asked Jim about somewhere in the city to rehearse last night, he said there is a storeroom at the back of the shop next door but it doesn't have air con." said Datch.

"Well, that might be a bit warm." Commented Fred.

"I could sort out the front bedroom if Hagger gives me a hand, we might have to keep the sound level down a bit but it might work." said Tank.

"I'll help, no worries." said a very enthusiastic Hagger who was now thinking he could show off his new house.

They were just about to start planning the room out when Datch's Vid com beeped, it was Zorm.

"Hi Zorm, what's up?"

"Err, I told to my dad about what you were doing and he gave me some info, he's also given me a light thing that might help, I missed you at school so we came down to the Barbers Inn, but there's a band on and we can't get in." Datch frowned and looked at Carina, she nodded.

"Ok, what are you wearing?"

"Err, my dark blue shirt and purple shorts, why?"

"Just wait there, someone will let you in. They will show you to a table stay there until you are brought to us, ok."

"What do you mean?"

"Just do what I say, you will see. Oh, and this stays in the Barbers Inn! Ok wait for them." With that Datch disconnected the call and waved at Jim.

Zorm and his team were standing outside in a very large group of people. They were a little confused to say the least when Zorm felt a very large hand on his shoulder. He turned around to face someone who was about a metre taller, twice as wide and none of it was fat.

"Excuse me, are you Zorm?"

"Err, yes?" he said in a squeaky voice.

"I've been asked to escort you and your friends inside. Please follow me." Zorm breathed out a very large sigh of relief.

They followed the bouncer to a side door and were taken in past the bar and over to a table near the stage.

"Err, where is Datch?" he asked.

"You will be seeing him shortly sir." replied the bouncer before taking up position in front of the stage.

"Well, the bands called 'THE PACK' I think." said Jen.

"How do you know that?" asked Zorm.

"That!" she said pointing at the stage.

Across the back of the stage was a large hologram spelling out 'THE PACK' in one-metre-high flaming green letters.

"It looks good anyway." said Japor.

They looked around; the place was getting really packed.

"I hope Datch gets here soon or there won't be anywhere for them to sit." Said Zorm.

"I'm not sure this is a sitting down sort of band."

"I thought Datch was already in here?" said Dando.

"Yes, he sounded like he was." replied Zorm.

The bar lighting started to dim and the manager went on to the stage.

"Ladies and Gentlemen welcome to the Barbers Inn. I know you're going to enjoy tonight's entertainment. Please put your hands together and welcome The Pack!"

There was huge applause, cheering and whistling. He jumped off the stage and ran for cover behind the bar.

Holographic lightening flashed all around the stage and the green flames expanded out across the bar as the music started. Then through the smoke and lightening The Pack appeared.

"Err, I just found Datch and the rest of them." said Jen.

"Where?" said Zorm looking at the crowd.

It took a few seconds before it sank in.

"Team Datch is The Pack! They have the bikers up there as well."

"That's not all," added Dando, "Professor Doji is there."

They sat looking in amazement as their fellow classmates performed on stage. The fourth song started and Jen grabbed Gardun and dragged him onto the dance floor. It wasn't long before the rest of team Zorm were dancing. Datch put a shout out for them and everyone cheered. The first set ended and Team Zorm went back to the table.

"Wow, that was different." said Zorm as they sat down.

"No wonder they didn't want anyone to know at school." Said Jen.

"The professor as well." Added Japor.

"I can't believe it." said Dando.

A shadow came over the table.

"Err excuse me sir."

It was the bouncer. Zorm turned around and had to look a long way up before finding his face.

"I've been asked to escort you to The Pack."

"Oh cool."

"Please follow me and mind your step, the floor is a bit slippery."

They got up and followed the bouncer across the stage and down the side passage past two more bouncers. They walk through a sliding screen and there was The Pack lounging around a large table with towels around their necks.

Datch looked up as they came in.

"Hi folks." He said casually.

"Wow, Datch now I know why you always disappear early on Patterday day. You're fantastic."

"Amazing." Said Jen.

"So cool." added Dando.

"You liked us then?" said Carina grinning.

They stopped trying to stumble for words and just nodded a lot. This had the effect of making them look like their heads were on springs which were wobbling about in unison just like the little characters that certain races put in their vehicles on the parcel shelve.

"Ok." said Datch, "We only have fifteen minutes but I wanted to say hi. If you can wait till after the gig, we'll sort security out for you. Then you can go back to school with us and we can talk."

"Err, yes, no problem."

There was another round of nodding much to the amusement of Clax, who nearly sprayed his beer over the table.

"Ok, now the man behind you will take you back to your table and Jim has been told to get you a couple rounds of drinks in on me."

"Oh cool, thanks." said Zorm.

With that they were shown back out to their table.

"Why did they come down anyway?" asked Carina.

"I asked Zorm about scattering fields. His dad makes force field generators and I thought it may help Don find the spider if we had a better fix on its position."

"Can't we just tell the security services where it is?" asked Rosey.

"No, my dad said if they went in to get it. It wouldn't need to eat for a couple of months. Don knows what they need to do to kill it. The security services just don't have the fire power."

"So, what are you planning?" Asked Tish.

"Well, if Zorm's dad comes through and I can make a sensor to cut through the scattering field, I'll fly over the area on my bike scanning for its nest, then when Don comes, I'll be able to tell him where it is."

"Is that all?" asked Carina who was slightly suspicious of the whole just find the nest bit.

"Yes, should be quite simple." He smiled instead of grinning as he thought it was safer.

"Anyway, that can wait till later, let's get our heads back into gig mode." he said and changed the conversation to the song list.

The second set was the normal run with Tank dodging underwear, the biker's song and the guitar song. It went down to screams and cheers. The crowd were shouting for encores and there at the front was Team Zorm shouting and screaming with the rest of them.

They had one song that they had been working on and thought they would give it a go, it was called 'Wild Wind' They started singing and the crowd went wild. By the time the song finished the bouncers were having trouble holding them back. They left the stage and waited a few minutes until it calmed down before going back out to sign the photos and T-shirts.

Afterwards they went back stage and waited for the crowds to thin out a bit more before heading out to join team Zorm.

They sat down and after another round of team Zorm telling them how good they were and how much they had enjoyed it, they started talk about normal things.

"So, what did your dad say?" asked Datch.

"He said you need a modulating scanner that can be set to block certain frequencies. He has a really old one kicking about somewhere if you want it?"

"That would be cool."

"Err, he also said that he'd be more than happy to demonstrate it if you wanted to come around. He sounded really interested in what you were doing."

Datch had to think fast, he couldn't remember what he had said. 'Ah that was it, an energy sphere with a changing frequency' he breathed a sigh of relief. He was going to have to find out about them, hmm.

"Yes, that would be great maybe next weekend, Hadday would be good?"

"Ok, I'll ask him and call you on your vid com."

"Cool, Thanks."

They carried on chatting and soon it was time to head back to school. On the way back Team Zorm stayed close together. However, The Pack was a bit more relaxed. They knew it had fed and wouldn't be about tonight. It was going to be another week before it was out hunting. It was hard trying not to tell people, but it was necessary. As they got back to school, they made team Zorm promise not to say anything about the gig and in return invited them down the following week.

The next morning everyone was up early ish. By nine thirty they were sitting in the restaurant having breakfast and discussing the big move. Hagger was very excited which was slightly strange with his dad being eaten by the spider less than a week ago but Datch thought that his excitement was down to his dad treating him badly and this was going to be a fresh start for him, Carina thought the same. They sat and sorted out who was doing what. Datch was going to take Hagger to his dad's apartment and start putting stuff into boxes while the rest of them waited for Tank. Tank would pick them up with their school bags and drop the bags off at Tank's, then they would all meet up at Hagger's to help with The Packing. They finished their breakfast and headed back to their rooms to collect their things ready for Tank's arrival. It didn't take them long and soon they were all outside waiting for Tank.

Tank's truck appeared down the street and flew into the parking area touching down just in front of them. The school bags and other bits were put in the back and off they went. Datch and Hagger got on Datch's bike and they headed to the apartment along with an assortment of flat boxes tied to luggage rack on the back.

They got to Hagger's and started sorting things out and packing them into the boxes. Hagger didn't have that much but Datch insisted on looking around in case there was stuff that he didn't know about. Some of Hagger's stuff had already been moved two days before but Datch wanted to make sure he didn't leave anything and was looking through some drawers when he found a small back box with writing on it. He wasn't sure what it was so asked his implant, 'The device is a memory cube, it is used to store memories which can be replayed and displayed on vid screens.' Datch picked the cube up to have a closer look. It had a woman's name on a tag stuck to the front, well Datch thought it was the front anyway.

"Err, who is Catiarna?" he asked.

"That's my mum why?" Datch went over to him.

"Look, I found this." He showed him the cube.

He took it and put it in a box with some other bits. Datch went back to looking for bits to pack. In the drawer where he found the first cube there tucked at the back was a second one. It was smaller than the first and had some markings that he didn't understand. He asked his implant again, 'The memory cube is encrypted and has markings that are unknown to the universal database.' Hmm that's strange Datch thought to himself.

"Hagger, did your mum or dad ever go off world?"

"Only my dad and that was just up to the space station one time, why?"

"I found this cube is it yours?"

"No. must be my dad's. You can have it if you want."

"Thanks." he put the cube into his pocket. He wanted to find out what it was and thought the bikers may know how to find out. He carried on helping Hagger to pack up what was left of his life. Datch felt very sorry for him. He found some more pictures of Hagger's mum and gave them to him. He smiled and that made Datch feel a little better.

The door pinged and Hagger said "Enter". The door opened and Carina walked in followed by the rest of the gang. By the time they had all got in there wasn't much room left.

"Wow this is small." said Dapo who was last in.

"What do you want us to do?"

"Well, you can take all the stuff off the cupboards and empty out the kitchen area."

"Where's the kitchen?" asked Tish.

"You're standing in it." said Datch.

"Oh, I see." she said realising that the shelf in front of her had a mister cooker on it and also a couple of empty plates.

They set about putting the rest of the stuff in boxes. There wasn't that much to pack and after an hour they had virtually finished it all. Then followed a steady stream of people with boxes going to Tank's truck and soon the apartment was empty. The only bits left were some bags with his dad's clothes in and some other bits of his dads that Hagger didn't want, like casino passes, work related things and stuff like that.

The others went and got in the truck while Hagger and Datch had a check around one last time before closing the door. Hagger didn't want to come back ever again. He closed the door and turned to Datch. He had a tear in his eye and Datch gave him a hug.

"Come on let's go and start your new life." he said.

Hagger wiped the tear away and gave a weak smile, they turned and headed to the bike.

Hagger was very quiet on the trip to Tanks. They arrived and were greeted by a steady stream of people going into the place with boxes. They were putting them into the spare room for now so Hagger could sort them out as he wanted. Rosey took him through to his room at the back and Tish followed them in. The two girls set about helping Hagger organise the room which was easy considering it was bigger than his entire apartment. The rest of The Pack set about unpacking boxes and carrying the contents through to the girls who asked Hagger where he wanted them. At one-point Dapo came through with an empty box on his head saying 'Let me out it's dark in here!' which made everyone laugh. While they got Hagger sorted Tank went off to the shop.

Two hours later they were all sitting in the garden having a drink and enjoying the sun.

"While I was at the store, I picked up some barbeque bits so if you want to stay for dinner, you can?" asked Tank.

"Yes, please stay." said Hagger who was now relaxing in a sun lounger.

After a bit of a conversation and a number of calls to their parents, Tank lit the barbeque. Also, the bikers were summoned and told to bring spare chairs and more beer. Carina, Tish and Dapo offered to help prepare the food and Tank took them into the kitchen and told them where everything was before heading back outside to start cooking the meat.

Rosey and Hagger were deep in conversation so Datch went to see if he could do anything to help inside.

The kitchen was a hive of activity when he walked through the door. He headed over to help Carina with the salad.

"What's Hagger doing?" she asked.

"Err, I'm not quite sure, he's either chatting up Rosey or being chatted up by her, I can't tell."

"I thought they would pair up at some point, she's had a soft spot for him for quite a while now."

"What was that?" asked Tish.

"Hagger and Rosey, look like they are going to be a couple."

"Cool, that means we'll be able to have a six some." said Dapo. Tish gave him a look of did you have to.

"Yes, it will be good, we can go out together for drinks!" Datch said with a certain amount of sarcasm in his voice. Dapo went quiet.

"Ok, now that it's out in the open, we can stop pretending." said Tish and then went back to the bread rolls she was sorting out.

Datch went to take a bowl of tomatoes outside and stopped in the doorway. Rosey and Hagger were in the middle of a kiss. He coughed and walked out.

"Err, I take it from that kiss that you're going out with each other?"

Hagger went red and even Rosey went pink.

"Sort of, we're just going to see how it goes." she said.

"Well, just for your information Tish and Dapo are also seeing each other and so as Dapo just put it, we now have a six some." added Datch.

"And what does a six some mean?" asked Hagger.

"Apparently it means the six of us can go out dinking together." Datch now had a slight frown.

"But we do that anyway." said Rosey.

"Yes, I know, I just pointed that out to Dapo." he said smiling again.

The kitchen staff came out with a number of bowls and plates. Tank steered them over to a flat metal table attached to the wall with a clear removable lid on. It was also cold and had cooling pipes running underneath it. They laid the food out and went back to their chairs to wait.

The door beeped. Hagger got up and went to let the bikers in as Tank was fighting a Jaxx steak. Clax had brought his pickup. Jep and Clax grabbed the chairs from the back and followed Peebop and Fred inside. They had brought an array of supplies which included Five bottles of alcohol-free wine, alcohol-free beer, normal beer and a bottle of something that Jep liked.

Fred came walking out into the garden.

"So, where's the party at dudes and dudets?" he said.

Tank turned to Hagger.

"Hagger, this is sort of your house warming party so go put some sounds on?"

Hagger had a blank look on his face.

"Just go to the panel in the hall tell it what you want on and to pipe it into the garden."

"Oh cool, come on Rosey you can help me choose." Hagger got up and headed off into the house with Rosey in tow.

"Err, did we miss something?" Fred said watching them disappear through the door.

"Hagger and Rosey are seeing each other on apparently a trial basis." said Carina.

"Oh, good for them." said Clax opening a beer.

The music started to play and it didn't take long before everyone was eating and drinking. Hagger was settling in well, he'd already taken Rosey to show her his mum's things and was looking very relaxed.

Datch fished out the small black cube from his pocket.

"Guys, we found this in Hagger's apartment and I wondered if anyone knew how to find out what was on it?"

"Let me have a look, I might be able to help you." said Clax who had spotted the cube.

Datch handed it to him.

"Wow, I haven't seen one of these for years, everyone uses their core storage these days, unless it's something they don't want people to have access to." He turned it over in his hands.

"Do you know anything about it?"

"Well, my implant told me it couldn't understand the markings." Datch said.

"What? The only markings not in the database are either very old or from an arachnoid star system, that's a bit of a coincidence."

"I would say so." said Fred suddenly taking a lot of interest.

"I wonder what's on it and why Hagger's dad had it?" added Clax.

"I don't know but I want to find out?" said Datch.

"I might be able to decrypt it; I have a decoder somewhere in the shop."

"You have a what in your shop?" said Fred.

"I got it off a trader friend of mine, they are sort of collectors' items now."

"Oh, will it still work?" asked Datch.

"Yes, I think so, it depends on the age of the cube. They stopped making them about eight hundred years ago, around the time the implants had the transmission upgrade." explained Clax.

"What upgrade?" said Carina joining in.

"The transmission upgrade, it allowed you to send your memories to a vid or any other compatible item."

"So, this must be about eight hundred years old at least?" asked Hagger.

"Yes, but the decryptor might not work, it's nearly a thousand years old."

"But it's worth a try anyway?" Said Tank.

"Yes, I'll have to dig it out, I was going to sell it at an antiques auction in the summer."

Datch gave him the cube.

"Here, you might as well look after it."

They carried on talking in to the evening and finally it was time to head home. Carina got on Datch's bike for a lift. Tank gave Tish, Rosey and Dapo a ride home in the truck while Hagger stayed with the rest chilling in the garden before going and having a very long bath with lots of bubbles.

Datch headed home via the city. He flew close to the static on his scanner but there was nothing much down there. One or two old warehouses and some industrial units. 'It must be there somewhere' he thought to himself and turned the bike for home. If he could just get a recording of it then the security services would have to call in the Inter-planetary space federation to kill it.

He got home and his mum came running out to him and gave him a very big hug.

"How are you doing?" she said and looked into his eyes

"I'm doing ok now; Hagger's got a new home and we just had a chilled-out party at Tank's place."

"Oh, I see and what do you have planned for the weekend, Carina's by any chance?"

"Yes, I've got to see Zorm on Hadday and then I'm going to Carina's from there."

"Does that mean we have you for two whole days?"

"Err, yes."

He gave his mum another hug and then went and put his dirty clothes in the washing machine.

"I'll say this much, Carina's getting you house trained." she said with a smile.

Datch headed upstairs to get changed. It was still very hot outside and he wanted a dip in the pool.

The next two days flew by and then it was time to go to Zorm's house and then two days at Carina's. If he carried on like this, he was going to need a bigger bike, either that or his own luggage drone. He put his bits together for school and closed the bag before heading down stairs to his bike.

Zorm's house was in a very up market area of the city. It had a small pool in the garden also a large sun terrace and barbeque area. The house itself was a large five-bedroom villa and had two large double garages.

Datch landed in the drive and got off the bike then pressed the doorbell. The door opened and there was Zorm.

"Hi Datch, Come on in."

He was taken through to the main room where Zorm's mum was sitting.

"Mum, this is Datch."

"Hi Datch, and welcome to our home."

"Thank you."

"We're so sorry to hear about your friend's dad, how is he doing?"

"Err, well, when I left him yesterday, he was sitting in the garden with the Barbers Angels having a drink. So yes, he's doing OK."

"The who?"

"The Barbers Angels, they are a very nice bunch of bikers who go to the Barbers Inn."

"Oh, well please send our condolences to him." she said with a puzzled look on her face.

"Thanks, I will."

"Zorm, why don't you take Datch to your dad's lair." Datch followed Zorm out towards one of the double garages.

"Your dad has a lair?" he said when they got outside.

"That's what mum calls it; he calls it his playroom." He opened the door and walked in.

There in the middle of the room was a large glowing ball of plasma surrounded by a forcefield. There was a bang from something on the bench near the window and the forcefield and plasma vanished.

"Dam, bloody thing..." muttered a man who was now looking at the smoking remains of the energy converter.

Zorm cleared his throat and the man turned around.

"Oh, Hi Zorm" he looked at Datch.

"Ah, you must be Datch." He came over.

"I'm very pleased to meet you sir." said Datch.

"Like wise young Datch. Welcome to my laboratory. Zorm has told me a lot about you." Datch looked at Zorm who smiled and nodded.

"So, you're doing an experiment with an energy sphere which has changing frequencies?"

"Yes, my dad has helped me set it up using a plasma generator, but I can't measure the central core because of the scattering field it produces. Zorm said you could help?"

"Yes, I have an old frequency canceller somewhere. It will detect the signals being given off and then you feed its output into your scanner."

"Oh, I see, so I would plug it in the calibration port?"

Datch's implant was doing overtime as he was trying to record everything and extract information from the database at the same time.

"Yes, the calibration input. Then it will be able adjust itself for the scattering effect."

"I see, cool."

"You don't happen to know anything about energy converters, do you?"

"Err, not really. My dad might and I know someone that does, but he's off world at the moment."

"Would you like a hand anyway?"

"That would be great. You can start by fetching me the quantum signal amplifier over there on the bench."

"Yes sir." Said Datch heading over to the opposite side of the room.

The next two hours were spent helping Zorm's dad and Datch getting a crash course in quantum force field design. Then, when they had got the experiment working again and managed to stabilise the field, Zorm's dad gave Datch the frequency canceller. It was a small box with a touch screen on the top and it had a small dish on the front and a fibre optic link to connect it to the scanner. Datch put it in his rucksack.

"Thank you for all your help, Datch."

"I've enjoyed it sir."

"Well, if you ever want to pop around just call Zorm and you will be more than welcome."

"Thank you, I'll ask my friend about the energy converter if I see him."

"That would be great, I'll message you with the unit details, oh and if you have any trouble with the frequency canceller just give me a call."

"Thank you again."

"No Problem, see you soon."

With that Datch left saying good bye to Zorm and his mum on the way out before heading off to Carina's.

When Datch arrived at Carina's she came running out and gave him a big hug and a kiss.

"I've missed you so much." she said holding him tight.

"I've missed you too." He said giving her a squeeze.

He wanted to talk about what happened to Hagger's dad and how much it had upset him but he hadn't had the chance to get Carina alone. He didn't quite know why, but he knew she would listen to every word. After a few minutes of hugging and squeezing Datch grabbed his bag and they took it to his room before heading back outside.

"Are you ok?" she asked.

"Err, sort of can we go for a walk?"

"Yes, sure." she could tell something was bothering him.

She told her mum they were heading off down the track and would be back later. They left the farm yard and started walking down towards the woods.

"So, what's up?" she asked.

"It's the whole thing with Hagger and his dad. I feel if I had done something sooner, he might still be alive."

"No Datch. you couldn't have done any more than you did. You can't blame yourself."

"But Hagger is part of The Pack and I'm meant to be looking after you all."

She looked at him and smiled.

"We all know how much you care about us. That's one of the reasons I love you so much, if you didn't you wouldn't be Datch. Now listen to me, I'm here for you, do you understand?" Datch nodded.

She stopped and gave him another hug. Datch just started to cry and melted into her arms. They must have stood there for ten minutes or more before Datch pulled himself together.

"I'm sorry." He said blowing his nose in a tissue that Carina happened to have in her pocket.

"It's ok Datch, you don't have to be sorry, just let it all out."

"I love you." he said giving her another hug.

They walked down the path telling each other how they felt. Datch told her how he wanted it dead and how he was planning to locate the spider so Don could kill it when he got back. He didn't hold anything back. She listened and told him how important he was to her and how much she needed him; they both let their feelings out and cleared their heads.

After they let it all out, they started to walk back towards the farm. They both were feeling a lot better. It was like a weight had been lifted off their shoulders.

By the time they got back to the farm house they were both laughing and smiling.

"Well look at you two." said Carina's mum coming out of the backdoor.

"What?" said Carina.

"Well, you were down in the dumps for the past two days and didn't say much at all. But now, a bit of Datch tonic and you're laughing again."

"I love him." she said and gave Datch a hug. He went a bit red.

"I can see that. Well, Datch looks like you're here to stay. Dinner will be ready in about thirty minutes."

She smiled and went back in after shouting thirty minutes very loudly at the barn. Datch and Carina went into the garden and talked some more until dinner time.

The Interview

Datch and Carina arrived at school and headed off to their rooms. When Datch walked in Hagger was showing off a new T-shirt and shorts he had got along with a cool cap. Tank had helped him go through his clothes and decided that he needed a new wardrobe. So, they had been shopping and Hagger was very happy with his new attire.

The only other time anyone had taken him shopping was when he went with The Pack. Carina said retail therapy always helps and it seemed to have done wonders for Hagger. Tank and Hagger had been busy over the last four days and the spare room had been converted to a rehearsal studio. It had also been fitted with a noise cancelling system so they could make as much noise as they wanted without annoying the neighbours.

"So, how do you feel about tomorrow night at Tank's?" Hagger asked quite excited about everyone coming around.

"It's good for me." replied Dapo.

"It's ok with me too, but we had better ask the girls?" said Datch.

"Oh, Rosey is ok, I asked her yesterday when she came around."

"She came around?" said Dapo.

"Yes, and the day before. We went swimming in the communal pool, it's got an automated bar that serves Gruck's and some really cool sun loungers."

"You don't hang about do you?" said Datch smiling.

"Err, I don't know what you mean?" said Hagger missing the point completely.

"It doesn't matter, I'll explain it one day." he said.

"So, did you see Zorm?" asked Dapo.

"Yes. His dad is really cool and very helpful, I have the frequency canceller and I know how to attach it to my bike's scanner. I should be able to track it to a building. I think if I hook it to the vid com, I might even be able to record it."

"What's the point of that?" said Hagger.

"I think it will give Don some reconnaissance information."

"You're not going inside though, are you?" asked Dapo.

"No, just the outside, they are mostly small buildings there anyway."

"So, when are you going to do it?"

"Err, next week just before we head home, Don comes into orbit the day after, I think he will need fresh information."

"You do realise, that's the weekend the new power plant opens, don't you?" said Dapo.

"Yes, the security services will be working overtime." added Hagger.

"Well, I'm sure they will leave me alone then."

They both looked at Datch and had a 'really!' expression on their faces.

"Ok, ok, I'll be very careful."

"Good, and you had better stay in touch all the time."

"Ok, I will. Anyway, we had better ask Carina and Tish about tomorrow night." Datch said changing the subject.

They left the room and headed up the corridor towards the girl's room.

The following night was rehearsal night. Tank and Hagger had done a pretty good job of the rehearsal studio. They had made a stage and set it out like the Barbers Inn. The room had a PA which they had setup to sound like the bar and there was a large vid screen on the opposite wall so they could see what they looked like when singing.

They took their positions and started the first song; it sounded a lot better than the last time. Everyone had been practicing at home and in fact, it did sound rather good. They tried the other songs and then played them back on the vid screen. They watched the playback and were very impressed. It was the first time they had seen themselves perform.

"I'd pay to see that." said Tank.

"Yes, it wasn't half bad." added Jep.

"I'll go with that; we just need a little more dancing in it I think." said Dapo.

"Yes, maybe if Jep, Tank, Peebop and Fred do a sort of dance thing like this." said Rosey.

They watched as she demonstrated a sort hip swaying dance.

"Ok, so like this?" said Fred trying to copy her.

"Yes, but a bit more of this." she moved her hips and Fred copied alone with the others.

"Ok, let's go through them again and see what we get." said Datch.

They went through the songs again and again until they were happy. Each time watching the vid and trying to criticise each other. That was Datch's idea, if anyone didn't like something they had to say so. That way they would be almost perfect. Finally, they all sat out in the garden talking and having a drink. It had been a long night but they were all happy with what they had done.

Datch sat quietly thinking.

"What's up Datch?" asked Tish noticing him sitting there.

"I think we should do this again next week and then perform the songs on stage." he said.

"What do you mean?" asked Carina.

"We have to get it right in the Barbers and we must not make any mistakes."

"I see what you mean." said Fred.

They carried on until it was time to head back to school, Tank gave them a lift back and it wasn't long before they were all asleep.

The rest of the school week was uneventful. Hagger had settled in at Tanks and seemed a lot happier than before, also more outgoing. Datch didn't know if it was Rosey or the fact he was now doing his own thing instead of being oppressed by his dad. Either way he seemed to be more himself now. Datch in a strange way was pleased for him and tried as much as he could to make sure he was ok.

The week's gig went as normal. The Barbers was full beyond capacity and apparently a reporter was in the crowd. he wanted to interview them but Fred said they were to exhausted and arranged for him to meet them the following week. That way they would have time to work out what to say. Datch arranged to have an extra rehearsal at his house over the weekend so they would be ready for the following week. He was trying to make certain that they got it right and also it was a good excuse to have everyone around.

The morning after the gig they got up and went out for breakfast at the cake shop. It was becoming an end of the school week thing before heading back home. Hagger had pushed for it as he had decided he liked pancakes for breakfast. They sat outside the shop eating,

"So, are you two going to be hanging out again this weekend?" asked Carina,

"Well, we are going out for lunch tomorrow." replied Rosey with a smile, Hagger just grinned.

"And what about you two?" Asked Tish.

"I'm hanging out with Datch, He's stopping at mine until the rehearsal and then I'm stopping at his until school, so what about you?" Carina said smiling.

"We're heading down to the city centre for a flat bread later and then the Barbers for a game of Solar Ball." Dapo said.

"Don't forget the shopping mall tomorrow." Added Tish.

"Oh, do you want to meet up?" Asked Rosey.

"Yeh, if you like. What about midday outside the Boom-boom room?"

"Sure." said Hagger.

They finished breakfast and started to walk back to school. There was a roar from overhead. It was the black ship again. This time it was heading into the city towards the centre.

"That's twice now we've seen it down here and in daylight." Said Datch while trying to get a picture using his implant.

"Yes, I wonder why, they are risking getting impounded flying like that." said Hagger.

"I think they are pirates." Said Dapo.

"Why pirates?" asked Rosey.

"Well, why else would they fly along the old pirate's route?" Dapo replied.

"That's the old pirate's route?" said Datch thinking hard.

"Yes, I looked it up and it's the old pirate's route. They fly below the scanners by hugging the hills on the way out of the city area. It is almost undetectable and then when they get near the mountains to the south, they would go straight up at full power kicking in the interspace drive as they went. It would look like a lightning strike on the planetary detectors."

"Err, surely they have stopped it?" asked Carina.

"They did, but that was over two thousand years ago." Dapo pointed out.

Carina looked at Datch. He had gone very quiet.

"Datch?"

"Yes."

"I know that look, what are you thinking?"

"Hmm," He wrinkled his brow, "Well, if you wanted to get someone or something into or out of the city without being seen, how would you do it?" he looked at the others.

"Yes, but surely the security services watch the route?" said Rosey.

"If it was two thousand years ago, would you still be watching it?"

"Well, no, not if it hadn't been used."

"I bet the planetary scanners are not set to look for it anymore."

"Do you think that's how the spider got here?"

"I don't know, but it is a coincidence don't you think?"

They looked at each other and agreed that it was a possibility. They headed up the road towards the school still thinking about it.

Back at school Datch sent Don a message telling him what they thought along with the image of the ship before heading to Carina's.

After a very good rehearsal at Datch's they decided that as long as the rehearsal at Hagger's and Tank's went well. They would give it a try in the Barbers.

The trip into the city was a bit more busy than usual. The bike was showing a large red circle around the new power plant indicating a no-fly zone. Datch and Carina landed at the school just as Dapo turned up with Tish, Hagger and Rosey were already waiting near the fountain.

"Well look at you two." Said Carina.

"I copied you two last night and stopped at Dapo's" said Tish with a grin. Dapo went a slight pink colour.

"So, are we all set for tonight?" Asked Datch.

"I'm a bit nervous about it." said Rosey.

"Me too" added Hagger.

"I'm sure it will be ok." said Carina.

"I've never been interviewed before," said Dapo.

"I don't think any of us have," added Tish.

"Well, Fred said to get there at about six thirty and we are to go to the big table on the balcony, Jim's going to make sure it's only us up there." said Datch.

"So, what are we meant to wear?" asked Tish.

"I think the T-shirts would be good." said Carina.

"Yes, T-shirts, I'll message the rest of The Pack, Oh and Fred said Jim's going to lay on some food for us, apparently a selection." added Datch.

"What sort of a selection?" Hagger asked.

"Err, knowing Jim, it will be one of everything off his menu, each with a little sign on saying 'Compliments, Barbers Inn' or something like that." said Datch grinning.

"Anyway, let's get our stuff in and get ready for the first lecture. I believe the first one is 'How to handle embarrassing situations.' which may be useful for later." Datch added picking up his bag.

They had the afternoon lectures and then it was time to head down to the Barbers Inn. They got ready and walked to the bar. The streets on the way there were quite busy and there were a lot of security officers about. Some were using hand held scanners checking the local buildings. The plant was only a couple of streets away and they were checking for anything unusual.

They got to the Barbers Inn and Jim waved at them and pointed to the stairs. They went up onto the balcony. Tank and Clax were already there sitting around a large table near the window. Next to them was another table with a verity of food on and yes it had little signs on it with 'The Barbers Inn' on them. They sat down and Jim brought their usual drinks up. As he went back down, he put a rope across the bottom of the stairs. It wasn't long before Fred came in with Jep and Peebop. They came up the stairs and sat down.

"So, are we ready for this?" Fred asked getting himself comfy.

"Well, sort of, we're a little nervous." the rest nodded.

"Don't be, we are making a name for ourselves, if we keep going the way we are, we'll be seeing more of the press."

"What do you mean?" asked Rosey.

"Well, in case you haven't noticed we are packing the bar out every week and people are now buying tickets three weeks in advance to see us, we're a big hit, I've started to get fan mail." He replied.

"Fan mail, how did they know where to send it?"

"They didn't, Jim was given it. He's got some for you dudes as well, just ask him for it?"

"You mean to forward it to us" corrected Rosey.

"Err, no, they are hand written letters."

"Hand written?" said Carina.

"Yes, they didn't have a mail ID to send it to." replied Fred.

"Oh wow, I don't think I've ever received anything hand written before." she added.

Fred waved at Jim and mouthed at him the words mail and then pointed at the rest. Jim nodded and went in the office. Two minutes later he came out carrying a very big bag and brought it up the stairs.

"Here you go, if this keeps happening, I'll have to start charging for the service, it takes up quite a lot of room in my office and also takes a while to sort out." he emptied the bag on the table.

To say it covered the table was an understatement, it was almost falling off the sides,

"I'll leave the bag; I think you'll need it." with that he went back down stairs to the main bar leaving them to wade through it.

During the next half an hour there was a lot of 'I think this one is yours' or 'who is '(some strange name with sexual context)'. Also, a number asking if they did private functions and how much they would charge. Fred was given them as he was their manager of sorts. Most of the others were saying how much the person or persons liked them and normally was addressed to their favourite member of the band. It would also normally contain a request for a signed photo or picture of 'The Pack'. They finally sorted it into piles. Jim brought some smaller bags so they could keep them separate and put them all in the big bag. The time arrived for the interview.

The reporter and vid operator came in right on time and went over to the bar. Jim chatted to them for a minute before escorting them up the stairs and over to the table.

"Folks, this is Joni Jabi of Channel 14's Joni's music movers."

"Please sit-down Mr Jabi" said Datch standing up.

"No, it's just Joni please and this is my vid operator Wen."

"Ok, Joni, I'm Datch, this is Carina and…" Datch went around the table introducing everyone.

"Right, let me start by staying I'm very pleased to be the first person to interview you. I want you to feel relaxed and don't worry if you want to stop at any point just put your hand up and the vid operator will stop recording."

"So, what sort of things do you want to know?" asked Tank.

"Well, I'll start by asking how you all met. Then I'll move on to how The Pack started and how you all are coping with the stardom."

"Err, Stardom?" asked Tish.

"Yes, I bet you don't know. Two weeks ago, someone took vid up here on the balcony and posted it in one of the music channels. It's been watched over three and a half million times so far."

They sat looking at each other in silence for a few moments then Fred spoke.

"Well, that explains the call then."

"What call?" asked Datch.

"Someone from a music company asked for a meeting to discuss a record deal. I thought it was just someone after free tickets to a gig."

Joni looked at them all and thought for a moment.

"Well, I've been dealing with the music business for many years. You don't want to say yes to the first offer and after this interview goes out on my show. You'll get a lot more I promise. Right, are you all ready to start?"

They all nodded and Joni started the interview. It was a lot easier than they thought. Joni was really nice. When anyone hesitated, he would stop the vid and wait until they were ready. It took about an hour and went very well. Afterwards Joni remarked on how well they had done.

"Thank you so much for the interview. Now you don't have to do this but I was wondering if I could have a vid crew here for your next gig, I will pay you of course, say two thousand credits each?"

They sat looking at him in shock.

"Yes, that sounds ok, I'm sure." said Fred trying to sound normal, "I'll sort in with Jim, would up hear be, ok?"

"That would be great. Then we have a day for editing and I'll send you a copy for your approval prior to broadcasting it on my weekend show."

"How much room will you need?"

"There will be three vid operators and a director. The vids we use are very small and you won't notice them. The three vid operators will be fine at the front of the balcony and the director will sit right at the back out the way. Just be yourselves and enjoy the gig."

"Ok, no problem." said Fred as he got up.

"Remember folks, channel 14, nine o'clock on Yuckiday"

With that Fred took them down stairs to Jim and The Pack set about eating the food Jim had put out.

"You know when this goes live, we're going to be celebrities. Everyone at school is going to know. There is bound to be a few that watch his show." said Rosey.

"I know. Still, we spend most of our time down here or around at Hagger's sorry, Tank's. Err, this is getting confusing, Hagger or Tank what can we call your home?"

"What do you think Hagger, does the Pad sound cool?"

"Yes, the Pad." agreed Hagger.

"Ok the Pad it is."

"Well, it's ok for you folks. But I have lectures to do and not to mention going in the staff room."

"I'm sure it will be cool." said Clax with a smile.

Once the feast had been demolished, they headed down to their normal table and a game or two of Solar Ball.

The next day, the rehearsal at the newly named Pad went very well. They went through the five new songs four times each without any problems. Afterwards they sat in the garden talking about it and agreed tomorrow was the night.

It was gig night. This time they all had their weapons of choice and were ready to rock the place. Datch went around and attached little pickup devices to the instruments and gave everyone an earpiece so they would be able to hear what they were playing. Outside the front of the Barbers Inn the security services had moved some barriers into place to stop people spilling onto the road.

Inside the crowd was buzzing and up in the balcony Datch could just make out three vid operators. Each had a holo visor over their face and you could just see the three vid bots hovering in the air just in front of the stage. They were about the size of an eyeball and black in colour with little thrusters on the side to let them move about. Datch realised that with the lights down they would be virtually invisible. He was glad about that. The rest of The Pack wouldn't see them and therefore wouldn't be nervous. It was going to be a big night as it was and they didn't need any more pressure.

The bar was full to busting point again. Datch wondered if they could keep this up and then a moment later, he went with yes. He walked back over to the table to address the troops.

"So, is everyone ready to go with the plan?"

'Yeh.' went everyone.

"Let's do this then." He nodded at Jim who was looking around the screen.

The lights dimmed and the bar quietened down and Jim went on the stage to introduce them.

The lights flashed, flames filled the air and the crowd roared. The Pack took to the stage.

"Hello Barbers!" Datch yelled and the crowd yelled back

"I can't hear you, HELLO BARBERS!" There was a massive roar from the crowd. The music started and they went straight into the first number.

The party had begun again and Datch loved the stage. It was where he came alive. The adrenalin pumped through his veins and his body crackled with energy. The others were carried along with him into the place amongst the stars. Song after song the crowd was screaming and dancing. The atmosphere was electric as the music vibrated across the bar. The bouncers were working hard to keep people off the stage.

"Ok you Barbers we're taking a break now and have we got something special for you in the second half."

They left the stage to cheering, applause and whistles.

They sat down getting their breath back.

"Wow, is it me or are they more excitable tonight?" asked Tish.

"Yes, they sure seem it." said Carina.

"Well, wait till they see the second set." said Datch.

"Do you think they can scream any louder?" said Tank trying to clear his ears out to stop the ringing.

"I have a feeling we're going to find out." added Dapo.

They sat cooling down and after another Gruck, beer, wine or strange thing with fruit in, they headed back out onto stage with their instruments to shouts and screams for the bar.

Datch grabbed the mic.

"Hello again Barbers and also hello to Joni Jabi and all of his viewers. We hope you're all enjoying the show as you can see, we're now armed. The first song in this set is for our parents and is called 'Space Dust'." The crowd went nuts, screaming at the tops of their voices.

Datch hit the first note and Tish hit the drums hard. The crowd erupted and started to dance and sing along to the song. The next five songs were incredible. The bar was just a heaving mass of people and the atmosphere was so intense. Every beat was like a blast of energy for the band. Datch along with the others felt so alive, they became the music. No one could stop them tonight. The crowd roared and cheered, song after song.

It came to Star Lovers, Datch and Carina did their stuff on the stage. When they came together at the end of the song for the kiss, it was as if sparks were flying from their lips and the crowd screamed. A woman had to be carried out after she collapsed at the front. Tank narrowly missed another set of underwear. This time they had planned what to do and did a very nice side step as they came flying towards them. The result is they flew by landing at the back of the stage without virtually anyone noticing.

The last song they did as an encore, Wilde Wind. Datch and Dapo did a sort of guitar dance with Carina and Rosey's drums. The bouncers had to be reinforced to hold the crowd back. Finally, the song finished.

"We thank you Barbers, and good night!" Datch shouted and they left the stage to chanting, whistling and cheers.

After the photo signing which this time needed all the bouncers there to keep control, they went and sat behind the stage cooling down.

Datch spoke first.

"Well, I think we can say that was a success."

"Err yes, just a lot!" said Carina.

"Did you see them take that woman into the office after she passed out?" asked Rosey.

"Yes, I asked Jim," said Fred "she was ok, just over heated in the crowd the medics said."

"Wow, what a night" said Dapo taking a gulp from his drink.

"I'll drink to that." said Clax raising his glass, "Cheers everyone!"

They all raised a glass.

The walk back was a little strange. They were all buzzing from the gig and the streets felt a bit safer as there was a lot a security officer's still around. The occasional security shuttle would fly overhead with active scans on the local area. The school was just on the edge of the security perimeter. Tomorrow night Don would arrive and they could be rid of the spider for good. They got to the school and said goodnight, Datch and Carina went down to their spot near the big windows to have their goodnight kiss before heading to bed themselves.

The Target

The next morning Datch was up at eight and packed his stuff ready for the trip home.

"Why are you up so early?" asked Dapo somewhat bleary eyed.

"I'm just going to scan for the spider before breakfast, I'll meet you down at the shop."

"You be careful."

"I will." With that he headed out the door with his rucksack over his shoulder.

Datch walked out the main doors and headed for his bike. When he got to it, he opened the rucksack. There in the top was the frequency canceller. He fetched it out and attached it to the side of the bikes console. He got on the bike and started its systems. It had taken him nearly three hours of messing about before he worked out how to interface the two units but now it was just a case of pressing a few buttons. He tapped the panel, the frequency canceller powered up and the system connected to it. Datch breathed a sigh of relief. He wanted this to work. He pressed a few more buttons on the display and a few on the canceller. The bikes screen flashed up 'systems synchronised'. Datch started the engines and the bike took to the sky.

The city was quite busy and there was a lot of shuttles flying in and out of the new power plant getting ready for the President's visit. The sun was shining down and it was already hot. Datch flew towards the static on the bike's terrain scan. As he got towards the edge he pulled up and hovered. He pressed a couple of buttons on the frequency canceller. it beeped. 'Hmm' he thought I need to get a bit closer. He flew the bike into the fuzz on his scanner. The bike started to complain that it was in violation of the safety protocols and stopped moving. Datch pressed the frequency canceller again. This time it found the scattering frequencies and started to feed them into the bike's scanner. The image started to clear. It looked like it was coming from a group of three buildings but it was hard to tell which. Datch decided that Don would need more precise information and moved closer until he was almost over them.

The three buildings stood on their own and were part of the same complex. One was an old industrial plant and had part of the roof missing showing some sort of mixing machines and a large mixing bowl of sorts with a hole in one side where the water had rusted through it. The roof looked like it had been damaged by a winter storm and had nearly a third of it missing and the windows on the outside were all broken.

The second building was an administrative centre of some sort and had a big glass front with a sign over the large glass doors. It read 'T__Rs _ood and Dr _nks compa__ '. Some of the letters were unreadable and one of the doors was broken.

There were a number of broken windows and you could see into the offices. There were desks and chairs scattered about inside. It looked like some of the homeless had been living in there as Datch could see clothes and piles of packaging grouped together to make bedding.

The third building was a warehouse. It had loading bays on the front with large shutter doors. It had a few broken windows and one of the side doors was swinging backwards and forwards in the breeze. The roof seemed to have been disturbed recently and there were some strands of white rope hanging down from the edge of the building.

Datch set the frequency canceller to recalibrate. It beeped a bit and then the image started to clear a bit more. The signal was coming from the warehouse. Datch took the bike a bit closer. The building looked deserted. He looked down and below him was a strange area near one of the loading bays that didn't have any weeds growing on it. Also, the ones around the edge had signs of burning and he realised that it must have been caused by thrusters when a ship lifted off.

Datch eyed the building up and down then took a few wide circles around it. It looked empty so he decided to take the bike down for a closer look. The reading was coming from the middle of the building anyway so it should be safe to look through one of the windows. He was feeling scared but any information he could get would help kill it.

The girls were waiting outside when Dapo and Hagger came walking out of the school. After a round of good mornings and a couple of kisses between couples, Carina asked.

"Err, where is Datch?"

"Oh, he got up early to find the spider." said Dapo.

"What! And you let him go alone." Carina screamed.

"Well, he said he was only going locate it and then meet us for breakfast."

"Oh, bloody Jaxx." Said Carina.

She got out her vid com and tried to call him.

"I'm not getting through to him, it keeps saying he's not connected to the grid."

"Err, should we call someone or something?" said Rosey.

Carina was starting to panic, Tish stepped in.

"Hagger, go and find Jep and tell him what has happened, Carina do you have his dad's vid ID?"

"Yes, but how will that help."

"Well, he'll be able to contact Don."

"Yes, but I can do that."

"Right do it, and let's hope he's in orbit."

Carina pressed a few buttons on the vid comm. There was a short pause and then it connected. Don's face appeared on the vid com.

"Hello, this is Captain Don Ronediamar how can I help you, oh it's you Carina, what's up?"

"It's Datch, He's gone to find the spider." she said nearly crying.

"Why the stupid…" there was a number of words that would make a hardened space pirate go red and then, "How long ago?"

"Err, about an hour" said Dapo.

"Crap, right don't worry, I'll get to him, hang tight." he ended the call.

Captain Don Ronediamar hit the ships intercom,

"All Hands, I want a tactical attack shuttle ready for launch in the shuttle bay by the time I get there and fully armed, also this ship had better be in orbit before that shuttle leaves the bay."

Alarms started to sound, he ran out of his cabin and headed for the shuttle bay. The med bay was put on standby and ten minutes later he was in the shuttle bay.

Back on the planet Jep came running out of the building followed by Hagger. At the same time Tank came flying into the carpark in the truck. He swung it around and stopped right next to them.

"Get in!" he yelled.

They jumped in the truck.

"Ok, where is he?"

Carina told him where the static was on the nav com. The truck roared into the sky rattling all the windows as it went.

Back on the Carpaycus a shuttle shot out of the shuttle bay and headed to the planet, Don told the crew what was going on and the pilot hammered the engines.

Datch disconnected the frequency canceller from the bike and reconnected it to a hand scanner he had in the rucksack. It was still showing that the spider was still in the centre of the building. He slowly edged his way to one of the windows at the side while watching the scanner for signs of movement.

A bird flew off from the other building and frightened him so much he nearly jumped out of his own skin but he carried on. He got to the window. It was dirty but Datch slowly wiped it so he could see in. The warehouse was empty inside except for a few empty cardboard boxes on the floor.

Datch wondered if it was in there or had gone out hunting. He had to find out. It wasn't far to a door so he thought a quick look inside wouldn't hurt. Slowly he moved to the door making sure not to make any noise and to stay out of sight. The place looked empty. If he could just see where it was. He reached the door and looked inside. nothing, it was empty. Just a dusty floor with foot prints and small circular indentations apart from a spot over the far side which had a large dark brown area. Datch realised with horror it was dried blood and was where the spider had been feeding. He slowly pushed the door open to get a better look.

Something flashed in the spider's nest. The arachnoid looked down at the box in front of it. 'Hmm' it thought, maybe one last snack before its mission is completed. After all it was a long trip home. It moved very slowly and looked out of the end of its nest. It was a young male. Not much of a snack but it should be enough till the next feed. It started to move from its nest.

Datch's scanner bleeped to tell him there was movement in the field. He stood still and looked around and then up towards the spider. The arachnoid stopped. This was something new. This little humanoid could see him. It could mean they were able to track it. The box around its neck started to flash at the same time the device in the humanoids hand beeped, it had to find out why.

Datch looked at the device. It was detecting multiple signals. That didn't make sense. He moved inside and crept along the edge of the room. The arachnoid watched him as he moved along the wall, then it took off the scattering field around its neck and placed it in its nest before starting to move slowly across the roof towards the male and froze as the device beeped again.

Datch looked around. He couldn't see anything. The roof was dark and there was no noise. He looked up towards the arachnoid but it was too dark to see anything. The arachnoid thought it had been spotted but the male looked away. Datch moved a bit further from the door and tried to see into the roof. He could feel someone was watching him. He got very anxious and started to move back towards the door. It was in there with him, he could feel it.

The arachnoid realised that it couldn't let him go and jumped.

Datch turned towards the door as the spider landed in front of him. Datch was terrified.

"WHAT DO WE HAVE HERE?" came a spine-chilling voice that sent icicles running down Datch's spine.

Datch froze to the spot. He was so scared he couldn't move and tried to think fast.

"I'm Datch, the IPSF know you're here." he said in a very shaky voice.

"DO THEY, SO WHY ARE YOU HERE AND NOT THEM?" the voice was worse than having a hundred nails dragged down a blackboard.

"I've told them and they are coming." said Datch hoping the spider would take fright and run.

"IS THAT SO."

"I know about the bots and the plant, but I don't understand why?"

"HMM, WELL AS YOU'RE GOING TO BE MY LUNCH, I MIGHT AS WELL TELL YOU."

The engines screamed and flames blasted the outside of the shuttle as it hit the thick atmosphere. Plasma streamed back from it as it plunged towards the planet like it was being driven by a madman. The craft shook as if it was in the centre of a tornado and the ground got closer and closer. Then the reverse thrust kicked in and the shuttle hit the ground. The back door shot open and thirty troopers ran out towards the building all armed to the teeth.

"LOOKS LIKE TIME IS UP." The spider lifted one of its arms and put it straight through Datch's head. his body dropped to the floor blood pouring out of the hole in his head.

The door was blown open and the troopers ran in shooting at the spider. It ran for its life losing one of its legs in the process. It went down a storm drain at the back of the factory blowing up the entrance on the way.

Tank's truck landed next to the shuttle and they all jumped out and ran towards the door. Don was standing in it stopping them from going in. Carina looked under his arm and forced her way past.

"DATCH!" she screamed running across to his lifeless body.

The others pushed through and followed her. Don turned and looked at them. He sighed and walked over to them. The others were standing around the body crying, Tank looked at Don.

"He's dead."

"Yes, I'm afraid so, well sort of anyway, this is going to cost me."

"What do you mean cost me, Datch is dead." screamed Carina.

"Err, I think you all need to come with me. Troopers secure the area and the body. I'll send another shuttle down. See if you can track where it went. I think it's left its scattering field up there. Right, I want all of you to follow me!"

Tank pulled Carina away from the body and helped her to the shuttle. She was shaking and the others had gone very pale. They went inside and the shuttle lifted off.

"Where are you taking us, Datch is down there." said Tish

Don turned and looked at them.

"Well, most of him is, but he had a lock on as soon as we hit orbit. He took the express elevator."

"The what?" said Carina.

"Let's just say, I think he may be a bit shaky for a few days."

"Err, you mean he's not dead?"

"No, not all of him anyway."

They all looked a bit confused. Don thought it was best just to wait and show them. The intercom burst into life.

"Captain it's for you, Commander Thome."

Don sighed again and told the pilot to pipe it through to him.

They didn't hear what Dechow said just the replies.

"Yes, he is… Yes, we have him… He's just died once, killing him again won't help…Yes, we had a spare on standby… No, we don't have another… Yes, I'll bring him down with me later. Give me at least till the end of the afternoon though… Yes, I will tell him. Captain out"

The channel closed, another sigh.

"Err, what was that about?" asked Jep.

"It was Datch's dad, I think Datch might be in a bit of trouble."

Carina looked at Don.

"Let me get this right, Datch is dead, well most of him anyway, but his dad wants to kill him and you're going to take him home by the end of the afternoon."

Don gave Carina a long look and then sighed.

"Just wait till we get to the Carpaycus, it will all become clear, remember he had his implant fitted, Jep maybe you could fill things in?"

Jep looked nearly as confused as the rest.

"Oh, never mind, we'll be there in about five minutes, just enjoy the view."

He turned back to the console and pressed a few buttons.

"Please can you contact the parents of Datch's friends and tell them they are staying with us for the rest of the day."

"Affirmative sir."

The shuttle left the atmosphere and banked left. Then there to the left of the shuttle was the Carpaycus. It was in a low orbit hanging just above the atmosphere with its nose pointing down as if it was about to dive into the planet. It was huge when you saw it this close. The shuttle flew alongside just as three shuttles flew past heading the other way. The shuttle slowed and turned into the loading bay and landed in bay eight.

Don stood up and said in a voice that would cause a dinosaur to roll over and play dead.

"Please do not panic, do not rush, stay calm and just follow me and above all listen to what I say. This way please."

They got up and followed him out of the shuttle. They went along the corridor and into a pod. Carina was still shaking from the shock of what had happened. The doors shut and Don said "Med Bay."

The pod moved off and soon was speeding through the ship, twisting and turning as it went like some sort of crazy rollercoaster. Eventually it slowed and came to a stop. The doors opened and Don stepped out followed by the rest of them.

"Ok, follow me." his tone was more like normal now.

He led them through a set of large doors with 'MEDICAL BAY' on them. Inside was a desk with an officer sitting at it. When he spotted them come in, he got up and saluted.

"Ok, where is he?" Don asked.

"Section seven sir, he will be at full integration in about thirty minutes sir."

"Ok, can we have a look at him."

"Yes sir, follow me."

The officer led the way down past a number of bays with beds in until he reached a room with a glass front.

There on a bed was another Datch. He was lying motionless and wasn't even breathing. Beams of light danced over his head as the computers reintegrated his brain.

"Datch." shouted Carina.

"He can't hear you; his brain is currently being held in stasis while it is attached to his new body." said the officer.

"So that's what you meant when you said he was mostly dead?"

"Yes, the express elevator is the term we use when someone dies but has a lock on, their brain is transported in stasis to the ship where it is fitted into a new body genetically grown from their own DNA. They will just feel a bit odd for a while, in Datch's case he's young so only a few days."

"The implant, oh now I get it, err I think?" said Rosey.

"I thought you had to be in a transfer centre for that to happen?" said Jep.

"No, if you're in the fleet and there is a ship nearby with a lock on. It automatically transports you."

"Oh, and Datch was in the fleet?" said Hagger.

"Err, not as such but I thought he might die in Asmove when the base started to fall apart and had a spare body made just in case. The ship still had him setup for lock on, that's what I meant about paperwork."

"Will he be any different?" asked Carina.

"Well, he might be missing a scare or two but other than that. No, that is the same Datch, but don't let him have a curry for a few weeks."

Carina sighed.

"Err why?" asked Tank.

"Well, it's a new gut, it takes a while to get going, trust me, no curries. I know someone who did it once and it took two weeks before you could go in his room. It's a wonder the paint didn't fall off the walls."

"Ok, point taken. No curries.".

"He'll be like that for another thirty minutes or so and then it will take him a few minutes to come around. Let's go have a drink while we wait. It will help steady your nerves."

"Can I stay?" asked Carina.

"Err, yes if you want, the officer will look after you."

"I'll stop with her, you lot go and calm down, we'll be fine." said Tish.

"Ok, come on follow me."

The rest followed Don out of the med bay and back into the pod.

Carina and Tish watched as the machines worked their magic. They watched as fingers twitched and toes wriggled. Then he started breathing and this was followed shortly after with him breaking wind. His eyelids flickered followed by his nose wrinkling. They sat watching as everything was connected to his brain. It was almost hypnotic to watch and then the officer came over.

"He'll be waking up in a few moments. Please don't rush him. He might jump a bit. Remember the last thing he saw was a spider about to put its leg through his head. His brain was transported as the tip went through his skull."

"Can I go to him?" Carina asked.

"Yes, but we have to wait till the light is green."

They watched and then the lights stopped flashing around his head and a scanner moved across his body. There was another blinking light and then the lighting in the room turned green.

"Ok, follow me. But remember he's going to be very shaky and a bit confused so don't rush him."

They went in through the door and across the room to the bed. The officer had a sheet with him and put it over Datch. Carina put her hand in his. It felt very warm.

"Datch, Datch, can you hear me?" he started to stir and then shuddered.

"Datch it's me Carina." His eyes started to flicker and then slowly opened.

"Carina?" he said in a quiet and slightly croaky voice.

"Yes, it's me, I've been so worried about you, I thought you were dead."

He turned and looked at her.

"What happened, I thought I was dead, where am I?" he started to sit up and then stopped. He lifting his hand up to his head, "What hit me?"

"Err, well you're on the Carpaycus and yes you did die sort of." said Tish trying to be helpful.

Datch put his hand up to the top of his head, "Err, there's no hole."

"Datch, do you feel ok?" asked Carina.

"Yes, just sort of light headed and my body feels a little odd."

"But other than that, you feel like you?"

"Yes, why?"

"Don said you took the express elevator."

"Oh, I did. I'm starting to remember, oh crap, I need to talk to Don right NOW!" he went to get off the bed and the officer caught him as he fell.

"Slow down. It's a new body give it chance to start working. The captain is on his way down, now just sit on the bed and recover." Carina helped the officer put Datch back on the bed.

"Err, where are my clothes?"

"Still on your body, well your other body."

"What, oh yes, err, any chance I can have something to wear?"

"Yes, the captain sent down one of your uniforms."

He walked over to the corner of the room and picked up a uniform from the table in the corner of the room.

"Carina can you help me please?"

"Yes, Tish please turn around a minute." said Carina.

Carina helped the officer to put Datch's clothes on. He sat back down on the bed. Tish couldn't help but glance over her shoulder at one point and then wished she hadn't.

"I feel a bit shaky is that normal?"

"Yes, quite normal. You need to get some food in you as your body is running on empty." said the officer.

"But no curries." Added Carina in a hurry.

"I quite fancy a Jaxx burger and fries with some ice-cream. I really do feel hungry thinking about it."

Carina thought that a Jaxx burger sounded safe.

"Ok, well as soon as the captain gets here, I'm sure he'll sort it out." said the officer.

The main doors opened and in came the captain with the rest following along behind. They came running through the door when they saw Datch sitting on the bed. The officer told them to calm down and take their time as Datch was still recovering. Tank stepped forward.

"Hey dude, how you doing?"

"I'm ok Tank, I just feel a bit shaky that's all."

"Hey you really scared us Datch, we thought we lost you, it was horrible." said Rosey.

"It takes more than a spider to kill me." he said smiling.

"Err, dude, it did kill you." pointed out Tank.

"Oh, good point."

Datch spotted Don at the back.

"Don! Don! I need to tell you something." Don came over and the others stepped to the side.

"What's the matter?"

"The spider, it wasn't the bots it was after, they were just its payment for the job."

"So why is it here then?" he said in a more urgent tone.

"It's the President, its after him. It told me before it, well I ended up here."

"Oh Crap! Comms! I need a link to planetary security Now! Oh, and tell commander Thome we maybe a bit late." Don said to his comms as he rushed out of the room.

They turned back to Datch; it was so good to see him.

"How do you know it's after the President?" asked Jep.

"It told me. It was about to eat me anyway so I couldn't tell anyone or at least that's what it thought. Oh." He put his hand to his head, "I feel so weak and tired."

"You will, your new body needs food and drink to get it going." The officer said.

"Is it ok if we take Datch for some food?"

"Yes, but I'll have to come with you. Datch, you need to sit in this wheel chair till you feel stronger, ok?" added the officer gesturing to a wheel chair next to the bed. Datch nodded.

"I'll push you." said Carina running around to get it.

Datch was carefully lowered into the wheel chair and they headed for the door. The officer went in front followed by Datch and Carina, with the rest walking along behind. They headed out of the med bay and into a pod opposite.

"Can I, I want to see if it still works?" asked Datch.

"Yes, if you want." answered the officer.

"Computer, Forward Lounge please."

"Welcome aboard ensign Thome, heading to forward lounge."

The Pod started to move and then picked up speed.

"Err, the computer knows you?" said Tank.

"Yes, I've been here before remember and I was introduced." said Datch grinning.

"Well, you're starting to look like yourself, that is apart from the uniform." said Dapo.

The lights in the lift started to flash yellow.

"What's happening?" said Hagger.

"The ships just gone on to tactical alert. We'll have assault teams on standby for immediate launch. Please just be quiet a minute. Bridge, this is med bay, please be advised, I'm currently escorting ensign Thome and the party to the forward lounge."

A voice came back.

"Ok. Commander Isbar will meet you there, then return to station. bridge out."

"I take it, he doesn't wear flowery shorts when on duty." said Tish.

There was a number of giggles and sniggers from behind Datch.

"Err, do you know the commander?" said the officer now feeling he had missed something.

"Well, Don, Alex and Fizz came to our bar for a drink and to watch the gig."

"Oh, so you are The Pack, Fizz didn't shut up about you for two weeks, I knew Datch was in the band but didn't realise you were the rest of it, I think Fizz must have told the whole crew about you."

"Did she think we were that good?"

"Well, she wouldn't shut up about you."

The pod started to slow down and then finally stopped. The doors opened and they stepped out into the corridor with Carina pushing Datch along. They rounded the corner and entered the forward lounge. It was quite busy and for some reason people kept saluting Datch and he would salute back. The waiter spotted Datch and came over and saluted.

"Welcome back sir, it's good to see you again, please follow me, we have a table in the quieter area for you. Commander Isbar suggested it when he told us you were coming."

They followed him across the room to an area with plants on the sides and two large tables that had been pushed together, they sat down with Datch being manoeuvred on to a chair and they then ordered the food.

Carina turned to face him.

"Don't you ever do this to me again, it frightened me to death." she said in a whisper. Datch looked at her. He wasn't sure how to react because she had the look of both concern and of being cross at the same time. It was not a nice look.

"Ok, I promise" he said feeling guilty.

"You said that the other day, I want you to mean it." Datch was now feeling very guilty.

"I mean it, I promise not to do that again." he said as he looked at her in the eyes.

"Ok then." she leant over and gave him a kiss, stopped and did it again to make sure it felt right.

A shadow fell across Datch and a voice spoke from above his head.

"So, ensign Thome, you weren't happy with saving my crew and half a dozen scientists, you now want to save the President of an entire planet."

"Alex!" Datch said suddenly brightening up.

"That's Commander Isbar, remember you're in uniform."

"Oh, sorry sir." Datch saluted but was still smiling.

"Officer Teeko please return to med bay. Your services may be needed at any time."

"Yes Sir."

The officer saluted and left them.

"Ok Datch, I'm here to make sure you have a good meal and get your strength back and then the captain needs to talk to you."

"Why?"

"He needs to know every last detail you do; The spider has vanished off the ships sensors, we're working on tracking it but so far nothing, we're hoping you might remember something."

"Ok, but I'm not sure if I'll be able to help much."

"We were hoping you could tell us about the scattering field. The one in the nest was being jammed by your device and exploded as soon as we got near it. The spider took your scanner with it."

"Err, well"

"Not now, you need food."

The food and drinks came out and Datch tucked in like he hadn't eaten in a week.

The Jaxx burger took about two minutes to demolish and the chips didn't fare much better. They sat watching in disbelief as food vanished into the bottomless pit that was Datch's new stomach. Alex ordered the same again for Datch and gave him a couple of energy pills as well for good measure. The second burger came out and that didn't take much longer than the first one but the chips did slow him down and finally the extra-large chocolate ice-cream finally brought him to a stop.

"Good grief Datch, I've never seen you eat so much. You sure you're not going to explode?" said Dapo.

"Err, no and can I have another drink of Gruck please?"

"Sure, why not, you just wiped out a whole day's energy intake in ten minutes, so let's wash it down with something full of sugar." said Tank in a slightly sarcastic tone.

Carina was staring down at Datch's expanding stomach. She hadn't noticed properly in the med bay how flat it was or rather had been.

"Err, I hope that uniform can stretch well." she said.

"Yes, they do." said Alex.

"How are you feeling now lover?" asked Carina.

"A lot better, I could almost go for a round of Solar Ball."

"Not so fast lover." She said with a 'you had better behave or else' voice.

Datch grinned at her.

"So, come on, what was it like dying?" said Hagger.

Carina glared at him.

"Well, I don't actually remember that bit as I was already on my way here, but the bit in front of the spider was really scary. It's all black and bigger than two Jaxx"

"So, what happened?" asked Dapo.

"Well, I traced it to the warehouse. The signal was in the centre so I looked inside and it was empty." The rest of the group were listening intently to him.

"I checked the scanner again and it hadn't moved so I carefully went in to see if I could spot it. I thought I could tell Don what it looked like. I felt it was watching me so I started to head back to the door and it dropped down in front of me. Then it spoke."

The thought of its voice sent shivers running down his spine again, he stopped and went pale.

"I think that's enough for now Datch." said Alex.

Tank's vid started to beep. He looked down at it. It was Fred.

"Tank, Thank the stars, I have been trying to contact you, the school said somethings happened to Datch."

"Yes," Tank stopped and looked at Datch who was knocking back another Gruck,

"Err, well the spider sort of killed him." he was not sure how to put it.

"You mean he's dead?" asked Fred with panic in his voice. Tank took another deep breath.

"Well, he was sort of dead, but he's now eating like a starving Jaxx."

Datch broke wind. Not just a little bit but an elephant couldn't have done better.

"Oh, and farting." Added Tank.

"What so he was dead, but he's not and now he's eating a lot and breaking wind. have you been drinking?" Fred said.

"Err, I might have had one to steady my nerves but I think I need a few more. Anyway, we're all ok and on the Carpaycus. I'm sure we'll all be able to tell you about it later, well apart from Datch who might be killed again by his dad."

He lifted the vid comm up so Fred could see everyone. There was a round of 'Hi Fred' and a large burp from Datch.

"I'll see you later in the Barbers. Oh, tell Peebop it was the spider taking the bots. It told Datch before it killed him."

Fred was about to ask what Tank was going on about but gave up.

"Ok, later dude."

Alex started to think, "Actually, that's not a bad idea." he said.

"What?" said Jep.

"We should all go to the Barbers later."

"Well, I think we could all do with a drink but don't you think Datch needs his mum and dad?"

"At the moment. No, not till his dad cools down a bit and the Barbers Inn is a good place for them to meet us."

They all were looking at him.

"Datch how are you feeling?" he asked.

"A lot better, Sir."

"Ok stand up and let me see."

Carina got up and put her hands behind Datch just in case. He moved his chair and stood up it was a little shaky but he took a couple of steps. Then found his strength and walked over to the bar and back with Carina in tow.

"Yep, my legs seem to be working, Sir." He said with a grin.

"Good" he hit his comms. "Captain we're all on our way to the bridge, we need to talk to you."

"Ok commander, come to the command room, captain out."

The others were looking at him.

"Ok, I have a plan, just follow me."

They headed off to see the captain. They soon arrived at the command room. It was a large oval room with a table in the centre and about thirty chairs around it. Don was sitting at the end of the table along with three other officers.

"Please all sit down." He waited till they were seated,

"So, what have you come to tell us then?"

"Captain, if Datch tells us how he found it, I may have a plan to catch it." said Commander Isbar.

"Datch take your time and tell us everything you did." Commanded Don.

Datch explained how he had got the detector, how he had used it and then the hardest part, what the spider had said before it killed him.

"So, how does this help me?" said the captain.

There was a discussion about detectors and how to modify them. Then another about where it would attack the President. The spider hadn't told Datch that bit. The captain had managed to pull authority over the case because the spider had killed an acting ensign in the IPSF. This over ruled the local security services by default.

"I have a plan…" Isbar said.

The Trap

Datch and The Pack boarded the shuttle to head back down to the surface. Isbar and a number of troopers were with them. The shuttle left the bay and headed to Yuland city and as it dropped down into the lower atmosphere it slowed right down. The traffic into the starport was stopped while the shuttle came down. It flew over the city in a very low circle with its air vents open before coming in to land at the school. They all got out and the troopers spread out on either side of them. They started to walk towards the Barbers Inn. The troopers hugging the sides of the streets as they went.

"Are you sure this is wise?" asked Tank who was getting a bit nervous.

"Yes, this is the only way, we need to flush it out."

"Oh, I wish you hadn't said that. I seem to need to go more in this body." said Datch.

"More like it's the six large glasses of Gruck's you drank." added Rosey.

"Trooper, bang on that door and please ask if Datch can borrow the, well you know." said Isbar.

Datch went over to the building and went inside. Five minutes later he came back out looking happier.

They carried on down the street. They were all looking up at the buildings as they went. They soon reached the junction and turned toward the bar. They headed over to the doors and went in.

Clax, Peebop and Fred were already sitting at the big table. It had been moved forward a bit. They got up when Datch came in and went over to him.

"Hey dude, are you ok?" asked Fred.

"Yes, I'm feeling a lot better now thanks."

"Hey, is it true you died?" asked Clax.

"Err, sort of, look, let's get some drinks and sit down."

They went over to the big table and Datch explained what had happened while the troopers came in and took up positions in the dark alcoves of the bar.

"So, what's with the Troopers?"

Before Isbar could answer Datch's mum and dad came in. Datch stood up and Tansya came running over to him,

"Are you OK?" she said giving him a very big hug.

"Err, I'm fine." he said letting out yet another burp.

Datch was glad to see her and was making the most of the hug. Also, his dad had just walked up behind her and he figured he wouldn't get a hug from him.

"You frightened the life out of me, don't ever do that again."

"I didn't mean to get killed, I just wanted to make sure Don knew where it was so he could kill it. It killed Hagger's dad." He started to cry and his mum gave him another big hug.

Dechow had herd what he said and part of him softened inside.

"Datch." he said.

Datch turned to look at him.

"Yes?" he had tears still rolling down his face.

"You did this for your team?" his dad asked in a calm voice.

"Yes, for Hagger's dad, it needs to be killed."

Dechow looked at him and remembered all the times he had put his life on the line for his team. He couldn't be angry at him anymore. He was just looking out for his friends.

"I have done the same for my teams in the past. You did very well, but please next time come and talk to me first."

"I just wanted you to be proud of me, dad."

Tank blew his nose and sniffed. Fred and Peebop were staring into their drinks.

"I am proud of you son, you are a Thome and I love you." he gave Datch a hug.

Tank burst into tears so Clax went and put his arm around him. Jim came over with a box of tissues and handed them around.

"Ok, Let's sit and have a drink."

"Err, Commander you may be needing this." Isbar gave Dechow an assault cannon.

"Are you sure it will come here?" he asked turning to Isbar.

"Yes, it will pick up his scent and come to find him. It doesn't have a choice. It's got to find out if Datch is alive and what he has told us."

"The spider is coming here?" said Fred suddenly realising what was taking place.

"Yes, it will be able to smell Datch right cross the city, but don't worry we have more than enough fire power to kill it before it can hurt anyone."

"Hagger, Dapo why don't you go and play Solar Ball?"

"I don't really feel like it." said Hagger.

"It's to make it hard for the spider to see the troopers, so you would be helping us out." added Dechow.

Rosey stood up,

"Come on." she said, "let's give them a show."

Tish got up as well.

The rest sat drinking while they went to play. Datch had to recite what had happened to his mum and dad. Carina sat next him and leant on his shoulder.

Across the city in an old building, an inspection cover lifted itself into the air and then was placed to one side. The spider squeezed out and stood upright. It had another scattering field generator around its neck and moved up to the roof to look around. It was almost dark and the city lights were bright after it had been in the darkness of the sewer pipe. 'Only one more cycle and it will be time to leave this world' it thought to itself. It tasted the air and detected something. It tested it again. 'That was impossible. It had been killed unless…' It had to be sure or the plan might fail.

It started to move from building to building using the alley ways and the shadows as cover. Slowly and surely following the scent of the male to the school. The scent was stronger now and it led down the street. It followed it along the buildings down the street. It stopped. The male had gone in there. It scuttled up over the building and in through a window at the back. The male was not inside it was just leaving the window again when a female opened the door. She saw it leaving and screamed. It stopped for a second debating a snack. 'No time.' It had to move and scuttled back up onto the roof. The scent led further down the street leading it to a junction. The spider jumped to the building on the opposite side. It looked up and down the street. Everything seemed quiet.

There were a lot of humans about so it moved slowly using the shadows for cover and minimizing energy use so that it didn't give off any heat allowing it to be tracked.

Isbar's comms beeped.

"Yes." he said.

"Ok, I'll let them know, Isbar out." he pressed the comms again.

"It's coming troopers, be ready."

There was movement in the booths and alcoves in the bar as weapons were made ready, Isbar turned to Dechow.

"It's just been sighted down the street where Datch stopped to borrow the bathroom. It was seen leaving the back window two minutes ago."

The Comms beeped again.

"Troopers orbital scans put it within 200M."

"You mean its outside now?" said Fred, Isbar nodded.

There was a subtle click and the sound of plasma being charged from under the table. Datch looked at his dad. Dechow gave him a smile. It was the sort of smile that a madman would give just before going on the rampage.

Across the street the spider sat on the roof of a low building. Its shape hidden by a large shadow from the building next to it. It looked at the bar trying to make out the inside. There were more scent trails going into the bar than people it could see. It scanned the tables. There at the back was the male. It started to move and the stopped again.

Datch felt a shiver go down his spine and shuddered. Carina looked at him.

"Datch, what's the matter?" she asked.

"It's watching me, I can feel it."

Dechow and Isbar turned to look at the door.

The spider waited to see what happened. Nothing, that was odd. It looked closer. The two males that turned to look out had something in their hands out of sight. It sensed danger.

Isbar's comms went again.

"We are detecting something sir, opposite the bar, it's a very weak signal but it's there."

They tried to look for it but the darkness outside meant they couldn't see anything.

There was a lot of movement in the bar. The humans were playing some sort of game and the light from it was stopping it from seeing clearly. The spider tried to look closer. Then, there in amongst the shadows was the glint of a trooper's gun. It studied the bar. Yes, more trooper's hiding in the dark. It was a trap! It jumped up on to the roof carefully checking the area as it went. Then it moved across to the adjacent building.

"Target is moving away sir." came a voice on the comms.

Once it felt in the clear it went leaping from building to building moving fast until jumping down a storm drain and running deep inside. It had to think, what had it said to the male?

"Target lost 1400M away sir." came the voice again.

"Dam, it must have caught sight of something." said Isbar.

"Will it come again?" asked Carina who had been holding on to Datch very tightly.

"No, not tonight but it might be a good idea if you stay on the Carpaycus tonight just to be safe. I'll have the ship contact your parents and you guys had better come to. Datch's scent is on you."

"Well, as we are currently not in danger let's celebrate Datch's safe return or rebirth, well something like that." said Fred who had been hiding behind Tank.

He tapped Jep on the back who then removed himself from under the table.

"I will arrange quarters for you on the ship and then after we're onboard, if you want, we can go to the forward lounge for another couple of drinks before retiring for the night."

The Solar Ball finished and the four players came back to the table.

"Err, what did we miss?" asked Tish.

"The spider apparently." said Clax.

They were told what had happened and what was going to happen.

Across the city the spider sat in a dark tunnel thinking. It decided that it needed to get into position now instead of waiting until the morning. It moved through the tunnels until it was under the power plant. Slowly it moved its way up to the surface and then into the main tower. The storm drain had a drainage grill that would stop any water getting to the control systems which gave it easy access to the inside. It carried on climbing up the inner core. It was close to the quantum singularities now and their shielding would also shield it. Down below was the main control area.

At lunch time the president would come in with all his entourage and the press. He would give a speech and then throw the switch that would bring the station online. The spider would wait until he was at the front before it would jump down and kill him. Then once sure of his death it would jump back up the tower before going back down the storm drain and off to a waiting ship and home. It settled in for the wait tucking itself into an air vent.

Back on board the Carpaycus the captain sat looking at the group around the table.

"We think it's going to attack at the power plant. Anyone got any ideas?" everyone just looked at each other.

"I'll take that as a no then."

They all carried on looking at their drinks and then Datch looked up.

"Err, I know I'm only an ensign but can I say something?"

"Acting ensign but tell me what you're thinking anyway?"

"Well, the spider wants me and the president. So, let's give him two targets."

"There are two problems with that. One, you're likely to die again which would take two weeks to grow you a new body and two, we can't put any troopers in there because it would see them." said Don.

"What about one trooper, my dad."

"I don't want you going into danger again." said Carina

"Me neither." said Tansya.

"I won't be, my dad will be there."

"It might work, Dechows scent will be similar to Datch's, it might not see him as a threat until it's too late. If Datch is at the front it might just distract it long enough." said Isbar.

"What do you think commander Thome," asked Don.

"It may work but I'm not happy about putting Datch in the firing line again."

"It will be ok dad, I don't want to die again, at least not yet."

"Has anyone else got any ideas before I have to agree to it." asked Don.

The table was silent while they all tried to think of another way.

"Ok, then Acting ensign Thome and Commander Thome you have a spider to kill tomorrow."

They had another couple of drinks before heading to their quarters.

The next morning started early with Datch and his dad being fitted with body armor before Dechow was given an assault canon. This was all followed by being fitted for a habit. Datch and Dechow were going to be visiting monks and needed to look the part. It was a Presidential event after all and also, Dechow could easily hide the assault canon. Isbar was also being fitted for a boiler suit and disguised as one of the workers.

It got to mid-morning and four shuttles left the bay heading for the surface. Three carried troops and the other had Datch, Dechow and Isbar.

They landed close to the plant and Isbar went on ahead. He had to look like one of the workers or the spider would see him for what he was. Dechow and Datch went over to the VIP area to wait to go in.

"Hey dad look, free food."

"Remember it's not dad its farther Thome."

"Sorry da.. I mean farther."

They went over and had a few pastries and a sandwich. They were posing as two visiting monks from Taul five, the temple world. They were wearing the monk's bright yellow habits and had hoods covering their faces. They mixed in with all the other dignitaries and before long it was time to go in.

The main control area was huge and had an array of panels showing the reactors and singularity status. The seats had been set out in a large semi-circle and each of them had a number on. Datch and Dechow found theirs at the front in the centre. Dechow's was behind Datch's so the spider would hopefully not notice him. They sat down. Isbar had worked out that it would take the spider about five minutes after Datch entered the room to smell his scent. So, they had only come in when it was getting close to the arrival of the President.

The spider stirred from its hiding place and looked out over the floor below. It moved itself to the drop point ready for it to pounce. The control area was full and people were sitting down. Soon an attachment of security officers formed a line and the President came in. Datch thought he looked smaller than on the vid. He was a small man who had a mustache, a short pointy beard and a little round hat. Everyone stood up as he walked to the front.

The spider watched him intently. Then it smelt something. The male. It looked at the crowd scanning for him but couldn't tell where he was. There were to many smells in here to pin point him. It looked around at the guards checking their weapons. 'Only small guns' it thought 'no threat there'. Then it looked at the people below looking for any troopers that might be hiding in the crowd. It couldn't see anything but looked again just to be sure.

The President walked up to the console and turned to face the crowd; he cleared his throat.

"Ladies, Gentlemen, Aliens and honoured dignitaries. It is my great pleasure to open…"

The spider pressed a button on the side of the scattering field. A light flashed on the doors at the back and they quietly locked shut. It got ready to jump.

"This new power plant will supply…"

The spider jumped falling through the air and landing in front of the President. People screamed and started to run for the doors. They didn't open. The security officers opened fire, but the weapons fire just bounced off the spiders armoured body. It raised itself up and said in an icy voice,

"THIS IS FOR TRAIMORE."

As the spider was about to strike and Datch dropped the habit to the floor.

"Aren't you forgetting something spider, I AM DATCH!"

The spider spun around.

"YOU!" it said.

Datch herd the click as his dad's cannon powered up and hit the floor. Dechows robe fell open and he lifted the canon. The spider was still looking at Datch when Dechow pressed the trigger. A plasma bolt hit the spider right in its head vaporising half of it and ripping the rest from its body, the spiders body fell to the floor and the scattering field rolled in front of Datch. There was the image of a man on it. Datch took a picture of him with his implant before the image vanished. He got up and walked over to the remains of the spider.

"That's payback!" he said and gave it a kick. Dechow started to laugh.

Isbar helped the President around the remains of the spider as the rest of the security officers came running over. They walked over to Dechow and Datch. There was a bang from the back of the room and the doors opened.

"Who are you people?" asked the President.

"I am commander Isbar of the Carpaycus, this is Commander Thome and this brave young man is Datch."

"Well, I don't know what to say, thank you, you saved my life."

"Dad, I have an image of a guy on the scattering device."

"Quick send it to me," said Isbar, "I have an active link."

Datch did as he was told and Isbar sent the image to the central database for recognition.

"Please come this way sir." said one of the security officers and the President was whisked away.

"Well, Datch. It's dead, how do you feel?" asked Dechow.

"A lot better dad, in fact, pretty dam good."

"Well, I don't know about you, but I fancy a beer." said Dechow.

"I can go with that." said Isbar

"Me too." said Datch, Dechow turned to look at Datch.

"What, I have the non-alcoholic one." Dechow laughed again.

"Come on." he said.

They turned and the three of them walked out of the doors into the sunlight, a shuttle landed in the carpark. Dechow and Isbar handed in their weapons. Isbar told the captain what they were doing and he agreed, the three of them left the carpark and headed to the Barbers Inn.

Across town the black ship lifted off and headed for the mountains, it was flying very fast hugging the hills as it went. Trees bent over as it flew past. The pilot was in a very big hurry. He hammered the engines across the lakes before he started to make a vertical climb. Priming the interspace drive as he went.

Up above the starship Carpaycus watched the ships route and moved into range.

The pilot reached for the interspace drive and pressed it. The ships engine whined and then stopped. The ship was still going up but not in interspace or even using the ships engines. It was being dragged into space using a force field. As it left the atmosphere, the pilot looked out the cockpit and there was the Carpaycus and five shuttles armed to the teeth and all pointing at him. He tried the self-destruct, that didn't work either. He sat back and waited for the inevitable as the ship was taken inside.

Back on the planet. Datch, Dechow and Isbar walked into the Barbers Inn, straight across the floor and up to the bar. All of them had big smiles on their faces.

Jim came over.

"What can I get you gents?"

"Three large cold beers please."

"Err, three dad?"

"Yes, three Datch." said Dechow.

Datch grinned.

Life is good

Tansya and The Pack were taken down to the city from the Carpaycus. They had been told that everything had gone to plan. The arachnoid was dead and the city was safe again. The shuttle landed in the street outside the bar. They left the shuttle and walked into the Barbers Inn. Standing in front of the bar was Datch, Dechow and Isbar. They all had a large half empty glass of beer and were grinning. Carina ran over to Datch and put her arms around him. Tansya did the same to Dechow and after a very big kiss Carina finally let go of Datch.

"You are incredible Datch." she said, "Err is that real beer?"

Datch grinned "Might be?"

The others came forward and patted and shook their hands.

Isbar's comms beeped.

"Yes sir." he said walking away from the rest of them

"Yes, I'll tell them sir, Isbar out." he walked back over to the others.

"Folks, that was the captain. They have just captured the ship you were on about trying to leave the planet. It had the owner of the casino onboard and after a scan he confessed. He wanted to kill the President for revenge after he had given the order to have his brother wiped."

"Brother?"

"Yes, the drug lord who became a doctor and saved all the people in the storms, that was his brother."

"Bloody Jaxx, now things make sense." said Clax.

They went over to the big table and sat chatting and relaxing content in the knowledge that the city was safe again. Jim brought out some complimentary food and sat with them for a while before heading off to sort something out in the office.

The sun started to go down the shadows grew longer in the bar. All of a sudden ten security officers came in the bar and there was a huge commotion near the door. Then the door was opened and the President walked in. Jim went into a blind panic and was calmed down by one of the security officers. The President walked over to the table.

"May I join you?" he said.

"Yes sir, by all means." said Dechow, "Tank, grab that chair for the President will you."

Tank got the chair and brought it over for the President to sit on

"Please call me Coola." He waved at one of the officers who turned to the bar.

"I wanted to come and thank you personally for saving my life and ridding the city of the arachnoid. The captain of the Carpaycus has told me all about what has been going on and how you have all been party to the destruction of the beast, especially you Datch."

"It was nothing sir." said Datch.

"I would hardly call dying nothing young man, I can't thank you enough for what you have done, if there is anything I can do just ask. I would also be very honoured if you, your dad and Commander Isbar would attend a banquet and accept the freedom of the Planet for what you have done."

"Err, yes." said Datch "Can everyone come?"

"Of course, you all did this together and as a small token of my personal appreciation, the food and drinks are all on me tonight, one of my officers will sort it out with the manager."

The officer he had waved at came over along with two other officers carrying drinks. Jim followed them across with various snacks and stated that the main food would be out shortly.

"I hope you don't mind, but I ordered the things you normally have and some other bits that you may like."

Datch got up and walked around to the President and whispered something in his ear, the president grinned.

"Yes Datch, I'm sure that can be arranged, next weekend?"

"Yes, that would be great, thank you." said Datch grinning.

He went back to Carina and sat down.

"Err, what did you just ask?"

"It's a surprise." he smiled again and kissed her.

"So, what do you all do for fun in here?" the President asked.

Dapo stood up, "Solar Ball, sir." he said.

"Well, let's play ball!" said the president.

They all got up and headed for the game…

The following week, was normal apart from Datch having regular check-ups to make sure his new body was ok. They also had an assembly where the principal told the whole school what hero's they had in their mist. Jep had to admit he was in the band and that this trimester was far better than the last one.

The Vid news channels had been full of the little hero and his dad and then came the connection with Joni Jabi's music show. Joni called them and told them the hits on their vid had got over four billion views and his show had the best ratings ever.

Then came gig night. Word had got around about where The Pack played and the Barbers Inn was swamped. To add to the chaos the President had turned up with his daughter and twenty security officers who had taken over part of the balcony. Jim was forced to put speakers outside and start an off sales service in order to stop a riot. The screen that he had put up to advertise the band now became a temporary outdoor vid screen. The bar was packed and so was the street. They had to be smuggled in though the back door in disguise. There had even been reporters outside the school waiting for them. They sat at the table a little more nervous than usual.

"Well, we really have a crowd tonight." said Datch looking carefully through the screen behind him.

"That's an understatement, it looks like Jim's had to get more bouncers, all of the normal ones are in front of the stage." said Clax peering through one of the gaps.

"No, he hasn't, the security services are manning the door because the President is upstairs with his daughter." said Fred taking another large gulp of beer,

"Oh, and there are three vid crews somewhere as well, each paying us twenty thousand credits a piece to put the event outlive."

"WHAT!" said Carina, Rosey and Dapo all at the same time and Tank sprayed his mouth full of beer across the table.

"Yes, folks, tonight we make sixty-five thousand credits each, Jim's promised us five thousand each, he's going to make more than that on the bar alone."

They sat looking at Fred.

"Err, you were going to tell us this when?" asked Carina.

"I don't know, I was waiting for the right moment."

"Right folks, looks like we have a show to put on, that means we pull out all the stops tonight, let's put on the best show ever," Datch said standing up, "Are we The Pack or what?" he put his hand out to the centre of the table.

They all stood up and put their hands out on top of each other's,

"Let's do this!" Datch yelled, and nodded at Jim who was the other side of the stage, they all shouted "Yes!!" and turned towards the stage.

Jim did the introduction and the cheering was so loud that it hurt their ears. Then they hit the stage and straight into the first song. The crowd went wild and were singing along with the songs. The buzz from the audience was incredible. Everything they did made them scream more and by the time they stopped at the end of the first set they all felt like they needed dragging down off the ceiling.

"Dare I say, that went better than normal." said Tank up ending a glass of cold water on his head.

"I think, I'll go with that." Said Carina, who's head was spinning.

"Err, well, all I can say is wow, I wonder if we get an after party?" said Dapo.

"Yes, all the big stars do." added Tish.

Datch sat looking at them. He felt happy. They had followed him and now they were reaping the rewards. He still didn't know why or how it came to this point. Yes, he could remember doing everything, but it just sort of happened. He watched them saying how good they felt and laughing. He smiled to himself and felt good inside. Carina saw him looking.

"And what are you smiling at lover?" she asked.

"I was just thinking, look at us all, would you even have thought this could happen when we first met?"

"No, it was just school, but I'm glad it did." she said.

Fred, Tank, Clax and Peebop just gave him a knowing look.

"Ok, I know what you are thinking."

"What?" said Fred "That we might need a new planet now that Datch has been unleashed?"

They all burst out laughing.

"Ok folks, let's do the same to the second set as we did to the first." said Datch, "Get your drinks down and let's rock the place."

To say the second set went well was an understatement. Three people were carried out after fainting and the local medical services set up a triage unit in the street to help people with heat exhaustion. Jim had to order two extra beer deliveries in one night. The barrels were being transported in and out like they were going out of fashion. By the end of the set even the President's daughter was down dancing. Which was in itself worth seeing as she was flanked by three large security officers all trying to dance while watching the crowd. Datch saved everyone more embarrassment by getting her up on stage and thus leaving the officers to what they were good at. In fact, they just helped reinforce the bouncers.

The second set finished to huge applause, cheers and whistles. They retreated to the table in the back taking the President's daughter with them for safe keeping. This was partly because there was no safe way to get her back to her dad until the crowd calmed down.

They sat behind the stage with four bouncers, three security officers and Jim who couldn't get back to the bar or to that matter even see it through the people.

"So, did you like us?" asked Datch.

"Yes, you were fantastic, I've had a really good time, the girls back home are going to be so jealous when they find out I've met all of you." said the President's daughter.

"And what about you Mr security man?" asked Carina.

"We like anything that mam likes."

Tank couldn't help but snigger.

"Jim, how did the bar do tonight?" asked Fred.

"I'm not sure, I haven't managed to get back to it in over half an hour, I think I need a bigger building."

"I like this the way it is." said Rosey before Jim had any ideas about remodelling again.

"Me too, it has character," said Hagger.

"I think we all like it the way it is." said Tish.

"Yes, please don't change it." said Datch.

"Ok, but we're going to have to do something with the stage, poor Timbo over there was nearly squashed." They all turned to look at the bouncer.

Timbo was a big man and built like a house. It was very hard to think of anything squashing him other than maybe a small moon. He shrugged his shoulders.

Datch had an idea,

"Timbo, would you like to earn a few extra credits this weekend?"

"Err, for what?"

"Well, I'm having a bit of a party and thought a man of your talents may be useful."

"How much?"

"Say one thousand credits for the weekend?"

"Ok, I'm in." Timbo said smiling.

"See me later and I'll tell you the plan."

"And what plan is this?" asked Carina.

"Well, we're having a party to celebrate me not being dead. I was going to tell you in a bit but now is as good a time as any. I want you all around my house for Nickaday lunch time and bring your instruments, ok?"

"Ok, but what are we doing?"

"It's a surprise and a thank you for being good friends."

One of the bar staff made it through with some drinks.

"It's starting to calm down now." he said getting his breath back.

"Ok mam, we have been asked to take you and the band up to your dad, please follow us."

"Well, I suppose if the President wants to have a drink with us, we can't really say no can we." said Tank with a grin.

They picked up their drinks and followed the security officers and the bouncers. The bar was still very busy so they were escorted around the back of the bar and along to the stairs. Half way along a pair of woman's underwear hit Tank in the head.

"Really!" he said.

"I did wonder where she was tonight." said Jep smiling.

"Yes, she is a very dedicated fan." said Peebop joining in.

"Thank you." said Tank in a loud voice.

There was a scream from the other side of the bar.

"Now you've done it." said Fred.

"What, that was a sarcastic 'Thank you'."

"With the noise in this bar, no it wasn't." said Clax.

"Oh crap." said Tank with a sigh.

They walked up the stairs and went to sit with the President. Chatting and drinking until the bar emptied out.

They walked back to the school in the cool evening air. Datch was happy. He had Carina arm in arm, the monster was dead and he had the best friends in the world.

The Party

Nickaday arrived and Carina was up early. She had gone home with Datch and was pretty much not letting him out of her sight. Datch came down stairs and walked into the bar. Carina was sitting at it eating a sandwich and watching Bob who was sitting in the globe behind the bar. Bob was in turn watching Carina and wondering if the sandwich she was eating tasted nice and if he could get one. Datch came in and walked over to her.

"Morning lover." she said turning to face him.

"Hi babes, did you sleep well?"

"Yes, how are you today?"

"I feel good, everything seems to be working."

"Good, now what do you have planned for this weekend, I asked you mum but she said it was a surprise."

"All I'll say is that it's a road trip and the President sorted it out for me, so you need to pack your bag."

She looked at him. This was Datch and she wasn't going to find out. His mum had told her that Datch took after his dad and could keep a secret.

"You sure lover?"

"Yes babes."

She gave him a hug and a big kiss but it wasn't working.

"Ok, the others will be here in about an hour, then a quick drink and we'll be on our way if all goes to plan." he said and gave her a kiss.

They put the vid on and watched it for a while, then Datch stood up,

"Come on I need you to help me with something."

"Ok, what are we doing?"

"Just follow me."

She followed Datch over to the corner where two large boxes were sitting on the sofa. Datch opened one up. Inside was several packs each with a name on. He found the one with Carina written on it and handed it to her.

"This is for you." he said giving it to her.

She opened it. Inside was a new T-shirt with 'The Pack' on the right breast and her name underneath, a set of knee length jeans, and a leather jacket with Her Name on and 'The Pack' in big letters and also had a picture of them all on stage with their instruments and flames all around them. Then there was a selection of T-shirts and shorts.

"Do you like them?"

"Yes, they look cool, but why?"

"We need to look the part for the trip."

"Ok, what's going on?" Datch grinned.

"I can't tell you; it will spoil the surprise."

She was just about to try to get him to tell her when the door pinged.

"That will be Timbo, can you start getting The Packs out and place them along the bar." he said as he headed towards the door

Timbo was standing there blocking the light.

"Hi Timbo."

"Good morning, sir."

"It's not sir this weekend, Its Datch, just use our first names, no need for formalities, this weekend you're part of The Pack,"

"Ok sir... Datch."

"Come in and follow me to the bar, do you remember the plan?" Timbo followed Datch in.

"Yes, Datch."

"Carina, Timbo is coming with us this weekend, there should be a pack for him." she looked through the pile and found it.

"I hope it fits ok, I had to guess your size, so went for extra-extra-large" said Datch as Carina handed him the pack,

"That will be fine Datch."

He opened the pack and inside was a T-shirt and jacket. The T-shirt had 'The Pack' on it and the Jacket had 'The Pack, Road Crew.' on the back.

"Thank you," he said "What do you want me to do?"

"Well for now, have a drink and chill until our transport gets here."

"Thank you Datch."

"Transport, so we're not going on the bikes and we have road crew, we have a gig, don't we?"

"Err, don't say anything to the others yet, it's a surprise, the bikers are going to freak out, and you're going to love it."

One by one, the others turned up. Soon, The Pack was assembled and they were all wondering what was happening. Datch finally stood up and cleared his throat.

"Ok, I know your all wondering what's going on. Well, we have a big gig and it's in a special place. Also, we're going to be living the high life until we go to the Presidents banquet in four days' time."

"Where is it then?" asked Rosey.

"Ah, now that would be telling, the transport should be here in about fifteen minutes, so get another drink if you want one."

Datch went around handing out the packs to everyone.

They got some more drinks and then sat trying to get Datch to tell them where they were going but he wasn't giving anything away.

Then came the sound of engines from outside and a large shuttle craft landed outside. It was a luxury one at that. The side door opened and two smartly dressed attendants came out. Timbo got up.

"I shall go and load the stuff up sir."

"Thanks, Timbo and its Datch remember."

"Sorry Datch, it's a habit."

Timbo took the bags and instruments outside.

"Err, what's Timbo doing?"

"He's our roadcrew for the weekend."

"We have roadcrew? When did that happen?" said Dapo and Tish in unison.

"Just now apparently." said Tank downing what was left of his beer.

One of the attendants came in.

"Err, I'm looking for Datch?"

"Yes, I'm Datch."

"Your shuttle is ready for boarding when you are ready sir."

"Thank you, we'll be out shortly."

At that moment Tansya stuck her head through the door at the end of the bar, she had a big smile on her face.

"Datch, you have a really good time and that goes for all of you, we'll be watching."

"Thanks mum." said Datch.

"Watching what?" asked Carina.

"Just wait and see."

They all got up and headed out to the shuttle.

"Bloody Heck. Now that's a shuttle." said Peebop.

It was a very nice shuttle. It had big luxury seats that you almost got swallowed by and tables with vids-built in. Also, at the back was a full bar with barman and the inside was decorated in the finest quality fixtures and fittings. They all sat down and got ready for the trip.

"Ladies and Gentlemen, flight time will be approximately two hours, there is a wide selection of refreshments onboard, please feel free to ask for whatever you wish and we will try our best to supply it, thank you for flying Presidential shuttles."

"Datch, did you get the President's shuttle?" said Hagger.

"Err, no, it's just the name of company who runs them. His was busy anyway."

"Oh…"

The trip was spent with everyone trying to work out where they were going. Fred and Jep seemed to think it was north because of where the sun was. Tank reckoned it must be the coast because Datch had put his trunks in and there was desert bellow. Hagger and Rosey both thought it was the capital. Tish and Dapo had no idea and Clax was waiting for a starship to turn up. They were currently debating the what to wear for the banquet when Hagger said there were rolling hills below. They all started to look out the windows. The hills became valleys and soon majestic peaks appeared in the distance; Fred turned to Datch

"It's Traxsent, isn't it?" Datch sat back and laughed.

"Don't tell me, we're playing the Dancing Jaxx aren't we?"

"Ok, yes we're playing the Dancing Jaxx well sort of, but we're doing it outside on a big stage."

"Err, won't the Snowmen be annoyed, Yuckiday is normally their gig night?"

"They are doing our support act."

"We have a support act?" said Tish.

"Yes, but they don't know yet, the signs don't go up until tomorrow morning and then it's the sound check in the afternoon."

"Let's just hope they are not there tonight because I'm crap at keeping secrets." said Peebop.

"You won't have to; they have been told they are meeting the band in the Dancing Jaxx tonight."

"So where are we staying?"

"We all have suites at the Excelsior."

"Wow, that's five hundred credits a night." said Peebop.

"Yes, all paid for by the President."

The shuttle flew through the deep valleys following the river until it flew up and over the huge waterfalls where the river Axecon drops over two thousand metres to the valley below. The sight in the summer was amazing as the spray was causing huge rainbows. It was one of the things Traxsent was famous for. The shuttle turned and slowed down on final approach to the Excelsior. The hotel was built into the side of one of the mountains and was forty floors of glittering glass and steel. The restaurant was on the top floor overlooking the city below. It also had its own landing pad for VIP's.

As the shuttle approached Datch looked out the window and standing at the doors to the hotel was an army of porters and a man in a very posh looking suit. The shuttle came in for a prefect landing. The door opened and they got up and walked out of the door. The man in the posh suit came over to them and walked up to Datch.

"Welcome to the Excelsior sir. I am Surju, the concierge. Please follow me to your suites, the porters will get your things."

"Thank you." Datch said and then turned to Timbo.

"Timbo, can you make sure the gear for the gig is sorted please."

"Yes, will do Datch."

"And Timbo, can you meet us in the bar in about an hour."

"No problem Datch."

They followed the concierge into the hotel.

"We have floor twenty-seven for you. It contains twelve luxury suites and private spa room. I hope they will be acceptable."

"I'm sure that will be fine thanks." said Datch.

They were taken to their rooms which turned out to be more like apartments.

Datch walked into his suite. It was huge with a large lounge with its own bar and a jacuzzi. He then went into the bedroom. It had a bed that made his look like a cushion and was so big you could sleep a whole family in it. He walked back into the lounge. In the centre of the lounge was a table with a big bouquet of flowers on, a large box of chocolates and a bottle of Champaign on ice complete with two glasses. Datch read the label attached to them. 'Welcome to the Excelsior, we hope you enjoy your stay with us'. He decided to try it and picked up the bottle. It had a strange thing stuck in the top. He looked at it and asked his implant what it was. It was a cork and you undid the wire around the top to open it. He removed the wire but it still didn't open so he pressed against the back of the cork. It started to move and then shot out like a bullet. Luckily a forcefield stopped it before it could do any damage. The Champaign bubbled out of the top of the bottle and Datch poured it into a glass. He looked at it closely, it was like fizzy pop. He took a sip and the bubbles went up his nose but it tasted ok. There was a ping at the door.

"Come in" he said.

The door opened and in came a porter with his bag and asked if he would like her to put the clothes away. Datch said yes and the porter sorted it out. Datch was starting his second glass as she left.

The door pinged again, this time it was Carina.

"Hello lover." she said walking in.

"Hi babes."

She walked over and wrapped her arms around him and gave him a big kiss.

"What do you think about the surprise?" he said.

"This place is amazing, what made you want to do this?"

"Well, I said I would like to bring you all here to see The Dancing Jaxx and the President gave me the chance to do it in style." he gave her a glass of Champaign, "To the Pack."

They took a sip and moved over to the large glass window.

"To us." she added.

They stood arm in arm sipping the Champaign looking out across the city and the river. Datch pointed out the Dancing Jaxx to her. You could see the outdoor stage going up in the large park to the rear of the bar. There was also a lot a people milling about. They watched while they finished their drinks.

"Well, let's head to the bar, the others will be waiting."

"Yes, we had better."

That night they all set out for The Dancing Jaxx with Timbo running security of sorts. It was only a couple of streets away and the evening air was a nice twenty-two degrees. They walked down the road discussing things like the bathrooms in the suites and how nice it looked also the bikers told the rest how different the city was in the snow. They arrived at the dancing Jaxx. It was a large building with a huge animated Jaxx on the roof which was lit up with colour changing spot lights. It was circular in shape with glass panels all the way around the outside. It was one of the larger buildings in that part of town and had a wide-open space outside with a number of benches and tables dotted around. It also now had a rather large stage being erected in the large park at the back. The fences had been removed to enlarge the area to accommodate a very large crowd.

They headed into the bar and a waiter came over to see them.

"Can I help you?" he said.

"Hello, I'm Datch and this is The Pack, we should have a big table in the corner." he said.

"Ah, Mr Datch, Please, follow me to the table and I will tell the owners you are here."

They followed the waiter across the bar to a large table in its own booth and sat down. The waiter gave them some menus and took their drinks order before heading back to the bar.

The owners came over and thanked them for requesting the Dancing Jaxx as the venue for the concert. The government had paid them fifty thousand credits to stage the event. They said the food was free for the length of their stay and the drinks were all being paid for by Joni Jabi of Channel 14. Datch had given him exclusive rights for broadcasting the gig. They said they would go and fetch The Snowmen but Datch asked if they could tell them to come over in ten minutes. The owners looked at him and he winked, they agreed before heading back across the bar.

"Why ten minutes?" asked Fred.

"Err, for theatrical effect." Datch said.

"Theatrical effect?" said Tish.

"Yes, I want to surprise them."

"Well, I think that's going to happen anyway." said Tank.

"Just watch!"

Datch gave a big grin and got up before heading across the bar. In the corner sitting down were The Snowmen. Datch walked around the area before coming back from the direction of the toilets. As he approached, he pretended to see them for the first time and went walking over.

"I've got to hand it to him, he acts just like a pro." said Fred looking around a screen so he could see him.

Datch walked up to the table.

"Hi Datch, wow fancy seeing you here," said Talia.

"Hi folks, how are you all?"

"We're good, what are you doing here?"

"I'm here for the concert, Carina said they are really good and wanted to see them but wouldn't tell me what they were called, do you know?"

"Oh, he's very good! remind me never to play poker with him." said Fred turning to Tank.

Talia smiled at Datch,

"No, I know what you mean though. We have to meet them in a couple of minutes, it's a secret, we don't even know who they are apart from the fact they wanted us as a support act."

"Oh, well I had better go. I'll see you with Carina later, then maybe you can tell me who they are."

"Ok, see you in a bit Datch, we'll look forward to meeting Carina."

With that Datch left them taking the long way around the bar so as not to give it away, he got back to the table and sat down.

"I take it you just went fishing and now you're going to reel them in?" said Clax.

"Err, reel them in? I'm not sure what you mean, but it will be cool."

The Snowmen got up and walked across the bar towards the big table. They came around the screen and there was The Pack which now included Datch with a very big grin on his face. They stopped.

"You're the big band?" said Talia.

"Err," Datch looked at the rest of them as if checking "Yes, we are The Pack."

They just stood there open mouthed. Finally, Jarna spoke,

"Wow, I really don't know what to say." she said.

"Well just sit down and have a drink."

Datch waved his hand at the bar and a waiter came over with round of drinks, The Snowmen sat down.

"Let me introduce everyone, the bikers you know, this is Dapo and Tish, Hagger and Rosey, this here is Jep and our roadcrew Timbo and finally this is Carina, my girlfriend."

"It's great to meet you all at last even if it is a bit of a shock, I'm Talia, this is Jarna, Starg and Bilow"

"So, where are you staying?"

"We have a whole floor at The Excelsior." said Fred.

"What! how the..." she tailed off.

Datch was grinning.

"Go on then spill the beans, what did you do?"

The next hour was spent telling the story of how they saved the President and killed the spider. Then the conversation turned to the gig.

"We do rock songs, I'm doing Star Lovers with Carina, also Space Dust, Wilde Wind, Rocking the City, Hot City Nights, Someone to Love, Bikers Dream and also No Place to

Hide. We normally do two sets but tomorrow we're just doing one with the encore's being Planet Rock and Super Nova, does that sound ok?" Talia looked at Th Snowmen and they nodded.

"Yes, that sounds good for us." she said.

"Oh, one more thing, the whole gig is going out live on channel 14, Joni Jabi will be hosting it. You will each be paid five thousand credits for the performance. Is that ok?"

"What! oh bugger I need to get my hair done and go shopping for clothes and err…" Jarna went into a bit of a panic.

"It's all in hand, Timbo has a Vid Comm, go sit with him to choose your clothes and he'll have them for you by the sound check tomorrow afternoon. There is a hair and makeup team coming from Channel 14 and half an hour before the concert starts, Joni is going to interview us."

"We have another interview?" said Dapo.

"Err, yes, just remember how much you're getting paid."

"You didn't tell us we're getting paid." said Clax.

"Oh, yes, we're getting paid."

"Well go on then, how much?" asked Fred.

"Err, fifty thousand each." Datch said quietly.

"How much!" said Jep.

There was a fountain of beer from Tank's direction.

"Fifty thousand." Datch repeated.

"Bloody hell, that's it, I'm buying a new bike." said Tank.

"Is there anything else you're not telling us?" asked Fred.

"Err, I don't think so, that's all of it."

"Are you sure?" asked Clax.

"Yes, as far as I know." said Datch feeling the pressure due to the fact that everyone was looking at him.

They changed the subject and ordered a large bucket of fried Hacks. Another hour went past and then a man came over to the table. Carina looked up

"Oh, Hi Joni, how's it going?" she asked.

"Ok thanks, I just wanted to touch base with you and see if there is anything you need?"

"I think we're good thanks, would you like to join us?" she said.

"No thanks, I have some work to do before the concert, so I'll see you all tomorrow."

"Ok Joni, have a good evening." said Datch, there was a chorus of see you later.

He turned and headed off across the bar.

"That was Joni Jabi!" said Jarna.

"Yes" said Tish then added casually "He's a lot shorter than he looks on the vid."

Rosey and Carina laughed, Datch watched them. They were starting to feel comfortable with the fame, he was too. It was like a party that gets better every time and tomorrow was going to be fantastic.

They carried-on drinking until after midnight at which point Timbo got a taxi to take them back to the hotel.

The Taxi dropped them off outside. They walked in and headed up to their rooms. Datch walked Carina to her room and stopped outside the door for a goodnight kiss.

"Not tonight lover boy." she said and pulled him in the room closing the door behind him.

"But my clothes are in my room" he said.

"Trust me, you're not going to need them."

"Oh…" and then the lights dimmed.

The next morning the door pinged in Carina's suite. She got up and headed to the door grabbing a dressing gown on the way.

"Who is it?" she said.

"It's Tank."

"Ok, door open." the door opened.

"Sorry to wake you. Datch said he would see us for breakfast but he's not turned up and he's not answering his door."

"Ahh, well, I might be able to answer that." she turned towards the bedroom.

"Datch, you're late for breakfast." Datch stuck his head around the bedroom door.

"Oh, sorry, it slipped my mind." he said.

"Oh, kay… I'll just go and err, tell them you'll both be along in a err, bit?"

"Yes, a bit is good." said Carina slowly closing the door.

Tank walked off down the corridor wondering how he was going to explain this to the others who had sent him up to find Datch.

The restaurant was quite busy when Tank got back. They had been given a big table in the corner. Apparently, it was down on a list somewhere that contained the things they liked.

"So, did you find him?" asked Fred.

"Err, yes."

"Err yes, you don't sound so sure."

"Well, he was with Carina."

"So, they're coming down then?" said Clax.

"Err, not just yet, they said they might be a while."

"Why, what are they doing?"

Tank was feeling very uncomfortable and was looking a little pink.

"Err, well he was in Carina's bedroom." he started to blush.

"Ah, I see." said Clax.

"Isn't it a nice view, wow look at that over there." Fred said quickly trying to change the subject.

They all started to look out the window looking for whatever Fred was on about but didn't find it. They had breakfast and sat having a coffee while the bikers took great pleasure pointing out all the good places to go.

Around an hour later Datch and Carina finally made it to breakfast.

"Sorry we're late, Datch stopped with me last night." said Carina apologetically.

"Well, Dapo stayed with me last night but we made it to breakfast." Tish announced and then realised what she had said.

Dapo and Tish went pink. Poor Hagger had gone very red. Fred at this point stepped in to save Hagger from exploding with embarrassment.

"Well, I think we should change the subject." he said hoping that it would switch to the scenery outside.

"You should stop with me tonight as well." said Rosey to Hagger.

He wasn't just red faced now but also had grin from ear to ear. Which had the effect of making him look like someone that had been really badly sunburnt and had gone crazy with the pain.

"Ok, look, let's just get away from the bedroom talk and let Datch and Carina have some breakfast so we can head out."

There was a general agreement on this and after several pancakes and another round of coffees, they headed out of the hotel.

"So Datch, where to?" said Fred.

"The River, I thought you could show us the sights." Datch replied.

What was left of the morning was spent walking around Traxsent with the bikers adding commentary on this and that. They stopped off at a café next to the river and had some lunch before heading back to the Dancing Jaxx for the sound check.

The Dancing Jaxx was very busy. There was a cordon around the area leading to the stage with a very large number of security officers and Timbo. They walked over to him. He let them in and handed passes to each of them. They hung them around their necks.

"Dressing rooms are at the back of the stage. The Snowmen are already there. Oh, and the President's daughter has arrived with her friends and wanted to say hi, I think she's in the bar."

Datch looked over to The Dancing Jaxx, a number of security officers were standing outside and trying to look very big.

"Ok, thanks Timbo, we'll do the sound check and then pop over to see her."

They turned towards the stage.

The stage was big. It must have been at least two metres high and fifteen metres wide. It had a lighting rig suspended about twenty metres above them which had hundreds of lights on it. The sound system was huge with two large speaker stacks. One on each side of the stage along with a large vid wall. About one hundred metres back from the stage was a sound and lighting booth on a raised platform. As people finished using their tables, they were being removed ready for the gig and the barriers were being placed further and further back. The Dancing Jaxx had put up a large outdoor bar and was busy stocking it up. They walked up the steps and stood on the stage looking out.

"Bloody heck, how many are they expecting?" said Tish looking out.

"The organisers said yesterday that all twenty thousand tickets had been sold." said Datch casually.

"Twenty thousand." Clax said slowly.

Then the number came into focus,

"Twenty thousand! Twenty bloody thousand!" he repeated suddenly realising what he was saying.

"Yes, that was what they said, the tickets sold out in fifteen minutes. People had seen us on the Vid and the planetary networks and wanted to come. There are fleets of shuttles inbound right now. The hotels are loving it, they are all full to bursting point."

"Wow, that's a lot of people." said Carina.

"Yep, and they all want to see us live." Said Datch.

"I thought it was a lot of people when we played the Barbers last week." said Dapo.

They stood looking at the area in front of the stage for ten minutes or more before heading to the back of the stage.

At the back of the stage were the dressing rooms and outside of each was a security guard checking their passes as they went in. The dressing room had various types of food and drink in it on a very posh looking table and also some fresh bouquets of flowers for the ladies and Tank.

"Wow, I'm loving this." said Peebop sitting down in a very posh looking chair.

"Yes, this is something else. I'm getting a little nervous though." said Hagger.

"Well, don't be, we won't see most of the people for the lights. We're going up there to have a good time. Ok, let's do the sound check and get used to the stage, I think we'll do Star Lovers and Wilde Wind. Does that sound ok?" asked Datch.

There was a lot of nodding and Datch poked his head out of the door. The security guard turned to look at him.

"Can you let them know, we're ready for the sound check."

"Certainly sir, I'll knock on the door when they're ready for you to go out."

Datch went back inside and gave everyone a pep talk before they were called. Timbo appeared and they followed him on to the stage. He showed them to their instruments and showed them how the stage was laid out. They were given an ear piece with a tiny mic attached to wear. They put them on and took up positions on the stage.

A voice came through the ear piece.

"Hi all, I'm Jass the sound engineer. Put your thumbs up if you can hear me."

They all put their thumbs up.

"Ok, start a song and I'll do the rest."

They started to play and the engineer worked his magic slowly altering the settings until they sounded perfect. It took a couple of attempts on each of the two songs before he was happy. The lights were locked into their ear pieces and would follow them across the stage. The check lasted about twenty minutes in total. Datch was right. The lights were very bright and it was like being at The Barbers Inn but with more space. They finished the check and gave the engineer the set list before turning to leave the stage. The Snowmen were standing at the back and clapped. After a round of congratulation, they arranged to meet in the bar after their sound check.

The Pack headed down the back of the stage and were shown a back way into the bar. It was very busy inside and an area had been cordoned off at the back. There were at least ten security officers guarding it. They went across and when the officers spotted them, they let them in. Datch told them that The Snowmen would be joining them soon as well. There was a table with five girls around it. As they approach the President's daughter got up.

"Hi, I was hoping you would come over."

"Well, your dad helped set this up so we thought we should." said Datch.

Then followed a round of introductions and then a lot of small talk, with things like, 'I love the Vid' or 'You're awesome' and 'I can't wait till later' and then The Snowmen came in. Another round of introductions followed and more small talk. The afternoon was soon over and the two bands headed back behind the stage to the dressing rooms.

The Pack got changed ready for the gig and sat waiting for Joni Jabi to come and do the interview. It didn't take long. He came in and then took them to a studio set that had been built next to the side of the stage. They went in and sat down. It had nice plush furniture and a coffee table in the middle. Around the set were pictures of them in The Barbers Inn playing and also a couple of pictures of them playing Solar Ball. He started filming and did his announcing bit before they were introduced and asked a number of questions that had been agreed to earlier. Then came the big one, 'how does it feel to be playing in front of twenty thousand people?'. The vid screen showed a view from outside. There were thousands of people and aliens crowding into the area in front of the stage.

"Err, I was feeling ok until you put it on the Vid." said Fred.

The others all agreed.

"How are you going to be on a big stage?"

"Well Joni, we're just going to do what we do in the Barbers Inn and have fun." said Datch.

"So, everyone wants to know, how are you coping with the fame?"

"What fame?" said Carina "We're just doing our thing."

The others all nodded.

"Well folks, that about wraps it up as its time for you to get ready. Thank you very much for the interview." He turned to the Vid, "This is the Joni Jabi show, we'll be right back after the break."

The light on the camera went out.

"I'll be having a few drinks after the gig if you want to join me?"

They said they might before getting up and leaving the studio.

As they walked back, they could see the crowd. It was huge and stretched from the front of the stage right across the park and up the sides of The Dancing Jaxx. The bar was almost lost in the sea of bodies, then the lights on the stage came on and The Snowmen hit the stage to cheers and shouts from the crowd. They stood at the side watching for a few minutes before going back to the dressing room.

"Err, I'm real nervous right now." said Hagger.

"I think we all are." said Tish.

Datch needed to do his team thing. He thought about it and then worked out what to do.

"Ok, We're all very nervous. It's a big crowd but just remember we were the same the first time we played in The Barbers Inn. This is no different. Yes, there are a lot of people but they want to see us. There're no big speeches, just us doing our thing. They have seen us on the vid and they love it because we're just having fun, so that's what we have to do." He stopped.

"Well, that was one heck of a pep talk Datch." said Fred grinning.

"Yes, talk about speeches, you should run for President." said Jep.

"I'm not sure the planet would survive that." said Tank laughing.

They all were now smiling again, it had worked.

They had a couple of drinks and a few snacks and then there was a knock on the door and it opened.

"Five minutes folks." The security guard said around the door.

Datch stood up.

"Well, its show time folks, now let's go out there and party, what are we going to do?"

"Party." they said.

"I can't hear you, what are we going to do?"

"PARTY!" They all shouted and left the room for the stage.

As they got to the edge of the stage The Snowmen were just coming off.

"Wow, what a buzz," said Talia, "you have fun folks."

The noise from the crowd was deafening.

"Huddle guys."

They all grouped into a circle and Datch put his hand out in the middle. They followed him and placed theirs on top and then Datch moved his up in the air.

"THREE! TWO! ONE! let's party!" he shouted and let go.

The Pack ran on the stage to an electric atmosphere. The lights flashed and crowd roared and then Datch remember what he had seen other bands do.

"Hello Traxsent, are you ready to party?"

The crowd roared again.

"I can't hear you, are you ready to party?"

The noise from the crowd went far beyond the loud level.

Datch turned to the others and nodded. Then he hit the first note and the crowd erupted. The next hour was the most incredible experience of Datch's life. They even threw in a song they were still learning. The whole city vibrated to the sound of The Pack and as for when Datch kissed Carina. It was like being plugged into a quantum singularity the feeling was so intense. They could all feel it. It felt like they were super heroes. The crowd was singing along with them. By the time they finally left the stage their heads were buzzing and spinning with energy.

They got back to the dressing room.

"Err, did anyone else think that went well?" said Tank with a big grin.

"Just a bit." said Clax.

"Bloody Jaxx." said Jep.

"I'll second that." said Dapo.

"I said we could do it." Datch said.

"Wow." said Tish.

"Wow again" said Rosey and Carina together.

"Err, I think I need a proper drink." said Hagger and everyone burst out laughing.

They sat down and opened a beer.

There was a knock on the door.

"Yes" said Datch, Joni Jabi stuck his head around the door.

"I just thought you might like to know. The shows viewing figures are in, we had four and a half billion viewers tonight. The feed was picked up by six other stations. People were even watching on the other side of the planet."

"Bloody Jaxx, four and a half billion." repeated Jep.

"I'm going for a drink now if you want to come over later?"

"Cool, we will I hope and thanks for the info Joni, that's amazing." said Datch.

He left them and they went back to chatting, drinking and trying to calm down. Ten minutes later Timbo came in.

"Hi Timbo, how you doing?" said Tank.

"Err," He looked a little stressed, "you can't go in the bar, it's not safe."

"What do you mean not safe?" asked Datch.

"It is totally packed out; the place is rammed. The security services have stopped the President's daughter from going in there. It's out of control over there."

"Oh, we wanted a beer or two with our friends." said Fred.

"Don't worry, The Excelsior has agreed to allow an after party in the spare suit on your floor if you want?" said Timbo.

"That's cool, but how do we get there?"

"I have a shuttle standing by for you."

"Oh, let's go then, oh can you get The Snowmen, the President's daughter plus friends and Joni Jabi plus friends."

"There are about a dozen VIP's that would like to come as well if that's ok."

"I suppose it's an after party, why not." said Fred.

With that, they were escorted out to a shuttle at the back of the stage. They were joined a few moments later by The Snowmen who hadn't been able to get to the Dancing Jaxx.

"So, where we going?" said Jarna sitting down.

"Party at our place!" said Dapo grinning.

"Oh nice!" said Bilow.

The shuttle lifted off and almost immediately another one landed in its spot. The shuttle turned and flew up over the streets at were packed with people and landed on the VIP pad at The Excelsior. They were escorted down to the spare suit where the staff were busy converting it into a bar. It only took a few minutes and when it was complete it was about a quarter of the size of the Baber's Inn but had much better furniture.

They sat around a coffee table with beers and various other concoctions that Tish and Carina were trying out. In fact, they were working their way through the cocktail list and Tank was helping them. Hagger decided he didn't like beer and started drinking something called Old Man's Boots and mixing it with Gruck. Clax said it tasted like jet fuel and it was making Hagger glow a bit.

They were just starting the second round when one of the hotel staff came over.

"Excuse me, we have some people asking to come to the party?"

"Yes, Timbo can you sort this out, oh and by the way your being paid double."

"Certainly." he said getting up with a very large grin on his face.

"Wow, he looks happy." said Carina fishing a piece of fruit out of her drink.

"He should be, he's just got two month's wages in four days." said Fred.

"And he's able to party at the same time." said Clax "Win-win I would say."

"Yes, it's a good weekend for all of us." said Datch, "Do you think we can do this again?"

"Well, let's think about it." said Rosey who was now helping Hagger with his Old Man's Boots and Gruck's,

"We have just played in front of twenty thousand people and the concert was broadcast to four and half billion homes, not only that, we came off the stage feeling like we were super human and are now hosting our own after party in the poshest hotel I've ever been in. Err what do you think?"

"I'm in." said Hagger and then he burped.

"Yep, me too." said Dapo eating a piece of fruit that he had acquired from Tish.

"Really! After tonight there's no going back is there?" said Carina.

The others all nodded in agreement. Datch stood up.

"Well then my friends, here's to The Pack!"

They all lifted their glasses and took a drink. Tank cleared his throat,

"On a personal note, I would like to say that at no point tonight did I get any underwear thrown at me." he said with a grin and everyone burst out laughing.

"Well, if you folks ever need a support band. The Snowmen are more than ready. However, we might change the band's name, it doesn't quite fit the gig." said Talia.

The Guests started to arrive and the party started to happen. The President's daughter and friends turned up along with a number of security officers. Then, Joni Jabi with his crew, followed by the sound engineer and a couple of his friends. Then there was a request from a couple of record company representatives who were let in on the understanding that they didn't talk about anything to do with work. Also, the owners of the Dancing Jaxx who apparently couldn't get a beer in their own bar as it was still rammed solid along with a number of VIP's who had flown in to see the concert and were staying in the hotel.

The party carried on until the early hours and was spent chatting to people. Then an impromptu sing along with The Snowmen followed by the arrival of a karaoke machine and a number of other people trying to sing. It was a good job the President's daughter had a powerful father because she couldn't sing to save her life. Joni on the other hand did have quite a good voice and funny enough so did one of the large security officers. Finally, people started to head off to their rooms. Hagger got up and fell over. He had found out why they called it Old Man's Boots. The top part of you wanted to move but the boots stayed planted to the spot. Rosey helped him back to her room. Then it was Datch and Carina's turn. They headed to Carina's room. The rest followed and went off to bed.

Next morning Datch woke up to find Carina stroking his shoulder. It was a wonderful feeling.

"Morning lover." she said and then he kissed her.

"Morning to you to babes."

He pulled her in close and she turned so that she was sitting on top of him.

"I have you now," she said pinning him down.

"So, what are you going to do with me"

"This…"

* The next hour has been censored due to adult content *

Mid-morning came and they headed up to the restaurant. The bikers were sitting with Jep having breakfast.

"Morning dudes" said Datch.

"Morning you two, sleep well?" answered Fred.

"Yes, we did thanks, have you seen the others?" said Carina.

"I've seen Hagger and Rosey." said Tank "Let's just say that they both now know what the term hangover means. They are staying in bed for the moment with a do not disturb sign on the door. I think they need to recover."

"Oh, we just took a couple of nano pills before going sleep." said Datch.

"We did too, apparently they didn't know about them." said Tank.

"Ouch! That Old Man's Boot was strong stuff too." said Jep.

"Yes, I gave Tish a couple of pills as well." said Carina.

"Talking about Tish and Dapo, here they come."

Across the restaurant came Tish with Dapo in tow. After another round of good mornings along with an explanation as to Hagger and Rosey's absence, a very large plate of pancakes was ordered and serval large coffees. It didn't take them long to polish it all off and then Fred turned to Datch.

"So, what's the plan for today then dude?"

"I thought we could go up the mountain."

"Err, we don't have our bikes?"

"Actually, we do, I had Timbo put them in the hold of the shuttle before we took off, they're down stairs in storage."

"Why?"

"Well, I figured that we'd get hassled by people wanting autographs today, so I wanted to get out of town, the mountain seemed like a good idea."

"Err, aren't we two bikes short." said Clax, "Sorry, one bike." he added remembering Hagger and Rosey were indisposed.

"No, I brought a couple of spares."

"Well, what are we waiting for, Oh and don't forget we can't stop on the lake this time, it's full of water." Clax was already standing up along with Peebop.

"Tank, go and tell Hagger and Rosey that we're going out and we'll see them later, oh and give them these." Datch got a couple of pills out of his pocket.

"Are these what I think they are?" said Tank looking suspiciously at the little blue pills.

"Yes, my dad gave them to me just in case."

"Oh right, I'll drop them in and then meet you down in the lobby."

"Err, Blue Pills?" asked Jep.

"Don't ask." said Fred.

Thirty minutes later they were flying though the forests having a great time. The sun was beating down and they were going for it. The mountains looked different in the summer.

Dust was being thrown up in the air now instead of the snow. He had Carina hanging on to him and his friends all around. This was the life, an hour and a half later they arrived on top of the mountain. It was so high there was still snow laying in drifts. The view was stunning with rolling forests stretching out into the distance. Some of the other peaks also had snow on the top and the contrast between the green of the forest below and the white snow on the top was breath taking.

Carina, Tish and Dapo jumped off the bikes and ran over to a big snow drift. They then found out that snow could be slippy and all ended up on their bums much to the biker's entertainment. Datch walked over and helped Carina up.

"Are you ok babes?"

"Yes, I think so." said Carina.

"I did that the first time I went on the ice; you have to move a bit slower."

"I'd never seen it before other than on the Vid."

"Just copy me." he said helping her across the snow. Dapo and Tish gingerly followed as they carefully walked over to the bikers who were heading into the bar. They went though and found some seats outside on the terrace. Even though the snow was still on the ground, the sun was hot.

"Err, that snow is tricky stuff." said Dapo.

"Yes, no one told us it was slippy." added Tish.

"Well, it is made of ice." said Clax grinning.

"I know, but I didn't expect it to be like that." she said.

"Everyone looks to be having so much fun on it in the vids." said Carina.

"Just to let everybody know. When I first came to Traxsent, I came out of the shuttle port and fell straight on my ass." said Datch trying to remove the embarrassed looks from them. "It was then I found out how to walk on it."

"And how's that then?" asked Dapo.

"Err, very slowly." he said and the bikers burst out laughing.

"Yes, or get some snow boots." said Fred.

"Snow boots? You mean the fluffy boots." said Carina.

"No, Snow boots, they have metal spikes on the bottom to give extra grip."

"I'll get some of them if we come again."

"I think we should all come next winter solstice, the snow will be deep and we can bring the bikes. If you liked the ride up here today, you'll love it in the snow."

"Yes, and you can learn to ski!" said Tank.

"And why would we want to do that?" said Jep.

"Well, we had to." added Clax.

"What do you mean had to?"

The bikers all turned and looked at Datch who was now grinning.

"Well, you have to admit, it was fun." he said.

"Please tell, they never said about being made to." asked Jep who was suddenly very interested.

"Let's get the food and drinks first." said Fred hoping to distract them enough so the story didn't get told again.

The dinks arrived and soon after so did the food,

"Ok then," said Jep picking up a hacks wing, "what happened?"

The bikers looked worried.

They sat eating while Datch filled in all the missing bits about the winter visit to Traxsent. There were various points where laughter was heard and one point were Fred wished he could hide under the table. After Datch had finished and the food was gone they went for a walk on the snow before heading back to the hotel.

The remaining couple of days were spent chilling out and having fun. Datch and Carina went in the spa and found out why his mum liked it so much. Then it was time to head home and to the banquet. Jep pointed out it would be a breeze and just to remember the lecture about etiquette at formal dinners. Tank said he had missed that one because he was in the bar either that or he had forgotten it as it was over three hundred years ago so Jep helped him remember.

The Banquet

They boarded the shuttle and headed home. They were going to Tanks first to get ready before heading straight to the banquet. The shuttle was due to arrive back in the city about two hours before. Timbo was going to sort out the luggage and the bikes. Then make sure they were all delivered to their respective homes.

They arrived at Tank's. The shuttle landing gently outside and they headed into Tank's apartment. The girls got to use the bathroom first as they needed to do their hair and then the boys went in. After an hour they were starting to look respectable. The boys had dress shirts and jackets. Datch had been told to wear his acting ensign's uniform. The girls were in very smart dress suits and looked amazing. There were a few moments of do I look ok and can you help with this but overall, it went to plan. They stood looking at each other.

"We don't look right." said Clax.

"What do you mean?" said Fred.

"Well, I'm used to going out in my jeans and leather jacket or T-shirts."

"I know but tonight we look posh, ok?"

"Yes, ok, but tomorrow I'm staying in jeans and T-shirt all day."

A luxury limo came for them. It was the size of a small shuttle and had smoked glass windows. They got inside and it took off heading for the government buildings on the other side of the city.

"Err, I think I'm more nervous about this than anything else ever." said Datch.

"Why?"

"Well, I'm going up there with just my dad."

"We'll still be there with you." said Carina.

"Yes, we've got your back, just enjoy it, you did die after all." said Tank.

"Ok." said Datch looking a bit apprehensive.

"Hey lover, come on, I've never seen you like this, why now?" asked Carina.

Datch looked at her with puppy dog eyes.

"We're always together, today it's just me."

They suddenly realised that Datch needed them as much as they needed him. He might always be the strong one but he got his strength from them. He was like a captain of a ship and they were the ship. Take the ship from under the captain and he would flap around helpless in the water. Take the captain away from the ship and it would head out of control and sink. The Pack was one unit and they only worked when they were together.

"You're not Datch, we're all up there with you even if we're not standing next to you." said Fred, the other all agreed.

They put their hands out and waited for Datch, he looked at them all and put his hand in and Fred said, "three, two, one, for the Pack!" they broke hands.

"Now go get them Datch!" said Tank.

The Limo landed outside and they were shown into the main stateroom. The place was decked out with long flowing drapes, it had a raised platform with a podium and there were a number of long tables, most of which were full of people. They were shown past the various members of government with their wives or husbands, past the rows of ambassadors from this world and others, past the rows of celebrities and various other people who had managed to get a ticket. Then there a headed of them was another large table with Dechow and Tansya along with the other parents. All were dressed up in their finest. Tansya and Dechow got up to meet them.

"Here is my little Hero." Tansya said giving Datch a big hug.

Dechow shook his hand and gave him a funny look that Datch hadn't seen before. Datch figured it couldn't be a bad one because his dad was still smiling. After a lot of hellos, they sat down. Dechow was next to Tansya then Datch and Carina and then her mum and dad followed by the rest in some sort of random order that somehow made sense. On the table opposite was Captain Don Ronediamar, commander Isbar, Fizz and the head of planetary security, all wearing their dress suits.

After fifteen minutes the lights dimmed slightly and the President came in and went to the podium.

"Ladies, gentlemen and aliens, it is my great pleasure to welcome you all on this special occasion. It is customary on these occasions to serve dinner first. That way you can all fall asleep during the speeches."

There was a lot of stifled laugher and then he continued,

"Dinner will now be served, please enjoy."

He left the podium and headed to the table opposite. Waiters came out and went around each table starting at the front. Datch was a bit worried about getting food on his uniform but Carina told him to take the serviette and tuck it in his front while he was eating. Tansya smiled to herself. he might be her son but he now did everything Carina told him to.

The food came out and looked incredible, they stared to tuck in, Jep was taking notes.

"Jep, what are you doing?" said Clax in between chomping his way through a very good-looking steak.

"Err, marking students."

"What, we're here for Datch, not to give him marks out of ten."

"It's not Datch, its some of the year two students, three of them are waiters."

"Oh, I see, well, err, mark away." Clax moved his attention back to the steak.

The meal really was nice and the wine was well wine with alcohol. Lucky for The Pack that they were used to it after the weekend. Then the sweets came out and then it was time for the speech. The President went up to the podium and cleared his throat. The room went quiet and he started his speech,

"Ladies, gentlemen and aliens, get ready for a tale of courage and valour. As you will all know by now, last week an attempt was made on my life. I came to the state opening of the new power plant in Yuland city and as I started to give my speech, an arachnoid dropped down in front of me. Its aim, to kill me. It had a scattering field around its neck that would have stopped my transport to a new body and thus resulting in my death. Three brave people stopped it, but the story didn't start there let me tell you. These three people along with their friends had been on the trail of the arachnoid for a few months. No one would have believed them so they created the call from off world to warn people. I'm sure there are a number of people alive today because of the warnings on the news. The leader of this group, is a young individual named Datch. He contacted the IPSF for help and Captain Don Ronediamar of the starship Carpaycus came to aid him. This one young man put his life on the line and died while trying to locate the monster that had been terrorising the city. But he had built a device that stopped the scattering field and allowed him in his moment of death to be transported to the

Carpaycus. Unphased by his death he came to the power plant along with his farther and commander Isbar. Datch distracted the beast long enough for commander Isbar to get me to safety while his dad retired commander Dechow Thome, fired at monster. All of which could have led to their deaths but instead, the beast was killed. You have all seen the vid of it on the news. This young man showed amazing courage as he faced the monster not just once but twice and, in the process, saved my life. This is a debt that I can never repay but I can reward. Please ladies, gentlemen and aliens please put your hands together for Datch, Dechow and commander Isbar."

He gestured for them to come up. Everyone in the room stood up and clapped as the three of them got up and headed for the podium.

"Ladies, gentlemen and aliens it is my great pleasure to give these three brave souls The Freedom of the Planet for their outstanding bravery."

He turned behind him, a man had a box with gold chains in. He gave him a chain with a decorative pendent on which had a number of jewels symbolising the planet and its moons. He placed each one in turn around their necks and then turned back to the room.

"Please put your hands together for Datch, Dechow and commander Isbar."

The room got up to their feet clapping. The President came and stood next to Datch. When the clapping started to die down and people sat back down Datch whispered something in the President's ear.

"Well go on then." he said.

Datch went up to the podium with his dad following for support while wondering what Datch was up to.

"Err," he said and the room went quiet.

"Go on then." said his dad quietly. There were a few titters.

"Ladies, gentlemen and aliens," Datch looked at his dad, his dad nodded, "I would not have been able to do this without my friends. They are the most err, wonderful people I know and I love them all. Dapo, Tish, especially Hagger who lost his dad to the spider, Rosey, Tank, Jep, Clax, Peebop, Fred and most of all, my girlfriend Carina, all of you please come up here." They got up and headed for the podium to rounds of applause. When they get got there the room cheered.

"Well, it's like a gig but without instruments." Fred said to Datch, the President over heard him.

"Well maybe I can fix that," he said with a wink, "I figured you might want to do a song so my daughter had a word with Timbo for me while you were in Traxsent."

He went back to the podium and said to the room "What about a song from The Pack."

There was another round of applause and then the President led them to the corner. There was Timbo with their instruments and a mini stage like at The Barbers Inn. They took up positions and Datch turned to the rest and said "Planet Rock."

They played and the room vibrated to the sound of The Pack. A number of old government officials looked like they wanted to stick their fingers in their ears but other than that everyone enjoyed it.

They finished the song and went back and sat down, an orchestra came out and took their place. They played somewhat quieter music than The Pack.

Tansya took a moment to talk to Datch.

"So, did you enjoy Traxsent?"

"It was cool, we had a great time, the gig was fantastic."

"Yes, we watched it on the vid. You looked like you were having fun. We tried to call your room after the gig, but couldn't get through."

"Oh, we had an after party."

"We, tried to call you the next day to," Datch's hairs were starting to stand up on his neck, something wasn't right.

"Err, we were out seeing the sights."

"Yes, I bet you were at nine in the morning." Datch realised that his mum knew more than she was letting on.

"Mum, what's going on?"

She looked at him, smiled and whispered in his ear.

"We were worried about you and called the hotel, they said you were staying in Carina's room." Datch wet red.

Dechow let out a laugh on seeing Datch, Carina looked around.

"Err, don't panic, we talked to Fred, it's all cool." Tansya said.

Datch breathed a sigh of relief.

"What's the matter?" Carina asked.

Datch whispered in her ear and she went slightly pink as well.

"Well, I think you had better clean your room up when we get back, ready for next time Carina stays with us."

Datch thought about this for a moment and then it clicked.

"Oh, Yes, as soon as I get back." he stopped and then continued "Err, well tomorrow morning anyway." he added.

He told Carina that they were cool with things and what they had told him to do. There was a quick conversation before they turned back to everyone else. Both of them were grinning which had the effect of putting everyone else on edge much to Datch's and Carina's entertainment.

As people mixed and mingled. Datch must have told the story a hundred times along with the rest of them. They were even taken to be introduced to the President's wives, all of whom were very grateful.

Don came over for a while but was soon dragged off by some ambassador from somewhere. Isbar made an early exit as he was heading up to Traxsent to see Jarna for a couple of days.

Datch and Carina sat watching the rest of the party.

"So, lover, you had better get your room ready for the weekend."

Datch laughed and kissed her.

"I will Babes, I will."

"So, what's next Datch?" asked Fred sitting down next to them

"I think it might be time to rock the galaxy."

Fred looked at him for a moment, unsure on whether he was joking or not. He turned to Tank.

"You know your uncle on Alcyone three."

"Yes?"

"Well, he might not be far enough away!"

They both looked at Datch and sighed.

The End...

Other Books in the Chronicles of Datch Series.

Datch – The Great Adventure.

The Mystical Gem

Arcaneus.

The Quest for Earthly Delights.

Hunting Jackars.

The Orphaned World.